Foreign
Correspondents

Also by Cindy Blake

GIRL TALK
BLOOD SUGAR
SECOND WIVES

Foreign Correspondents

CINDY BLAKE

SIMON & SCHUSTER
A VIACOM COMPANY

First published in Great Britain by Simon & Schuster Ltd, 1997
A Viacom Company

Simon & Schuster Ltd
West Garden Place
Kendal Street
London W2 2AQ

Simon & Schuster of Australia Pty Ltd
Sydney

A CIP catalogue record for this book is available
from the British Library

ISBN 0-684-81727-6

Typeset in Goudy 11.5/14pt by
Palimpsest Book Production Limited, Polmont, Stirlingshire
Printed and bound in Great Britain by
Butler & Tanner, Frome & London

With love to my mother, Rosemary S. Blake
Who made Club LXI the best, the only place to be

The ideal love affair is conducted by post

George Bernard Shaw

Chapter 1

January 1

308 W. 93rd St.
NYC, NY

Dear Angela Rae,

I read that article about you in People Magazine and although it was short, it made an impact. I mean, how many 72-year-old women swim the English Channel? I promise you, I don't know one other.

I'm writing because I really don't understand. Why do it? I bet you couldn't look me in the eye and tell me it was fun.

The People piece didn't say whether you did the breaststroke or the crawl. Maybe you were really brave, maybe you did the backstroke. Or what's that thing where you throw both arms over your head like they're Ferris wheels and then kick like a mermaid?

What are the chances of a passing ferry or a dumb deep-sea fisherman or an overzealous Oxford crew running you over? All that effort would be for nothing, Angela. All for absolutely nothing. You'd be dead in the water.

What are your family doing? Aren't they concerned for your health? This is really, really sad.

I want to know. Did someone tease you at school? Did some

psycho girl bully throw you into a pool before you could swim? Did you get bitten by a rabid dog – a bite, which of course would render you temporarily hydrophobic or permanently dead? Is this your way of getting your revenge on water?

WHY DIDN'T THEY TELL YOU ABOUT THE TUN-NEL?

Will you marry me?

With much respect,

Carl Lioce

January 14

7 St Peter's Grove
LONDON W4 8NB
England

Dear Mr Lioce,

I should start by explaining why I read your letter addressed to Miss Rae. After swimming the Channel, she decided she needed another challenge and has gone on a round-the-world solo sailing trip. As she has no idea when she'll return and no interest in any letters received in the meantime, she asked me to open any post addressed to her and, if need be, deal with any emergencies. Otherwise, I'm instructed to toss everything in the bin.

I think a marriage proposal is something of an emergency, so I am writing back on her behalf to refuse your kind offer. Miss Rae is an old friend of mine and has told me on numerous occasions that she 'can't imagine anything worse than being shackled to some idiotic man'. Of course, you might be the person to change her mind so I should hate to dash your hopes, but I'm afraid you'll have to wait until her return to try your luck.

Meanwhile, I should tell you that Miss Rae has never been 'bullied' or, to my knowledge, bitten by a rabid dog. (We have

2

strict quarantine laws in this country.) I wouldn't try to woo her with any appeals to childhood victimization. I suspect she was a fierce young girl.

The swimming stroke you refer to in that contorted description is the 'butterfly'.

I wonder how you could have Miss Rae's address.

SHE KNOWS ABOUT THE TUNNEL.

Sincerely,

Clare James

Anna Howland took a sip of coffee and wondered what the hell had happened to Clare to make her hand in a manuscript with a beginning like this. It was certainly different from Clare's usual work, but where was it leading? Would it continue in this light-hearted vein or tail off into another of Clare's stories of human misery? Deciding to cheat and take a short cut, Anna selected a page at random from the middle of the bulky manuscript.

Letter Twenty-five

Dear Carl,

I woke up this morning feeling dreadful – and then your letter came. Yes, this correspondence has become obsessive. No, I wasn't bored. You're right about female friendships – they are, or can be, remarkably strong. Why? I think it's because a female friend will listen carefully to whatever another female friend has to say, whether it be a conversation about men or work or food shopping. We listen. Men listen only when the subject has something to do with them.

What I'm trying to say is that a man will listen if he is involved somehow or thinks he can give advice or help; but he will not listen, his eyes will begin to wander, if the subject has nothing to do with him. This isn't to say that men are all hopeless egocentrics. I think people in general would prefer to talk about themselves. But women have been trained to be good listeners. From birth, . . .

Anna stopped at the comma, murmured 'blah, blah, blah' and yawned. Her eyes skipped down long paragraphs and focused on the end of the letter.

Love,

Clare

Oh dear. A romantic epistolary novel. The Englishwoman and the American man develop a relationship by post. Hasn't Clare read *84 Charing Cross Road*? Hasn't she heard of e-mail? What a derivative concept. Besides, Clare attempting to write like an American man is about as authentic as me trying to look like Cindy Crawford. How can I possibly sell this to a publisher?

And how am I going to let her down gently? Telling an author you can't sell his or her work is like telling a patient he or she has cancer. You can try to soften the blow, but the plain truth of the matter is that you've just injected disease into what was probably a healthy ego.

Being a literary agent sucked sometimes, Anna decided. But it was preferable to being a doctor. At least you could take your client out to a good lunch when delivering the bad news. And uncommercial writing wasn't, after all, fatal.

Anna put the manuscript aside and picked up the next on the pile.

Clare James looked up from her paper when she heard the roar. 'A superb catch,' the commentator exclaimed. 'A truly remarkable catch. He's done it again.' She watched as the replay showed Jeremy racing to the edge of the boundary and catching the ball at full stride, then performing a perfect somersault. He didn't touch the rope. He held the ball high but didn't toss it in the air. Jeremy never tossed the ball in the air after a catch.

She bowed her head and re-read her last sentence.

'In answer to your question: yes, Carl, you would like Jeremy. Jeremy is the quintessential perfect English gentleman. I know you would never understand a sport like cricket, but let me try to explain anyway.'

Picking up her cup of tea, Clare rested it against her forehead. How can I possibly explain cricket to an American man? she wondered. Where would I begin? But I can't explain Jeremy without explaining cricket. An athlete's character is bound up in the nature of his or her sport. If Jeremy had been a figure skater, Jeremy would be a different man, wouldn't he?

'Jeremy is playing in a match right now – an international Test match against South Africa. It lasts for five days and it's very possible there won't be a result – I mean maybe neither team will win. Sometimes you can win, in a manner of speaking, by forcing a draw. Sometimes a team will pray for rain so that the match will be stopped.'

And sometimes, Clare thought, as she bit the end of her pen, that's what I think Jeremy and I are doing in our relationship. Waiting for a storm to stop play.

'Clare. People don't write letters any more.'

Anna said this with the special kind of disappointment she reserved for lamentable but unavoidable truths. She could have been saying 'Sainsbury's don't stock seedless grapes any more', or 'Men don't dance the rumba any more'. Each of these statements would be accompanied with a sad shake of her head and a faraway look in her eyes.

They were sitting at a cramped table against the far wall in Kensington Place and Clare found herself wishing Anna had picked somewhere quieter and less trendy. You could measure the 'in' factor of a restaurant by how many different kinds of bread it served, she thought, as the waiter removed her uneaten

5

slice – studded with walnuts and olives. Which would be the first establishment to offer sardine-and-vodka-infused loaves?

'That's exactly why I thought the manuscript might work, Anna. It's so old-fashioned. People would be intrigued by the idea of a relationship growing *slowly* – a man and a woman getting to know each other over a period of time.'

Clare had practised this sales pitch for at least an hour before lunch. It sounded better when there was no one else about to hear it.

'And?' Anna leant forward.

'And what?'

'And what happens? Does this Carl character meet your Clare character? Which, by the way, surprises me. The fact that you're using your own name. Do they fall in love, have fantastic sex and ride off into the sunset together?'

'Anna, that isn't the point. This is a story of unfolding—'

'Because if nothing happens, Clare, nothing happens. It's as simple as that. And if nothing happens, I can not sell this book.'

Clare blinked. Anna wondered whether she was fighting back tears of rejection. Unlike some rebuffed authors, Clare would never weep openly. Anna was sure of that. She was too repressed. And, unfortunately, it came out in her novels. Clare's wasn't a *Remains of the Day* type of repression. If only it were. No, it wasn't a repression that *sold*.

'A lot happens,' Clare protested. 'It happens in the letters. *That's* the point. Carl and Clare get to know each other gradually, without any sex to muddle things up. They don't even know what each other looks like. They become friends, close friends, through this correspondence. They can be honest, tell each other everything because all the usual complications in a male–female relationship aren't there.'

Anna had Concorde eyes. They travelled around the restaurant at an ungodly speed, checking out every table, every newcomer, every person who went to the toilet, yet she was so quick it was impossible for Clare to accuse her of not paying attention.

'So, what we have here is a *When Harry Met Sally* scenario except Harry never meets Sally. Is that it?' Anna pressed.

Clare stared at the dessert suddenly placed in front of her. Anna would have been one of those children at birthday parties who refuses to pass the parcel when it is her turn. 'Why does trying to sell myself make me feel so small?' she wondered, reluctant to look up and meet Anna's gaze, so small and so shabby?

'Which means, Clare, that there is absolutely, no dramatic tension. Boy doesn't *meet* girl, boy doesn't *get* girl, boy doesn't *lose* girl.'

Wake up and get commercial, Anna wanted to add, but decided to edit herself and scale down a full-frontal attack.

'Listen, Clare. You know I adore you and there's nothing I'd like better than to make you a star. You've got everything going for you – you're young and bright and you've got the kind of face I wish I had – the kind where the initial impact just keeps getting better, you know? You would look great on TV – with that slightly sleepy aura. I thought about it the last time I saw you and I think I've figured it out – you always look as if you've just woken up after a great night of sex. The point is, you're a publicist's dream. But the dream can't come true unless you write for the public.'

Clare didn't know whether to be offended or complimented by this description of her supposed physical attractions. And she wasn't sure she liked being labelled 'young with a slightly sleepy aura'. These weren't attributes an older, relentlessly energetic woman such as Anna would normally 'adore'.

'This *is* for the public. I'm trying to say something important about male–female relationships.'

'All right, all right. You're trying to say not to have them.' Lowering her voice and glancing at the two tables flanking theirs, Anna murmured, 'Are things going *that* badly with Jeremy?'

'No!, no!' Clare quickly looked from left to right as well. 'Everything's fine. He's playing in South Africa. He called me yesterday.'

'Good.'

Clare could hear the relief in Anna's voice and pressed on.

'Did you read *all* the letters? You know, Carl's really funny.' Clare knew that the desperation she was feeling wouldn't come out in her voice; she was a master at hiding despair. Anna wouldn't have any idea how difficult it was for her to listen to her letters being dismissed so decisively.

'Of course I did. Carl's a wonderful creation. I'm sure you could use him in some other form. Really.'

They had almost finished their coffee. It was time, Anna knew, to placate, to offer some hope for the future.

'You're an excellent writer, Clare. You can do great things. But sometimes . . . you go wrong. Take Carl, for example. I know I just said he was a wonderful creation, but he has some flaws. I think it's ambitious to try to portray an American male. You've never even—'

'Carl's not a creation.'

'What? You mean Carl actually exists?'

'Yes.' Clare smiled. A first. Finally she'd managed to surprise Anna. 'Carl definitely exists.'

'The letters are genuine?'

'Anna. How many letters *did* you read?'

'You told me this was a novel.'

'No. I handed you the manuscript. I didn't say whether it was fiction or not.'

'But you write fiction.'

'This is real.'

'So.' Anna began to click her fingers. 'The whole correspondence is real. Which means . . . ?'

Clare waited, as she always did, when Anna said, 'Which means?'

'Which means this Carl fellow actually wrote to Angela Rae;

which means – wait a minute – it means you weren't just using Angela Rae's name, you *know* Angela Rae. You never told me that.'

Angela Rae. One of the wonderful female eccentrics. Were there any recent biographies of Angela Rae? Were there *any* biographies of Angela Rae? Anna wondered. She'd have to do some research when she got back to the office.

'There was no reason to tell you about knowing Angela – and no, before you ask, I won't do an intimate, informed biography of her life. That's out of the question.'

'Why?'

'Because Angela lies constantly. I'd take years sorting out the truth from the fiction. And she'd be a terror to work with. I'm frightened of her – as you would know *if* you'd read my manuscript. A biographer shouldn't be scared of her subject.'

'All right. I take your point. But I honestly don't know what to do with your manuscript, this correspondence. It's a lot like *84 Charing Cross Road.* It *could* be a lot like *When Harry Met Sally.* Or maybe The *Bridges of Madison County*, if Carl came to England and had a wild affair with you and subsequently disappeared and tragically died. But then again, you're not married. Is Carl married?'

'No. Anna, you didn't read beyond the first page, did you?'

'Does Carl have any special talents? Does he whisper to horses? Or is he a criminal lawyer? An ER doctor? A forensic pathologist?'

Clare gave up on her cappuccino and pushed it away from her. It was sad, really, Anna truly believing that she'd renounced her native country, that she'd become a bona fide Brit after a decade and a half in London. Anna trashed her fellow Americans at every opportunity; she had an impeccable English accent, but she was steeped in American ways. She worked the room with a vengeance at any party; she had no sense of irony, perfect teeth, and dressed like a character from an up-market soap opera.

'Of course Carl could be a mass murderer,' Anna mused,

studying the bill. 'You could have developed this terrific, perfect relationship with a man who turns out to be a psychotic killer. How would you find out, though? Who would tell you? Or would he turn up on your doorstep and . . .'

'And what? Rape, torture and shoot me?'

'Poison's better. The book could be called *Poison Pen-pal.*'

'Anna, you're depressing me. Does everything *have* to have a hook?'

'Oh look – there's Clive Anderson! All right, pretend you don't care. Don't look. No, every book does *not* have to have a hook. Not if you have a name that's a hook already. If you're called Amis or Rushdie or Trollope or any other name of note you can write whatever you damn well want. James would be fine if it were preceded by Henry or P. D., Clive, even. But Clare does nothing for you. Your only claim . . .' Anna skidded to a stop.

'Go ahead.'

No, Anna knew she'd gone too far already. Occasionally she wondered whether Clare had seen the gleam in her eyes the first time they'd spoken about a possible business relationship – the gleam she couldn't dampen when Clare had casually mentioned her boyfriend's name.

'I thought for a second that woman with Clive Anderson was Anthea Turner.'

'No, Anna. You were just about to tell me that my only claim to fame is being Jeremy Letts's girlfriend.'

'That is *not true.* Honestly. You're so sensitive on that topic. It's not Anthea Turner, I can see that now. But she does look a lot like her. She's got that bouncy kind of hair. Actually, you might consider copying Anthea's style. You could afford to dress up a little more. I mean, if you're worried that putting on more exciting clothes would make you look like a bimbo, you don't have to be. Really – your face can carry a lot – you don't have to understate yourself.'

'Anna, do me a favour. Forget what I look like, just read the manuscript. I'm aware that my previous books haven't sold well.

10

But this one is different. I can feel it. You'll understand when you read the whole thing.'

'All right. I will. And I'll think long and hard about what we can do with it – if anything. I'd like to make this concept work, Clare, but you have to understand. People don't read books where nothing happens any more.'

The faraway look clouded Anna's eyes for a moment. When it cleared, she threw her Visa card down on the table.

Letter Three

January 29

308 W. 93rd St.
NYC, NY

Dear Ms James,

Well, OK, I was drunk. I admit it. I have no recollection of writing that letter, much less putting a stamp on it and mailing it. I think I wrote it in the small hours of the morning, the midget, dwarflike hours of the morning of January 1, having indulged in a New Year's Eve binge which was misjudged and very debilitating. It seems that the People Magazine with that article in it was two years old. What the hell am I doing with a two-year-old copy of People Magazine? And what in the world prompted me to read it? I don't think even a total drunken stupor is a good enough excuse for that.

Still, it sounds like I picked a winner. Miss Rea must be a real piece of work. I'm sorry you think she won't accept my marriage proposal. I believe it might be a good idea to marry someone who travels constantly and was a fierce child. I wonder if I proposed to anyone else at the same time. Maybe I've set myself up with a mail-order bride from Bangkok. Maybe she's winging her way here as I write this and I will soon be in a state of connubial

11

bliss. I also believe it might be a good idea to marry someone who doesn't speak my language. So many misunderstandings could be avoided.

Didn't someone once say that America and England are two countries separated by the same language? Problems start when someone thinks that he or she knows what the other person is talking about but actually has no idea at all.

People tell me that I'm a very idiosyncratic man. Mostly women tell me this. Miss Rae would probably skip the 'syncra' and settle for the 'idiotic.'

One of my quirks is my collection of foreign telephone books. I've never been out of this country, but I have in my possession the telephone books for Santiago, Bangkok, Sydney, Marseilles, Oslo, Cairo, Marrakesh, and London. I must have found Miss Rae's address in the last one. Sometimes I write to people I read about in articles in newspapers or magazines, but sometimes I pick random, unknown people and send Christmas cards or just cheerful notes along the lines of 'keep up the good work.' So far you are the only person who has responded to any of my letters at any length. I did once get a postcard saying 'Who the hell are you?' from a guy named Shane in Sydney.

So. Who the hell are you, Clare James? How did you ever become friends with the indomitable Miss Rae? Where do you live? Do you play polo? Have you had an affair with any member of the royal family or their staff?

I suppose that sounds pushy and crass and obnoxious and all the adjectives I know foreigners apply to Americans. I promise I don't wear Bermuda shorts. I wouldn't want to rip down St Paul's Church and put up a McDonald's. I'm not entirely uncivilized. Yet. I need a few more years in New York City to achieve total depravity.

Right now I'm just curious. I'd like to find out more about another human being. I don't want to know how old you are or what you look like or what job you do or don't have. I want to know what you think about things. Things? Yes, things like friendship and *love and how the hell we're supposed to lead our lives of very noisy desperation.*

Maybe you've never felt desperate. Maybe you've always sailed through life easily. Maybe you think I'm crazy. And maybe I've used the word maybe too much in this letter.

With sober good wishes,

Carl Lioce

Noisy desperation? St Paul's *Church*? Anna smirked. Typical bloody American.

Chapter 2

'It's very sweet, Carl. This correspondence is very cute. And I don't want to hear another word about it. It bores the shit out of me.'

'That's nice, Art. That's supportive. Friendly. I appreciate your thoughtful remarks.'

'Look. You're writing to a woman you've never met. Great. You have no idea what she looks like, how old she is, what she does for a living. Great. You share deep thoughts and feelings. Great. She's English. Not great. Lousy. End of interest as far as I'm concerned. I *know* them, Carl. I *lived* there. And I hope they all run like little lemmings and jump off the cliff at Beachy Head. Which, in case this wonderful woman hasn't told you, is the primo suicide spot in Merrye Olde England.'

'I can sense you're building up to a diatribe, Artie.' Carl leant back in his chair, put his hands behind his neck and assumed a patient expression.

'How can I explain this to you?' Art, reversing Carl's movements, leant forward, his elbows resting on his knees, his chin in his hands. 'When you think of England, you think of Buckingham Palace or you think of James Bond, or you think of cheery chappies having a fab time in a Liverpool pub chatting to someone like Michael Caine, right?'

'Wrong. I think of King Arthur. I think of legends.'

'OK, fine. The point is, you don't think of people sitting around dinner tables talking about which boarding school their eight-year-old kid should go to, do you?'

'No,' Carl smiled. 'I can't say that I do.'

'And you don't think of a group of zenophobic zombies who hate all other nations and have utter contempt for Americans, do you?'

'Nope. When I stop thinking about King Arthur, I start thinking about Shakespeare.'

'Of course . . .' Art nodded. 'But that's just my point. If you were sitting at a dinner party in London with the people I used to sit with at dinner parties in London, you'd realize that they don't believe you could have any understanding of Shakespeare, except as he is delivered by Hollywood studio heads who have a belief in the bankability of Kenneth Branagh. You're an American, Carl. Which means that you are vastly inferior. As am I. We have no history, we have no culture, we have no education – we're savages, and we're not even noble ones.'

'Artie, who did you hang out with when you were over there?'

'Back in the bad old days when I was an investment banker at Langhursts? Men with names like Rupert, women with names like Fiona. All of whom were consumed by the process of getting their kids away from them and off to an absurdly expensive, socially correct school as soon as humanly possible. Take it from there, Carl, you get the picture.'

'So, . . .' Carl crossed one blue-jeaned leg over the other. 'I'd say that you saw the wrong kind of English person. The snobby, rich kind. Those types exist here too, you know – they have their American counterparts. Just take a walk along Park Avenue . . .'

'I know, I know. There are some similarities, I agree. There are those types all over the world, people who seem born for the sole purpose of putting others down. But there's a *finesse* to the way the Brits dismiss the people they regard as inferior. I know, I've been on the receiving end. Without actually feeling the blow, you are suddenly lying on the floor, winded and gasping for air.'

Art paused. Casting a glance around Carl's tiny, quintessentially Upper West Side New York apartment, he felt for a moment as if he were back in college, surrounded by scattered books and newspapers, drinking coffee and discussing life. The feeling made him smile briefly.

'I remember going to a party when I first arrived in London. The man who was responsible for hiring me led me up to one of his fellow Garrick Club members and said, "Ian, I'd like you to meet Art Rolfe, he's over here from New York, working with us at Langhursts." After we shook hands, Ian said, "Pleased to meet you. Welcome to London." He waited for a microsecond, then said, "So, Art, when are you going back to the States?"'

'He was probably trying to be polite.'

'I thought so too. Until about twenty other people I was introduced to that night said exactly the same thing. They can't bring themselves to say "Get the hell out of our country, you foreign scumbag," so they say "Oh, by the way, I was just wondering, old chap, when *are* you going back?"'

'Aren't you being just a little paranoid?' Carl regarded Art, wondering how many of these supposed slights he'd received in London were imaginary and how many real. He couldn't envision Clare being dismissive at a dinner party, but then he couldn't envision Clare at a dinner party full stop. The only place he could imagine her being was right there in his apartment, sitting where Art was sitting, looking at him with wide, clear eyes.

'Maybe a little,' Art admitted, 'but England is a truly tribal nation, Carl. As a nation, the tribe can't stand foreigners, I promise you. Ask any English person his views on the French or the Germans. And within the nation, there are all sorts of other tribes. You should go to a soccer match sometime. The passion is intense – far more than in any sport here. I mean, in my days there, rival fans were knifing each other. Literally. It was actually *frightening* to go to a Chelsea match and watch the tribes at war. Ask your ladyfriend. She'll know.'

'Her husband plays cricket. I don't think she goes to soccer matches.'

'Oh, right. Cricket. The sport where you can play five days and no one wins. You blink at the wrong time and you can miss the only excitement of a whole day's play.'

'I've heard it's a very subtle game.'

'Sure. So subtle you have to be dead to appreciate it.'

'Have you finished now, Art?'

'No. I want you to know what you're getting into here. You've established this wacky relationship which you seem to believe holds the key to the meaning of life. Strangers telling each other the truth. But it's a dangerous belief.'

'Because she's English?'

'Partly that, yes. As I said, it's a tribal nation and tribes don't like outsiders. Whether you're from the wrong class or support the wrong football team, or come from a different country, you are on the outside looking in. In the old days the Brits solved the irritating problem of foreigners by colonizing them. But please don't tell me they accepted those colonists as equals. The point is, you're probably an object of curiosity to this pen pal of yours.' Art picked up a pillow from the sofa and threw it at Carl. 'Object being the relevant word. Anyway, lecture over. The point is, you should think about forgetting her. If she's married to a guy who spends his life playing cricket, she'll never understand a normal American male. I think you should stop this correspondence. It's not healthy.'

'You haven't read any of the letters.'

'I don't want to.'

Watching Art adjust his tie, the signal that he was getting ready to go, Carl realized he wanted at least a hint of approval from his friend before he left. Although Art could occasionally be overly critical on certain subjects, the English being the foremost of those, he had authority in Carl's life, as if he were his teacher or coach. Although they were approximately the same age, Art

17

struck Carl as being decades more advanced in the subject of Life and How to Live It.

'Read one. Just one. Here—' Reaching towards the pile of correspondence on the table beside him, Carl leafed through a few pages and found what he was looking for. 'Here's her second letter to me. Read it and see what you think.'

'Do I have to?' Art was standing up now. 'Shit, just look at that rain, will you? It reminds me of my days in Blighty. I used to think of the sun as an unidentified flying object, an unexplained wonder of nature which appeared infrequently, and always to our astonishment – like corn circles.'

'Art—'

'Alright. I'll read it. I'll take it home with me and read it in bed tonight. I hope it's sexy, but I think sex is an experience English-women have yet to discover. Basically because Englishmen prefer to keep it to themselves.'

Letter Four

February 16

7 St Peter's Grove
LONDON W4 8NB
England

Dear Mr Lioce,

Who the hell am I? Like Shane, I wonder who the hell you are. Why have a telephone directory for Marseilles and not Paris, for example? Other women may find you idiosyncratic. I think you're simply crazy.

So why am I bothering to answer your letter?

I'm not a Catholic and I've never been to a psychiatrist or therapist of any sort. I've never actually told anyone whom I don't know any details of my personal history. I think I would prefer a priest to a shrink because I like the idea of secrecy and absolution. Perhaps you are a Catholic and will know how many Hail Marys I should say for whatever I choose to confess to you. Perhaps I'm a little crazy too. And perhaps I've used the word perhaps too often already.

I met Angela Rae on a plane trip. I was twelve years old. She was sitting beside me when the plane, just after take-off, veered sharply to the left and downwards. I was eating a banana at the time and I knew we were going to crash but I thought I had to finish the banana before we did crash. I was a victim of good table manners.

Angela reached over, grabbed the banana from my hand, ordered me to swallow what was in my mouth and then pushed me into the standard 'be prepared to die' position. I don't remember the actual impact, although I have had nightmares when I hear the same kind of screams I heard then. Angela had a tight grip on my wrist, as if she were going to take me with her wherever we were going – to heaven, to hell or to blank extinction. I didn't know her, had never met her, but I knew somehow that with her beside me, I was safe.

I have absolutely no idea how we got out of that plane. I know that we did get out – all sixty of us – and that no one was killed, but I also know there were ambulances and stretchers everywhere and Angela and I were standing in a field, watching everything.

'The authorities here are useless,' she said. She still had a hold of my wrist. 'It will take them ages to organize a room for us.'

We were in Spain. She was right. We had to wait hours and hours, standing in that field. I kept thinking that the plane looked like a huge beached whale and I finally got up the nerve to speak to her, to tell her this.

'Don't be silly,' she said very sharply. 'I'm sure you've never seen a beached whale, or any other sort of whale for that matter. Except in pictures.'

Of course she was right again. Angela is always right.

'You shouldn't make bad analogies,' she said. I didn't know what an analogy was. 'And you shouldn't make things up until you are much older.'

I thought that I might cry, but I surprised myself by laughing instead.

'I'm glad you find this funny.' She let go of my wrist then. 'That means you can take care of yourself. You won't be a burden to me. When they finally find us a room, I'll call your parents and you can begin this day again.'

'I don't know my father's telephone number,' I said. I had stopped laughing. 'It's in my bag.' I gestured to the field, littered with luggage from the crash.

'Do you know your mother's number?'

'Yes, but she's in England. That's why I'm flying back. I've been with my father here and I'm going back to my mother's.'

'Oh, I see. Shuttle diplomacy.'

Do you think I'm making this conversation up, embellishing it? Well, I'm not. I've forgotten everything about the actual crash, but I remember every detail of the afternoon afterwards.

When we finally arrived at our hotel – a small one, I remember, with masses of flowers in the lobby but none in our room – Angela called the number I gave her. My mother had heard about the crash, and she knew there were no fatalities, but of course she was worrying like crazy. I heard Angela reassuring her, then I heard Angela go very quiet suddenly on her end. I had thought she'd pass the receiver to me, so that I could talk to my mother, but she didn't. She turned to me, still holding it and told me to go down to the lobby and 'fetch' her a Coke. I was upset, terribly upset, that I couldn't speak to my mother, but I was scared of Angela. She had made me feel safe when we were about to crash, but on the ground she looked like the Wicked Witch of the West.

When I came back with the Cokes, she had hung up the phone and was sitting in the only chair in the room, looking very businesslike.

'I suppose you're wondering why I haven't allowed you to talk to your mother,' she said. I didn't reply. 'The reason is this. Your mother doesn't know how to tell you that your father is dead. I know this must sound strange because you have just escaped death, but it's true. He had a heart attack in his swimming pool – probably around the time the plane was taking off, as I understand it. Your mother doesn't seem too upset by this news, but she is worried about you. Obviously she is lacking in the maternal knack or she would never have allowed me of all people to tell you. How old are you, Clare?'

'Twelve.'

'Well, you had the misfortune to be placed next to me on that plane. I am not a sympathetic or empathetic woman. I can't comfort you.'

'I'm all right.'

'Good. Well, I'll set about the tortuous prospect of getting us back to England in one piece.'

She did just that, while I sat imagining my father in the swimming pool. I remembered him waving to me from the pool as I left to go to the airport in a cab. I remembered thinking how glad I was that he hadn't kissed me goodbye. During the holiday, I'd watched him floating, face down in the pool a few times, when he'd take a break between laps. So I could picture how he would look, but I couldn't decide whether he'd be doing the dead man's float at the deep end or the shallow.

When we got back to England, my mother and Miss Rae shook hands at the airport. She patted me on the shoulder and disappeared. I thought and hoped that was the last I would see of her.

I didn't go to my father's funeral and I didn't feel in any way sad. I had hated my trips to see him in Spain. He'd always drive me to visit his friends and he would chain-smoke the whole time in the car. My lungs weren't in good shape – I had asthma – but he wouldn't let me open the window because he said it would interfere with the air-conditioning system. We hardly ever spoke. He was flabby and looked horrid in his little bikini/jock-strap of a swimsuit. I wasn't rude to him, but I couldn't wait to get away.

Isn't that a sin, Mr Lioce? Not to honour your father?

I have no idea why I'm writing this.

Yours sincerely,

Clare James

Whoa, Art thought. A mixed-up, shook-up girl. What has Carl gotten himself into here?

It wasn't completely surprising, however. Carl had some strange and hidden pockets in his personality. He *seemed* like a normal guy – occasionally wild and crazy, like all born and bred New Yorkers – but basically sane. Yet there were times lately when you'd be talking with him, having a decent conversation, and you'd sudenly hit clear air turbulence. Carl would start in on the plight of homeless people. As if no one else in the world had noticed, as if there were anything anybody could do about it. Or he'd go off on a riff about the Greek myths. He'd talk about Zeus and Athene and whoever, like he believed in them, like he *knew* them.

OK, sure, Carl had been having a hard time lately. His career was on a downswing and had been for a long time. His wife had left him. He'd had to move into a miniscule apartment on the Upper West Side. Still, he should have kept more of a grip on himself. Ranting on about Aphrodite and writing reams of letters to some unknown English bird who was obviously a sad case were not good signs. It might have been a lot healthier if he'd acted like most guys his age – if he had hit the bottle too much and ended up in some twelve-step deal. At least then there were rules, there was a *programme*.

Art sometimes worried that he'd walk into Carl's apartment and find the guy sacrificing a goat to appease the gods.

Carl was a dreamer, a charming, endearing, funny dreamer, who slipped in and out of fantasy worlds of his own fashioning. Art, while he had sympathy and regard for his friend's whimsical nature, was concerned that Carl appeared to be carrying it too far, and feared he would end up a Peter Pan at the mercy of a host of Captain Hooks. 'He's naïve,' Art thought, putting down the letter. 'Sometimes he can be quick and witty and even sarcastic, but at heart, he's pure-spirited and naïve, and he's looking for The Answer. What will he do if he doesn't find it?'

It might be a good idea to read *all* this so-called correspondence, Art decided. Then he could get a take on the true status of Carl's psyche.

Art reached over and turned off his bedside light. He wouldn't watch Jay Leno tonight. Instead, he'd concentrate on what he could do for Carl. Men had to stick together these days. Women sure as hell weren't going to help them.

Chapter 3

Anna put down letter number four, sighing as she did. How could Clare have such an exciting childhood and never mention it to her, much less write about it in her novels?

A plane crash. Her father's simultaneous heart attack. The meeting with Angela Rae. Excitement, drama, death – all perfect for a book. But not Clare – oh, no. Clare wrote about people's inner thoughts, journeys into the desert of strangled emotions. You had to read so much between the lines, it really wasn't worth buying the actual book – as the punters had proved by their conspicuous failure to fork out any money for *Between Pauses* and then *Breathing in the Dusk*.

Anna still didn't know how she'd managed to sell those two novels. She'd pitched them as small but perfectly formed jewels which the public would discover and take to their hearts, because the public were tired of blockbusters. Sure. Try feeding the same line to the men in suits armed with sales figures the third time around and she'd be laughed out of town.

Clare was on Anna's B list of clients anyway, but she was heading rapidly for C. Basement level. What Anna dreamt of, whenever she thought of Clare, was the Big One – the book about Clare's relationship with Jeremy. Jeremy Letts – Hero of Our Time – worshipped by men, fancied by women, respected by all, even people who had no idea what LBW stood for.

Jeremy Letts the golden boy: better looking than David Gower, better batsman than Brian Lara, better sportsman than anyone in cricket, or even football – and that included the sainted Gary Linneker.

Jeremy, the man who single-handedly saved English cricket. Who wouldn't want to know what the reticent Jeremy was *really* like when he was at home? Who wouldn't gobble up every word offering a close-up of the man who never gave interviews to the press, the Greta Garbo of sporting achievement? Jeremy was a phenomenon, mostly due to his extraordinary talent, but partly because of the air of mystery surrounding him.

The public knew where Jeremy had gone to grammar school. They knew he'd been to Cambridge. And that was it. End of story. Jeremy's parents didn't talk, his friends didn't talk, his team-mates didn't talk. He was protected by a moat of secrecy the royal family would have killed for.

Anna sighed, yet again, thinking of the possibilities of such a book and the seeming impossibility of convincing Clare to write it. She knew from the first that she'd have to tread carefully on the subject of Jeremy, that she'd do best to bide her time. Yet she'd waited two years now and there had been no chink, not the tiniest opening for her to exploit. Nothing seemed to happen between Clare and Jeremy, no fights, no infidelities splashed in the *News of the World*, nothing which would lead to the kind of conversation Anna needed to have with Clare in order to introduce the subject of a book about them. Clare's life with Jeremy seemed as uneventful as Clare's writing.

Or else Clare was as addicted to keeping secrets as her boyfriend. Certainly, judging from letter number four Clare held things back as a matter of course. Anna couldn't remember any occasion when Clare had talked about her childhood; in fact, now that she thought about it, Clare hardly ever offered any personal information at all.

So why was Clare baring her soul to some stranger in New York? Perhaps further on in the correspondence Clare would tell this Carl Lioce about Jeremy. A lot about Jeremy. Then there'd really be something *to* this manuscript. Nobody gave a damn about Carl Lioce, whoever the hell he was. But there might be precious nuggets in these papers. It was time, Anna knew, to mine the source, to read on.

I've gone stark raving mad, Clare thought. I'm actually watching *Neighbours* for the second time today. What's the matter with me? She turned off the television with her remote control and rubbed her eyes.

What *was* the matter with her? Why did she give that manuscript to Anna in the first place? She could never publish it. Those letters were private. Carl's letters belonged to him, morally and legally. How could she have shown them to Anna? Wouldn't she be offended if Carl had given her letters to someone without her permission? She was betraying Carl – Carl, who had been nothing but honourable and kind to her.

Why?

She wanted to share their correspondence with someone. That, more than a desire to sell it as a manuscript, may have been what prompted her to hand it over to Anna. She wanted people to know what an extraordinary relationship she and Carl had developed through their writing.

And she wanted people to stop thinking that Clare James was just an extension of Jeremy Letts.

Everyone she knew thought that the most interesting aspect of her life was the fact that she was living with Jeremy. They made the mistake most people make regarding celebrities – they couldn't distinguish between the public persona and the private one. People believed that Jeremy Letts at home was the same as Jeremy Letts on the cricket pitch.

Could she really blame them? Clare asked herself. After all, part of what had attracted her to Jeremy in the first place was his star status.

*   *   *

26

Three years before, she had gone to meet her friend Bernice in a wine bar in Hammersmith. Looking around the crowded room, she had spotted one unoccupied table with two chairs. At the same time as she went to claim it, a man appeared, a brown-haired, tall, lean man Clare immediately recognized as Jeremy Letts. 'Oh, I'm sorry,' he said, backing away. 'Go ahead. Take the table.' 'No, no,' she protested. 'My friend hasn't even arrived yet. *You* take the table.' 'Absolutely not,' he said softly, then turned and walked off.

Throughout the evening Clare kept sneaking glances in Jeremy's direction as he stood at the bar with a male friend and and found him returning her gaze, sometimes accompanying the look with a quick smile.

'Who *is* that?' Bernice, arriving ten minutes late, asked as soon as she caught sight of him. 'For one happy second I thought he was looking at me.'

'He's a cricket player,' Clare answered. 'A very good one.'

'I wish I cared about sport the way you do,' Bernice said wistfully. 'I'm sure it would help me in my quest for Mr Fabulous. Actually, Mr Anybody at this point. Time is running out. We're twenty-four years old, Clare. Doesn't that scare you?'

'No,' Clare said, wondering if Jeremy would come up to her, and if he did, what he would say.

As closing time approached, he did come up to her.

What he said was, 'How was the table?'

What she said was, 'Very nice, thank you.'

'Would it be presumptuous of me to ask you to join me at another table, a different table, tomorrow night? Would you like to go out to dinner with me? My name is Jeremy, by the way.'

'Jeremy Letts,' she said. 'I know. I follow cricket. In fact, I'm a fan. And I'm Clare. No, it wouldn't be presumptuous. Yes, I'd like to have dinner with you.'

It had all been so easy, so straightforward after that. Neither of them was involved with anyone else at the time, both gravitated quickly toward a serious live-in relationship. They'd been together now for three years without even one fight.

For at least a year of that time, Clare knew, she remained slightly awestruck by Jeremy's athletic prowess and his growing fame. She'd watch him single-handedly win matches, and feel a secret 'look at *my* man' glow suffuse her. He was a national hero and she knew she shouldn't really bask in his reflected glory, but she did allow herself to sometimes, she couldn't help it. Yet the Jeremy Letts she watched playing such beautiful shots at the crease was not exactly the same as the Jeremy she watched potter around aimlessly at home.

The more famous he became, the less he wanted to go out. Weeks and days and months would go by and Clare would wonder what they'd done with all their time. Occasionally they'd see friends, but mostly, when Jeremy wasn't touring, he'd stay in. He liked to cook, a process which could take him all day. When he wasn't cooking, he would read magazines or watch whatever was showing on Sky Sports 1, 2 or 3. Clare began to feel as if she were in a permanent state of hibernation.

'Can't we go out a little more often?' she asked once, when the walls were beginning to close in on her.

'I go out too much,' he'd said quietly. He always spoke quietly and politely. 'I go away so much, Clare. The travelling can be exhausting. The constant pressure. I just want to lie back and relax when I'm home. Besides, when we go out, people stare. You know they do. I hate feeling like some animal in a zoo. You understand, don't you?'

She did. She eased the problem somewhat by inviting friends over for dinner more frequently, but her sense of alienation from the outside world still lingered. She worked all day by herself, writing. To live in a cocoon-like state with Jeremy all night as well made her, as the years went by, anxious and twitchy.

Waiting for a storm. The phrase reappeared in her head. That's what it felt like lately – as if she were waiting for a storm.

The amazing relationship she'd built up with Carl over the past fifteen months had become an unexpected source of excitement for her. How many people had corresponded so closely with a complete stranger for so long? Wouldn't everybody be fascinated by such a unique story? She didn't know Carl's age, his job, or what he looked like. Wasn't that special, wasn't that *different*?

That was why she had showed the letters to Anna. She had wanted Anna to read them and say 'My God, this is remarkable. How amazing that this is happening between two people! Clare, you're involved in something really interesting and incredibly *exciting*. And without Jeremy! All on your own, without the hero!'

Instead, what Anna had done was to tell her the correspondence wasn't commercial because nothing happened in it.

Oh, and of course she'd also asked how things were going with Jeremy.

How could Clare have assumed that Anna or anyone else would be as fascinated by this exchange of letters and thoughts as she was? 'I can't abide these women who think I want to hear all about their children,' she remembered her mother saying. 'You should never talk about your children and you should never tell your dreams – no one else is interested.'

The correspondence with Carl was both her baby and her dream, Clare thought. Infinitely interesting to her and probably deadly dull to anyone else. She had been stupid to give it to Anna.

Non compos mentis, she murmured to herself and then grinned as a memory pushed its way into her thoughts.

'*You may have weird habits, Carl,*' she had written in one of her earlier letters, '*you may collect phone books from foreign cities and write letters to strangers, but I – and I don't often admit this – I like Latin. I'm the only person I know, in fact, who likes Latin. There's something a little kinky about that, isn't there?*'

'Et penitus toto divisos orbe Britannos . . .' he ended his next letter. 'I have an unnatural interest in Virgil myself, Ms James. If I had to choose, I'd pick Virgil and Alfred Hitchcock as the two men I most admire in human history. I don't know if that makes me very learned or very twisted or just plain nuts.'

'Which Hitchcock do you prefer?' she'd written back excitedly. The question had comprised the entire letter and she'd felt like a little girl when she sent it off.

His reply arrived ten days afterwards, which meant, she knew, that he had sat down and written back as soon as he'd received the question.

'Aha,' the first paragraph began. 'Tricky question. Do I pretend to be someone I'm not and say *Vertigo*? Just to impress you? No, that goes against our ground rules in this correspondence, doesn't it? No false notes. OK. I'll come straight out with it. *Notorious*.

'Is this a problem for you? Is this the end of our glorious relationship? Do you loathe and despise Cary Grant? Christ, have you *heard* of Cary Grant? I mean, you could be a very bright eight-year-old for all I know.'

How unlikely was it, Clare wondered, still smiling as she remembered the entire exchange, that two people on opposite sides of an ocean should have the same liking for a dead language most people loathed? And the same favourite movie? Wasn't it uncanny? Especially as she was, she knew, supposedly too young to pick a Cary Grant and Ingrid Bergman film as her Number One. She should have chosen *Trainspotting*. Or something with Liam Neeson. But she'd seen *Notorious* one day when she was fifteen, ill and home from school. For those two hours, she forgot everything else in the world. To fall in love for the first time with Cary Grant seemed to her one of the truly wise choices she'd made in her life.

Now, staring at her blank television screen, she was over-whelmed by a yearning to break the rules. She was desperate to know what Carl looked like, how old he was, what he did for a living. She knew it wasn't fair to imagine he looked like Devlin, the Cary Grant character in *Notorious*, so she forced herself to conjure up the image of a hairy, plump, dwarflike man.

What if that picture were true? What if Carl were hideously ugly? Wouldn't that colour her response to him? And if he were eighty years old? Or eighteen? Or someone who worked in finance, repossessing homes?

The beauty of their relationship was the purity of it, their refusal to acknowledge the arbitrary aspects of each other, like age and looks and social position.

Even a quick telephone call could destroy everything with awkward voices, long pauses, idle talk. Hearing him speak would make him human – right now, he was a presence, a perfect soulmate. He didn't interfere with her life, he made no demands, he couldn't chew too loudly or wear too much aftershave or do anything to disappoint her. As much as curiosity made her want to, she couldn't bring herself to break the rules because she dreaded the possible outcome.

The telephone rang, and she reached out automatically, expecting to hear Jeremy's voice.

'Are you watching the *Six o'clock News*?' Bernice demanded, a little breathlessly, Clare thought. Had there been another IRA bomb? 'They're about to show Jeremy. Did you know he'd scored 146 not out?'

'Bernice, you don't know a thing about cricket. You hate *all* sports. Why do you care?'

'I care because my best friend is living with a superstar and I was there when you two first met, so I feel some proximity to fame. You really should be watching.'

'If I watched television every time Jeremy might be on, I'd spend my whole life in front of it.'

'I have no idea what 146 not out means, but it sounds as if it's important.'

'It is.'

'Do you think Jeremy would take me along on one of these tours if I asked nicely?'

Clare pictured Bernice with her long, dark, braided hair, her throaty voice, her omnipresent silver dangling ear-rings and her penchant for bottles of wine and wild behaviour, cutting a swathe through the English cricket team.

'I don't think they'd have a hope in hell of winning if you went along, Bernice. I think the Test Board would ban you.'

'What a shame. Anyway, turn on the tube. Tune in to your hero.'

'I will,' Clare said. 'Talk to you later.'

Clare reached for the remote contol but instead of pushing the on button, she left it lying on the table, got up and as if in a trance walked down the hallway to the study. Opening the left-hand drawer of the desk, she pulled out the pile of Carl's letters. There was one in particular she wanted to re-read right now.

Letter Five

> *March 4*
>
> *308 W. 93rd St.*
> *NYC, NY*

Dear Ms James,

You capture my thoughts. The Wicked Witch of the West saves Dorothy and what happens next? You say that you didn't go to your father's funeral. What did you do? Please tell me. What does a twelve-year-old escapee from death do when she gets back to Kansas?

I grew up in the ethnic atmosphere you see in movies. Italian mamma cooking pasta, Italian father listening to the opera. Three brothers, two sisters. No table manners. However, unfortunately, no Mafia connections either. A lot of religion. Don't talk to me about confessions. I used to confess that I'd listened in to the last confession. I was a practiced eavesdropper on other people's sins.

The charmed anonymity of the confessional box fades when you realize the man you've just been confessing to is also the guy who has done nasty things to various choirboys in his parish. I wouldn't recommend it.

As for shrinks, well, I just don't know. It's a lottery, I guess. There are good and bad ones and you have to hope you pull the right number and don't end up with the person who has been instrumental in Woody Allen's emotional development over the past twenty years.

I'm interested in how many children really don't mourn a parent's death, but can't tell the truth because society expects them to be devastated. It's like New Year's Eve – you're supposed to have fun and get drunk and kiss everybody, so that's what you do. Why not go to bed before midnight and escape the routine? I am not railing against society's expectations in general. I'm no rebel, really. I just happen to believe people's responses to situations shouldn't be rehearsed. No, that's not what I mean. I mean that certain responses shouldn't be expected.

Once I walked in on a girlfriend of mine who was involved in an intimate act with my best friend. What did I do? I apologized for interrupting. That was my first and I think, in the end, my most honest response. Later, I became jealous and angry and self-righteous. But my split-second reaction was the human one. Here were these two people whom I had no right to barge in on.

Or maybe I was a victim of manners myself?

Miss Rae (Angela to me – after all, we're practically married) seems refreshing in her candor. She admitted she had no sympathy and she dealt with you straight from the hip. That doesn't mean that people should get away with being ogres just because they openly admit to being ogres. But at least she knew her limitations and she wasn't out to harm you in any way. I need to know how she came into your life again, and why.

Don't worry about being crazy. My best friend, Art, thinks I'm a nutcase, I know. He tries to hide it from me, his concern for my sanity, but I can see. He makes drop-by visits to check up on me and his round face squeezes into an oblong-shaped picture of gloom whenever I say more than two sentences. To keep him happy, I let him do most of the talking. He's a divorced man and he sometimes trashes his ex-wife. He refers to her as the Swamp Creature. I've never met her, so I don't know the true story, but his hatred of

33

someone he once loved seems as crazy to me as my oddball takes on life must seem to him. So I believe we're all a little crazy. At least I hope so.

The idea of perfection worries me. I don't like symmetry. I'm like William Blake, I suppose. I find it fearful. People's foibles, their mistakes, their strange passions, make me hopeful for humanity in general. Everyone in this country seems to be yearning for balanced, healthy, centered lives. They go to the gym or to their analysts or appear on television talk shows to iron out their imperfections. 'I used to be a shopaholic, now I only spend ten dollars a month on essentials' – that kind of thing. It makes me nervous, all this balance.

A beautiful married woman fell madly in love with a beautiful young man. As a consequence the Trojan War was waged. And the Trojan War made possible the Iliad *and the* Odyssey. *I'm sorry about all those soldiers who died, I really am. But where would Homer have been without adultery?*

Uh-oh. I must sound like a serious pro-sinner. I don't want to be misunderstood here, but I think I won't be, so I will not apologize or explain myself further. I'll just say a few Hail Marys. And goodbye.

All my best,

Carl Lioce (pronounced Lee-oh-chee so maybe there's a Chinese connection somewhere in my antecedents' past)

Clare replaced the letter carefully in the correct sequence. He'd responded to her aircrash story in a way she could understand. He'd thought about her feelings with a sympathy which had taken her a few readings to grasp fully. He hadn't pressed her for the wrong details, as some people in her life had; the ones who'd say 'So what exactly was wrong with the plane?' or 'What were the stewardesses doing? Why weren't they looking after an unaccompanied minor?'

Carl had wanted to know what had happened next, which as

far as Clare was concerned was the important question to ask. What happens to Dorothy back in Kansas or, in her own case, back in Kensington?

Jeremy, after hearing her story of the crash, had given her a nice hug and said, 'That must have been awful. I'm so sorry for you.' She'd felt comforted and protected in his arms. Yet she'd also felt slightly empty, she remembered. As if there were a huge amount more to say, but no possible way of saying it. That wasn't his fault, she knew. He would have sat and listened attentively to whatever she chose to disclose to him, no matter how mundane it may have been. Why she never did go any further, why she so rarely talked about her past with Jeremy or anyone else, were questions which often worried her.

Was it because that past might make people look at her differently, judge her in a way she didn't think she wanted to be judged? Would people have thought she was too strange a child to grow up to become a normal adult? She *was* normal now, she knew. Somehow, once she'd left home and gone to university, she'd managed to keep her terror at bay, to avoid the feeling she'd had constantly as a child that doom waited around every unseen corner. Unable to understand where her fear had sprung from in the first place, she'd refused to question why it had finally left her.

Yes, some scary things had happened in her life; she had had severe asthma attacks ever since she could remember, attacks which made her feel that a dark and frightening monster was squeezing her lungs in a grip which would never loosen. The terror came from not being able to breathe, from a deadly constriction which tightened with each second.

Often she would end up in the Brompton Hospital, attached to a drip, but the supposedly comforting presence of doctors and authority never managed to reassure her. She had to wait until she felt the hands clenched around her lungs gradually let go and give up, until she was sure that the monster had, even if only momentarily, gone elsewhere.

The asthma episodes had started so early on in her life, that she knew she should have grown accustomed to them, but each time one came, she would be as panicked as the previous time.

Yet asthma was not a sufficient reason for her hysterical reactions to everyday life. Not every asthmatic child thought that each ambulance she saw was carrying the corpse of someone she knew. No other asthmatic child she happened to meet listened to the radio all night every night just to reassure herself that the world wasn't being blown up in a nuclear attack while she lay in bed. And what other little asthmatic girl on the planet thought that if she raised her voice too much, she'd literally explode?

The monster might let go of her lungs for weeks or months at a time, but that didn't mean he had left her. He was always in her mind, always threatening, crouching over her world, just waiting to pounce.

Why had she been so gripped by visions of death and destruction?

Her parents had divorced when she was only nine and didn't understand what was going on, but her terror had started at an earlier age, she knew. Besides, her parents had been reasonably civilized in their breakup. Clare remembered overhearing her father shouting at her mother, but she also remembered that her mother never shouted back. They didn't throw plates at each other or pull out kitchen knives. On the whole, she knew, they had acted in an adult fashion; they would have had to, because adult behaviour was important to them, so important that Clare understood instinctively she could never allow herself to act in childish ways herself. She kept her fears hidden when she was with her mother in London. And even when she went to Spain to visit her father, terrified of a possible trip to an unfamiliar foreign hospital, she remained outwardly calm.

Despite the hours spent in her father's smoke-filled car, Clare never had an asthma attack during her brief visits to Spain. She had to ask herself why this should be. Was it the Spanish weather or could she, if she *really* wanted to, control the monster? If she could keep him away from her in Spain, why couldn't she manage to do so in England? These questions plagued her, and the only answer she could find was a growing belief that her monster would choose not asthma but a different method to get at her in Spain.

After the plane crash, she calmed down for a while. Since disaster of a kind had, indeed, struck, and she had been so close to death and extinction, she thought for a brief, happy period that she'd experienced the worst and wouldn't have to worry any more. The monster had attacked and she had survived. Perhaps now he would leave her alone.

Two weeks after she returned home, she had another asthma attack. And soon afterwards, all the old terrors came back – with a vengeance. No one, not anyone in her life, knew how haunted she was by small, everyday occurrences. If the light bulb didn't go on in her room, she'd fall into a panic, thinking that the entire supply of electricity for the world had suddenly been cut off for ever. If she answered the telephone and someone hung up without speaking, she became convinced the caller was an alien terrorist, listening to the last human voice before it blew up the planet.

She spent afternoons fashioning long windpipes from straws. These contraptions, she hoped, would save people when the earthquakes came and buried them alive.

Ninety-nine per cent of her waking life was spent secretly pondering potential disasters and how to stop or, if that were impossible, survive them.

Had Anna read the letters yet, the ones where Clare confessed all this childhood horror to Carl? Did she now know what Carl knew – that the only antidote to this massive *Angst* had been moving away to university in Bristol, where, inexplicably and magically, the monster had vanished? She no longer suffered from severe asthma attacks, or any of the other terrors. When Clare turned eighteen, she also turned into a normal human being.

Before writing the letters to Carl, Clare had fooled everyone into thinking she'd *always* been calm and centred and well-balanced, everyone including Jeremy.

There was no reason not to tell Jeremy about her childhood craziness – she had simply chosen not to because it was no longer relevant to her life. She had outgrown it.

No, even if she did watch *Neighbours* twice in one day, at least she wasn't hiding in her bedroom terrified. There were worse things than a surfeit of daytime TV.

Clare put Carl's letter away, went back into the kitchen and switched on the News to watch Jeremy. But it was too late.

This Carl fellow is interesting, Anna thought, putting down letter number five. Strange, but interesting. Surprisingly enough, the manuscript had some potential, certainly a hell of a lot more potential than any other of Clare's strained novels. If the whole correspondence were jazzed up; if, for example, they were doing it on e-mail and all the boring bits were cut, it might just work.

Of course to get anything really buzzy going, Clare and Carl would have to meet. That was the key. If Carl were fairly presentable and Clare fell for him; well, that would be a decent premise. Especially given the Jeremy situation. Clare would have to make a choice. A real-life struggle between Italian rough-trade Yank and dashing Brit sports star would be spicy. Use different names in the book and give Clare a pseudonym so she'd feel safe. But then leak the true identities to the press pre-publication. A *roman-à-clef* to whet everyone's appetite.

Anna suddenly dropped the pen she was holding. She twirled her chair around so that she could see out of the window and onto Hampstead Heath. Why, she asked herself, was she bothering to come up with these far-fetched ideas for a book which had no hope of selling? These were kneejerk responses, ones she was getting sick and tired of having.

She was equally sick and tired of being regarded as a pushy, commercial American woman. She knew that's what they all thought, her 'fellow' Brits. No matter how hard she tried to fit in and to be one of them, in the end she couldn't and never would be. She could see it at parties, at any social gatherings, the way people's eyes narrowed slightly and their faces tautened whenever she talked too loudly or came on just a bit too strong. She could see the ticker-tape running through their brains. 'Anna is an American' it ran. 'Anna could live here fifty years and she'd still be an American.'

Not for fifty, but for fifteen years Anna had attempted to have it both ways – to mix socially with the British at the same time as maintaining a high-profile *selling* job. This was normally a contradiction in terms; her adopted fellow countrypeople didn't like anything as obvious as selling. They seemed to think that money should arrive like Christmas presents under the tree, delivered by an unseen Santa Claus.

There were still certain parties she wasn't invited to, she knew. And most probably there were jokes at her expense in the publishing world. Known as an in-your-face kind of agent who pushed hard and worked fast, Anna was not exactly everyone's cup of tea.

Feeling a rueful smile creep over her face as she thought of how calculatedly she'd switched from coffee to tea when she first arrived in London, Anna twirled her chair back to face her desk. She'd tried to pull off the impossible, to be both British and American. Now she felt neither. She wished she could climb aboard a plane, head for New York and stop midway over the Atlantic. Somewhere between the two countries she might possibly find a place where she felt she belonged.

Anna picked up letter number six. Clare James was never going to write a word about her relationship with Jeremy Letts, she knew that. The fact that she'd entertained that concept as a possibility for so long demonstrated how far-fetched and fantastical she could become in the hot pursuit of commercial ideas.

Clare's and Carl's letters would not make a book, either. But she liked them. There was something about them that appealed to her. What was it exactly? Why did she want to read on?

Romance.

The thought of Clare and Carl meeting and falling in love. Could she arrange it somehow? Could she set up a meeting between them?

What about Jeremy?

What about him? Anna had never liked cricket. She'd fallen asleep the only time she'd been taken to a match and the man who had taken her had been so condescending and patronizing to her afterwards, in the most cutting British way, that she'd thought seriously of hailing a cab outside Lord's and asking the driver to take her straight to Terminal Four.

The fact was, she had always hated *84 Charing Cross Road* as well. It irritated the hell out of her that those two never met, it just wasn't natural.

If she could set up a meeting between Clare and Carl – well, it wasn't work, it wasn't commercial – but it might be fun.

Anna, in her heart of hearts, was a true romantic.

Chapter 4

There was absolutely nothing to say.

Carl imagined a paramedic rushing into the restaurant with one of those machines they use in hospitals to kick-start the heart and applying it to each person in turn at the table. That was the only possibility of jump-starting the dead conversation into life. The two females, Cathy and Elizabeth, were sitting there expectantly, blue eye shadow glinting, lip glitter sparkling, waiting to be entertained. But entertained how? Not with conversation, Carl thought. They looked as if they expected Art and Carl to pick up guitars and break into an Oasis riff or invite them on a yachting trip around the Greek islands.

'So, Cathy . . .' he started, but he couldn't come up with any words to finish. She looked at him vacantly, then turned to her friend Elizabeth with an expression of boredom on her face.

'Carl probably wants to know if either of you have been involved in a plane crash.' Art was fixing Carl with an 'I'd kill you if I could' glare. 'He's interested only in women who've had near-death experiences. Isn't that right, Carl?'

'Don't.'

'Don't what?' Art asked in mock innocence.

'Just don't.'

'You see, Carl has this English friend who was in a plane crash once and was what I'd call pretty damn stoic about the whole thing. Now that's not surprising, given the British attitude to pain and suffering. You know, I lived over there for awhile, and I think it was in the first month or so, I was listening to the radio. They have a program called *Desert Island Discs* where some famous person gets to say what records he or she would take with them if he or she were shipwrecked on a desert island . . .'

'Wow. That's kind of a cool idea,' Cathy said.

'Yeah. Sure. So anyway there's this guy on called Douglas Bader, choosing his records. And the interviewer is asking him about his life and it turns out he was a pilot in the RAF during the war. Which isn't that amazing except the guy has no legs.'

'What?' Elizabeth asked, suddenly showing some interest.

'Right. No legs. I mean he had fake legs. He'd had some, plane accident before the war started. But the deal was he was desperate to fly in the war and beat up the Germans so he managed to fly with these fake legs. The interviewer is talking about all this and says, "It must have been difficult for you, when you were shot down over the Channel or wherever and you crashed and you didn't have any legs."'

'You're kidding.' Cathy perked up as well. 'Anyway, what kind of fake legs did he have? I mean, were they made out of plastic or what?'

'I have no idea,' Art sighed. 'And I'm not kidding. The point is, this Bader guy says, "Difficult? I wouldn't say that. A lot of people were worse off than me." And then the interviewer says, "But afterwards you escaped from Colditz. How did you manage that, what with the leg problem and everything?"'

'What's Colditz?' Elizabeth asked.

Carl grinned at the ceiling.

'A refrigeration company,' Art sighed. 'A prisoner of war camp, Elizabeth. The other side's, not ours, in case you were wondering. And the war I'm discussing is World War Two, not our incursion into Grenada. Anyway, you see the *point* of this story is that this guy, Douglas Bader, says, "No problem. A lot of people in that POW camp were worse off than I was" and he says it totally deadpan, like how could this interviewer be so stupid as to think not having legs in Colditz was a big deal, you know?'

'I'm not sure I get it.' Cathy frowned.

'It's this British shit.'

The two women looked at Art blankly.

'I mean it. It's bullshit. It's stiff upper brain, arrogant bullshit.' Art looked wildly around the table. 'I'm not getting my point across here, am I? Carl, help me out here, will you?'

'No.'

'Carl becomes monosyllabic after ten p.m.' Art turned to Elizabeth and struggled to lower his voice. 'That's one of his more endearing traits.'

'I don't know what you guys have going on here,' Elizabeth rose from the table, 'but I think we should leave. It's like, I mean, are you saying something against some poor man who has fake legs? That's not nice. I think Cathy and I are out of here.'

'Come on, ladies. Stay for an after-dinner drink. I didn't mean to trash a cripple, really I didn't. And I'm sure we can get Carl to utter a complete sentence. I know he hasn't managed it yet tonight, but some short one . . . maybe "Jane goes up the hill." At which point I could reply "*See* Jane go up the hill."'

'Thanks for the food,' Cathy said, already backing away from the table. 'But we have to be up, like, kind of early tomorrow.'

'Oh,' Art replied. 'I see.' He rose but then sat down again as the two women headed quickly towards the exit.

'Fantastic,' Art muttered, removing his glasses. 'You were great tonight, Carl. Sparkling, witty, debonair. Every young lady's idea of a dream date.'

'You're the one who set this up, Artie. I'm sorry if I didn't perform, but you could have gone out on your own with one of them. You didn't have to drag me along.'

'I was *hoping* to give you a good evening out. Two beautiful young women I met in a bar. OK, they're not sparkling conversationalists. In fact, English may be their third language. But so what? I thought I'd share my good fortune. I didn't know you were going to sit here acting like Forrest Gump on Valium.' He shoved his glasses back on in weary frustration.

Carl regarded his friend with affection. Even in his attack mode, Artie was somehow genial. Perhaps it was the way he constantly fiddled with his round tortoiseshell glasses, a nervous habit Carl empathized with. The first day Carl had walked into Art's office, five years previously, he had taken an instant liking to the slightly older man. Art had stood up behind his desk, offering an outstretched hand to Carl who, upon taking that hand in his own, had simultaneously recognized Art's weak eyesight and generous heart.

'Sorry,' Carl laughed. 'The girls were perfectly nice. I didn't have anything to say to them, that's all. And you blew yourself up at the end there, anyway. Dumping on a legless war hero was not a good move. They're kids. They're not cynics like you. They're *fresh-faced*. Almost scarily so.'

'You want me to bring the embalmed corpse of Bette Davis next time out?'

'I don't think I'm in the mood for dates, Artie.'

'No? Well, dates certainly aren't in the mood for you, judging from tonight. Christ, I never saw two people leave so quickly. They didn't even have time for the chocolate mints.'

Art picked up a mint, tore off the wrapper and popped it in his mouth.

'If I didn't know how poor you are, I'd say you should pay for this fiasco,' he commented, munching. 'I was expecting to have sex tonight,' he laughed. 'Well, all right. Maybe not sex, but at least a nice long kiss. Instead, I'm landed with looking at your sour face. *And* a fat bill.'

'Art, you don't have to make me feel guilty, I already do. I was a bore. But they were in their early twenties. I mean, I don't know what to say to people that young.'

'Your advanced age of thirty-five does not qualify you as geriatric. And your sweetheart over the sea may be nineteen, for all you know. You seem to know what to say to her.'

44

'Clare's different.'

'Clare's different. How many times have I heard that? This is getting bad, Carl. You were thinking about her all night, weren't you?'

'Yes.'

'That's part of the reason I set this date up, to try to get you to visit planet Earth for a few hours. What were you doing during dinner? Composing letters to her in your head?'

'I was wondering what *she'd* think of this place, of you, of Cathy and Elizabeth.'

'Listen . . .' Art reached out and grabbed Carl's elbow. 'You're living in a fantasy world, my friend. This isn't good. I know those women weren't going to be the loves of our lives and maybe I shouldn't have invited them. I know I was acting like an asshole, but you scare me sometimes, Carl. You take everything to heart too much. You have created this woman out of thin air and—'

'She exists, Art.'

'I know. I understand that she is alive. Maybe I should see more of the correspondence. I mean, that letter about the plane crash was fine. I get it. It was an interesting letter. But Jane Austen, she ain't. And chances are she isn't Kate Moss, either. You're setting this whole deal up as the correspondence of the century, as some almost other-worldly experience. And I'm afraid if you're ever let down by it, you'll feel as if you've been pushed off the top of the World Trade Center. What do you do all day, Carl? Sit in your apartment composing letters? What do you do all night? Wonder what she'd think about everyone you meet and everything you do? This is becoming obsessive. You need some distance from it. Let me read some more, let me try to help.'

'I can't give you all her letters. They're private. I shouldn't have shown you that one before, but I wanted you to understand a little about her.'

'Carl. Please. You're on the rebound from a bad marriage. I know what it's like – the Swamp Creature kicked me in the balls and it took me a long time to stand up straight again. But I didn't fall in love with some . . . some, *stranger.*'

'I'm not in love with her.'

'Right. And Pamela Anderson Lee is going to spearhead a campaign against cosmetic surgery.'

'Art.' Carl sighed. 'Do you know one of the reasons I like you so much? Because you never wear sunglasses.'

'So?' Art looked at Carl with a glance which said in effect, 'What the hell are you talking about?'

'So, you obviously don't need to be protected from the light. Which means you should be able to distinguish between friendship and romance by now.'

'OK. I don't understand you, I have no idea what you're talking about, but so what? The point is, I want you tell me something. Tell me – if you were writing to a man, would you have the same responses you're having now? I don't think so. You see, we're not talking about simple friendship.'

'She's married.'

'And you're an honorable guy. I'm aware of that. All your responses are really ethical, Carl, and I have always admired you for that. I'm even sure when you finally meet her, you'll refrain from jumping on her bones.'

'We're never going to meet.'

'I can't take this anymore.' Art put his head in his hands. 'I really can't. The only way you can stop this craziness *is* to meet her and find out she's not the same in person as she is in print. The longer this fantasy goes on, the more painful it will be when it ends – and it will end at some point, you know.'

'Why would I want to meet her? And why does it *have* to end?'

'Carl, please show me some more of these letters. For my sake, OK? I need to know what all this is *really* about.'

'It's about paying attention, Art. It's about time. Look at all these people in this restaurant. They're all anxious, they're all hurried. No one is listening to each other. Take that guy over there . . .' Carl nodded in the direction of a table by the window. 'He's sitting across from an attractive woman and he's talking. He's probably telling her a story, maybe about the time he had his appendix out when he was five. And she's pretending to listen. In fact, she's waiting for him to finish, so she can tell him *her* story about the tonsillectomy she had as a teenager. Right? They're trading bits of information and they're not concentrating.'

'So?'

'So, they're missing out. Everyone's life story is an epic narrative. You can't rush an epic. You shouldn't speed-read. But that's what we all do, we effectively speed-read each other's stories while we talk. *That*'s what's different about Clare, about Clare and me. We take our time. I can spend a week or more replying to a letter of hers. I can think about what she's said and why she's said it. I can't interrupt her out of some ego-driven impulse to get my own point across. We have time to consider each other, to listen.'

Art leaned forward. He looked at Carl for a moment, before replying with unusual passion in his voice, 'Life *is* about trading silly stories, Carl. Life is about not listening sometimes. You can say we're all living in the pages of *War and Peace*, but most of us are the guys who sweep the hall before Prince Andrei arrives. We're *not* all epic characters. You know how everyone decides they were Cleopatra or Hannibal in a past life? Well, my guess is that if I were to regress a few centuries, I'd find out I was the man in charge of ancient garbage disposal.' He reached out to put his hand on Carl's arm before continuing. 'We like to delude ourselves, to think we're all heroes. I don't want to depress you, but by and large we're normal human beings. We have normal marriages and sometimes they work and sometimes they don't. Everyone starts off in a romance thinking he's Romeo and she's Juliet, but reality comes tiptoeing in. After a few years, it comes stomping in. Wearing army boots. I love the romance, Carl, but I also love the reality. And that's the hard part, to love the reality.'

Carl leant forward as well. The two men looked as if they were about to start arm wrestling.

'Why can't romance be the reality? You're missing a whole level of life, Art. Making romance real. You can do it, but you need time, you need the right attitude. I have a perfect relationship with Clare because we started out in the perfect way – and we can continue in that way, we can keep things perfect. If we never meet.'

'You're screwy, Carlo. You know that? You're saving the only way to have a great relationship with someone is to write letters. I know Dee-Dee hurt you. But you can't become a hermit. This is Howard Hughes territory. You'll end up with five-foot-long fingernails and floor-length hair, scribbling away in some attic to a lady you've never met.'

Looking at Art's anxious, pinched face, Carl suddenly laughed.

'All right. Stop by my apartment on the way home, and I'll give you the whole correspondence. You'll understand what I'm talking about when you've read it.'

'What happened to privacy?'

'Well, I have a hidden agenda. I've often thought that Clare should be a writer. She *should* be read. I'd like to know if I'm right about that, and you could tell me. You know, I'd like to help her. Whatever she's doing now, she should use her natural talents.'

'Yeah,' Art shrugged. 'No problem. But if she's not talented, I'm going to be honest. Are you prepared for that?'

'Yes.' Carl mimicked Art's shrug. 'No problem.'

'Good. Now that that's settled, which one do you think I should call? Elizabeth or Cathy?'

'That's a joke, isn't it, Artie?'

'Kind of. I mean, sort of. Like. You know?'

'So, you think I have a *round* face? You don't understand why I hate the Swamp Creature? This sucks, Carl.'

'Art, just keep reading, all right? Let me get back to sleep.'

'A *round* face? My face is *not* round. My face is and always has been very, very *masculine* and *attractive*.'

'I'm hanging up.'

'You are *so* wrong. I'm looking in the mirror right now.'

'Don't look too long. You might disappear into your own reflection. Goodnight, Art.'

'Fuck off, Carl.' They were both laughing as they simultaneously hung up.

Art grabbed a box of chocolate chip cookies from the kitchen, poured himself a glass of dessert wine and settled back down on his capacious living-room sofa.

Letter Six

Dear Mr Lioce,

I think Salman Rushdie once wrote a long piece about The Wizard of Oz. *He couldn't understand why Dorothy would want to go back to Kansas, such a dull, bleak, tornado-strewn landscape. After meeting the Scarecrow, the Cowardly Lion and the Tin Man, who needs Aunty Em and Uncle Henry?*

Reading about your childhood, even those few short sentences, I picture so much noise and colour. Masses of children, all those pasta sauces, tenors booming out heart-breaking arias.

I lived in noiseless black and white.

My mother is a very controlled and defeated woman. She doesn't speak much; when she does, it's often hard to hear what she says. I have no siblings. At school, I tended to make friends with the most raucous girls. In effect, I would play the straight man to their comic routines and chaotic lives. They liked having me around, and I liked being around them. They didn't seem to mind that I never got into trouble, whereas they always did.

My friend Bernice, whom I have known since I was ten, is an effervescent mischief-lover. She was kicked out of our all-female school when she was thirteen. Why? She called our history teacher a 'cunt'. Our class sat in stunned disbelief. I don't think we really believed Bernice had said what she had. The history teacher, Miss Hall, certainly did, though. She walked straight up to Bernice, said 'You're gone' and smiled malevolently. You see, Miss Hall had always hated Bernice and had been goading her, Iagolike, to commit an offence heinous enough to get her booted out.

I suspect this may have had something to do with the fact that Bernice looked wanton when she was ten years old, so you can imagine what the elderly spinster Miss Hall felt when faced with Bernice at thirteen. Every class Miss Hall would pick on Bernice, asking her unanswerable questions and gloating when Bernice didn't reply. 'Do you all see how stupid Bernice is?' she'd asked that fateful day. 'Take note. Bernice will end up married to a stupid man and she will lead a stupid life. You will never get anywhere, Bernice. You're just a silly, dirty, little girl.'

'And you're just a dried-up cunt,' Bernice replied.

Bernice moved to a state school. (My school was what you call private, and what we call public.) She didn't last long there, either. Now she's in advertising and she calls her boss a 'cunt' every other second. He takes it as a compliment, she says.

Back to Kansas. I worked hard at school, I came home afterwards to my mother's house in Kensington and studied hard there. My mother and I watched the occasional show on television. She cooked me dinner and, at a fixed hour, I would go straight to bed. She didn't like conversing with children, even her own.

Every summer, from the age of nine to twelve, I would spend a gruesome week with my father in Spain.

Any passion or craziness in my life was vicarious. When I was a teenager, my friends provided me with wild tales of parties and boys and drugs and fun. They assumed I wouldn't want to attend these parties myself, and they were right. I wouldn't have known how to behave.

I watched. Sometimes I wonder whether I was always waiting. But if so – for what? I still don't know.

If I were to find my husband in bed with my best friend, I would apologize as well. And then I'd probably serve them tea.

My father was brash and manic and driven. Why my mother, who was a quiet, reserved and haughty woman, married him, I will never understand.

My father didn't refer to my mother as the Swamp Creature. I used to overhear conversations, when I was in Spain, in which he called her the Perfect Patrician Prig.

Were your parents happy together?

Was Helen happy with Paris before the Trojan War started? Can two passionate people coexist, or does too much intensity in one relationship burn it out?

Angela Rae re-entered my life when I was eighteen and back from university for a weekend. She simply showed up at our door and told my mother she wanted to take me to the Ritz.

'I'm going gambling,' she announced. 'I need a chaperone. Could you lend me your daughter for the evening?'

It's hard to explain why it's impossible to say 'no' to Angela. I'm sure you'll understand when you're married to her.

All my best,

Clare James

Art finished his wine and stared at the letter on his lap. They were strange people, Carl and Clare. But that wasn't the point. The point was that he wanted to keep reading.

And that gave him an idea.

Cursing Art for waking him from a deep sleep, Carl lay in bed and stared at the ceiling. He didn't know the couple who inhabited the apartment above his, but he found it interesting that their floor should be his ceiling. He could hear their footsteps, and occasionally sounds of what could have been either aerobic exercises or Spanish dancing. What did they hear of his life? Did they ever put their ears to the ground and eavesdrop? No, that was something only he would do.

On nights like this – well, on every night, if he were honest – he missed Dee-Dee. He longed for her sleeping body beside him, the way she thrashed her legs in scissor-like movements when she was in the midst of a dream; leftover muscle responses, he supposed, from her days spent teaching jazz dance to hopeful amateurs.

Right now, he would have liked to wake Dee-Dee up and do some dancing of his own. Their marriage had worked for long enough to make him believe it would work for ever. Yet eighteen months ago she had taken her dancer's legs and walked out on him, spouting incomprehensible – to him – phrases about discovering her own balance of power.

He couldn't blame her for leaving. He didn't even want to blame her. She'd made the right decision. His career was going nowhere fast, his temperament was unstable and his sex drive had gone from phenomenal to non-existent. He had tried to sympathize with her desire to fufil her own potential; he listened to her monologues on self-realization, and he nodded approvingly when she told him she needed space. He did everything and anything to keep her with him, but one day she took off and raced out the door as if she'd been locked in for decades.

Carl knew he wasn't having a mid-life crisis. He wasn't old enough. He'd just lost the plot, he didn't know who he was supposed to be in his own epic narrative. The hero? Or, as Art had suggested, a minor character who walks in and out of the story with no apparent purpose?

Art had a drive, a certainty, that Carl admired. Art knew he wanted to succeed in life and that was just what he was doing. Art was making money. He could criticize the Swamp Creature and date young women and make speeches and have too much to drink occasionally, all the while taking pleasure in himself and his possessions.

Also, Art had a head-down, eyes-blinkered-to-everything-but-the-ultimate-goal walk. He never meandered or ambled aimlessly. Art was impossible to distract; whereas Carl found it increasingly difficult to sit on a subway without asking the person next to him what he or she thought this world was all about. He had to restrain himself from going up to homeless people on the street and asking them what exactly had happened to bring them to this point in their lives. Tonight, when they'd left the restaurant, Art had put on a silly little plaid cap, so silly and ridiculous, it had touched Carl's heart to the core. He'd wanted to put his arms around Art and kiss the top of that cap.

Carl knew he was acting like a drunk without drinking. What he didn't know was how much this should worry him.

He thought about Clare. It would be six o'clock in the morning her time, so she was probably asleep. Did she have children? He suspected not. No mother could have sustained that lengthy a correspondence without mentioning her children. Did she go out to work? Probably. But doing what? Was she a bank teller? A policewoman? A call-girl?

What was this husband, this Jeremy like? Did he dote on her? Had they been married for a couple of years or a quarter of a century? Carl had been brave in the last letter he'd sent, he knew. He'd taken a risk and asked Clare if she thought he would like Jeremy. That was a small yet definite infringement of the ground rules. But he'd needed to know.

Who the fuck was this Jeremy guy?

And why had he, Carl, lied? Why had he told Clare he'd never been married himself?

He didn't want to admit to his failed marriage with Dee-Dee. He'd re-written the script and taken her part out. How crazy was that? How could he possibly think he was having an honest relationship with Clare when he had lied like that?

He was human. Humans lied. He could remember his first lie when he was five years old. He'd told his mother he hadn't had a candy bar before dinner. And she'd believed him. The small triumph he'd felt, the wonder of getting away with something, had been astounding. So *that's* what lying is, he'd thought. Boy, it's easy. And kind of fun.

His lie about the non-existence of Dee-Dee thirty years on had been what lies become the older you get. Shabby. No fun at all.

Carl gave up any hope of sleep and went to the corner of his living room where the computer lived. He turned it on and tapped into the file of his letters to Clare. He wanted to find the genesis of the lie. It had been in response to what she'd said about finding her husband in bed with another woman, he remembered. The word 'husband' had hit him, jumped off the page straight at his solar plexus. He'd assumed, for no good reason, that she wasn't married. It unnerved him – the picture of Clare all settled into her English domestic scene. Cosy tea and crumpets or whatever the hell they all ate and drank over there. How could he tell her he hadn't been able to make his own home the kind of place no one could bear to leave?

Letter Seven

> *Dear Clare,*
>
> *I'm sorry, but I don't think I can refer to you by your full name anymore. It's wonderfully old-fashioned and polite, I know, but it sounds false at this point. As if I were trying too hard not to be American. Which I am, Clare. American, I mean. Which I decidedly am.*
>
> *I learnt about trying too hard when I was a boy, seeing this little runt of a kid who lived a few blocks from us, little Danny, who wanted so badly to be a part of everything that he would actually give his treasured bicycle away to get a pat on the head. Danny hounded people. Followed them down the street, his head pointed like a dog's, his eyes following their footsteps, his mouth in a permanent expression of eager hope. God was this kid eager. And God was this kid reviled.*
>
> *'That boy, he tries too hard,' my mother announced one afternoon when Danny came over to our house uninvited and proceeded to loiter, thrilled as anything to be within the walls of our family's house. As if it were a passport to popularity to cross our threshold. And I suppose it was, in a way. We had juice, our family. My brothers were all cool, my sisters were beautiful. We were immensely popular, all of us. And Danny was doing his parasite act, hanging on to our backs for dear life.*

I wanted to know why it was that Danny did try too hard. So I suggested to him that I go with him to his house one day. We lived in Brooklyn. Not in a tenement. We lived in a tree-lined street and had nice neighbors and none of us touched drugs until we were at least sixteen. Which was when Danny finally found his place in life. He became a dealer.

But on that afternoon when we were ten and I asked to go over to his house, Danny fell into a panic fit.

'You can't, Carl,' he said. And then he added, 'I'm sorry. I'm really, really sorry.'

'Why can't I?'

'You just can't.'

My mother could hear all this going on.

'Carl,' she commanded. 'Don't be pushy, OK?'

'OK,' I said, not only because I respected my mother's wishes, but because I knew from the way she said it that she knew why I couldn't go over to Danny's and I figured she'd tell me as soon as we'd managed to get Danny out of our kitchen. Which wasn't easy, but we did it.

'So?' I asked, when he'd finally given up and gone. I was ten years old and cocky and I knew she loved me. 'Why can't I go over to Danny's?'

'Because he doesn't want you to.'

'Why not?'

'That's not for you to find out. That's his business.'

'But you know.'

'That's my business. There are things I know about you; you want me to tell Danny every little thing about you when you were a baby boy and how scared you used to be of swimming, for example?'

'No.'

'OK.'

'OK.'

'That boy, he tries too hard,' was all she would say.

Later on, when Danny became the Dealer and people needed him, he told me he'd always wished my parents were his parents. We were stoned at the time and this information didn't particularly interest me. I was concentrating on the music coming out of his car radio.

'Yeah, well,' I said. 'They're not flawless, you know. My parents.'

'You know nothing about flaws, Carl,' he shot back. 'You know fuck all about flaws.'

After that, I knew that I could have found out whatever I wanted to about Danny and why he'd tried too hard when he was a kid, but I didn't want to anymore. I had a feeling that that knowledge might overwhelm me.

We all learned from Danny how fatal it was to try too hard. And that helped a lot, especially later when it was dating time.

But I also think I took the principle of not trying too hard way too far. Which is why, I suppose, I've never settled down with a woman. Unlike you, I couldn't quite make it to the altar. I never tried hard enough.

There it was. Carl stopped at the sentence, pinpointing the moment of untruth. A whole complex story leading up to a whopping lie. Why? 'Because I'm human. And these days I know a whole hell of a lot about flaws.'

He turned the computer off and ambled back into the darkness.

Chapter 5

'You're setting them up on a television show?' Bernice asked, wondering, as she always did when she saw Anna, what Mr Anna had been like and where he was now. Everyone seemed to know that Anna had been married, but no one could say what had happened to the man. Anna didn't have any pictures of him, never mentioned his name and immediately cut Bernice off the one time she'd asked her about him.

'What's wrong with that?' Anna stared at Bernice across the table.

'Isn't that a little over the top? Meeting on a television show?'

'Funny – that's the phrase everyone used when I explained Simon's potential in the market-place. Over the top, they kept repeating. Have you forgotten how I succeeded with Simon?'

'I wish I could forget.' Bernice felt her shoulders sag in despair. Simon the Skunk. Her nemesis. The very mention of his name brought back memories of a whole childhood spent listening to her father's bedtime tales of Simon the Skunk and his Robin Hood-like exploits in the Forest of Dean. She hated that shitty skunk almost as much as she supposed Fergie's kids hated Budgie the bloody Helicopter.

Every night when her father came to tell her another episode in Simon the Skunk's life, Bernice would recoil from the smell of his Paco Rabanne aftershave, as if it were an odour let off by Simon himself. She had no interest in Simon's cute antics and was horrified when her father announced he was trying to sell the tales of Simon to a publisher.

Anna was his agent. Anna and Simon together made her father famous. The fact that Bernice's father was named Simon and he had called the skunk after himself was somehow so embarrassing that Bernice cringed with shame every time she saw *any* kind of animal. Upon hearing that Simon the Skunk was to become a national figure, a new version of Paddington Bear, she punched her bedroom wall and wept with despair.

'I can do for Clare what I did for Simon,' Anna said proudly.

'What, you're going to turn her into a skunk and send her into a forest?'

'Very funny. No, I'm going to bring her to life. I'm going to force her into a situation she'd never have the nerve to bring about herself by setting up this meeting with Carl on American TV.'

'But—'

'Do you have any idea how intense this correspondence has become?'

Anna interrupted, her eyebrows moving up and down with a rapidity Bernice found disconcerting. How old was Anna? Hard to tell, and Bernice had never asked. Somewhere in her late thirties, possibly early forties. Closing fast on past it, anyway. Is it hard to pull after forty? she thought of asking Anna but, noticing the silver penknife on Anna's desk, decided to stick to the subject at hand.

'It doesn't sound too intense to me. Clare talks about Carl fairly often, but always as if he's a good friend, a pen-pal type of bloke.'

'It's more than that. I've seen the letters – she gave them to me. She's terribly close to him, you know. She confides in him.'

'You think she's fallen in love with Carl?'

'Do you?' Anna cocked her head to the side and smiled.

'Anna – God! – you really think they'll get together if they meet?'

'Maybe.' Anna's smile transformed her momentarily into a young girl.

'What is all this? Are you giving up being a literary agent and starting a dating agency?'

'Don't *you* think they should meet?'

'I don't know. I suppose so. But on TV?'

'It's as good a place as any. Plus, then we all get to watch it. What's the point of arranging a meeting if we don't get to see it ourselves? Cupid likes to watch his arrow hit, you know.'

'It's certainly dramatic.'

'Romantic *and* dramatic. Exactly.' Anna clapped her hands. They were ringless, Bernice noted, and fairly plump. Yet Anna's frame was thin. She could wear miniskirts or tight jeans with ease and grace, but she had never deviated from just-above-the-knee-length power suits. Today she had an ice blue number on with a white silk blouse. Bernice found herself looking at her own deep purple fingernails, black baggy jeans and black sweatshirt. The contrast was faintly alarming.

'Look, Bernice – let me put it this way – if you knew the Prince was out there with the slipper trying to find Cinderella, and you also knew exactly where Cinderella lived, wouldn't you do something to get them together?'

'I'm not sure. Aren't you supposed to let the Prince find his own way?'

'Come on – everyone needs a little help these days, even Princes. *Especially* Princes.'

'Excuse me, but where exactly does Jeremy Letts fit in to this scheme?'

'I'm not sure. He may end up winning, as usual, I just don't know. Listen, Bernice, it's simple. I read all the letters and I got caught up in them – in the possible romance of them – those two together. And once I'd decided that they should meet, I went for it one hundred per cent. Which happens to mean, in my case, television. It *is* over the top, I agree. But that's the way I work, that's the way I think. It's the American in me I've been denying for too long, all right? If they met in a bar or at the top of the Empire State Building or whatever it would be the typical, usual story. This way, it's different. It's glorious.'

'So Jeremy be damned?'

'I figure Jeremy can take care of himself. Besides, even though my gut instinct tells me Carl Lioce is a good-looking, presentable man, I can't be sure, can I? Clare could be sick at the sight of him. He could be a real dog.'

'Anna.'

'You know what I mean.'

'So you've already talked to the producer of the show?'

'Mmm,' Anna nodded. 'Actually, he's an old flame of mine. He's just the type to be running a show like *Magic Moments*.'

'And it's like *Surprise, Surprise!*?'

'Right. It's the American equivalent. People meet people they haven't seen for years, couples get re-united, all that heart-rending stuff. Clare and Carl meeting for the first time will be right up their street.'

'I don't understand. Why don't *you* go with her? Why me?'

'Because I am pulling the wool over her eyes, Bernice. I'm telling her that she's going to appear on this show to plug *Breathing in the Dusk*. How many times do I have to explain this to you? She *thinks* she's got a new, trendy American publishing company which has bought the rights to *Breathing in the Dusk* and is now going to publicize it. She doesn't know it is all a set-up to get her on the air, on a live television show in New York where she will meet Carl. I know she'll be angry with me at first for tricking her, no matter how well it goes with Carl. She'll need a cooling-off period. That's what you're there for.'

'I think this could all turn out very badly,' Bernice frowned. 'And I still don't understand. How are you going to get Carl to be on this show too? Are you going to tell him he's there to meet

Clare? He doesn't sound like the type of man who would like to have a first date on nationwide TV.'

'Leave that to me. I guarantee it will be a surprise for him too. For both of them. And don't worry if it does go badly, if they dislike each other on sight, for example. It's a cable show based in New York. It's not broadcast nationwide.'

'Oh. Well, that's a *huge* relief.'

Bernice stopped silently comparing clothes with Anna and started silently comparing hair-styles. Anna often changed the way she wore her hair. Today it was in a bun on top of her head, fashioned into a mound like Patsy's in *Ab Fab* – a beehive.

The last time she'd seen Anna, a month ago, her hair had been à la Jennifer Aniston in *Friends*. Was Anna conscious of modelling herself on female television stars, Bernice wondered, or was this reflecting a deep, hidden, unconscious desire for screen fame? Was that why Anna was so keen to get Clare on television? Was she living vicariously?

Bernice forced her eyes from the top of Anna's head, then forced her mind back on track.

'Do you think Clare will really believe a television show wants to plug *Breathing in the Dusk*? You need a plumber to *un*plug that book. It's so stiff, the pages have arthritis. Oh, Jesus—' Bernice sighed. 'I didn't mean that. But this plan is totally absurd, Anna. Clare is not a good candidate to be surprised on live television, even a non-national cable programme. She's not going to gush and enthuse, you know. She's not like that. It's as if you wanted to turn Maggie Thatcher into Paula Yates or something.'

'Bernice,' Anna leant back in her chair, 'I'm paying for this trip.'

'Does that include,' Bernice leant forward, 'an up-market hotel?'

'Absolutely.'

'And restaurant meals?'

'As long as they're not excessive.'

'And what's my part in all this?'

'You calm her down afterwards. Explain to her that I set this up for her own good. Also, make sure she doesn't catch on to anything beforehand.'

'What's in it for you, Anna? You're paying for our trips, putting us up, what do *you* get out of it?'

'You know something?' Anna swivelled her chair and looked out of the window, her eyes travelling across Hampstead Heath. 'I have no idea. Maybe I'd like it if someone did something like this for me. Or maybe it's the story. I want to find out what happens next in the story. The letter-writing part is finished, as far as I'm concerned. Now it's time for some action.'

Cricket was in a bad shape in this country before Jeremy came onto the scene. We'd been humiliated in the World Cup, which is, I suspect, like the World Series over there, or the Super Bowl – in other words, the really big match. But you don't play other nations in baseball or American football, do you? The difference here, you see, is that we do. When other countries consistently beat us, we feel ashamed. There's a national malaise. My husband changed all that . . .

Clare stopped, staring at the words 'my husband'. Why was she carrying on this absurd charade? Why lie to Carl of all people? And what would Anna think, if she *did* ever manage to read the entire manuscript? How humiliating. She could try to explain by telling the truth, of course. She'd made a comment in a letter, saying that, if she were ever to find her husband in bed with her best friend etc., etc., and Carl had misunderstood, had taken her literally, instead of realizing that she was positing the worst-case scenario of discovering someone you love with someone else. Carl had written back and said that unlike her, he'd never married. Well, she *could* have set him straight in the next letter, but she hadn't.

Why not?

Partly because she liked the idea of stopping any romantic

thoughts which could spring from this correspondence dead in their dangerous tracks. It made life simpler and the letters easier to write. If she had protested, if she had said, 'Carl, I'm *not* married. Jeremy and I are a couple but we're not married,' wouldn't that have sounded as if she were opening some kind of door, particularly as Carl had just told her *he* wasn't married? With this one deception, she'd managed to squelch any potential embarrassment.

Now, after almost a year and a half's worth of letter-writing, she knew Carl well enough to believe he wouldn't have forced any romantic issue between them even if he had known she was single, but back then, back at the beginning of it all, she wasn't as confident. After all, he was a man, and men were always *thinking* of sex, weren't they?

Wasn't that what Billy Crystal had said in *When Harry Met Sally . . .* that it was impossible for men and women to be simply friends? Well, it wasn't impossible in letters, especially if one of the letter-writers was married.

But it was more complicated than that, Clare knew. She was practising in her letters, getting used to the idea of being Jeremy's wife. He hadn't asked her to marry him yet, but he might, and if he did, she wanted to be prepared.

'Clare, you ginormous bitch!' Bernice had exclaimed after Clare had announced that she and Jeremy were going to live together. 'Why does everything in your life seem to work out so perfectly?'

Bernice had asked this in a tone of undisguised, though supposedly light-hearted jealousy. Bernice believed Clare led a golden, trouble-free life. To protest, to say, 'Hang on, it's not always the way it seems, *I* have problems too' would appear to be begging for undeserved sympathy.

Clare knew that Bernice had been adopted as a child and that for very good reasons Bernice felt misunderstood and unloved. Clare also knew that Bernice saw the good-looking, attentive, famous Jeremy and assumed all was idyllic in Clare's life, just as she had assumed, when they were little girls together, that Clare's asthma was nothing more than a minor medical inconvenience.

How could Clare explain her unhappiness to Bernice? The task was similar to explaining cricket to Carl. The subtleties, the nuances seemed ineffable and, at the core, faintly ridiculous.

What would happen if she said, 'Jeremy's too good. He's too nice. Everyone tells me how lucky I am to have him and it drives me wild. His constant good behaviour makes me want to do something wicked. He is robbing me of my self, bit by bit. When we have people round for dinner, he insists on cooking. When we've finished eating, he leaps up and clears the dishes while I sit there listening to other women marvel at his helpful nature. He doesn't lose his temper. He pats me on the head like a dog when he leaves the house.

'If he is so clearly the "nice" one in the couple, who am I? If he is so clearly the successful one in the couple, who am I? I could sit back and decompose slowly and he would carry the weight of this relationship in his handsome arms with consummate ease. Sometimes I think he could point to an ashtray on a table and say "This is Clare" and everyone would nod and smile.

'I am living with a perfectly nice, caring man and I yearn for a tough, difficult character whom I could scream bloody murder at – someone whom my friends would occasionally come round and console me about. "I don't know how you do it, Clare," they'd murmur. "You're amazing." A man who was dangerous and tricky and not entirely safe.'

But what would Bernice do if I said all this? Wouldn't she say, 'Spare me the sob story. You don't know what it's like *not* to have anybody – you've had it all too easy – all your life. How can you possibly whine about a man being *too* nice and *too* supportive when I am aching for any man who will offer me any kind of love on a permanent basis? *I* would take Jeremy's love and run on it happily for the rest of my life.'

She would be right, of course.

So I don't say anything to Bernice. I just nod and smile like some lucky dumb animal when she tells me how perfect my life is. And only once in a while, at times like this, do I admit to myself that my life isn't perfect. And I wonder what it would be like to be Mrs Jeremy Letts.

Pushing her unfinished letter to Carl away, Clare picked up the postcard she'd received from Angela Rae that morning. It showed a white beach with a grass hut in the background. Turning it over, she re-read the one-line greeting.

'What are you doing with your life?'

'I'm taking care of your house.' Clare answered the question out loud. 'I'm trying to keep it clean and tidy and I'm answering your mail occasionally and I'm waiting for Jeremy to come back from South Africa. If I knew how the hell I could find you, Angela, I'd write to you and tell you how grateful I am for this house, how pleased I am to live amongst your few possessions.

'I won't tell you I've bought a television; I suspect it might drive you mad. I won't ask you when you're coming back because I know you won't answer. I won't mention that I'm afraid you might die at some point during this seemingly endless sailing trip. I certainly wouldn't dare to say how much I've missed you. Or how lost and alone and strangely *thirsty* I often feel. Carl's the only one I can talk to about you. Carl's the only one who understands.'

It was getting to be a bad habit, Clare realized. The way she kept re-reading letters from her correspondence with Carl. She'd go to her study desk in the same way Bernice went to the refrigerator. Guiltily, yet savouring the prospect of a treat. No one would understand this particular addiction, or what craving it satisfied, but more and more often she'd go and pull out the letters, devour the words and then place them back in their drawer.

This time she tried to excuse herself by pretending she had to file Angela's postcard in its proper place, in the drawer below the Carl–Clare letters. As soon as she'd put away the postcard, she gave up any pretence and indulged herself.

Letter Eight

March 30

Dear Carl,

You're right. It's time we were on a first-name basis. You know, this is a fairly tiny island nation on the large scale of the world, and living here can be claustrophobic. That's why, I suspect, people tend to keep their distance, be more reserved than in an open, ranging country like America. An American friend of mine here who now says she hates the States, still admits to missing the idea of getting in her car and driving across country for days on end. 'Hitting the end of the road in Scotland is a lot different than hitting the end of the road in California,' she sighs. 'And the M1 doesn't really live up to Route 66.'

So we're physically and psychologically bound. Country lanes are beautiful but very, very narrow. There are hedges everywhere. People need their space, obviously, so they keep it inside themselves. Americanisms have crept in on us – people in shops often say 'Have a nice day' too, but it's very rare to enter into a conversation with a stranger.

The English are known to be eccentric, particularly members of the upper classes, but we're not idiosyncratic. I think eccentrics are often quite similar in their eccentricity – they share many of the same peculiarities – so they're easily recognized and satirized. People who are truly idiosyncratic – well, let me put it this way – I don't know one English person who would write letters to unknown names in foreign telephone directories.

That's why it was strange to come downstairs and discover Angela Rae in my mother's house that evening. I found it hard to believe that she would have remembered my name, much less looked me up again after six years. I thought she had been pleased to get rid of me in the airport. Pleased to be shot of me for ever.

After we'd shaken hands, she ordered me to change my clothes. 'Dress for roulette,' she said. 'That means no jeans.'

My mother, who, I suspect, was relieved whenever I left the house, nodded to me, motioning for me to go back upstairs and get ready. I did just that, throwing on a skirt and blouse, wondering what the hell was going on.

Angela had a black cab waiting outside. And Angela, being Angela, didn't speak on the ride to the Ritz. I'm wrong. She said one sentence. 'Your mother should never have married your father, but she should have had you even though she doesn't seem to know that, so I suppose there's some sense in it all.'

We strode through the lobby of the Ritz. Angela never walks, she strides. I was having trouble keeping up with her. She was dressed impeccably, in a tailored dark blue suit. But she still looked like a witch.

'Stand beside me at the roulette table,' she commanded. When we entered the casino she told me to keep my mouth shut and watch.

She then proceeded to win four hundred pounds. I think it took her about half an hour.

We left the table and she strode to the Palm Court, where we sat down. She ordered two glasses of champagne.

'You're old enough to drink now, thank God,' she said. 'I'm not in the mood for Coca-Colas.'

'How did you find out where I live?' I asked.

'Clare, there are a few important points to understand in life. The first is that you shouldn't ask questions which aren't relevant to the occasion. The second is that you deserve to be surprised.'

'Why did you bring me here?'

'So that someday, any day in the future, when you want to, you can tell this story to someone. Who will be just as interested in the answer as you are right now.'

'Will you tell this story to anyone?'

That was the first time I heard Angela Rae laugh. She has a girlish laugh, Carl. A tantalizing laugh. Flirty and fun and enticing.

'Yes, she answered, 'I'm sure I will. But I'll probably change some of the details.'

'Which ones?'

'None of your business.'

That reminds me, you see, of your mother, that day with Danny, the boy who tried too hard. Your mother knew what was best left unsaid, just like Angela.

Angela Rae gave my life meaning. She wasn't a fairy godmother. Oh, she gave me a glass of champagne that evening, she gave me many glasses of champagne on many subsequent evenings. But she wasn't a warm person, or a visibly affectionate one. We've never hugged or even kissed each other on the cheek. I've always been frightened of her. But she's the only person who believes in me.

Clare felt the same shock she did whenever she came to re-read this sentence. Before she'd written it, she'd never thought of Angela in that way, but as soon as the words were on paper, she knew it was true. Each letter to Carl revealed more and more of her psyche, as if she were doing a psychological dance of the seven veils, except in this dance there was no set number of veils, they just kept falling off, surprising herself probably a lot more than Carl.

Had she let him think she was married because she wanted him to keep his distance from her, or because she needed to keep her distance from him?

'Jesus, Carl,' she said to the air. 'You're dangerous.' Then she smiled.

Bernice pulled a Dime bar out of her coat pocket and looked at it longingly, before pitching it into the bin at the foot of the Tube station stairs. Clare had never had to worry about eating. She burned calories in her sleep, it seemed. She could eat ten Dime bars a day, if she wanted. It wasn't fair, but then life wasn't fair. Hadn't some American president announced that once as if it were a new and startling concept? Bernice tried to remember which president, but gave up. She'd probably heard about it in school and she knew she'd forgotten almost everything she'd ever heard at school.

Bernice had gone through schools like a snooker ball in a trick shot, bouncing off educational establishment after educational establishment and finally landing in the pocket labelled 'give up and get a job'.

It hadn't been her fault, not really. She had a habit of blurting things out, that's all; saving the wrong thing at the wrong time to the wrong person. Teachers had hated this propensity, headmistresses and masters had booted her out for it. She couldn't keep her mouth shut and that one simple failing had landed her in more trouble than she cared to remember. Now, finally, she'd found a job where her boss actually enjoyed her uncensored views and statements. However, she'd also discovered a whole new area to cause havoc in . . . her romantic life.

Why did men hate it so much when you told the truth? Why weren't you allowed to say when you liked them? It didn't make sense to Bernice, but she knew it was one of those immutable rules in life you had to take on board if you were ever going to sustain a relationship. Bernice wished she had taken a course in Creative Lying or could find a book entitled *How to Stay Silent*. Sometimes she thought she was on the verge of learning the basics, but then she'd screw up yet again.

The last man she'd fallen for had been the worst. Paul had been tall and blond and devastating and she'd cautioned herself over and over again not to reveal to him how hard she'd fallen. All was proceeding fantastically well when he took a business trip to Amsterdam and asked her to meet him there the following weekend. On the Thursday evening before, she'd decided to have some fun and visit a psychic whom a girlfriend of hers had recommended.

Marie, dressed all in white, sitting in a council flat in Harlesden, took Bernice's hand in hers and foretold marriage. 'You will marry the man you are going to meet soon on a trip,' she'd said.

'Is he blond?' Bernice had asked.

'How should I know?' Marie had responded.

The following night, sitting in a bar in Amsterdam with Paul,

Bernice had too much to drink. Christ, she'd been nervous, that was all. Was it so terrible to light into a bottle of white to steady her beating heart?

'So,' Paul asked after telling her all about his business meetings, stories which she had listened to with an intense look of interest on her face, 'what have you been up to this week?'

Bernice racked her brain. What *had* she been up to? Well, she'd been thinking about him every second, plotting what she was going to wear, buying new underwear. But no, that would not be a good way to carry on the conversation.

'I've been to a psychic,' she finally said, finishing another glass. 'A woman named Marie. She was incredible. Incredibly astute.'

'Really? What did she say?'

Even as she answered Bernice knew she was making a major mistake. She couldn't help herself, though. It was somehow impossible not to babble on.

'She said I was going to marry the man I was about to meet on a trip. Which must mean you, I guess.'

His eyes turned from hers instantaneously. The air between them grew still. It was over. One wrong sentence and the entire fabric of her life had been torn to tiny bits.

The rest of the weekend was filled by his desperate efforts to extricate himself from the relationship and hers to keep it going.

Clare would never have been so stupid, Bernice found herself thinking enviously. Clare was like some Zen master of control. She never indulged in the excesses which ruled Bernice's psyche, but never judged those excesses, either. She seemed to love tales of adventure and craziness and passion. She would absorb them the way she absorbed food, without any visible effect.

Sometimes Bernice felt as if Clare *waited* for her stories, as if she lived vicariously through them, just as it now seemed to her that Anna was living vicariously through Clare. Some-times – Bernice watched the train pull into the station and unsuccessfully scanned the carriages for any attractive man – sometimes, very occasionally, Bernice felt Clare was a little like an emotional vampire, draining all Bernice's blood for her own private use.

Until she read Clare's novels, Bernice had had more than a few troubling thoughts when it came to her friend. She felt that Clare had been favoured at birth. She lived in a big house on Victoria Street in South Kensington with an aristocratic type of sexless, slightly fucked-up mother and an absent, then dead, father. Bernice considered this wildly preferable to her own desperate-to-be-aristocratic adoptive parents – a mother who drank too much and a father who wrote about skunks.

That was how she and Clare had first become friends – through their parents. Bernice's father, a middle-middle-class businessman had gone way out on a financial limb to buy the sought-after Kensington house right next to Clare's mother. He'd scampered out to the very edge of that limb in order to enroll his daughter at the same private school as Clare. Luckily, Simon the Skunk had pulled him back to financial safety at the very moment the bough was going to break.

Bernice's parents had pushed Bernice at Clare, constantly inviting Clare round and trying to set up a socially acceptable friendship between these two girls. Bernice understood the transparency of it all and hated her parents for foisting Clare upon her – but when she'd found that despite all her antipathy, she couldn't help but like Clare, she'd given in and allowed them the pleasure of making the 'right' connections for their daughter. This was the one and only time Bernice's parents had derived any pleasure at all from their daughter's choice of friend.

Often, Bernice found herself wondering not whether her father and mother wished they could have traded her in for a different adopted baby, but exactly how early on in her childhood they had had that wish. Had they discussed with each other how unsatisfactorily she had turned out? No, it was more likely that they had kept their thoughts to themselves. Disappointment was a private emotion. Bernice understood that herself.

Clare had had it easy, there was no doubt about it. Of course, she'd suffered from asthma, but it never seemed to affect her particularly badly. Occasionally she'd have to pull out her puffer and inhale away, and every once in a while she'd have a short stint in hospital, but as far as Bernice was concerned, the asthma was a godsend for Clare.

It meant she was in the enviable position of being let off games at school.

Then, when Clare was older and out in the world, determined to make it on her own, she ran straight into Jeremy Letts' handsome arms and was given Angela Rae's house to live in rent-free.

Bernice didn't have any Jeremy Letts or Angela Raes in her life. She didn't have any unknown male foreign correspondent sending her letters, either. What she did have were *nouveaux riches* parents who considered their adopted daughter mad, bad and dangerous to give money to.

It really wasn't fair.

Bernice would chastise herself for feeling envious when these thoughts assailed her, decide to be a better, kinder person, and ring Clare up for lunch or a chat. After finishing the last page of *Between Pauses*, though, Bernice closed the book, and allowed an unaccustomed feeling of depression to swamp her. It was a story of missed opportunities. Characters would start off on a trip and never arrive at the destination. Women would begin a love affair only to have it fizzle out. There were never any confrontations or dramatic scenes, just some flickering and then fading and finally dead hopes. The book was no fun at all.

When *Breathing in the Dusk* was published, Bernice opened it with a premonition of dread. Which was, in time, fufilled. The same stalled action, the same unrealized dreams, a relentless parade of losers wiling away their empty lives. It was appallingly forlorn.

At that point, Bernice decided it was time to confront Clare. She rang her, told her she'd just finished *Breathing in the Dusk* and wanted to discuss it with her. 'Did you like it, Bernice?' Clare had asked. Bernice heard the eagerness in Clare's voice but couldn't match it with her own enthusiasm. 'I thought it was, I don't know . . . interesting, I guess,' she'd replied lamely.

'Oh,' was all Clare said.

'Listen, Jeremy's away, so why don't we go out for a night on the town?' Bernice quickly suggested. 'It's time you experienced a little night life.'

She didn't say, 'It's time you experienced *life*.' She didn't say how much she wanted to cheer Clare up, to give her something entertaining to write about, something optimistic. She certainly didn't say that for the first time in her life she felt really sorry for Clare.

When Clare agreed, Bernice planned an evening of total revelry. They started in a pub in Notting Hill, moved on to Soho and were drinking pitchers of *sangría* in a club called Barcelona at three a.m., while hordes of sweaty bodies danced to wild salsa music. Actually, Bernice was the one drinking the *sangría*. Clare sat with a pleased expression on her face, watching. Bernice inhaled her way through three packets of Bensons; Clare didn't complain about the smoke. Finally, Bernice dragged Clare onto the dance floor.

Clare could dance. It was a revelation to see her. She came out of herself, took the beat of the music and moved with it like a piece of flowing silk.

In the taxi back home, Bernice was telling Clare she should get out more. 'You see how much *fun* you can have? Fun, fun, *fun*!' she was shouting when the taxi was rear-ended. Clare went flying into the partition, while Bernice somehow managed to remain in her seat. At five a.m, Bernice waited in the emergency room of the Charing Cross Hospital as Clare's face was being stitched up. The scar on Clare's chin faded, but it was still faintly visible and reminded Bernice, every time she saw it, of that evening when life turned out to be not entirely different from Clare's books. Fun ended badly. She'd wanted to give Clare a good time, and what was the result? Dawn spent in a cold, antiseptic hospital.

'Shit,' Bernice thought. 'If I *were* to go with Clare to New York, we'd get mugged and raped and knifed. I'm bad luck for her. Still,' she sat on the tube, considering the idea, 'I can't resist a free trip. And maybe Anna's right. Maybe it's time for Clare to meet Carl. He's probably ninety years old with a hunchback – she might as well find that out sooner rather than later.' She shut her eyes, reached down again for the Dime bar, before realizing she'd thrown it away. 'And maybe, while we're there, I'll find a bar full of men who just *love* slightly overweight English girls with bad attitudes.'

Chapter 6

They were sitting in a submarine, or rather in a restaurant designed to look like a submarine. It had a real periscope in the middle of the floor and a terrible, airless atmosphere.

'Jesus, Art, what's that noise?'

'A dive bell. You know, it's supposed to sound like the horn they blow when it's time for the sub to dive,' Art answered. 'Get with the program, Carl.'

'If we had to go to a theme restaurant, couldn't you have picked the Christmas Bar? Even on a warm April day I'd rather listen to Bing Crosby on the juke-box and be surrounded by reindeers on the walls than feel like I'm about to get torpedoed.'

'Come on, the fish here is great. Stop complaining.'

'When do we surface? Do we get to watch the waiters in those bell-bottom Navy outfits swab the decks between courses? Is this a *nuclear* sub?'

'Carl. Shut up and eat. And try your hardest to listen to me. I'm saving your career here.'

'You aren't making any sense. This is an absurd proposition. There is absolutely no way it can work.'

'Bullshit. You've got the makings of a great story . . . a great love story. Everyone loves a lover, remember. This could be as big as *The Bridges of Madison County*. Bigger, because it's for real. When the book comes out, you two can do the talk-show circuit. You can pitch that line of yours about getting to know people slowly. All that crap will be fantastic.'

'She's married, Artie. I haven't met her. We don't plan on meeting each other, much less declaring our undying love on national television.'

'Listen, it might work. Clare – the quintessential English rose – falls for you, the ethnic American male, leaves this cricket-playing wimp of a husband and is allowed, for the first time in her life, to express her emotions, her inner self. The rose blooms and you write the book. You tell it like it is. How two people can reach across a vast ocean and find a soul mate.'

'I'm not going to be used in your one-man assault on the British Isles, Art. I know you had a lousy time there, I've heard all the stories. Stealing Clare away from Jeremy may be your idea of revenge, but, even if it were possible, it's not mine. I can not write a book about Clare's and my relationship. Forget it.'

'Fine . . .' Art wiped his mouth with his napkin, placed it back on his lap with exaggerated care. Why did this so often happen when he was with Carl? Why did he end up playing the brash, insensitive businessman to Carl's idealistic caring-sharing artist? Something about Carl's wilful romanticism goaded Art to heights of ruthless pragmatism. He knew Carl must see him as a stone-hearted wheeler-dealer, he was irritated by that knowledge, and yet he took on the role as if he were hoping for an Oscar. 'Then what are you going to write, Carl? Why don't you tell me the plot of your new novel?'

'I don't have any new novel.'

'How do you pay the rent then?'

'It won't be long before I can't pay the rent.'

'Do you have any other skills for the marketplace? Are you a secret electrician? A rodent exterminator?'

'Art . . .' Carl sighed.

'Then for God's sake, why don't you use what you have? You've got a book out of this correspondence, a possibly commercial book, if we play it right. Your side of the story, your letters – not hers. No legal problems then. No shared royalties.'

Art paused. Why didn't he give up right now and drop the subject? What did it matter if Carl couldn't pay his rent? Literature wasn't supposed to be about money, was it? Art knew he'd like to ditch all thoughts of commercial projects and take on the part he preferred, the part of Carl's friend, not his agent. That would be a hell of a lot more pleasant. They could drink wine and discuss Herman Melville, William Faulkner, Henry James. Still, he had an obligation to be the bad cop because sooner or later Carl *would* run out of money and Art didn't want Carl out on the street, no matter how romantic the plight of a homeless, starving author might sound. He had to try to push Carl's career, whether Carl wanted it or not.

'But you have to meet Clare,' he continued. 'The story goes nowhere unless you meet her. OK, the best scenario is if she's a babe and you two get it on and fall in love and you steal her from the wimp. And don't go all moral on me. How many times have I heard you talk about Paris and Helen of Troy? But even if she's a dog, you've got a story. I'm not sure how it plays out yet – if she *is* a dog – but I can think of something, I know. You're on the ropes, Carl. You don't have much of a choice. Use what you've got.'

'Why would I have to meet her?' Carl asked. 'Why couldn't I do the book and make up meeting her? Why couldn't it be fiction? That way I don't involve her and I still have a book.'

'Then you've lost the hook. It's not a real-life story. Less human interest. No TV.'

'*The Bridges of Madison County* was not a real-life story. Besides, if I write it as fiction, I can make sure she's not a dog, as you so delicately put it.'

'You know you want to meet her, Carlo. You know you're dying to meet her. Look, I'll advance you the money for a trip to London. How could it hurt?'

In one of her recent letters Clare had asked, '*Do you ever, when you're in a restaurant or at a party, look around the room for someone who would instinctively, with just one shared glance, understand everything you're thinking and feeling at that second?*'

You asked me once, quite a few letters ago, to tell you what kind of person I'd like beside me if we were both buried up to our necks in sand and an army of red ants were approaching. I didn't answer properly then. I said I'd like someone who would make me laugh. Yes, that's true. But there's more to it, Carl. I'd like to be able to look over at my fellow soon-to-be-devoured sufferer and with just that one look, feel an instinctive, unassailable empathy. Us against the world, against the ants. Us fighting common doom together. I know this sounds histrionic. I'd still like to have that person tell a joke, but I think what I missed in life, being an only child, is a sense of having someone on my side.

Jeremy has it in his career. I mean, he has a team, a group, and I envy him. I watch an American sitcom like Friends *and I think, yes – that's what they have as well – they're all on the same side, the same team. Can you imagine them lined up in the sand together, facing those ants? I can.*

Well, maybe I should join a female volley-ball team, right? One which practises on the beach. Then we'd all be good in the sand.'

Carl considered Art, who was digging out mussels from their shells. Art would pass the 'red-ants-in-the-sand' test, he'd be one of the better people to share your last minutes with, but he was not, in the end, *truly* simpatico. He didn't comprehend Carl's relationship with Clare and he never would. He was too much of a businessman, not enough of an artist.

'I'm not going to London, Art. I *am* getting out of this hellhole of a restaurant. I know you're trying to help me, but you just don't get it. You don't understand.'

'No. I'm not supposed to understand, am I? After all, I'm the money man. All I understand is that your career has stalled bigtime. You had one book that did OK, the next two went south. I'm offering you a chance. Maybe you're right, maybe you don't have to meet her. But I know in my bones that meeting her is the key.'

'You—'

'And you know something else?' Art thumped the table. 'You gave me that correspondence because you wanted me to get hooked on it like you are, not because you want to give Clare a writing career. Sure, she can write, I'm not denying it. But you can write too. It's what you do for a living. She probably sits at home and knits cricket sweaters. You *want* this stuff published, in one form or another. That's your job.'

'But—'

'And you want this woman. Face it. Meanwhile get it through your head that she wants you too. You think she'd be writing to you the way she's been writing to you all this time if she were real happy being Mrs Cricket? No dice. Christ, she didn't have to answer that first letter, did she? It wasn't even addressed to her. Think about your career and think about your love life and I'll call the airlines for cheap deals to London.'

'Don't do that.'

'All right. But promise to think about the book?'

'I'll think about the book.'

'Good.' Art sat back and relaxed. He wished fewer of his clients were his friends as well. How the hell could you sit down and tell someone what to do and how to do it when what you really wanted to do was ask him or her to a movie.

'Art, what happened to that little plaid cap you sometimes wear?'

'Shit, I don't know, it's in my closet somewhere, I guess. Why?'

'I miss it. I love that cap.'

'I don't like that statement.' Art's face scrunched into a grimace. 'That statement worries me, Carl. It makes me think there's a sanity problem looming on the horizon.'

'Up periscope,' Carl smiled.

Dear Clare,

My friend Art wants me to write a book about our relationship. Why? He thinks it is romantic. Or does he? He thinks we should meet and fall in love. He wants my career to resume. Oh, I haven't told you, have I? I'm a writer. I was a writer once, I mean. I've published three novels. What would you call them? They don't fit into any genre, exactly. The critics compared the first, which was a minor success, to Kurt Vonnegut's Cat's Cradle. I have to say, that was heady praise. As far as the next two books were concerned, well, the critics didn't compare me to anyone. They wrote the inevitable 'not fufilling his promise' stuff. I can't remember promising them anything. Oh shit, never complain, never explain. Always maintain, always stay sane. The rain in Spain stays mainly in Madrid.

My wife, Dee-Dee – an absurd nickname for Desiree, which is, I think, an even more absurd name – was very happy when my first novel did well. She's beautiful, Clare, you should see her. I didn't tell you about her. How could I? I'd have to tell you how she left me when I didn't want her to and all the rest . . . the rest is pity.

Supposing I were to write a book which was somehow centered around our relationship? What would you think? What if it became popular? Would you feel used, Clare? I mean, you shouldn't, not really. After all, you have Jeremy, star of cricket field (and bed, I assume). It's just that Art seems to think it might work. And I admit, I'm pretty desperate at the moment.

Still, I wouldn't use you, Clare, I couldn't. You mean too much to me. You're always out there, the person I confide in, the person who has the same responses to life I have, the same sense of humor, my psychic twin, the person to whom I correspond. Wait, let me get the dictionary . . . Right. Now. Here it is. Correspond: 1) a. be analogous or similar b. agree in amount, position, etc. c. be in harmony or agreement 2) communicate by interchange of letters.

You do see, don't you? You're my other half, you're—

Carl stopped typing, pushed Apple One, then Apple Delete, then scrolled down the page highlighting the words. When he reached the bottom, he pushed Return, and the screen instantly went blank.

The marvels of science, he thought, how convenient they are. They can whisk away a page of crazed writing into the emptiness of the airwaves, but they can't erase the thoughts from my sick, addled brain.

He reached over and picked up the telephone to the right of his computer, and punched in Art's home number. He didn't want to talk to Art at work. He wanted to leave a message. When Art's voice answered and commanded him to speak after the beep, Carl stated firmly, 'I can't do a book that has anything to do with the correspondence.' He paused for a second before adding, 'But thanks for thinking of me, Art. I'll come up with another book soon, something great, something different. Hey, how about a thriller?

'Maybe the President of the United States could assassinate the pope or maybe the pope could assassinate the president. Or maybe the pope could have an affair with the First Lady or – hold on a second – maybe the First Lady could be a serial killer. You know, that's not such a bad idea – FBI stalks serial killer. The last place they'd look would be the White House. Or has that been done already? I don't think so. The president could know that his wife – wait – no, the chief of staff knows the First Lady is a raving killer on the rampage, but doesn't know how—'

The machine cut him off. Carl smiled at the receiver before replacing it.

She had that sleek, greyhound-out-of-the-gate look. Skin like a sheer satin coat, legs stretching to a distant finish line and eyes which kept the rabbit in sight at all times. How Carl had bagged her in the first place, Art couldn't fathom. Not that Carl wasn't a good-looking guy and everything, but Dee-Dee – well, she needed a handler, a trainer and most probably a stud farm to keep her in line.

'So, I was thinking, Art . . .'

That was it. He'd almost forgotten. The short grey cashmere skirt and button-up grey cashmere sweater leaving a nicely visible slice of gleaming flat stomach had distracted him. She wasn't too bright. Not dumb, exactly, but verging on it. The bit of personality lacking in her came across when she spoke. Hers was a perfectly palatable voice but a completely emotionless one. Dee-Dee had only one facial expression as well, now that he thought about it. She looked ever so slightly dissatisfied. Even when she smiled, the lines of her lips went straight across her face, they never curved up.

'You know I'm still teaching dance classes, and all that is going fine. It's just I've come up with an idea, and I thought you might want to hear about it.'

'Of course.'

'I thought I could write a novel. In my spare time, that is.'

'Oh.' Art continued silently, 'And I'll take up teaching jazz dancing in *my* spare time, sweetheart.'

'It would be about a woman . . . someone my age, who is into dance. She's married to a writer, but he isn't – well, he isn't—'

'Successful.'

'Right. Anyway, she leaves the marriage and – this is where it gets really interesting – she goes off with another woman.'

'I see.'

'You know, lesbians are big these days.'

'Are they, Dee-Dee?'

'Absolutely. This woman has to struggle with her sexual iden-tity. What would be a better word, Art? Struggle sounds so obvious.'

'Wrestle?'

'Exactly. She wrestles with her own sexuality.'

'And who comes out on top?'

'What?'

'I mean, does she continue with women or go back to men?'

'She renounces both!' Dee-Dee's lips formed the line signalling a smile.

'Does she become a nun, then?'

'No, she goes to Tibet.'

'Uh huh. And that's where she meets Richard Gere?'

'Actually, I hadn't thought of that. It's a possibility, though. Someone a lot like Richard Gere, perhaps.'

'How did you do it, Carl? How did you live with this for two years? Was she *that* good in bed?' Art looked away from Dee-Dee and out of his office window. There was nothing to see but other offices peopled with men and women in suits.

'The thing is, Art, this woman has led a very exciting life. At a young age, for example, she worked for a music promoter in a sleazy office in midtown Manhattan and he actually took a bite out of her arm once, when he failed to book the Jackson Five for a concert in Meadowlands. She finds peace through her dancing, but not in her head. That's what she discovers, as the book goes along. Peace.'

'And how much of this novel would feature her writer husband?'

'Oh, I'm not sure yet. A couple of pages, I think.'

'Not a chapter? Carl doesn't even rate a chapter in this bimbo's brain?' Art mused.

'Tell me something, Dee-Dee. Off the subject of the book for a moment. Then we'll get back to it. What drew you to Carl in the first place?'

Dee-Dee exhaled softly and tilted her head. Her straight black hair covered half of her face in an alluring manner.

'He was thoughtful. He cared about me. He loved my dancing. He made me laugh. He's very intelligent.'

'So – excuse me, but I feel compelled to ask – why did you leave him?'

'There wasn't any peace of mind in his presence, Art. He wasn't a content man in himself, so he couldn't offer me any true contentment. Carl needs help. I just wish I could have been the one who could help him.'

'Carl, you poor bastard,' Art thought, placing his elbows on the desk in front of him and resting his head against the palms of his hands. 'You fell for her looks. You fell for her dancing. And you really believed she had a brain.'

During most of Carl and Dee-Dee's marriage, from what Art could observe, Dee-Dee had kept her mouth shut. She was the sexy, silent type and Carl had interpreted her silence as mysterious intelligence. It was a manoeuvre dumb people used well. Don't talk and people will assume you're smart. Now Dee-Dee seemed to enjoy spouting on at length, but now was too late for Carl. She'd already changed the channel on him.

'Right. Well, then, back to your book idea. I'd need to see a synopsis, first of all. And it would help if you could write a few chapters. I'm sure you're a hell of a writer, Dee-Dee, but I need to see the proof in print. Does that sound reasonable to you?'

'Yes, that sounds fine, Art. I truly appreciate your help. Thank you for seeing me at such short notice. I realize this will be my first time as a writer, and it's asking a lot to expect to be an overnight sensation, but I know I have a book in me, I can just sense it.'

'I'm sure you can.' Art stood up, and stretched his hand across the desk. He didn't want to come into too close proximity to her. She had a visceral effect on men, that was for sure. Clearly she had an effect on women as well. It was a wise idea to keep a healthy distance.

Why had he typed her hand-written letters so scrupulously into his computer file? Had he been thinking of a book before Art had mentioned the idea? Had he unconsciously been setting things up, recording all their correspondence in the hopes he could make something out of it from the very beginning?

Carl stared at the Carl–Clare file entry on his screen before pushing the Return button to retrieve it.

No, he thought, as the first letter flashed up before him. He had put it all on the computer for easy access, that's all. For nights like this when he felt alone and tired. What does she look like?

he asked his computer. Would it matter if, as Art so tactfully put it, she were a dog? How much did Clare really figure in his life, anyway?

Yes, he re-read her letters often, but more often than that he would re-read his own. The vanity of a writer, he supposed. Or the vanity of Carl. This correspondence was as much a private diary as a communication between strangers. He could push a button and come up with a letter he'd written months before, thereby finding himself at a different point in his life. How much had changed since, for example, six months ago? It would take no time at all to find out.

Letter Twenty-one

October 12

Dear Clare,

I'm writing this in the dark, with the blue screen glowing in front of me. It sheds just enough light to let me see the keyboard. It seemed right to keep the lights off. Whenever I write to you, I am sending my thoughts off into the dark. Across a dark ocean. Will this letter sit in the bottom of a heavily laden 747, full of holidaymakers and business people and visiting relatives? Or does it fly on its own mail plane? I don't know the mechanics of how it will reach you. I don't know if you have a mailbox outside your place or a little slot in the door. I know nothing, Clare.

There's an impressive sounding thunderstorm going on outside my windows. After every boom, another car alarm goes off. The signals of theft in the city are mixed with the gods' bowling game. (A flash of lightening is a strike. Or don't you aliens know about tenpin bowling?) New Yorkers long ago ceased paying attention to any form of siren noise. People scurry in and out of the rain, they order Chinese food to be delivered to their apartments, they flee the streets, while the alarms sound around them. And the lightening flashes. Strikes.

I had a friend in my college days who was a very Ralph Lauren type of guy. But funny along with well-dressed. He had parents who had money. I went to his Long Island pad for a weekend one summer. Hey, I'd read The Great Gatsby. *I wasn't worried about infiltrating the upper echelons of society. I wouldn't wash my face in a finger bowl. I might put a goldfish in it, but otherwise I'm hip.*

There was a monumental thunderstorm on the Saturday night. It didn't interrupt the dinner party, it didn't do anything but make polite conversation even more polite: 'Can you believe this storm?' 'Oh, no, I can't, can you?' 'Do you think we'll have a power cut?' 'Oh, my Lord, did we leave the window open in the conservatory?'

But afterward, after the storm had passed and taken its ticket to another town, I took a walk outside. The land smelt fresh and all those things the country is supposed to smell like, but I was disappointed. After a deluge, New York City is like a place transformed. Streets which are not used to being thoroughly clean ever in their lives suddenly shine. Only for a moment, of course, but yet . . . that moment. A clean city smells like nothing else in life. Grass and trees expect water. Sidewalks don't. It's a sight to smell and see.

By the way, do you listen with your eyes?

Clare. Everyone, everyone in this life needs someone to believe in him or her, in his or her soul, I mean. I believe in you. I don't know what you do or what you look like or anything about you except for what I understand as your essence. None of the rest of it matters. Clare. You're like the city after a storm. I feel the same way when I get one of your letters. Fresh and invigorated and alive. I've known you forever, you know. Ever since I could understand my heart.

You must miss Angela Rae. Do you know how pleased I was to read that she'd taken you to the Ritz for the purpose of a future story you could tell? What a present. What a lovely story. The mystery of it intrigues me. Do you think that she might feel that you are the only person who believes in her? Maybe you were, but now I believe in her too. Not as a fairy godmother or even the witch you say she resembles, but as someone I can never hear enough about. Why do I picture her wearing a tailored suit and high heels in her one-woman sailing boat? Setting down on an outer Pacific island and playing blackjack with the natives or whoever happened to come along? I want to sit in the shades of dusk listening to her stories.

I was one of those kids who always had a book in his hand. And also the kind of kid who tells stories well. A lot of my popularity – you see, I'm not going to be falsely modest, because I know I was popular – anyway, a lot of that popularity stemmed from the fact that I could tell the best ghost stories on the block. I was a real entertainer, of real value, because I could make up scarier, more terrifying stories than anyone else had heard or read. The people in my brain, Clare, the people in my imagination, were and are so real to me that I sometimes wonder whether I'm one of those guys who will soon hear voices. I don't understand the people I come in contact with in the real world. Oh, I like them – a few of them I love, especially my family – but I worry about my ability to relate, to seriously relate (to split an infinitive for the hell of it) to a human being.

You have told me about your secret terrors as a child, how you hid and are still hiding a side of yourself. Well, that's me as well. I have a secret, many secrets. You want to know my monster? My monster is the thought that no one will ever live up to my imaginary friends and lovers, to characters I have either read about or made up for myself. My fear is that I will never truly understand another living, real person. What kind of a man does that make me, Clare?

I'm thinking of taking up Ping-Pong. It seems like a wonderful sport, doesn't it? You have to have great hand–eye coordination, fabulous reflexes and good-grip shoes. There's a Ping-Pong parlor down the street from where I live. The players there are all very deft, however. I wouldn't want to face any of them without private lessons beforehand.

I have to go out into the streets now. The rain has stopped. I need to catch the clean moment.

Love,

Carl

'Shit,' he thought, quickly turning off the computer. 'Nothing has changed. If there had been a thunderstorm, I could have written that same letter tonight.

'I'm wandering around a mega department store called Life and I'm lost and even if I could locate a map I wouldn't be able to find the pointing arrow, the You Are Here sign.

'I'm writing to a formless, featureless being. I'm – it's time to admit it, if only to myself – *in love* with a spirit.

'I'm lost.

'Something's gotta give.

'Soon.'

Chapter 7

Clare returned to her car and headed back to the A3, pleased with herself for having had the idea to come to Chessington World of Adventures. She had had a mania for rides ever since she had been taken to Blackpool for the weekend by a school friend. She'd been seven years old and amazed by the excitement and sense of freedom she had experienced, but most of all by the Big Dipper. How she was able to drop all her fears when she got on a roller-coaster, she didn't know. But she could and she did. She loved them, with a passion bordering on addiction. She could go on *any* ride a theme park could dream up, the scarier the better. The only problem, given that her mother would never take her to far-flung fairgrounds with rides, was finding willing friends who would.

What was it, she wondered, that appealed to her so much? The fact that she could let go, could scream with all the other riders when they plunged together down a defiantly steep slope? Or the fact that this was the one time in her life she felt really brave? The only time in her past when other children looked at her with wonder. 'You're not *really* going on that one?' friends would ask. Even Bernice, wild and free-spirited as she was, shrank from some of the rides which Clare embraced.

The rides freed her – for a brief time she forgot her doom-ridden thoughts. The heart-pounding excitement of it made her feel as if she could do anything in the world. Until she got off and turned back into her normal self.

For one moment, in Spain, when that plane had veered to the left and downwards – just before the crash – she remembered feeling a sense of exultation. She was going to go on the ride of her life. The moment vanished as soon as she heard people screaming, and knew they were screaming not out of fear mixed with excitement but out of fear alone.

Taking a trip to Chessington had been a treat she'd given herself after good news from Anna about the Americans buying *Breathing in the Dusk*. All on her own, she had gone on ride after ride, feeling happier than she could remember ever feeling before.

Perhaps, she thought, as she neared Kingston, perhaps her life was going to change now. 'I always asked myself if I would go onto a spaceship were one to visit my apartment and disgorge little creatures who politely invited me on board,' Carl had written. 'And I think, because I have a brave streak lurking in me, I would. I'd say "to hell with it", climb on and prepare myself for take-off. Can you imagine the ride? My real worry would be landing on Mars only to find shopping malls and a large population consisting entirely of male dentists and female talk-show hosts.'

Clare had laughed when she read that sentence. When she wrote back, she said, 'My worry is that I'd step out of the spaceship and onto the Mars M25, but you wouldn't get that joke, Carl, and there's no way I can explain it to you. Unless you come over here and I treat you to a morning of motorway madness. But, of course, you can't come over here. Or you could, but you couldn't see me if you did, could you? God, we're complicated, aren't we? Maybe we'll end up meeting on Mars.'

Clare turned up the volume of the car radio and began to sing along with the old Bee Gees' hit 'Staying Alive'.

I am a witch, Anna said to herself. A conjuror. A supreme and clever plotter. Madame Machiavelli.

Looking around at her fellow passengers, she felt the seed of happiness lodged in her heart sprout another inch. Not only was she a sharp cookie, but she was also about a thousand times better off than any of the travellers surrounding her. That wasn't saying much when flying Aeroflot, she knew, but every little bit helped.

Who were all these ugly, fat, chain-smoking people *en route* to Moscow? What did they expect to find when they got there? Vodka lakes? Perhaps. Or new business opportunities in the anarchic atmosphere of post-communism.

Anna herself was on a 24-hour trip looking for an author. She'd been led to believe she could sign a female ex-KGB agent who would re-open the whole spying can of worms with her tales of double and triple agents in the good old days. Translators had been arranged, a hotel room booked. It was a tip worth following up, if only because Anna had never been to Russia and was curious. She'd had an unhealthy interest in Lenin's Tomb since childhood.

Opening up the Aeroflot in-flight magazine and giving it a quick read-through, she was slightly taken aback by the advice to visitors printed on the last page: 'Never take a taxi alone at night. You might be hijacked. Be especially careful if the driver says he has to stop to get cigarettes.' Why? Anna wondered. And why don't they bother to explain why wanting to stop to get cigarettes is 'especially' dangerous?

Given the amount of smoke in the cabin of the plane, she reckoned that Russians must run out of their fags constantly. Why would it be so awful if a taxi driver ran out of them in mid-trip? He might stop at a wonderful, dimly lit place with balalaika music. He might look like Omar Sharif. In the days when Omar Sharif still looked like Omar Sharif, not an old rug salesman.

She replaced the magazine in the shredding seat pocket in front of her, and pulled her clipboard out of the travel bag at her feet. Before scanning the checklist again, she gave herself another moment to savour her own handiwork. It hadn't been easy. She had managed to manoeuvre every piece on the chessboard into the strategically correct position; it had taken great patience, tact and deceit.

Yes, Clare and Bernice were going to New York. And yes, Clare *thought* she was going to promote *Breathing in the Dusk*, because the Americans had shown sudden interest in it. Poor, gullible Clare. Anna felt a momentary pang of regret when she remembered how happy Clare had been at the news.

'They even want you on a television show,' Anna had confided excitedly. 'This is a very, very good sign.'

'Which show?' Clare had asked.

'It's called *Magic Moments*.'

'*Magic Moments*?'

'It's a kind of art show. Specializing in showcasing new, fresh talent. The host will interview you, you'll do your bit and that will be that.'

'Why is it called *Magic Moments*?'

'I'm afraid I have no idea. Maybe they think art is a series of magic moments, I don't know. Your publishers' publicity department set it up, Clare.'

'And the publishers are called Raphael and Co.?'

'Yes. I know you haven't heard of them. They're new to the game, but the buzz is that they're a hot company, that they're making waves already. All the big boys are running scared. These people are bringing *literature* back into the market-place.'

'That sounds wonderful,' Clare smiled. 'Of course I'm nervous, but I'm excited, too. Incredibly excited.'

Anna wondered if she was losing her scruples. Was it fair to lead Clare up the garden path like that? Probably not, but she couldn't think of any other way to get her into a television studio. Although she'd conceived the whole plan of arranging a Clare and Carl meeting with nothing but the best of intentions, as time went by she found that the means became more important than the end. She wanted to prove that she could do it, that she could organize such a difficult project, get two people across the world from each other into a television studio with neither knowing what they were there for. It was like the sorority challenge she'd had to do as a student at New York University – find a goat, a policeman and a pearl necklace and bring them all to the sorority house together – by midnight. She'd managed that way back then; in fact, she'd been so good at it, she'd been put in charge of those challenges for her remaining years there. Now she could prove she was as competent and inspired as she had been in the old days.

Recollecting with pleasure her triumphs at university, Anna suddenly grimaced. That's when she had met her ex-husband, the one person she'd prefer to banish from her memory.

Like some latter-day version of Scarlett O'Hara on her knees raging against the Yankees, Anna had pulled herself together after he'd left her and promised herself she'd never speak his name again. He didn't deserve to be remembered. He'd abandoned her, fourteen years ago. He'd left her, not for another woman, but for another country.

After graduating from NYU, they'd married and moved to Montclair, New Jersey. Both of them had jobs, both of them were happy. But he hadn't considered, when he walked into their apartment one evening and announced that they should pack their bags because he was taking a new job in England, he hadn't considered *her*. He'd assumed she'd tag after him, and he was right. She did. She'd had to build a new life for herself in London, to start from scratch making friends, finding work, settling into a foreign atmosphere. And she'd done it. She'd cultivated friends very carefully, she'd found a job in a literary agency, and she had *adapted*.

But *he* hadn't.

He hated his new job and his new life in London. In fits of pique, he'd yell at her for 'selling out to the Brits'. In the biggest fit of all, he walked into their Notting Hill flat and announced once again that it was time to pack up. She'd just begun to spell color with a u, to pronounce vitamin with a short i, to understand the jokes in *Private Eye*; and he expected her to up and leave with him just like that. He had no clue how difficult it had been for her to blend into the British landscape, or how proud she was of herself for managing to do it. Follow your man to the ends of the earth – or in this case, back to New Jersey – that was his take on the situation.

As Clare had said in one of those letters – who wants to go back to Kansas when you've seen Oz? Or did Clare say that Salman Rushdie had said it? Whatever. The principle was the same. New Jersey was the armpit of America. London, where she had managed to establish herself, was the heart of all cultural life, the emerald city of her dreams. When the time came to make a stand, she effectively clicked her red shoes together three times and said, 'There's no place like London, there's no place like London.' The next day she woke up alone.

No one had any idea how much Anna had once loved that man or how much he'd let her down when he walked out. No one knew how much of a heart she had. She tried to exile him from her thoughts completely, but he'd sneak back in – at times when she was feeling on the defensive, when she'd hear anti-American cracks or when her work was going badly. She would picture sitting down with him and pouring out all her woes, but that picture would fade and dissolve into anger when she realized that it was just that – a picture. He would never be there for her in person.

He would laugh now if he knew how uncomfortable she could still feel sometimes in the midst of her adopted countrypeople. He'd say 'Told you so' and laugh his head off.

'I wonder what he feels about me now,' she mused, before fighting down the rising, dangerous thoughts of him. She was far better off without him. They'd met young and married young. Some day, perhaps, she'd meet someone with whom she could have an adult relationship.

Maybe some day some man would write to her out of the blue and she could have a correspondence too.

No, Anna decided, she wasn't being unfair to Clare – on the contrary – she was giving her a shot at true romance, and if that took a little lying, then fine. If all went well in New York, Clare *would* find a real American publisher, not the imaginary Raphael and Co. She would break out of her repressed shell and discover something exciting to write about. Anna was doing Clare a huge favour – whether Clare would see it that way or not would depend almost entirely on the X factor – Carl Lioce.

Clare–Carl Checklist

1) Clare and Bernice take off on BA at 9.45 a.m., arrive NYC approximately noon, proceed to hotel.

2) Bernice makes sure Clare is unable to watch or ask anyone questions about *Magic Moments* show. Bernice *occupies* Clare for the rest of that day, also making sure Clare can't get near a phone book or phone box. She *must not* be allowed to look up or try to call Raphael and Co.

3) The following day, 10 a.m., Clare and Bernice go to *Magic Moments* studio for live broadcast.

4) Tame, friendly producer of MM assures Clare that she will be talking about *Breathing in the Dusk*.

5) Tame, friendly producer (who by the way, in case anyone is going through my files after my death and happens to read this, was a lousy lay many years ago) manages to get Carl into studio audience without letting him know what is going to happen, either. This will not be too difficult; the producer assures me he will take care of it at his end.

6) Clare, introduced as English writer, comes on stage. Segments of her correspondence with Carl (which, for the record, I previously edited and faxed to NYC) are read out. Host of

Magic Moments explains Carl and Clare have never met, don't know what each other looks like, etc. SHOCK!!! SURPRISE!!! Clare is introduced to Carl for first time – on television.

7) Qué será, será.

8) Book/made-for-TV movie written by yours truly? (Only kidding)

Bernice had just called the stewardess back to ask her for another packet of peanuts. Clare, careful not to smile, unhooked her seat-belt and attempted to watch the news on the screen in front of her. She was grateful but puzzled by Bernice's sudden decision to accompany her to New York. It would be nice to have a friend with her, but she hoped Bernice wouldn't try to drag her out on the town. This trip was about work. Finally someone had recognized what she believed she'd written in *Breathing in the Dusk*, an intricate story of human relationships.

For Americans to accept *Breathing in the Dusk* – actually think it worth a television slot – struck her as strange because it seemed to her a quintessentially English book. Yet if the Americans wanted to put her on TV, who was she to question them? Americans were wonderful. America was a great country. She'd never been there before, but she knew she was going to love it.

It wasn't going to be easy, though. Being in New York City and not calling Carl seemed close to impossible. She could be sly, if she chose to be, hang around his apartment building and surreptitiously find out who he was. Follow him into a restaurant or bar and just observe him. That's what she really wanted to do – watch him from a distance, get some knowledge without having to disclose herself. However, that plan of action wouldn't be fair, so she wouldn't do it.

Or would she?

Letter number nine was the one which had done the damage to her heart. Up till then, she'd believed she was in control, that she was indulging in a fairly harmless, friendly correspondence with no subtexts, no hidden emotional agendas, nothing she wouldn't be able to tell Jeremy about, if he were ever to ask her about the airmail letters she kept receiving.

She thought that Carl must have written Letter nine under the influence of a lot of wine. She pictured him sitting at his computer around three o'clock in the morning, alone and tired and defenceless. In this picture, the window was open and the air was riffling his dark hair. He looked like a sailor. There was an open bottle of red wine on his desk. He was exhausted. But he had to write. To her.

Letter Nine

March 5

Dear Clare,

We send each other so many thoughts, but not the ones we really want to express. Am I right?

The horizon of infinite possibility recedes. Dreams get shunted onto abandoned railway lines. Passion puts its thumb out and doesn't get a lift. Death starts stealing bases.

The night is not going gently. None of us are.

Am I no better than maudlin?

Do you want to know what I did tonight?

Do you have a choice?

I had a date. OK? She's a nice woman with a terrific smile and a bubbly personality. We met at a bar and had a few drinks and then she went to the bathroom. She left her purse at the table, right by my feet. Unusual for a woman to do that, right? I picked it up and started to look through it. Why? Because I wanted to know. I wanted to see if she carried lipstick, a comb, mace, reading glasses. What kind of keychain did she have? Were there any pictures of loved ones?

Of course she came back in the middle of my search. I saw the look of horror on her face, mixed with disbelief. I think she thought I

97

was robbing her. Anyway, she took the purse from my prying hands and walked out of the bar without another word.

What am I doing, Clare? What kind of psycho am I?

I want to know everything, that's all. I want to get straight to the heart without any bypass operation. I'm too interested in the details of other people's lives, possibly because the details of my own are mysterious to me.

No, wait, I've been untruthful.

When I was looking in her purse . . .

I was looking for you.

Love,

Carl

Clare had been ambushed by that last line, completely shaken by its stark frankness. For a long week, she pondered a reply. How could she respond in kind, and did she actually want to? He had made two bold moves in that letter, the first being the words I was looking for you, the second, a quantum leap from his standard All my best, Carl to Love, Carl.

In the end, she decided on what she considered a middle ground. She would write back a harmless, chatty letter which made no reference at all to his last one and sign it Love. Yet when it came time to put pen to paper, the letter turned out differently. This was the first of her letters in which she described her childhood fears. Once she had started, she couldn't stop herself and all her secrets came pouring out. Stranger still, she signed it Yours sincerely.

What a schizophrenic response that was. Even now she shook her head in disbelief thinking about it. She'd emptied out her soul to a stranger but pulled back from that final word which really meant very little in letter form. Carl hadn't flinched, though. He'd replied with what was practically an essay on the power of childhood fear which had made her both laugh and cry. And he'd signed it Love again.

Bernice nudged her, signalling that she should take off her earphones. 'Listen, I was just thinking. When we get there, after we get checked in, I reckon we should go out on an all-day tourist trip. Do the whole city – the Empire State Building, World Trade Center, Staten Island ferry, Statue of Liberty—'

'Bernice, hold on. That sounds exhausting. We're going to be jet-lagged. And I'd like to see if I can arrange a drink or something with my publishers. Anna told me the name of the man I should talk to there, but she didn't give me his number; still, it should be easy enough to find.'

'Why don't you wait until after the television show? Wait till tomorrow.'

'Why?'

'Why not?'

'Bernice! What difference could it possibly make! We're arriving around noon. I could schedule a drink around five or six.'

'No, no, no. That's not a good idea. You should wait. As you just said, you're going to be jet-lagged. Much better to be fresh, right? I work in an advertising firm, remember. I know about this stuff. People come in jet-lagged all the time and they look like complete losers. They have problems talking. Their eyes have these circles. And their mouths are dry and they smell like aeroplanes.'

'OK,' Clare laughed. 'OK. You've convinced me. But we don't have to do *everything* in one afternoon, do we? I'm going on television for the first time tomorrow. And I'm scared, Bernice. I'm really nervous.'

'Don't worry, you'll be perfect. You'll surprise yourself.'

'I hope so.'

'Clare . . . relax. Put yourself in my capable hands. Tomorrow's going to be excellent, honestly. Absolutely excellent.'

Excellent was one of Jeremy's favourite words as well, Clare thought, turning away from Bernice and looking out of the window onto the clouds below. He'd used it the previous night when ringing up a mutual acquaintance. 'George,' he'd said, 'it's

Jeremy here. Yes, I'm back. Did you? I'm glad. We played liked princes for a while there. The series was difficult, but it was excellent, really excellent the way we managed to work together. Anyway, it's been a while since we've spoken. I thought we shouldn't lose touch. We must get together soon . . .'

Clare was watching him, sitting at Angela's kitchen table, address book in his hand. This was a ritual of his. Every couple of months he'd ring round, touching base with all the people they knew, lobbing in phone calls to keep their various friends happy. 'Jeremy just rang,' she could imagine George saying to his girlfriend, Sandra. 'He's just back from South Africa. That's nice of him to think of us, isn't it?'

Isn't it?

Of course it's nice of him to think of others, to maintain friendships, Clare said to herself. His ability to charm with a simple telephone call was not something she could ever fault him for.

The process itself seemed so *considered*, that was Clare's only problem with it. He'd get his book out and go down the checklist and charm all the people on the other end of the line. It didn't or shouldn't matter that half of these recipients of Jeremy's charm were people who been *her* friends originally, and the other half were upper-class twits Clare occasionally ran into whom she would have never pursued except in her darkest nightmares. Jeremy had come to her without his own circle of friends. He'd adopted hers, and some acquantainces she could have lived without as well – but what was wrong with that?

Sometimes, when Jeremy was in the midst of these calls, Clare imagined him putting a tick beside each name, as if with one phone conversation, he could ensure himself of a year's worth of bonhomie. He didn't need to do anything more. Clare was sure, for example, that the fact that Jeremy would never follow up the call and meet George for lunch or drinks didn't matter in the overall scheme of things. The call itself would be sufficient to make George think of Jeremy as a thoroughly good chap, great athlete and extremely close friend. Of course, Jeremy could always sense when that goodwill period was running out, at which point he'd pick up the telephone to ring again.

What did Jeremy get out of all this? Clare found herself wondering. Not *real* friendship. But what? Did it matter? Only in so far as it made Clare nervous about her own recent responses to Jeremy.

Whenever he came back from a tour abroad, he would walk through the door with his self-assured gait, and not even pause to say hello before taking her straight upstairs to bed. This was definitely a romantic scenario and one Clare had loved for a long time. But two days ago, on his return from South Africa, she'd found it slightly stage-managed, as if he'd decided a long time before that this was what a star athlete *should* do with his girlfriend whenever he came home to her. She'd wanted to interrupt him, postpone the love-making, but felt, very strangely, as if it would be tantamount to her taking his address book and throwing it in the bin.

Watching the last day of the Test Series the week before, she'd astounded herself by feeling irritated that he didn't once throw the ball up in the air when he made a brilliant catch. This coolness of Jeremy's, his trademark refusal to be visibly pleased with himself, suddenly seemed childish to her. An attempt to be what? Some aristocratic character out of the Golden Days of the Raj? Clare really wanted him, just once, to throw away his superior stance and act like all the others, be more of a player and less of a gentleman. She wished he would hug his team-mates wildly, shout for ridiculous decisions, do a little jig when he scored a century. Anything to make a tiny dent in his 'excellent' behaviour.

But what was so different about her own behaviour? she asked herself. She too was basically even-tempered, slightly aloof, cool. At least that's how her friends viewed her. She never drank too much or gave vent to rage or lost control. 'To Clare – the calm, cool, collected one' – was the greeting on a birthday card from a friend the previous year. That inscription would have fitted Jeremy just as well. So why should she blame him for exhibiting the very traits she did herself?

Occasionally Clare would imagine the child she and Jeremy might produce. She could visualize a blond, blue-eyed wonder boy with good-looking features and incredible coordination. He would be bright and polite and look terrific in his school uniform. And he would be completely devoid of feelings. That was what she feared a union between them would engender, a perfect frame with no picture in it. As soon as these thoughts entered her brain, she would try to push them away. She would concentrate on the stability and love Jeremy and she would have to offer. Their child would be safe. No monsters would be able to attack him. He would be fearless. Before long, though, the image of this boy, wearing pristine white, never smiling, never crying, never yelling, would invade her brain again and she'd have to stop thinking about children altogether to rid herself of these notions.

Turning away from the clouds, Clare focused on the stewardess who was offering her a choice of chicken or lamb.

'I'll have the chicken, please,' she said.

'Can I have both?' asked Bernice.

Chapter 8

'Yeah, I know the guy's name from somewhere. Wait a minute. I think he used to—'

'Artie,' Carl wrapped the telephone cord around his wrist, then tightened it as if it were a handcuff. 'Can you figure out why the hell he has asked me to be in the audience of this show? What does *Magic Moments* have to do with me?'

'I don't know. Do you have a long-lost brother you haven't spoken to for thousands of years?'

'No.' Carl imagined Art fooling with his glasses in much the same way he was fooling with the cord. Sometimes they were both little boys playing at being grown-ups.

'Maybe he's trying to fill seats?'

'You told me at the beginning of this conversation that the show is reasonably popular.'

'It is, it is. For cable.' Art paused. 'Actually, I've seen it. It can be kind of fun.'

'Kind of fun?'

'Yeah. As Cathy and Elizabeth would say, kind of fun. People are confronted with their first love whom they haven't seen for twenty years and, you know, you can tell they suddenly hate each other on sight. Disaster on live TV always cheers me up.'

'I'm not sure I want to be in the audience of this show, Art.'

'Oh, come on. Why not? It's a mystery why they've asked you.

You should show up and solve it. Look, I'll come with you, if you want. I'll make the right calls and get a ticket.'

'Alright, that makes it bearable, I guess.' Carl amused himself by imagining Art in a television studio, grinning at a camera and waving wildly, mouthing 'Hi, Dad!'. 'And I have to admit I am curious. The producer guy said he'd send a car to pick me up at nine tomorrow morning. He'd already called three times yesterday and twice today to make sure I'm coming. Anyway, I'll get the driver to swing by your place on the way.'

'Good. Listen, Carl, maybe this producer is a lot like you. Maybe he flicks through the telephone book and instead of writing letters, invites the people he's chosen randomly to be in the audience of his show. You know, there's no guarantee that there aren't other people in the world as crazy as you are.'

Bernice was exhausted. All her energy had been spent keeping Clare away from the hotel room, away from telephone books, away from the imaginary Raphael and Co. Anna owed her for this one, she really did, Bernice decided. It wasn't as if they were staying at the Plaza, either. No, Anna had booked them into the Sheraton Towers on Seventh Avenue and 53rd. It was perfectly all right and serviceable but it was no luxury spot. Ivana Trump wouldn't want to buy it.

They were sitting in Siena, an Italian restaurant across the street from the Sheraton. Conversation had petered out not long after their trip up the Empire State Building, and even Bernice was struggling to finish her huge dish of spaghetti alla marinara.

'What do you think I should wear tomorrow?'

'The cream suit,' Bernice responded immediately.

'What if I get sick to my stomach?'

'You won't. Come on, Clare, you know how to handle yourself. Even when you were eleven years old, you came across as twenty-five going on forty.'

'That's because I was never allowed to be a child.'

'Did you ever want to be?'

'I *always* did. I still do. I want to have a temper tantrum. I want to have a birthday party. I was never allowed a birthday party because my mother thought too many children would make too much of a mess.'

'Your mother definitely wasn't a party animal, I remember,' Bernice grimaced. 'She used to look at me as if I were slightly dirty, some gypsy urchin with a worryingly dark complexion who had walked in off the street. I suppose I *had* in a sense, being adopted and all, but I remember her attitude made me always take a bath whenever I stayed over at your house. And I made sure your mother *knew* I was taking one.' Bernice shuddered, then examined her silver-coloured fingernails. 'Listen, we *could* order some ice cream now and you *could* have a temper tantrum afterwards if I tell you you have to go to bed early. I could manufacture a childhood for you right now.'

'It doesn't work that way, I'm afraid. You can't manufacture a giggle, for example. Do you realize I've never giggled, not once in my life?'

'Do you know why women fake orgasms?' Bernice leant forward, whispering this question to Clare.

'No. Why?'

'Because they think men give a shit.'

Clare emitted a half-laugh.

'You were *supposed* to giggle at that one, Clare.'

'I *almost* did.'

'That's like *almost* having an orgasm. You don't have problems having orgasms, do you?'

'No.'

'Well, then, I really wouldn't worry about not giggling. There are priorities in life you know. I wouldn't rank giggling that highly.' Bernice leant back. 'Relax, Clare. Chill out. The show will be fine. You'll be fine. What's the worst that could happen?'

Clare had so many responses to that question, she decided to keep her mouth shut.

*   *   *

Before she'd really taken in what was happening to her, Clare was in make-up in the *Magic Moments* studio on West 57th Street, being brushed, powdered and pulled together by experts. The two men working on her were having an intense conversation amongst themselves and Clare was trying to get control of her nerves.

No one knows me in this country, she reminded herself. If I do something stupid, it won't wreck my life. Besides, I can talk about *Breathing in the Dusk* without making a fool of myself, I know I can.

'Could you look up now?'

Clare obligingly raised her eyes to the ceiling.

'All right. Great. Now look down. You'll like Mick Nelson, he's a sweetheart,' one of the make-up men said. Clare thought for a second that he was still talking to his co-worker. 'Mick's a very professional host. He's great with first-timers like you. Eyes straight ahead now, please. What are you on for anyway?'

With his New York accent, it sounded like 'What are you in for?' and Clare imagined answering 'Fraud'.

'My book. I'm promoting my last novel.'

'Oh, you're one of those.'

'Those?'

'The ones who don't know.'

'The ones who don't know what?'

'That's for us to know and for you to find out,' the other man chipped in, winking at Clare in the mirror.

'I don't understand,' Clare felt like pulling the protective cloth from around her neck and running away from the studio.

'You don't have to. You look terrific anyway, sweets. Those languorous eyes will knock the camera out. And I love the English accent.' The man twirled her around on the stool, unwrapped the cloth and patted her shoulder. 'Knock 'em dead.'

Yet another man suddenly appeared in the room, sporting a long blond pony-tail. He motioned for Clare to follow him.

'Listen,' he said, grabbing her elbow. 'This is the deal. We have to keep you away from the stage for a few minutes while Mick introduces the show, all right?'

Clare nodded dumbly.

'Then, during the commercial, we'll mike you up and get you ready to roll. Is that cool?'

'That's cool,' she nodded again. But it wasn't. She didn't understand. Why wasn't she being taken to the greenroom where guests could sit and chat before the show? That's what was supposed to happen, wasn't it? Everyone who was scheduled to be on the show sitting together amiably, waiting their turn, maybe even drinking some coffee. Clare felt faint and confused when Pony-tail took a sharp right-hand turn in the corridor and deposited her in a windowless room with one chair sitting conspicuously in the middle. Why couldn't she watch the introduction of the show?

She had seen posters of Mick Nelson when she'd been led through a maze of corridors from reception to make-up, but she would have liked to see him on air. Presumably he would have said something about his guests at the very beginning. She *should* have been allowed to listen to his description of her, shouldn't she?

Clare took off her cream jacket and placed it carefully on the top of the chair. She couldn't sit, she was too nervous. She had to pace around the room. What were the make-up people talking about? She was 'one of the ones who didn't know'. Didn't know what exactly? If only she'd had that conversation with them at the start of the make-up session. They might have told her something then. Pony-tail had left her before she'd had any chance to protest.

She coughed. A horribly familiar wheezing breath accompanied the cough. And then the hands suddenly came, circling her lungs, squeezing. Within a few seconds there was no air. She was choking.

Reaching for her handbag, she quickly emptied its contents onto the blue carpet and sank to her knees. Her inhaler was there, she knew. She went regularly to her GP for check-ups and always kept a current supply of medicine with her just in case she had a minor attack. She remembered specifically putting the inhaler in her handbag that morning, but where was it? Her keys, her scent bottle, her tissues lay right before her, but the inhaler wasn't in sight. She couldn't breathe. She was on her hands and knees, her eyes watering, her heart pounding unnaturally and it wasn't bloody there. But it had to be there, she knew. It just *had* to be.

Groping desperately, she felt the terror she hadn't experienced for almost ten years, the terror of life shutting down from within. The outlines of the room blurred, then vanished from sight, replaced by a vision of cemeteries stretching to an endless horizon; row upon row of headstones, with young, childlike bodies lying in front of them, waiting to be buried. In a blind panic, she reached out further and finally felt the shape of the inhaler in her right hand. She opened her mouth, placed it around the nozzle, pushed down and inhaled at the same time. Ventolin. A spray of Ventolin. The smell, the taste, were instantly familiar. The terrible vision began to recede as her breath returned, but she couldn't quite shake the spectre of the gravestones and the image of mass death.

If only she could have some human contact, someone to calm her down, reassure her that the world wasn't about to collapse, but no one appeared. She was all alone, confused, a helpless child. Tears were sliding down her made-up face. In a few minutes she was supposed to expose her most pitiful self to an entire television audience. *Everyone* would know how pathetic a human being she really was. Clare crawled to the chair, pulled herself up onto it and tried to think herself back into her adult self.

The attack was over. She could breathe. She was all right. She had to be. There was no choice but to be calm, to survive. No other option was available. The childhood fears had to be banished. She was twenty-seven years old now, she had had two novels published and she lived with Jeremy Letts. Concentrate on Jeremy, she told herself. Jeremy was her safe place.

Jeremy would have never got into this mess in the first place because he wouldn't appear on a television talk show. He'd been pleased when she'd told him about it, certainly, although now that she remembered, he'd looked slightly sceptical.

'Why don't you get a tape of this *Magic Moments* programme, so you'll know what you're in for?' he had suggested. 'I know how vicious the media can be.'

'But I'm not famous. So why be vicious to me? They can't be interested in me, only my work. And I can't believe my publishers there would set me up on a television show which would pan my book. It doesn't make sense.'

'No,' he'd agreed. 'It doesn't.'

'I don't know the mechanics of getting a tape of the show,' she had continued. 'Besides, Anna was thrilled about it and she wouldn't let me make a fool of myself. It's not in her interest.'

'No.' Jeremy practised an imaginary swing of the cricket bat. 'You're right. I suppose it all seems strange to me because this is the first time you're leaving *me* instead of the other way around. I'll miss you, you know.'

'I certainly hope so,' Clare had replied.

'Pull yourself together, Clare,' she whispered to herself, 'nothing bad is going to happen. The world is not such a scary place. It's not made up of cemeteries with childrens' bodies everywhere. I've been living in it happily enough for a long time. When this is all over, I can call Jeremy and laugh. Meanwhile, I have to stay calm. My tears can't have completely ruined my make-up. And I can breathe – that is the most important part.

'I can breathe and I can talk and I'm going to be all right. The monster has gone.'

Rising slowly, and going to pick up the items scattered on the carpet, she told herself, 'This is my chance. This is my chance to promote my book and I can't blow it. I *can't* lose it, not now.'

'Who *is* this jerk?' Carl whispered to Art as the theme tune to *Magic Moments* struck up and Mick Nelson gave a little hello wave to the camera.

'Who cares?' Art replied. 'I wish I hadn't come with you. I have a feeling this is going to be one of the painfully boring ones. Someone

109

will be thrilled to meet his long-lost second cousin who's had five liver transplants.'

'Shh,' the woman beside Art said with menace. 'Listen to the show or get out.'

'We're all in for a thoroughly fantastic show today,' Mick Nelson grinned.

The audience applause light flashed on and people clapped wildly. Art and Carl sighed simultaneously.

'So pip, pip, and hurrah, folks, because we've got an English theme. Later on we're going to get a couple together who haven't seen each other since the war – that's World War Two, when we Yanks were oversexed and overpaid and over there in Britain. Our ex-GI Sam met Deidre in a pub, they had a brief but passionate romance and then poor Sam was shipped home and he and Deidre lost touch. Now Sam's wife has unfortunately passed away and he's anxious to see his wartime gal again. Won't that be fun?'

More wild applause, accompanied by whistles.

'But first, before we bring Sam and Deidre on, and remember, Deidre knows *nothing* about this meeting, we're going to introduce two people to each other who have been having a whale of a correspondence. For almost two years, Carl Lioce, a man living right here in New York City, has been writing letters to a woman in England he has never met. Her name is Clare James, and she's a honey, folks. Carl doesn't know what Clare looks like, poor Carl doesn't even know why we've asked him to be in the studio audience here today, he—'

'I don't fucking believe this,' Art said, stunned.

'I'm not fucking doing this,' Carl replied. 'I can't believe you did this to me, Artie.'

'Carl, I didn't! I promise—'

'So when we come back, these two letter-writers from different countries will meet for the first time and share that experience with our studio audience.'

In a phenomenally quick movement, Carl ripped off the lapel badge he'd been given when he entered the studio, ripped off

Art's, stuck his own name on Art and Art's name on himself.

'You fucking set me up for this, *you* do it,' Carl hissed. 'You go up there and meet her.'

'I didn't do a goddamn thing. I just came along for the ride. I know nothing, Carl. Absolutely nothing.'

'Then *she* set me up. I'm not doing it, whoever's idea this was. I won't be cornered like this on television.'

A young woman was suddenly kneeling beside Carl on the aisle.

'So, are you ready?' she asked him. 'When Clare comes on and she's introduced, you go up on the stage, we'll get you a mike and—'

'Don't look at me,' Carl said evenly. 'I'm Art Rolfe. This guy beside me is Carl Lioce – *he's* the one you want.'

'But Carl was supposed to be on the aisle,' she protested.

'Yeah, well, things don't always work out perfectly. Carl—' Carl turned to Art. 'Switch places with me here and it will be easier for you to get on stage.'

'Just a second—' Art protested.

'What?' The young woman sounded fraught. 'You should switch places *now*. The commercial's almost over.'

'Well, the show will be over if you don't give me a second,' Art replied. 'I'm not so sure I want to share a stage with that asshole Nelson. Or some floozy English girl, who, for all I know, might be overaged, overweight and over here.'

Pony-tail rushed back into the room, grabbing Clare by her shoulder this time.

'OK, OK, this is groovy. Time to party. We've got to make tracks fast.'

He hustled her back out into the corridor and then onto the sound stage where Clare could see Mick Nelson sitting in a comfortable blue chair, talking to a cameraman. As yet another unknown man strapped a mike to her blouse, Clare took her eyes away from Mick and glanced at the audience in a semicircle around the stage. Bernice was sitting there somewhere, she knew, and that fact gave her a little comfort.

'He's in the fourth row, far left-hand side, on the aisle,' a man beside her said into a headphone.

'In twenty seconds I want you to go and sit beside Mick in that chair over there, all right? The commercial will finish and we'll come back on air with you sitting there.'

'All right,' Clare nodded. She was beginning to feel like a calf being herded into a crate bound for market. All she could do was nod her head and look bewildered.

Somehow she managed to get across the floor and into the chair at the right moment without tripping over cables or being sick to her stomach or wheezing. When she settled in, Mick Nelson leant over and whispered, 'You're going to love this. Let me do all the talking at first.' Mesmerized by his contact-blue eyes and the teeth which matched the whiteness of his gleaming shirt, Clare sat back, relieved that he was taking control. She didn't have to say anything for a while and she knew she was good at being silent.

'Stop tugging at my sleeve, sweetheart. Oh, right, there she is now, there's the famous Miss James.' Art grinned. 'Move over, Artie, I'm ready to take my place.'

Music began to play, the red light on the camera in front of them went on, and Mick Nelson started to speak.

'Now, our first guest, Clare James is over here from England. She has written a book called *Breathing in the Dusk* and she *thinks* she's on here to plug that book. Isn't that right, Clare?'

Nodding, Clare looked at Mick Nelson with terror in her eyes. She could feel her chest constrict.

'But she's not here to plug her book, is she, folks?'

On cue, the audience screamed, 'No way!'

She was in the middle of some crazed pantomime, and she had no idea how to get out of it. Clare caught sight of her own face in the

112

monitor and was stunned by its contorted appearance. The plane was veering out of control; why wasn't Angela Rae sitting beside her now? And where was her bag with the Ventolin? On the side of the sound stage – she'd left it on the side of the sound stage.

'No, Clare's here because she has a very special friend in her life, one she's never met. For almost a year and a half, Clare, you've been writing letters back and forth across the ocean to an American man named Carl Lioce. You don't even know what he looks like, do you?'

Clare shook her head. Her lungs hurt. She couldn't speak. Carl? This was about *Carl*?

'Well, you're going to find out what he looks like now, Clare James, because sitting in the audience, right here, is that very guy. Carl?'

The camera panned to the fourth row. Art beamed and stood up. 'Carl Lioce, Clare James, take a deep breath, you two – here is your magic moment!'

Art did a quick sprint to the stage. When he reached Clare's chair, he took a step back, suddenly bashful. Clare found herself standing up as well.

'Carl?' she asked, searching his face for help.

'Clare,' Art said quietly, holding out his hand. She immediately shook it and they stood staring at each other.

'Sit down, Carl, Clare. Please,' Mick said effusively. A chair had magically materialized beside Clare's. 'This must come as a real shock to you both. Neither of you had any idea this was going to happen, did you?'

Art and Clare shook their heads at the same moment, looking like twins. The audience laughed appreciatively.

'Oh my God, that's him!' Bernice strained forward to see his face. 'He's quite sweet-looking in those glasses. But he's definitely not Clare's type.'

'So tell us, Carl – Clare looks a little dumbstruck at the moment, so we'll let her get herself together – how did this correspondence begin?'

'Well,' Art leant forward in his chair, 'I read an article in *People Magazine* about an elderly woman who had swum the English channel and I decided to write to her. She's English, you see, and I happen to keep a telephone book for London in my apartment and I sent this letter off. Clare is living in this woman's house and handling her mail. So Clare opened my letter, replied and I guess you'd say "that's all she wrote," or that's *part* of what she wrote.'

Mick nodded happily. Art could tell Mick was pleased with 'Carl''s televisual ability.

'So you continued writing to each other for over a year. How fascinating. And Clare, what do you think now, seeing Carl?'

'What do I think?' Clare asked herself. 'I don't know what the hell I think about anything. He's so *different* but he's somehow the same. And the moment I saw him, I stopped panicking, I relaxed. What does that mean?'

'Clare?' Mick pressed.

'I think you've really shocked her, Mick,' Art said quickly. 'We were never going to meet. I mean, that was one of the groundrules of our writing to each other. So she must be really confused. But, Clare . . .' he turned to face her and his voice became soft, 'I never knew you were a writer – that's fantastic!'

'Isn't it?' Mick jumped in. 'Especially as my happy campers in the research department of *Magic Moments* have found out that you're a writer as well, Carl. That makes you very well matched.'

'*You're* a writer?' Clare burst out. 'Carl, I can't believe it.'

'Were my letters that bad?'

'No. No,' Clare said quickly, stopping the laughter welling in the audience. 'No, your letters were wonderful. It's such a coincidence, that's all.'

'Does he look the way you imagined?' Mick asked, stretching his smile to the limits.

'I guess he does,' she managed to mumble. 'I don't know, really.'

'Uh-oh,' Art covered his face with his hand in a melodramatic gesture. The audience guffawed.

114

'And you, Carl, what do you say? Does she look like you imagined?'

'No. Not at all,' Art replied, taking his hand away from his face and staring at Clare. The studio became preternaturally silent. 'I could never have imagined that she'd be this beautiful. I mean, that's not the kind of luck I would expect. It's too much.'

Applause boomed out from all sides.

Carl, watching from the fourth row, buried his head in his hands.

Clare blushed. She sneaked a look from the corner of her eyes, trying to see if Carl had been genuine or was giving her this extravagant praise for the benefit of the television cameras. But he couldn't have faked it, she decided. Carl wasn't like that, he didn't have a imposter's bone in his body.

'It's the make-up,' she said, smiling. 'Normally I'm sure you'd pay a lot of money not to see me at this time in the morning.'

Mick Nelson smiled back at her. This time even his smile semed for real.

'I think you've just won the hearts of everyone watching this show, Clare,' he stated and the audience clapped their assent. 'So *Magic Moments* has reserved a table for you two at O'Neal's Balloon tonight. We thought that would be a nice place for you to sit down and get to know each other, face-to-face.'

'Thank you, Mick,' Art said. 'That's very generous of you.'

'And we definitely want to know if anything serious happens between you two in the romantic stakes, OK?'

'No problem,' Art grinned.

'Cilla Black,' Clare found herself saying.

'What was that, Clare?' Mick looked slightly irritated.

'She's an English woman who sets up blind dates on a television show,' Clare explained, realizing how silly she must sound.

'Well, jolly for her,' Mick beamed. 'We all love romance, don't we?'

The audience cheered.

'And soon we'll meet our next transatlantic couple, Sam and

Deidre. Let's hope it goes as well as this meeting between Clare and Carl. We'll be back right after the break.'

The theme music sounded and various stage-hands were motioning for Art and Clare to leave the set.

'Well done, guys,' Mick stated in his best host's voice. 'Good spot.'

Art took Clare's elbow, guiding her to the edge of the set.

'Boy,' he whispered, 'that was hell, wasn't it?'

'You thought so too?' she asked, looking up at him gratefully. He was a few inches taller than her and, she noticed for the first time, had amazingly deep, dark eyes behind the glasses, with eyelashes which looked so black and long, they might have been painted. His face wasn't conventionally handsome, but his eyes were almost frighteningly compelling.

'Absolutely. I hope you realize that we – I – knew nothing about this, Clare. It was an honest-to-God bombshell.'

'You really didn't know either?'

'No way. Oh, my God!' Art hit his forehead. 'What's the cricket player – your husband – going to think when he hears about this?'

'I don't know.' Clare suddenly noticed her handbag on the floor and picked it up. People were waving them away from the set and Pony-tail reappeared, saying, 'Follow me. I'll show you the way out.'

Art kept his hand on Clare's elbow as they were guided back through all the winding corridors and finally emerged in the lobby.

'Have a blast tonight, guys,' Pony-tail said gaily. 'Just show up at O'Neal's Balloon at seven-thirty. Here's a card to show to the maitre 'd. The table's reserved in your name, Carl. The bill's on us. That includes one bottle of wine.'

'Thanks,' Art replied, holding the door open for Clare. 'One whole bottle of wine. Wow!'

'Oh my God, Bernice,' Clare remembered, as she emerged onto the pavement. 'She's in the audience. My friend Bernice. Do you think they'll let her leave now?'

'Well, I guess they will, unless she has some unknown connection with GI Sam or pub lady Deidre. Bernice? Isn't she the one who called your history teacher a "cunt"?'

'Yes,' Clare actually managed to laugh. 'I keep forgetting you know everything about me.'

'Hey,' Art spread his hands in the air, 'I don't know half enough.'

'Clare—' Bernice came rushing through the door and out onto the street, but she stopped when she saw Art. 'Hello,' she said. 'Carl.'

'Hi, Bernice. Nice to meet you. I've heard, I'm mean I've read a lot about you.'

'About me? Wh—'

'And here's *my* friend Art,' Art quickly interrupted, seeing Carl. 'Art Rolfe. Art, I'm glad you managed to get out of there so quickly.'

'So am I,' Carl replied sullenly. 'Who set this up, anyway?'

'I didn't,' Clare said immediately. 'I honestly thought I was going on to talk about my book.'

'Well, I—'

'I didn't either,' Art interrupted Carl. 'I was asked to be in the audience. Art came along for the ride.'

'The whole thing is a joke,' Carl muttered.

'No, no, no, Art. Don't say that. It's not a joke. You see it gives me a chance to meet Clare, to get to know her in person. Although, I have to admit, I'm a little concerned about what her *husband* will think when he hears about all this. Wouldn't you be, Art, if you were me?' Art narrowed his eyes, staring at Carl.

'What?' Bernice stopped staring at Art and focused on Clare. 'What's he talking about?'

'He's talking about Jeremy,' Clare said.

'I know, but he said—'

'Listen, it's crazy standing around here on the sidewalk, like this. I have a great idea,' Art rubbed his hands together briskly. 'Why don't we expand this dinner tonight and make it the four of us? I'll cover whatever the other half of the bill comes to. It will make everything easier if we all get together, don't you think? Clare and I have been put under a lot of pressure in this whole deal. We should have our seconds with us, as it were. And I'm sure by the time dinner rolls around, one of us will have discovered who arranged this meeting on our behalf. What do you think? Is that a good program?'

'Good program,' Clare asked.

'A good idea, he means,' Carl said, staring intently at the pavement.

'You never used that word before,' Clare turned to Art.

'It's a conversational type of word,' Art replied. 'It's not a big deal, is it?'

'No, no,' Clare shook her head. 'Of course not.' She tore her look away from his black eyes and noticed what he was wearing. A conservative dark blue suit, white shirt and blue and white polka-dot tie. He looked so *comfortable* in these responsible-looking clothes, a fact which surprised her. She would have bet Carl would dress more haphazardly. Still, she liked the way he kept touching his glasses nervously.

'So, what about dinner . . . the four of us?' Art persisted.

'That's a nice idea,' Clare found her gaze drawn right back to his eyes. That's where she could see the Carl she had daydreamt about for all these months, right there in those amazing eyes.

'See you at O'Neal's then. It's on Columbus Circle, by the way. But you can check out the exact address in the phone book. 'Art put his arm around Carl and began to lead him away. 'It was nice to meet you too, Bernice.'

Finding herself unable to reply, Bernice simply stared at his retreating back.

'I can't believe that's Carl,' she finally said after they'd disappeared around the corner.

'I know,' Clare nodded. 'I can't believe any of this. Who arranged this, Bernice? Was it my publishers here? Raphael and Company?'

'Clare, listen, I know it's still early, but we've got a lot to discuss and I think the best place to discuss it is in a bar.'

118

Chapter 9

'Come off it. You want to keep being me because you think she's sexy and stunning and you want a chance with her, it's as simple as that.'

'No, honestly, Carl. I admit she's something to look at, that's obvious. I thought she'd look like a horse, I mean that's my experience of Englishwomen. But that's not the point. Her looks aren't the point. The point is that you should have some time to check her out without putting yourself on the line. I mean, she's married, for one. You've got to be careful. And she *says* she didn't know anything about the show today, but how can you be sure? She's a writer, she might be planning to write a book about this whole deal.'

'Why do I think I've heard that idea before?'

'Well, it's one thing for me to indulge in sleazeball, commercial book-selling tactics, but another for her. Honestly, she could be using you, and this way she can use *me* instead.'

Art took a sip of the coffee from the plastic cup in front of him and stared at the waterfall cascading down the back wall of the tiny park they were sitting in. Carl, he knew, was annoyed, but Art wasn't sure what was irritating him so much. Had it been the television program? The switch of identities? Or the fact that Clare James was an actual, flesh-and-blood woman, not a goddess from the spirit world of writing?

'Oh, that's wonderful, Artie. That's just wonderful. So kind of you. Really. I'm impressed by your magnanimity.'

'Tone, Carl. Careful about the tone.'

'Well, you've put me in one hell of a bind. If I suddenly announce at this dinner that *I'm* Carl, she'll be so confused she'll probably kill us both.'

'You seem to forget that you're the one who put yourself in the bind. *You're* the one who switched nametags and made me go up on stage. Now you want to switch back – I'm saying it's not a wise idea. I mean, we don't even know where Jeremy Cricket is hanging out, do we? He could be with them. He might show up at dinner. *I* can handle that scenario gracefully, I'm not so sure *you* can.'

'Why not?'

'Because you're more involved than I am. You've got more at stake. Look, let's just play it the way it is at the beginning of this meeting, all right? We can tell her the truth after I've done a little digging – you're free to come out and say who you are whenever you want to after the first fifteen minutes – what about that? Instead of fifteen minutes of fame, I'll have my fifteen minutes of being Carl Lioce. How's that for a good solution?'

'It sucks.'

'So you're going to walk in to O'Neal's Balloon and tell her immediately?'

'I don't know. I don't know why I didn't set things straight right there on the sidewalk. I was too overcome by the whole thing, I guess. Seeing you on that show pretending to be me . . . well, for a while there, I thought I was going crazy, that you might actually *be* me.'

'Carl.'

'I know, I know. My sanity problem isn't looming on the horizon anymore, it's coming to shore full speed ahead. But you were so convincing. The way you explained how the correspondence got started. I was watching the monitors instead of the stage. Seeing it on television somehow makes it real. And then, there you were, standing on the sidewalk with her, looking so protective and proprietorial. I was paralyzed. I couldn't say anything.'

'I noticed. Alright, as soon as you want to tonight, you go ahead and spill the beans. I can't stop you, can I?'

'No, Artie. You can't.'

'Does she look the way you imagined her to look?'

'That's the strangest part of all. She *does*. Exactly.'

They were sitting in a bar on 53rd Street called Chapmans. Bernice had ordered two Sea Breeze cocktails and was smoking a Silk Cut. Clare reached over and grabbed one out of the packet for herself.

'Clare? You don't smoke.'

'So you're telling me that Raphael and Company doesn't exist.' She said this in a monotone, while she took Bernice's Cricket lighter off the table between them and lit up.

'It was all Anna's idea and I know I shouldn't have gone along with her, but she convinced me it would be good for you. She thinks you had to meet Carl, as soon as possible. Clare, what about your asthma?'

'Fuck my asthma.'

Bernice was amazed to see that Clare didn't cough or splutter as she inhaled. She was even more stunned when Clare took a huge belt of the Sea Breeze.

'Well, that's just excellent,' Clare remarked. 'My own agent lies to me and I end up looking like a complete prat on American television.'

'You didn't, Clare. You looked terrific. We should get a tape of the show. You were a little out of it at first, but you rallied. I loved the make-up comment. Everyone did.'

'Excellent. Fabulous.' Finishing her drink in another huge gulp, Clare looked around for the waiter. 'Could I please have another of these?' she asked as he approached their table.

'Rough morning?' he asked, smiling.

'You could say that. *I* couldn't possibly comment.'

'Excuse me?' he hovered for a moment beside them.

'Yes, she's had a tough morning,' Bernice stated, staring at his peroxide crew cut. 'Do you have any food here?'

'Peanuts.'

'Fine, could we have a bowl of those, please?' Bernice waited until he had left, then turned to Clare. 'Is he the way you imagined he'd be?'

'Carl?'

'No, the waiter.'

'He's different. I didn't think his hair would be so curly, I thought he'd have a more angular face and a deeper voice. But then, when I saw those eyes –' she stopped and took another deep drag.

'What eyes?'

'Didn't you notice? He has truly amazing, dark eyes.'

'Oh,' was Bernice's comment, as she tried to remember Carl's eyes. He was a decent-looking man, but not one to write home about, she thought. Compared to Jeremy, he was pretty lame, actually.

'So what exactly does Anna have planned for me now? I mean, what's the next step in her twisted, screwed-up mind?'

'I think she wants you and Carl to have a romance.'

'Oh, wonderful. That's just wonderful. I hate her, Bernice. I really loathe her. Can you imagine how I felt when I was put in a room by myself waiting for the damn show to begin? I started to have an asthma attack again, the first really serious one since I was eighteen. I was down on my hands and knees searching for my inhaler. Do you have any idea what she has put me through?'

'No,' Bernice shook her head. 'I guess I don't, really.' The waiter placed another Sea Breeze in front of Clare and a bowl of peanuts in front of Bernice. 'She thought it would be romantic.'

'Romantic? Is torture her idea of romance?'

'Is there anything else I can do for you ladies?'

'You can leave us alone for a while,' Bernice answered.

'Sorry,' he said, backing away. 'I love your accents. We don't get many Brits in here.'

'What a shame. I'll ring Paul Gascoigne and tell him to come over; you'll adore him.' As the waiter retreated, looking puzzled, Bernice took a fistful of peanuts and regarded Clare's miserable face for an instant. She'd never seen or heard Clare betray such raw emotion. Even in the emergency room on the night of the cab crash, Clare had been calm and unfazed.

'Do you want to fly home as soon as possible, then? I know we're booked to go back Sunday night, but we could get a flight tomorrow. One day less won't make any difference, I'm sure we can arrange it somehow. And we certainly don't have to go to this dinner tonight.'

'No, I want to see Carl. I can't leave it like this, it's so abrupt. But I feel, I feel . . .'

'What?' Bernice prompted.

'Unbelievably pissed off. Used and betrayed and pissed off.'

'Are you pissed off with me too?'

Turning her profile to Bernice, Clare gazed at the far wall of the bar.

'Angela sent me a postcard the other day. She asked me what I was doing with my life. Well, nothing is the answer. I'm doing fuck all with my life and I'm incredibly unhappy. I don't know who the hell I am and I don't even care.'

'Clare, slow down. Where did that all come from? You shouldn't let this get to you so much. It's not *that* big a deal, meeting Carl, is it? I mean, crikey, it's not the end of the world. He seems . . .' Bernice faltered and stopped. The two women stared at their drinks for a moment in silence.

'You didn't answer my question, Clare, are you pissed off with me, too?'

Clare pondered for what seemed to Bernice an agonizingly long time before she replied, 'No. I would have gone on this trip without you. At least you're here with me now. Did you notice how Carl was able to handle that show so well? *He* didn't fall to pieces. I guess I believed we were more alike than we are. I would have thought he'd have the same reaction as I did, that he would have been too surprised and stunned to speak for a while, at least. But he had a grip on things, he rescued me.'

'What?' Bernice smiled. 'The knight on the white charger rescuing the damsel in distress?'

'Something like that, yes. Don't make fun of me, Bernice. You don't know how terrified I was.'

'All right, I'll stop grinning and go to the loo.'

Clare stubbed out her cigarette as Bernice left the table. She slipped another from the packet, all the while thinking of Carl. He'd written her a letter fairly recently about the way he felt when he fell in love. 'You might not understand this,' he'd begun. 'I'm not sure I understand it myself, but I know that when I fall in love with a woman I feel the same way about her as I would feel about a child, if I were ever to have one. She is not so much my companion as part of my blood. Joined at the heart. I *guess* that's what parents feel for their children, anyway. A primeval bond.

'And sometimes, I confess (as I confess everything to you now, Clare, so I hope you're reading this in the sanctity of a confessional box), I confess that I have daydreams about rescuing the woman I love from a house on fire or a flood or any life-threatening situation I can think up. I see myself charging in and saving her. I would *love* to be able to charge in and save her; now how bizarre is that? Oh, Christ, why am I telling you this? You will laugh at my image of myself as Sir Lancelot and I don't blame you. In fact, if I were you, I'd recommend some good foreign clinics in your next letter so I can go away and hide my crazy soul elsewhere. Out of sight.'

The rest of the letter had been bright and breezy and very funny, but Clare had fixated on Carl's passionate desire to rescue his loved one. The night after she'd received it, she'd sat with Jeremy in the kitchen and despite all her determination never to make comparisons between him and Carl, she asked; 'Do you ever dream or daydream about rescuing me?'

'Rescuing you from what?' he'd parried.

'From any kind of danger. You know, a fire or a flood or something.'

'I can't say that I do,' Jeremy responded, cutting up a clove of garlic.

'But you dream about beating Brian Lara's 376, don't you?'

'Of course,' he laughed. 'In fact, I can't believe I haven't done it yet.'

'So you dream about being a hero on the cricket ground but not at home.'

'Yes.' He paused, knife in mid-air. 'That's true. But I don't see what point you're making. Do you dream about rescuing *me* from a fire?'

'No.'

'Do you ever daydream about being on the bestseller list?'

'Yes, I guess I do. Sometimes.'

'Right.' He took another clove of garlic and began to peel it. 'Then we're even in the dream stakes, aren't we?'

He'd made her feel foolish for bringing the subject up, but she knew that her heart had chosen Carl in the crazy competition she'd set up; she'd preferred Carl's zealous, all-encompassing commitment to a woman he fell in love with to Jeremy's practical, almost *laissez-faire* attitude. She didn't know, when she received that letter, what Carl did for a living, but she reckoned his real job, his true career, was the pursuit of romantic love and she was amazed a man like him still existed in this cynical world.

Now that she'd seen him, now that she'd been rescued by him, albeit in a very different fashion than any she supposed he would have dreamt up himself, she was surprised that he could combine the old-fashioned knight in shining armour with the new-fashioned, take-charge *competent* man she'd seen on stage. It was a baffling combination, certainly, one to which she didn't quite know how to react. She'd envisioned Carl, before they'd met, as a sexy, wild, Byronic figure with a touch of Don Quixote. Now that she saw how modern and cosmopolitan he was, she was slightly disappointed and at the same time, surprisingly, she was slightly pleased.

Carl may not have been as romantic as she pictured him, but she was intrigued by the strength he had shown, his ease in strange surroundings, the aura of power he exuded. Yet she guessed that Carl would not want to be described as powerful. He'd rather stick with the adjective Byronic. And she felt guilty that she had responded to his wordly side in equal measure as she had to his soul.

'So,' Bernice said, coming back from the loo and sliding into her seat, 'have you been thinking about your rescuer?'

'Yes,' Clare admitted. 'I still don't quite understand how he managed to calm me down, as soon as I saw him. What do you think that means?'

'I'm not sure. Men are generally supposed to excite women, not calm them down, aren't they? What about Jeremy? Does he calm you down?'

'I've never been in a state of panic with Jeremy. But he might have the same effect.' Clare shook her head. 'I don't know.'

'I wouldn't think Carl's much like Jeremy. He doesn't *look* like Jeremy, anyway.'

'No,' Clare sighed, 'Jeremy doesn't have those eyes.'

'There go those eyes, again,' Bernice thought. 'The eyes obviously have it.'

'Clare, why does Carl think you and Jeremy are married? Is there something you haven't told me? Did you two elope to Gretna Green when no one was looking?'

Clare squirmed slightly before saying, 'It's a long story. There was a misunderstanding and I never set it straight. It seemed like a good idea at the time to let Carl think I was married.'

'Well, it might be a good idea to remind him about Jeremy now. I saw the way he was looking at you. He fancies you rotten.'

Catching the waiter's attention, Clare held up her empty glass.

'Carl's not like that.'

'Oh, yes, he is.'

'Here we go again,' Clare thought. Pantomime time. Oh, yes, he is, oh, no, he's not. How could Bernice think she knew anything at all about Carl?

'What the hell am I going to tell Jeremy when I *do* get back?'

'You could blame everything on Anna. That's what I would do.'

'Well, that would be fair. Bernice, you've known me since I was ten. How do I strike you? I mean, how would you describe me to someone else?'

'I suppose I'd say you're very attractive and intelligent and you're . . .' she hesitated, wanting to choose her adjectives carefully.

'Yes?'

'You're incredibly calm and self-contained.'

'Well, it's all bullshit. I'm a mess. What's taking that sickeningly friendly waiter so long? I need another drink.'

'Are you sure?'

A quick slideshow of pictures flicked through Clare's brain. She saw herself on her hands and knees scrambling for her asthma inhaler. She saw herself sitting on stage, next to Mick Nelson, in a state of mute panic. She saw, with X-ray vision, her heart collapse as she understood, finally, that Raphael and Company didn't exist, that there was no wonderful American publisher who understood what she'd been trying to express in her fiction. When *Between Pauses* had first been accepted by a publisher, she'd thought her entire life would change, that being a published author would make all the difference. She wasn't sure exactly what difference all the difference was, but she knew, as soon as she saw a copy of her book on sale in a bookshop, she would understand. Her life would be transformed.

Yes, she had experienced a thrill of pleasure when that moment had occurred. She had blushed when she walked into Waterstone's and found it on a far corner of a far table. But that was the extent of it. Nothing changed. Her life continued as it had always continued. The book didn't sell. No one took her seriously, except in her role as Jeremy's girlfriend. Everyone seemed to think her life as a writer was unimportant, and because she never made a fuss or admitted how important it really was to her, people assumed she didn't really care that the books had done badly. Well, she did care. Passionately. She was embarrassed and ashamed and hurt that no one was interested in what she wrote.

Being duped about an American sale was an indignity she didn't know how she could cope with. Obviously Anna thought she wouldn't be offended by it because – hell – why would Clare care? Clare took everything in her stride. And, even if Clare *did* care, Clare was the least likely person in the world to express any anger, wasn't she?

Clare stared at the cigarette she was holding, and watched the smoke waft away.

She was, and always had been, a failure. All she'd managed to do was hide her own inadequacies in the feeble guise of being self-contained.

'I'm positive I'd like another drink, Bernice,' she said. 'I'm absolutely sure.'

'They're fifteen minutes late already,' Carl muttered. 'Maybe they're not going to show up. They might have flown back to England for all we know.'

'Calm down, Carl. I've never seen you so jumpy. They'll be here, I'm sure of it.'

'How can you be so sure?'

'Because she's curious. She wants to find out more about me. I mean you. Trust me. I understand women better than you do.'

'That's not saying a whole hell of a lot.'

'I know, I know.' Art sighed. 'But look, here they come now. Score one for my expertise. Shit, look, she's . . .'

'Carl,' Clare stumbled over to the table. Bernice, a pace behind her, had an anxious look on her face. 'God, it's wonderful to see you again.' Clare aimed a kiss at Art's cheek, but missed and her lips landed briefly on his.

Carl, sitting across from Art, winced.

'Clare,' Art exlaimed, shooting Carl a troubled look. 'Are you all right?'

'She's had a few drinks.' Bernice quickly waved away the maître d' who had shown them to the table and managed to pull out the chair beside Art for Clare to collapse into, then seated herself on the other side of Carl.

'I've had a few drinks,' Clare repeated. 'Sea Breezes. I'm being blown by the fresh breezes of a stormy sea.'

'That sounds poetic,' Art smiled. 'We'll have to do some catching up pretty quickly.'

'I thought you didn't like to drink, Clare,' Carl stated, more to himself than to the group, but everyone heard him.

'What?' Clare rounded on him. 'How would you know whether I like to drink or not? Did Carl show you my letters, Art? Carl, did you show him my letters?' She turned back to Art. 'You did, didn't you? I don't believe this. This is horrendous. But why should I be surprised? It's typical news for this day, isn't it? Who else have you shown, Carl? Don't tell me – you're a writer too so you've probably got an agent. You've shown all my letters to your agent.'

Art waited a beat, but Carl didn't say a word.

'Art *is* my agent,' Art replied, thinking, 'Fine by me, if Carl wants to keep playing this little game for a while, I don't mind.'

'What about you? Do *you* have an agent, Clare? Did *you* show your agent Carl's letters?' Carl leant forward as he asked this, zeroing in on Clare's drunken eyes.

She knew she had to respond, but her mind was taking longer than usual to digest what was being said. Carl had shown her letters to someone. To whom? To Art. To Art who was both Carl's friend and his agent. And now Art wanted to know whether she had shown Carl's letters to *her* agent. She'd been happy for a brief moment, because she'd felt justifiably angry. She could remember the unaccustomed pleasure in knowing she had a right to be pissed off at somebody. Normally, any feeling of anger would change quickly, mutate into self-doubt and then guilt.

So many times she'd been on the verge of anger with Jeremy only to back off quickly, realizing she had no legitimate excuse to be mad. There was never any reason to be mad at Jeremy, which made her realize how much she'd like to have a real argument with Carl.

Only now, it turned out, as she put the pieces of the conversation together, she *couldn't* get justifiably angry with Carl – she'd done exactly the same thing as he had. Still, in this new state of alcohol-induced hazy release she was feeling, she decided that she didn't have to retreat totally, she could continue to go on the offensive for a while, just to see what it felt like.

'Absolutely, Art,' she said with spirit, turning to face him full on. 'Yes, absolutely, I showed Carl's letters to my agent. And she's the one, Bernice tells me, who set this whole thing up. She wanted Carl and me to meet. For all I know, she wants to write a book about it. After all, we're all in this for the book deal, aren't we? Everyone except for Bernice here. Or are you going to write a book about this too, Bernice?'

'No, not me.' Bernice shook her head. 'I'm here for the food.'

'Why did you show the correspondence to your agent in the first place? Were you planning to publish Carl's letters without his permission, Clare?' Carl persisted.

'Hold on, hold on everybody!' Art thumped the table. He didn't like the fact that Carl, having taken his name, was behaving so obnoxiously. After all, *he* was trying to be a nice, affable Carl Lioce, so why couldn't Carl be a decent Art Rolfe? Carl was taking his name in vain. 'Let's forget about books for awhile here. We should get to know each other, shouldn't we? We're here for a friendly dinner.' He glared at Carl. 'Not an inquisition. I don't mind whom you showed my letters to, Clare. I couldn't care less.'

'Jesus,' Carl muttered. 'You're a real piece of work.'

'Who's a real piece of work?' Bernice asked, taking notice of the other man properly for the first time. Art had a rugged, slightly dark face, thick black hair and brown eyes. An inch or two taller than Carl, and obviously a few years younger, he had broader shoulders and a much deeper voice. He was definitely a good proposition, she thought. If she played her cards right and didn't drink too much and didn't talk too much, she might be in with a chance.

'Clare,' Art put his hand on her forearm, 'I think you should have something to eat. There's some very decent pasta here. Bernice, how about you? Would you like some pasta? Should I order for you both, would that make things easier?'

'That would be wonderful,' Clare sank back in her chair, suddenly swamped with a feeling of utter exhaustion. She blocked out the others at the table from her thoughts, trying to work out exactly what she was doing and why. The morning's events had wrenched her soul and psyche, leaving her deflated, vulnerable and angry; angry with Anna for tricking her, angry with herself for losing control. The thought that she could succumb to her childhood fears again, even if only for a few moments, enraged her. So she'd had an asthma attack, so Anna had set her up, so what? She shouldn't have been as freaked out by it all as she was. Her revenge had been to lose control *purposefully*, to get drunk and try to blot out her overwhelming sense of inadequacy.

Now that she *was* drunk, for the first time in her life, she realized that inebriation did not stop you from thinking or feeling. Yes, it could give you false courage for a while; but as the effects of the alcohol slowly wound down, the bravado wore off. She realized that all her drunken spree had managed to accomplish was to make her feel even more hopeless.

Clare wanted to collapse into Carl's arms, she wanted him to forgive her for being weak just as he had forgiven her for showing his letters. She sensed that he was, in his own way, looking after her by doing something as simple and straightforward as ordering pasta. Only a few minutes ago she had wanted to argue with him, now she wanted his total, blanket understanding and sympathy.

'I don't want to trap you in this letter-writing, Clare,' he'd said in the last letter she'd received. 'I occasionally forget that you have your own life and that this corespondence of ours may be impinging on it. The correspondence doesn't have to go on the way it has been; I write, you write back, I write again, ad infinitum. We could break the rhythm. You could take some time out, if you want. I can continue to write to you without needing you to reply. All I need to know is that you're out there. Somewhere. I will do anything to protect what we have from harm.'

Clare looked at his profile beside her. He was so physically different from her image of him, and his speech was so gramatically different from his letters, but his instinct to protect, his essence, was the same.

'Thank you, Carl,' she said as the waiter approached to take their order. 'Thank you for being so understanding and kind.'

'Is this country having a bad-hair century?' Bernice asked. 'Is it mandatory for all waiters to have peroxide heads that look like they've been run over with roller blades?'

'She fell for it,' Carl said to himself, listening to everyone laugh at Bernice's comment. 'Clare fell for Artie's little ladies' man routine of "Oh, let me help you, damsel in drunken distress, let me order pasta for you".'

He was unreasonably aggrieved, he knew, but he couldn't help himself. At first, that morning, Clare had seemed so perfect, almost too perfect to believe, but now, now she had rolled into the restaurant totally hammered, acting like some put-upon dizzy blonde. As far as she was concerned, it was fine for her to show his letters around. But it was heresy for him to do the same. What hypocrisy. He never would have believed she was capable of it.

Now, watching Clare focus her semi-glazed eyes on Artie, Carl thought of Dee-Dee, her dark beauty, her proud face. In comparison, Clare looked washed-out, as well as edgy and slightly bitter. He'd always been careful not to make comparisons between Clare and Dee-Dee, but they would slip through his mind occasionally, almost slyly. He'd find himself thinking that Dee-Dee was incapable of constructing a sentence with fewer than four adverbs, or that he'd be truly amazed if Dee-Dee thought

Virginia Woolf was anything but a weird name in an Elizabeth Taylor movie. His feelings for Dee-Dee didn't suffer because of these observations, however. He could never feel anything but love for her. Still, this was the first time he'd ever compared the two women in his life when Clare had been in the less advantageous position.

The glorious relationship he and Clare had fashioned out of their letters was fast crumbling, as he'd always suspected it might if they were ever to meet. Nobody could be Clare on paper, especially not Clare in person.

Where were all those childhood fears he'd found so compelling and appealing? Had she made them up? She was, after all, a writer; she probably invented the plane crash story as well. It could all be lies and deception. She could have been fooling him from the very beginning. He had *needed* her, he had *counted* on her and there she was gazing into Art's eyes with something approaching adoration. If she could actually believe Art was the man she'd been writing to all these months, if she couldn't discern the difference between them, she was indiscriminate and, frankly, stupid.

Carl had always wondered what a snarl looked like, exactly. Now he knew that if he had a mirror he would have been able to see one on his own face. Art had been right. This woman wasn't worth his trouble.

'Let the charade continue,' he decided. 'Let Art be me for as long as he damn well wants to be.'

Carl turned to Bernice as he heard Art begin to explain to Clare the plots of his, Carl's, books. The whole situation would have been hilariously funny if it hadn't been so devastatingly disappointing.

'So, Bernice, since, thanks to Carl, I *have* read all the letters, I know you like trouble. Have you been in any lately?'

'Well, I've been here today. I guess that counts, doesn't it?' Bernice smiled. Carl felt himself immediately warm to her. At least she was honest, she had a sense of humour and she wasn't shit-faced. However else Clare may have been dishonest in her

133

letters, she had managed to give a very accurate description of her friend. Bernice *did* look wanton. Her eyes were a lovely shade of green, her dangling silver moon- and star-shaped ear-rings set off her long black hair, plaited in a braid down her back, and her smile was contagious.

'It counts,' Carl caught her smile and reflected it. 'Definitely. Tell me something. I'm curious. What's Jeremy like?'

'I'm not sure, really. I've only met him a few times. He's away a lot. He's handsome, of course. He's got athlete's legs – do you know what I mean?'

'Probably like a dancer's, in which case, I *do* know,' Carl replied.

'Jeremy seems very conservative, but he's not a stuffed shirt. I don't know, it's hard to say. I thought he and Clare made a great couple, but after today, well. Clare seems so – I can't explain – I feel as if I've never properly understood . . .' Bernice realized that she was managing to finish fewer and fewer sentences as the day progressed.

'She seems to be getting along well with Carl,' Carl tried to keep the fury out of his voice.

'Carl seems like a fabulous bloke,' Bernice said.

'He sure is.'

'Are you two close friends?'

'We're so close sometimes people can't distinguish between us. They think I'm Carl.'

'But you don't look like him.'

'Don't I?'

'No, Carl has very different features to you. And his eyes . . .'

'Yes?'

'Clare's the one who made me notice them. I think she's completely obsessed by his eyes.'

'Really?'

'She's been banging on about them all day. I think they've made as big an impact on her as his letters.'

'I see.' Carl paused, staring at Clare across the table. 'One pair of dark eyes equals a year's writing. That's interesting. You know, Carl described *me* as having a round face in one of his letters. Would you say that was accurate?'

Bernice scrutinized him. 'No,' she said. 'Not at all. That's strange. But I reckon all people see each other differently.'

'Art, Art!' Art was snapping his fingers at Carl, but it took a few seconds for Carl to respond to his new name.

'Yes, Carl?' he finally said.

'Do you want some pasta too?'

'You bet. Everyone can have the same dish, what about that? Isn't that togetherness for you? I was just telling Bernice that people think *we're* very similar, Carl. She found that difficult to believe.'

'So,' Art said quickly. 'Clare, how's that swimmer? Angela, Angela . . .'

'Rae,' Carl finished.

How strange, Clare thought, glancing back and forth between the two men. *Carl* had forgotten Angela's last name, but *Art* had remembered it. Still, Carl must be feeling as nervous as she was.

'I'm not sure where she is at the moment, but I'm sure she's fine. Fine, I'm sure she's fine,' she replied.

'Clare's exactly like me,' Bernice thought. 'When she gets drunk she repeats herself. But at least she's not telling Carl a psychic predicted their marriage.'

'That's settled, then. Angela is *fine*,' Carl said in such a way as to ridicule Clare.

Why is Art so bolshy? Bernice wondered. He was certainly attractive. In her eyes, he was much more attractive than Carl, but Carl's personality was far preferable. Carl, at least, knew how to enjoy himself. Art was sullen and morose.

'And *Art* calls his ex-wife the Swamp Creature?' Clare thought, reeling from the verbal blow. 'He's the bloody Hound from Hell.' All right, she *had* repeated herself, she now realized, but it wasn't necessary to draw attention to it. She was doing her best to sober up and she was trying hard to be what everyone wanted her to be – which seemed to be what everyone had always wanted her to be, since the day she was born – good-natured, quiet, friendly and no bother. It seemed she couldn't even take one evening off to be immature, get drunk and act silly, not even in a foreign country, not under any circumstances. If she weren't so conscious of how inappropriate and whingeing it would be, she'd feel sorry for herself.

'This agent of yours, Clare. The one who set this meeting up. Can I ask what she expects to happen next?' Carl growled in her direction.

Art, she decided, was a thoroughly unpleasant person.

'I haven't the foggiest, Art,' she glared back.

'The foggiest? The foggiest what? The foggiest sky? The foggiest glasses?'

'Artie, please,' Art now glared at Carl, 'ease up, that's an English expression. It means she doesn't have any idea.'

'I thought you hated all English expressions,' Carl shot back.

'No, Art. That's you, remember? You're the one who hates the English.'

'This is getting ridiculous,' Carl stated, standing up. 'I'm going to leave. Bernice, would you like to come with me? I know a nice place we could go, a nice little quiet bar.'

Bernice hesitated, thinking of the pasta Carl had ordered. She was hungry, all she'd eaten during the entire afternoon was a large quantity of peanuts. Looking at Clare and Carl, though, she decided leaving them alone would be a good idea. Besides, Art was clearly having some kind of problem with this dinner. He might cheer up when he left, and she wouldn't mind seeing what Art was like when he was in a better frame of mind. If she stayed, she'd definitely be the unnecessary third person.

'All right,' she replied, standing as well. 'Clare will you be OK?'

'She'll be *fine*,' Carl muttered.

Clare felt the hostility directed at her and found herself on the verge of tears. Why was Art being so mean to her?

'I'm sorry about the pasta, I can give you my share of the money.'

'Don't worry, Bernice,' Art said quickly. 'I'm sure I can cancel your order.'

'Oh, thank you, Carl. You've been very generous, really. I'll see you back at the hotel, Clare,' Bernice said, giving her a quick kiss on the cheek.

'Don't count on it,' Carl silently fumed. 'Clare will probably end up in bed with Art. Art is so *generous*, so *kind*, so *understanding*. And Artie has "those eyes", after all. What more could a girl want?'

How could Clare be so unobservant? She hadn't even blinked when he had come out with Angela's last name, which Art had obviously forgotten.

This was as disillusioning an evening as he had ever spent in his life.

'Would the real Carl Lioce please leave the restaurant?' he said to himself, grabbing his jacket from the back of his chair and heading out.

Good riddance, Clare thought, watching him exit, Bernice following a pace behind. Poor Bernice, stuck with this nasty man for the evening, although Bernice might have focused on his brooding good looks instead of his personality.

Clare knew, after the years spent with Jeremy, how nice it was to wake up beside a man who was lovely to look at. But looks were beginning to seem less and less important. Carl wasn't as physically attractive as Art, but Carl had passion. Carl cared about her. He knew her. He was, after all, *Carl*.

Chapter 10

Clare looked up at the sky. It was starless. She felt a little ridiculous and vulnerable, standing outside the restaurant on her own, but she'd needed to get some fresh air. While she and Carl had been eating their pasta, she'd had a sudden strange flash of recognition. The restaurant reminded her of the one in the Al Pacino movie *Sea of Love*. That movie, she remembered clearly, had been all about people meeting each other through lonely hearts newspaper ads; as it turned out, one of the people putting those ads in the papers was a serial killer whom Al Pacino, the streetwise New York cop, was assigned to track down.

The thought that she and Carl were not so different from those people who wrote lonely hearts ads had hit her with a breath-taking force. She'd had to excuse herself from the table, saying that she needed to go to the ladies. If Carl knew she was standing on the street alone, he'd probably rush out to protect her from the evils of the Big Apple.

What exactly, she had to ask herself, was she doing having dinner with him, a man she'd met through the post? And what was going to happen next? She'd never cheated on any man in her life. Her two relationships pre-Jeremy had ended, if not wholly amicably, at least without any sexual betrayal. She trusted Jeremy himself totally, despite all the time he spent away from her. And Jeremy obviously trusted her, for he certainly never showed any signs of jealousy.

Was she going to climb into bed with Carl just because they'd exchanged letters for a long period of time? Or because she wanted to be adventurous and daring for once in her life? To do something possibly wildly passionate and definitely wildly naughty?

Would it make a huge difference to her relationship with Jeremy if she *did* sleep with Carl? Would Jeremy have to know? Would it be possible not to tell him?

She jumped as a taxicab driver leant heavily on his horn a few feet away from her. There she was, debating the ethics of a sexual liaison with Carl before he'd even made a move to touch her. How could she assume he looked on her as more than a friend? Why was she churning herself up, asking herself all these impossible to answer questions, on a subject that might never be at issue?

She *wanted* to spend the night with Carl – that's why. She wanted to feel his arms around her. Most of all, however, she wanted to laugh with him in bed. She could imagine giggling with him as they negotiated their first time together, and that thought made her smile. Jeremy was wonderful in bed, yes, but he took it so seriously, as if he switched sports as soon as he entered the sexual arena and turned into a professional tennis player. He made her feel as if she was his mixed doubles' partner in the finals at Wimbledon. As far as Jeremy was concerned, you didn't have good sex or win Wimbledon being silly. And you sure as hell didn't laugh.

Carl struck her as someone who could have fun in bed and still be sexy. When the time came, *if* the time came later on in the night, Clare thought she'd probably back away from any physical contact. But the fact that she had these desires in the first place gave her reason to take a few very deep breaths before going in to rejoin him. What kind of woman was she if she couldn't be satisfied with someone like Jeremy? Why was she suddenly courting trouble?

'My life is very undramatic,' she had written in one of her letters to Carl. 'I like it that way. I wonder sometimes, though, whether I am addicted to soap operas (which I am) because all these other people's event-filled lives seem so real and so vibrant to me. Honestly, I suspend all my natural desbelief when I tune in. I'm one of those people who would call a soap-opera character by his soap opera name, if I saw him in the street. So that's what I am at heart – a drama junkie – but a junkie shooting up on other people's dramas.'

Well, she was in a very strange episode of her very own soap opera at the moment. It was time to go back into the restaurant for the next episode.

They were sitting in the corner of the bar, at a small, pine table. Bernice liked the atmosphere, the sawdust on the floor, the juke-box playing old Springsteen hits. And she especially liked Art. He had, indeed, lightened up as soon as they left the restaurant. In fact, he'd been pretty damn charming the whole evening, asking her questions about her life, and actually listening to her answers. He had a good sense of humour which jibed with hers and during the times when he'd go off to the loo, she found herself contemplating moving to America, starting afresh in the States. What did she have to lose, after all?

'I suppose it must be fun being a literary agent,' she offered after she'd returned from her own trip to the ladies.

'I suppose it must be,' Carl replied. 'Bernice, listen . . .'

'Clare's agent, Anna, she's American, actually. She has a posh flat in Hampstead and she's always flying off to Frankfurt and all these places. Sometimes the advertising world I work in seems so phony. I can just about bear it, and when it gets bad, I know I should be grateful not to be working in a bank in the City or some other horrible place like that. I'm not cut out for that sort of life. I'm not a suit-and-tie type of person.' She stopped herself from putting her hand on his jeans.

'I had a very strange impulse the other night,' Carl said, smiling. 'I went to a party given by a friend of mine who works on Wall Street. Most of the people at this party were bankers. There was one man there, he was really very ugly and he looked

140

miserably sad. When I was leaving, I went up to him and I kissed him.'

'You snogged him?' Bernice sat back, aghast.

'If that's your word for kissing, yes. I kissed him on the lips and walked out.'

'Jesus,' Bernice thought. 'The guy's a fruitcake. Just my rotten luck.'

'So do you kick with both feet?'

'Excuse me?'

'Are you bisexual? Or one hundred per cent gay?'

'Oh, I get it. No. No, I'm not gay. Or bisexual. I can't explain it, I thought he needed something and the thing I thought he needed was a kiss, that's all.'

'Was *he* gay?'

'No. Not as far as I know. I'd never spoken to him. I saw how sad he was and I thought I should do something about it.'

'Oh,' Bernice said. She was searching to find something wonderful about this story, but all she could come up with was the thought that Art might be a little too weird for her taste. She then did her utmost to dismiss that thought.

'Haven't *you* ever done something spontaneous like that? How about when you called your history teacher a "cunt"?'

'Oh, well, I always say the wrong thing at the wrong time, but I don't snog ugly women at parties, if that's what you mean.'

'I guess I was foolish.' Carl sat back in his chair. 'But was I charmingly foolish or stupidly foolish?'

'I don't know. I don't know what kind of kisser you are.'

Carl laughed and rubbed his chin.

'Well, neither do I. I mean, I've never kissed myself.'

'That's a relief,' Bernice commented, then wondered what to say next as Art appeared to be suddenly lost in thought. 'Art?' He turned his eyes toward her but remained mute. 'Art, don't do this to me. I can't take silence. If you keep silent I'll say something incredibly stupid just to break the silence. I'm like that.'

'Bernice, come on. You must be able to sit silently with some people.'

'No,' she shook her head. 'Well, my parents, but I don't count them.'

'I don't believe this.' He leant forward. 'Let's try an experiment. Let's sit here without speaking for a minute, all right? I'll time it. I'm sure you can last a minute.'

'I'll try,' she said sheepishly.

'OK. One minute starting . . . now.' Carl looked at his watch, smiling. Bernice, after ten seconds, began to shift uncomfortably in her chair. After twenty seconds, she began to laugh nervously. And after thirty-two seconds she cracked.

'I can't. I just can't,' she groaned.

'You're unbelievable,' he laughed.

'Charmingly foolish or stupidly foolish?' she asked. 'No, don't answer that.'

'I will answer it,' he protested. 'Wonderfully foolish. It's a whole new category of foolish.'

He shrank back slightly when he saw the smile suffuse her face; it was so grateful, so heart-breakingly eager to please.

Carl had recognized early on at the bar that he was longing to fall in love with Bernice; he was aching to feel passion for Clare's friend and wipe out the horror of his lost dreams, but he also recognized that he couldn't simply substitute her for Clare; nothing was that pat or easy in life. Yet he felt driven not to give up the quest. She was nice, she was friendly and funny and more intelligent than he would have guessed from looking at her heavily made-up eyes.

'This skunk your father writes about – Simon – is *he* gay?' he asked.

Bernice laughed and Carl laughed with her, feeling relieved to be back on the safe shores of humour.

'I think Simon the Skunk is asexual, although now that you mention it, he does have an unnatural interest in Michael the Mouse.'

'Bernice, it's time I explained something to you. I'm not . . .'

'You're not interested in me, is that it? I talk too much, don't I? Oh, God, I'm getting pissed. All afternoon, I sat with Clare and watched her get pissed and I was being careful not to myself. So I could look after her properly. Then I come here and start in. I can't believe it.'

'Bernice . . .'

'I've done it again. I've said too much. Just now, I mean. I interrupted you and said you weren't interested in me as if you *should* have been interested in me in the first place. Oh, God . . .' Bernice dropped her head in her hands.

Carl was astounded by how suddenly she'd turned tipsy, as if the last sip of wine had set off a chain of chemical reactions which caused immediate intoxication. He had been planning to tell her that he was Carl, not Art, explain the whole mix-up, but he could see now that she was surreptitiously wiping tears from her face. She didn't need to be surprised, she needed to be comforted. His heart went out to her.

'But this isn't your address, is it? This isn't where I send my letters.'

'Think fast,' Artie told himself. 'No. This is Art's apartment.'

'Why are we going to Art's apartment?'

'Because . . . because Art is staying in Long Island this week and he wanted me to house-sit for him.'

'Oh, I see.' Clare looked around the plush lobby as they headed for the lifts. She didn't quite understand why Carl would flat-sit when he had a flat of his own to take care of. Still, she didn't have the energy to cross-examine him. After the large plate of pasta, two bottles of Perrier and a double espresso, she had returned to a reasonably sober state, but the alcoholic binge she'd gone on had taken its toll.

'Don't worry,' Art smiled reassuringly. 'I'm not getting you up here to jump on you.'

'I know,' Clare returned his smile. 'You're not like that.'

143

'What *am* I like, Clare? I want to know what you really think of me.'

Art asked this, unsure whether he was referring to Clare's reaction to Carl or to himself. Now *he* was getting confused by this charade he'd perpetrated. Suddenly he pictured Carl, with a demented gargoyle face, clinging on to him, digging animal claws into his back. Art wanted to shake him off, but Carl wouldn't budge.

They rode in the lift in silence while Clare contemplated Carl's question. She didn't know what he was like, not any more. He had a complicated, multi-faceted character, that was for certain. There was a brashness to his speech she hadn't anticipated, and a take-charge attitude which continued to sur-prise her.

Having pictured Carl as an observer, a man who watched and waited and had his own silent thoughts and emotions, she was faced with someone suave, someone who knew how to handle waiters and fancy restaurants and who was now walking with ease into an expensive flat, holding the door open for her with a flourish. He looked and acted like someone who had travelled around the world, yet she knew from his letters that he'd never left New York City. Again, she felt a little uneasy about her positive response to his sophisticated side – a side he hadn't revealed in the correspondence.

He seemed as if he owned the place and Clare found herself wondering what his flat looked like. Was it as neat and tidy and as masculine as his friend's? How could this man have been caught rummaging through a woman's purse? Her eyes pursued him as he walked around the living room turning on lights, and she tried to picture him wanting to play ping-pong. The effort failed abysmally.

'Art has good taste, don't you think?' he asked.

She nodded.

'You haven't told me yet what you think of me, you know. Is my end-of-term report that bad?'

144

'No, Carl.'

He approached her, holding out his hand. She took it, and allowed herself to be led by him to the sofa.

'Tell me something,' he coaxed, sitting down a few feet away from her. 'If I hadn't written those letters, if I were – let's say – the man who arranged for a modern day Cyrano de Bergerac to write those letters for me, what would you think of me now?'

'I don't know.' She looked down at the dark green carpet, fearing to meet those eyes of his. 'You couldn't be exactly as I had imagined, of course, any more than I could be how you imagined me. I'm sure you weren't expecting me to walk into the restaurant drunk tonight – that's not in my letters, it's not really in my character. Something inside me snapped today and I couldn't control myself.'

'I think you're cute when you're smashed. In fact, now that you've sobered up, I'm a little nervous.'

'Well,' she smiled, still gazing down. 'That makes two of us.'

'Oh, my God,' Art thought, looking at her profile. 'What's happening here? I don't know what's happening here any more. This was supposed to be a joke. I was getting my own back on the Brits and having some fun with Carl and his crazed obsession, and I knew I wouldn't do anything fundamentally wrong. I wouldn't take advantage of her – not when the time came, *if* the time came. But I've been ambushed, snuck up on. The way she said "That makes two of us" set my fucking jerk-off heart spinning. Is it possible to fall in love in a matter of seconds?'

Art flashed back to a scene when, in his early twenties, he had been driving to visit a friend in Princeton, New Jersey. For a second he had taken his eyes off the street to turn the dial on his radio, and when he'd looked up, a tiny child was running across the road, just a few feet in front of him. Slamming his foot on the brake, he'd narrowly missed this toddler, who had darted out from between parked cars. A woman, presumably the mother, was screaming. Art sat there, shaking in fear, his brain racing through the ramifications of what might have been. He could have killed a child. If he'd been one foot further down the street, he *would* have killed a child. How would he have felt? What would the rest of his life have been like? Time had saved him and the child as well, but just a tiny fraction of time. Only a few seconds.

And now, within that same time frame, he had fallen drop-dead in love. Perhaps everything really important in life happened in the space of three seconds.

She's so damn lovely without being vain and sweet without being gushy and smart and funny and trusting and . . . and everything. It's as if I recognize her from somewhere, from some place in my heart I've always wanted to travel to. But I could never find the right ticket to get there. This is absurd. Fuck Carl for switching those nametags and having his temper tantrum and walking out tonight. What am I supposed to do now?

'What are we supposed to do now?' Clare asked, finally meeting his stare.

She wanted him to kiss her and she didn't want him to kiss her.

'That's what I was wondering myself. We could sit and talk for awhile. Or we could watch television, I suppose.'

Why did she have to wear such a fucking cute dress? Pale blue with tiny flowers dotted over it. And Jesus, she had one of those anklets on, too. A simple thin gold chain which made his heart lurch everytime he looked at it. Pretty soon, she'd think he was a foot fetishist.

What could she be thinking of? Clare asked herself. As far as Carl was concerned, she was a married woman. Of course he thought that watching television or talking were the only activities available to them. He was honourable . . . and most probably not attracted to her anyway. Clare put her hand to her face to hide her blush. She hoped to God Carl hadn't seen the willing look she feared her eyes might have expressed.

'I'm incredibly knackered.' She faked a yawn. 'Tired. So much

146

has happened today. I don't think I can talk or do anything,' she paused. 'And that includes watching TV. You know, it's funny. I was writing to you the other day. I wanted to tell you about this Australian daytime soap we have in England. It's called *Neighbours*.'

'You know we get *Eastenders* over here. I'm the only person I know who hated *Upstairs Downstairs*, but I love *Eastenders* – despite myself.'

'I'm surprised you didn't tell me that when I admitted to being a soap addict.'

'I guess I didn't want to admit to being one myself. You know, in case the letters turned into the Soap Opera Digest.'

'I adore Grant,' Clare sighed. 'I mean, I used to like Phil, when he was having his affair with Sharon. But now I love Grant.'

'Do you think he'll ever meet his kid over here?'

'Michelle's baby? I don't know. I hope—'

'Arthur's death was tragic.'

'Don't you love Pauline's hair?'

'I like Kathy's – when the roots show.'

'She's had a tough life,' Clare yawned. This time she wasn't faking.

'Listen, you've had a tough day. Here's the program. There's a nice spare room here. You can get some sleep and we can talk in the morning. There's something I have to confess to you. I'd rather do it in the morning.'

'But I should be getting back. Bernice is on her own. Jeremy might call. I should go now.'

'Relax. Bernice is with . . . Bernice is with Art. He'll look after her. I can vouch for him. And it's four or so in the morning English time, so I don't think Jeremy will be calling. Stay here. I'll wake you up early – at eight. I really want to talk to you about something in the morning.'

'Well, I am completely shattered. And there's something I have to talk to you about as well. There's something *I* have to confess.' Clare simultaneously yawned again and sighed. 'Do you still listen in?'

'What?'

'You know, you used to listen in on other people's confessions.'

'Oh, yeah,' Art nodded. 'Right. So I did. Let me show you to your room – I'm going to get in trouble soon if we stay up any longer.'

'What kind of trouble?' Clare mumbled as she rose to follow him.

'All kinds. Every kind of trouble there is.'

'The red light is flashing,' Carl said, as Bernice made her way unsteadily out of the bathroom.

'There must be a message.'

'I think that's a safe bet.'

'Right. OK. I'll get it then.' She weaved to the telephone, picked it up, studied the front to find which numbers to push for messages, managed to hit the appropriate ones and listened for a moment.

'One call from Anna, one from Jeremy,' she announced, hanging up. 'They wanted to know how things went for Clare. Looks like they've gone well,' she eyed the empty bed beside hers.

Carl didn't speak. He watched as Bernice collapsed on her bed.

'I'm sorry,' she said. 'I'm sorry to flake out like this. I must be jet-lagged. I think I'm jet-lagged.'

'Bernice—' he moved from the wall he'd been leaning against and sat down beside her. 'You're lovely, you know.'

'No, I'm not,' she groaned. 'I'm fat and I'm ugly.'

'Please—' he laughed. 'Don't use two such inappropriate adjectives.'

'Inappropriate,' she repeated wearily. 'If you think I'm fat and ugly you might snog me to make me feel better.'

Why was it, she wondered, that she saw every man she met as a potential husband and father of her children? Why didn't she really give a toss about work, about her career? Why was the prospect of having her own family the only one that interested her? Because she'd been adopted? Or because she'd had enough of running around being wild and crazy?

'I'm tired,' she thought, as she yawned. 'I want to marry Art straight away, this very second, and then settle down and have tons of children. Let *them* be wild and crazy.'

Leaning down to kiss the top of Bernice's head, Carl found himself staring at Clare's unoccupied bed.

What had he done? What the fuck had he done?

He'd thrown Clare straight into the arms of Artie, that's what he had done. And all because she'd been drunk. What kind of reason was that? *He'd* been drunk when he first wrote that letter to Angela Rae. He'd been drunk plenty of times in his life, yet he'd acted as if Clare had committed a shocking crime. Then, having decided she didn't measure up to his dream picture of her, he'd been rude and aggressive and had stomped out of her life. What an idiot he was, and how could he possibly make up for his incredible imbecility?

It was too late. She was with Art. She was cheating on her husband with a man she didn't even know. Christ – he gently moved a handful of silver necklaces aside and rubbed Bernice's neck – Artie shouldn't have taken advantage of Clare, of the whole situation, like that. That wasn't the way for a gentleman to behave, not to mention a friend. Artie knew how much Carl cared for Clare; how could he have been so selfish?

'Human passions,' Carl told himself. 'Human mistakes. Why did I ever think they were so appealing?'

'Bernice—' he bowed his head to whisper in her ear. 'I have to tell you something. I'm Carl, not Art. I'm Carl.'

'That's nice,' she mumbled, closing her eyes.

'Clare—' Art appeared in the doorway of her room just as she was about to fall off to sleep.

'Yes?' she sat up in bed, quickly. What did he want? Was he going to try it on? What would her reaction be now?

'I'm sorry if I woke you up, but I thought you might like this—'

He switched on the light in the room and approached her bed, holding something in his right hand.

'What is it?' She was wearing a T-shirt he'd given her. The picture on the front showed two men holding cups of coffee. One of them was saying, 'If it weren't for caffeine I'd have no personality whatsoever.'

'This is Eddy. Eddy Elephant.' Sitting down on the foot of her bed, he stretched out and handed her a stuffed animal. 'He's pretty battered, but he's good company. I got him when I was seven years old. He has great character, Eddy. He's a prince among stuffed animals.'

Clare examined Eddy carefully. He was literally falling apart at the seams, and one of his button eyes was missing. She hugged him to her and smiled at Carl.

'You even take him with you when you're flat-sitting?'

'What? Oh. Yes. I take him everywhere. My mother gave him to me for my birthday when I was seven.'

'How old are you now, Carl? I *can* ask, can't I? It's not breaking the rules any more.'

'I'm thirty-nine going on a nervous breakdown. How about you?'

'Twenty-seven.'

'Do you think that's a huge age gap?'

'No,' she shook her head, 'do you?'

'No.'

'Eddy's the perfect present for a seven-year-old.'

'I know thirty-nine's a little old to be so attached to a stuffed animal, but I can't help it,' Art felt his spine stiffen.

'Oh, please. No. I didn't mean it that way. I've always loved stuffed animals. I still have a lot of my old ones in my mother's house. I wasn't criticizing, really.'

'That's a relief. I was beginning to feel – I don't know – kind of—' Art took off his glasses. 'Silly. Anyway . . .' he stood up. 'I just thought you might like him with you tonight.'

'You were right.' Clare couldn't stop smiling.

'And if, when you wake up, you find that he's down on the floor somewhere, you should know that he's taken a late-night visit to the refrigerator, gorged himself, and is too full to get back up on the bed.'

'Carl, you're really cra—' Clare found herself emitting a sound which came surprisingly close to being a giggle.

'You have no idea how crazy I am. Goodnight, Clare.'

'Goodnight, Carl. And thanks.'

'I hope you'll thank me in the morning,' he said softly, turning off the light as he left the room.

She woke up disorientated, with no idea of where she was or how she came to be there. As soon as she began to remember the previous evening, she found herself flooded with toxic shame, regret and a desperate sense of guilt. Jeremy. She'd been on the verge of betraying Jeremy. Not only that, she'd also completely neglected him. She hadn't rung him. Not once since she'd arrived in New York. What if he had phoned the hotel? How would Bernice explain her absence? She looked at the sleek clock-radio beside her bed and immediately panicked. It was seven-thirty, which meant it was twelve-thirty in London. Jeremy could be phoning her right now, for all she knew.

A hazy remembrance of Carl's last words stopped her in the middle of dressing. Where was Eddy Elephant? She searched the bed, then looked down and found him lying on the floor. As she picked him up, smiling at his button eye, she recalled that Carl had wanted to have breakfast with her and to confess something. Yes, that was right, and *she* was going to tell him about not being married. Well, she might not be married to Jeremy, but she needed to get back to the hotel and talk to him as soon as she possibly could. When she heard his voice perhaps she'd come back to her senses. Yesterday had been an aberration – the drinking, the disloyal thoughts – everything would return to normal, she'd be safe again, as soon as she heard his voice.

151

After laying Eddy carefully on her pillow, she quickly brushed her hair and slipped out of the room.

'Clare—' He was sitting on the sofa, in the same place he'd occupied the night before. He had a green and black striped dressing gown on and a mug of coffee in his hand. 'Come here . . .' he patted the sofa beside him. His glasses slipped off as he bent down to put his coffee cup back on the table and he took a moment to retrieve them. 'Sorry. Would you like some coffee?'

'No, no thank you. I've got to go. I've got to get back to the hotel.'

'What's the rush? I thought we were going to have breakfast together.'

'I can't, Carl, really. I have to get back. Jeremy may have rung and I need to speak to him.'

'You can call him from here.'

'No, that wouldn't be right.'

'Principles,' Art thought. 'That's so refreshing. She has principles.'

'Well, then, can we meet for lunch? Should I call you at your hotel? Where did you say you're staying?'

'The Sheraton Towers.'

'Fine. I'll call you there. Around eleven?'

'Around eleven,' Clare hesitated, wondering whether she should give Carl a kiss on the cheek. He solved the problem for her by waving his hand in a sweet, almost bashful goodbye.

'*Forsan et haec olim meminisse juvabit,*' she said, waving back.

'Excuse me?' he asked, startled, but she had gone.

'Clare, calm down,' Bernice sat up in her bed, her head reeling. 'You can call him now. He hasn't called yet this morning, he won't be worried. Just tell him you had such a hectic day yesterday, you had no time to get in touch. Tell him the truth . . . up to a point.'

'I told you – nothing happened. I went to bed in Art's spare room.'

'So you say Art's staying in Long Island? He didn't tell me that. How far away is Long Island?'

'I don't have a clue.'

'OK, OK, don't bark at me. Ring Jeremy. You'll feel better. But tell me something first. Are you in love with Carl?'

'How should I know?'

'I doubt anyone else does.'

The phone rang, startling both women.

'Why don't you answer it?' Bernice stared at Clare.

'I will.'

Slowly, Clare approached the telephone, a look of anxiety on her face. Picking the receiver up, she said 'Hello' very softly. Within seconds, her expression had hardened.

'No, Anna, you haven't woken us up.' Clare turned to Bernice and shook her head, her teeth gritted in anger. Covering the mouthpiece, she whispered; 'I'm going to kill her.'

'No, no, of course I'm not upset. You wanted me to meet Carl, I understand. You wanted it to be a surprise. Of course.' Bernice, watching Clare's eyes narrow and her lips curl, couldn't believe the voice could convey such a pleasant, carefree tone. 'Actually, it all went amazingly well. Carl's very nice, we get along wonderfully, but—' she stopped, and Bernice could see her search for inspiration. 'But it's Carl's friend who I think is really wonderful. He's a literary agent here, and he says he can make me a star. You wouldn't belive how many plans he has for me. I hope this doesn't come as too much of a shock to you, but he convinced me that he should take over my career. In fact, Monday morning he has a meeting with an editor at Random House about the book on Carl's and my correspondence.'

A smile snuck over Clare's features, and she signalled a thumbs up to Bernice as she listened to Anna.

'I understand that my meeting Carl was all your idea, Anna. But this is America. You know – this is *major*. And—' the smile broadened. 'And I think I've fallen in love with Art.'

'Art,' she was positively grinning now. 'Art Rolfe.' Clare sat down on the bed and leant against the headboard. 'Art Rolfe,' she repeated. 'Haven't you heard of him? He's a big agent here. Of course it will be hard to tell Jeremy, but I think it's all for the best, really, don't you? I *love* this country. I don't understand how you could ever have left it.'

'Anna? Anna?' Clare waited for a moment before putting the phone down. 'She hung up. Why don't I feel the slightest twinge of guilt?'

'Not even one twitch?'

'No.'

'You certainly hit her where it hurts – if you left her and became a megastar here, I think she'd go round the bend.'

'I also like the whole concept of my falling in love with Art – if she wants romance so badly she can have it – but not the way she planned. Turning Art into the romantic dark horse is pure genius, if I say so myself.'

'Absolutely . . .' Bernice unplaited her hair, and shook it out until her head hurt even more. 'I never knew you could be so evil – it must be all those steriods they put in the asthma medicine you took as a child – they're coming out now. Your muscles will probably begin to bulge. Soon you'll be throwing the television out the window.'

Bernice got up out of bed to get a bottle of Perrier from the minibar. Something was bothering her, pulling at the back of her brain, something simple, like a name or face she couldn't remember. 'I have to tell you—' she took a swig from the bottle and returned with it to her bed. 'Art's wonderful. I know he seemed pretty dreadful at the restaurant, but as soon as we left, he was transformed. He was like a different person.'

'Oh.' Clare looked bemused and preoccupied. 'That's nice. God, I really should ring Jeremy now.'

'I'll leave you in peace,' Bernice struggled off the bed again and headed for the bathroom. The words 'That's nice' kept echoing in her mind. What was nice? The fact that Art had turned into a different person. Art had turned into – Bernice found herself, tooth-brush half-way to her mouth, transfixed by the look of amazement she saw in the mirror.

'Everything went well,' Clare tried to sound bright and breezy. Explaining the entire fiasco to Jeremy over the transatlantic wires was not a good idea, she had decided as she was dialling. The best plan was to wait until she returned, when she could do it all properly. 'I went out to dinner with Bernice last night. I'm sorry I didn't ring. We celebrated. I had too much to drink, actually.

'I know,' she sighed. 'I know that isn't like me. It was a special occasion, that's all.' Why couldn't Jeremy let her do something different for once in her life either? Clare wondered. Why did he have to sound so shocked and disappointed?

She listened as he changed the subject and told her whom he had invited over to dinner the previous evening – an old Etonian who was now an investment banker in the City. She could picture them discussing vintage cricket and vintage wine all night. In the course of their relationship, Jeremy had sent back at least ten cases of wine he'd ordered from Oddbins, claiming they weren't up to standard. That seemed an unnaturally high number to her, but then she wasn't a wine connoisseur, whereas Jeremy had taken a course at Christie's.

'I'm not surprised,' she commented, when he told her that Andrew, the old Etonian, hated Ian Botham as much as he did. 'Botham's not Andrew's type either.'

Much of the conversation must have centred on one of Jeremy's favourite topics, sporting lager louts who let down the image of the nation. Clare could never bring herself to admit that she quite liked what she'd seen of Ian Botham.

'Yes, our flight's leaving on Sunday night. Tomorrow night. We get in around eight-thirty in the morning. I'll make my own way back, don't worry.

'I miss you too. See you soon.'

Hearing his voice *was* reassuring, Clare thought thankfully, as she replaced the receiver. Jeremy was a still point in the midst of the recent storms she had experienced. At this precise moment in her life, she was in danger of feeling blown about like a weightless, worthless piece of trash. Her asthma had come back as soon as she'd experienced a moment of deep stress, she wasn't at all sure what she felt about Carl, and she was beginning to doubt whether she wanted to write anything ever again in her life.

At least she had a safe option. She could go back to London, take up where she had left off with Jeremy and find a job which wouldn't require her to put her soul out on the washing line. Writing was too personal, far too personal a way to make a living. You could get profoundly hurt.

Yet the sound of Jeremy's voice, reassuring as it was, hadn't wiped out the effect of his words. He'd been upset, almost angry, that she'd had too much to drink. He was, at heart, an old-fashioned man. He might do housework and the cooking but he expected his mate to act as well-mannered as he did. Jeremy would have been shocked if he'd seen her last night; he wouldn't have thought, as Carl had, that she was 'cute'. No. Jeremy would have been embarrassed by her.

Bernice wandered out of the bathroom, looking as bedraggled as she had when she'd gone in.

'Clare—' she was massaging her forehead. 'Could you tell me again how Carl described Art in his letters?'

'He said Art had a round face,' Clare replied. 'He also said that Art thought he – Carl – was crazy.'

'Carl is the kind of bloke who would do off-beat things, then?'

'Carl described himself as idiosyncratic. You know, writing that letter to Angela was pretty strange when you think about it.'

'So Carl's the type who might kiss some ugly man to make him feel better?'

'What?'

'Never mind.'

'Bernice, are you all right?'

'I'm hung over, I feel like a dead mad cow and I look like one too. Yes, Clare, I'm perfectly all right.' Bernice answered, feeling her heart fall and knowing it hadn't packed a parachute.

Was it possible? Had she remembered correctly? Did Art tell her he was Carl as she was passing out? If, for some reason, the two men had switched identities, Carl was Art and Art was Carl. Obviously Clare wasn't aware of this yet. But what would happen when Clare *did* find out? The logical answer was unavoidable. Clare would switch her feelings and fall in love with the real Carl. Just as she had.

'Tell me again why Carl took you back to *Art's* flat?'

'Because Art is staying in Long Island, wherever that is,' Clare answered, trying to be patient.

'I see,' Bernice nodded. 'When you were with him last night – I know nothing happened – how did you feel about him?'

'It's hard to explain. He's wonderful in so many ways. He was kind and thoughtful. We didn't *really* talk, not the way we communicated in our letters, but we were both a little shy and nervous. He did something really touching – he gave me his stuffed elephant to sleep with.'

'He has a stuffed animal? At his age?'

'I know, it sounds silly, but it wasn't. I can't explain. Eddy Elephant is special.'

'Jesus, he should team up with my father.' Bernice began to pace around the hotel room in her pyjamas. 'Is he . . . would you—'

'Yes?'

'Would you like him even if he hadn't written the letters?'

'That's a strange question. He asked me the same thing last night. Is there something I don't know?'

'No, no, no.' Bernice waved her hands in the air. 'I was wondering, that's all. I was just wondering how important the letters are to the way you feel about him.'

'Bernice, at the moment I don't know how I feel about anything or anybody.' As soon as she'd said this, Clare regretted her outburst of honesty. She didn't want to discuss her feelings with Bernice, at least not right now. Maybe later, back in London, but not here.

'Still, you think Carl's attractive? Those eyes and all.'

'Mmm,' Clare studied her friend, at a loss as to what could possibly be making her so nervous.

'You think he's a lot more attractive than Art?' Bernice pressed.

'Listen, I'm glad *you* like Art so much, I really am. But *I* don't – at least I don't like what I've seen of him so far. He wasn't very nice to me at dinner, if you remember. I know I was in bad shape, but I didn't think he had to be as aggressive as he was.'

'Absolutely not,' Bernice said with conviction. 'He was a bastard to you.'

'Did he tell you why?'

'Pardon?'

'Did Art explain, when he had transformed himself into a decent human being, why he was so awful to me?'

'No,' Bernice said quickly. 'We didn't talk about you at all, I'm afraid.'

'Well, I'm glad you like him so much. He's a friend of Carl's so I'm sure he's very likeable. He was probably feeling protective of Carl – and when he saw me drunk and heard that I had shown the letters to an agent as well – he must have thought I was on the make in some way.'

'Right,' Bernice finally stopped pacing and sat down. 'That must be it. Are you seeing Ar – are you seeing Carl again today?'

'We're supposed to be having lunch together. He told me he has something to confess to me.'

'Oh, shit.'

'Bernice?' Clare couldn't understand what was going on in Bernice's head, but then whenever Bernice liked a man she became fairly irrational. Art had obviously thrown her off balance.

Sometimes Clare envied Bernice's loss of sanity when she was smitten, but right now she wished Bernice would just be coherent about whatever it was that was bothering her.

'I think you're getting in way over your head here, Clare. I mean, you've spoken to Jeremy and everything's all right as far as he's concerned, isn't it?'

'Yes. So?'

'So why don't you fly back to him now? I'm sure we can change your ticket. What difference can one day make to a huge airline? This thing with Carl – it isn't healthy. It might screw up your whole life. You say you don't know how you feel about anything. You're horrendously confused. The only way to sort yourself out is to go back. Soon. Immediately. I'll look up the airline number, if you want.'

'Hold on. I'm not as confused as you seem to think I am.' Actually, Clare thought, I *am*. But I'm not going to tell you any more about it. Approximately twenty seconds after I put the phone down on Jeremy I was wondering what lunch would be like with Carl. I can't share this problem with anyone, though. It wouldn't be fair to Jeremy to broadcast my doubt. 'The point is, I don't want to go back right away, Bernice.'

'Why not?'

'I'd like to see Carl again, for one. We didn't get much chance to talk. During the first half of the evening I was drunk, and when I sobered up I was jet-lagged. And I wouldn't mind seeing more of New York while we're here, either.'

'Oh,' Bernice hung her head.

'Do you have some kind of problem with this, Bernice? Why don't you want me to stay?'

'I . . . I think I've fallen in love.'

'I figured that. And I think it's wonderful. As far as I know, Art is a divorced man so he's available. Your relationship with him doesn't have anything to do with me seeing Carl again and staying till Sunday night, though.'

'You'd be surprised,' Bernice said in such a low voice Clare couldn't make out the words.

Chapter 11

'Dee-Dee!' Art, tipped back in his chair, his feet up on the desk, came close to toppling over backwards. 'What are you doing here?'

'I came by yesterday but you were out of the office. Your secretary told me you work some Saturday mornings, so I thought I'd take a chance and see if this was one of those Saturday mornings.'

'Oh. Right.' He motioned to the chair opposite his with a vague gesture. 'Sit down.'

'You looked lost in thought when I came in.'

'Mmm. I was. What time is it?'

'Art? Is your watch broken?' Dee-Dee stared pointedly at the Rolex on his wrist.

'Oh,' he looked at it himself. 'Right. It's ten-thirty-two.'

'Anyway—' she leant down and took some papers out of a leather briefcase. 'I've brought the synopsis of my book and the first two chapters.'

'Great. That's fantastic.' When Dee-Dee held the papers out to him, he took them without a glance and tossed them onto the side of his desk.

'Aren't you going to look at it?'

'Of course. Later, when I have time.'

'Whine, whine whine,' Art thought. 'Clare would never whine. I wonder who Clare's agent is. *I* should be her agent.'

'Art, you seem a trifle distracted.'

'Dee-Dee? This may sound like a strange question, but indulge me for a moment, will you?'

Dee-Dee flicked her dark hair in such a way as to signal willingness.

'Is there a significant difference between Carl and me?'

'I don't think I understand the question, Art.'

'No. Of course not. What I mean is . . . oh, forget it.'

'When you read my synopsis, I think you'll see what a world-wide appeal this book will have. It's not bound by geography, Art. That's the beauty of it . . . *one* of the beauties of it.'

'I think you should seriously consider going back to Carl, Dee-Dee. As soon as possible. Immediately, if possible.'

'That's *not* possible, Art. Anyway, you'll see that my heroine embraces all religions, all races, all sexes.'

'*All* sexes? Exactly how many sexes are there?'

'Oh,' Dee-Dee attempted to laugh, but it came out sounding as if she were about to sneeze. 'That was just a figure of speech.'

'I see. What time is it, anyway?'

'Well, it begins in the 1990s, but it transverses centuries.'

'No. Oh, shit—' Art made a huge effort to pull himself together, to concentrate. Dee-Dee was here on business and she deserved his attention no matter how crazed a book she had planned and no matter how preoccupied he was with Clare.

'Leave it with me, Dee-Dee, and I'll read everything and get back to you.'

'When?'

'When?' Art closed his eyes to hide the exasperation he knew they were expressing. 'As soon as humanly possible.'

'Great,' Dee-Dee stood. She was dressed in skin-tight lycra black pants and a skimpy, lacy, black top. 'Is Carl in some kind of trouble, Art? Is that why you're so anxious that I go back to him?'

'Carl's fine. I'm the one in trouble.'

'Oh,' Dee-Dee commented. 'I'm very sorry for you. However, I think you should regard whatever trouble you may be in as an opportunity for enlightenment. If, for example, I have a sore throat, I decide not to let myself be brought down by it, but to take the time that illness gives me to, for example, read a book. Or do some mental work on my own book. Use it, Art. Use that trouble. I'll call you tomorrow, then.'

'Tomorrow? Dee-Dee, tomorrow's Sun—'

She was out the door, and Art found himself pounding his desktop in frustration. 'I could weep,' he thought. 'Or I could kill Dee-Dee. Or I could kill Carl and assume his identity forever. What I can't do is tell Clare how she's been tricked and then stand by and watch as she runs into Carl's arms.'

When the telephone rang, Art answered in the tones of a man about to be executed. 'Art Rolfe. Yes?'

'This is Bernice,' a voice whispered.

'Who?'

'Bernice McKay. Clare's friend.'

'Oh, God. Of course. Bernice, how are you?'

'Wait . . . wait a minute.' Art thought, feeling panic seize his body. 'I'm supposed to be Carl. But I answered saying Art Rolfe. Have I blown it all without meaning to?'

'I'm fine. Listen, I have to say this quickly, while Clare's taking a shower. I tried to get you at home and your answerphone gave me this number and I know who you are – I mean – I know that you're Art, not Carl and vice versa. I also know Clare doesn't know. And I know you're planning on telling her at lunch.'

'Bernice—'

'And I think that's not such a good idea. Are you aware that Clare suffers from asthma?'

'Bernice—'

'She does. She has ever since she was a child and it used to be really bad. She used to have to go to hospital and be put on drips and all that medical palaver. I'm worried that she could have an attack again – stress can set off an attack, you know. Think how stressed out she'll be if she finds out what you and Carl have done to her. Yesterday was bad enough. That's why

162

she got drunk, because she had a mini-recurrence. So what would happen if she had a major attack and she was in a strange city? She could die.'

'Excuse me?'

'Right. Cancel the coffee I just ordered. I've changed my mind.'

'Bernice?'

Art listened to the disconnected tone for a moment before hanging up.

'What the hell?' He stared vacantly around his office, trying to work out how he should react to this news. Yes, he remembered now, Clare had written about her asthma – letters he'd skimmed through because they had turned her into an invalid in his mind – a sickly, pasty Englishwoman who most likely spent her life reclining on sofas. Carl had replied with great feeling, as he recalled. Well, Carl would probably be the perfect partner for Clare. Except Carl seemed to gravitate to weakness in women and Clare was not, in Art's opinion, weak. Despite the asthma.

Should he tell her who he was at lunch or not? How upset *would* she be? Musing on all the possible consequences of the truth, Art idly picked up the title page of Dee-Dee's book, which had the word Shescape printed on it in capital letters. Turning it over, he came to Chapter One and read the first line, 'Caught in the woof and warp of time's great web, SHE struggled to find a persona which would encapsulate the sexual burgeoning of Eve, of Woman.'

Art put his head in his hands and struggled to control a frighteningly manic laugh.

'Bernice?'

Quickly cradling the receiver close to the right side of her head, Bernice moved as far away from Clare as she could.

'Yes?'

'This is Carl – the real Carl. The one you thought was Art.'

'I know.'

'You remember me telling you last night?'

'Yes.'

'Are you OK?'

'Fine.'

'Is Clare there?'

'Yes.'

'Have you told her about me?'

'No. Not yet.'

'That's probably a good decision. I should tell her myself. When is a good time to come over?'

'Lunchtime?'

'Alright, I'll come around twelve-thirty. Bernice, is Clare OK?'

'Absolutely fine.'

'Has she told you anything about last night? With Art?'

'Mmm hmm.'

'Did he – no – forget it. I'll see you later.'

'Sorted.'

'What?' Carl asked, but Bernice had hung up.

'Was that Art?' Clare asked. Bernice nodded. Lying was somehow a less egregious sin if you didn't have to speak.

'Oh, good,' Clare smiled, combing out her hair. 'Just one more, that's all,' pleaded Bernice silently. 'Just one more time alone with him. I deserve that, at least. It's evil and wicked and unhealthy, I know. But I'm desperate. Calling Art to try to keep him from telling Clare the truth was *seriously* desperate, but the phone book was here and his name was in it and Clare was in the shower and it all seemed like fate telling me to go ahead.'

'So you're having lunch with Art?'

Bernice nodded, and then a thought struck her. 'But that's when I always get in trouble. When I say "Just one more". Just one more drink. Oh, Christ. What am I doing?'

'God, Bernice, you must be smitten. You can barely speak.'

She nodded again. 'I deserve it. Clare has Jeremy. Clare could probably have Art if she wanted him. I should be allowed to have

Carl, or at least another chance with Carl. A time alone with him when I'm not babbling. The truth can come out *after* I've had the chance to recoup, to even the odds.' Grabbing the ringing telephone, which was thank heaven, on the table beside *her* bed, Bernice answered 'Hello' in a breathless voice.

'Clare?' God, Art thought. Her asthma really *is* bad.

'No, it's Bernice. Hello, Carl.'

'It's Art.'

'I know.'

'Oh, shit. Oh, shit. I don't think I can keep this up, Bernice.'

'Of course you can, Carl. She's right here, actually.'

Bernice handed the telephone over.

'Hi.'

'Ah, hi,' Clare had thought she'd conquered her nervousness in regard to Carl, but she hadn't quite, not yet.

'I said I'd call you at eleven, remember. It's eleven.'

'So it is,' Clare laughed.

'Um, I thought we could have lunch at a restaurant I know called the Submarine. It's on 63rd Street, between Second and Third Avenue.'

'Wait a second, I'll get a pen and take this down.'

Bernice had anticipated her needs and was thrusting a pen and pad into Clare's hands.

'Could you give me that name and address again?'

Art repeated it, wondering, as he did so, where Carl would have chosen to take her. Some dive, no doubt. A low-rent bar with sawdust on the floor. Or the park? A picnic in the park?

'Would you prefer a picnic in the park?' he asked.

'Ah—' Clare looked out the window. 'It's raining.' Did that make her sound boring? Unromantic? Should she be willing to brave the elements for him? 'Unless you want to have a picnic, I mean,' she added hastily. 'I don't mind the rain, really.'

'No, no, a restaurant would be better, I think.' Art stumbled through this sentence, relieved to ditch the picnic in the park idea. He wasn't a picnic-in-the-park-type of guy.

165

'So what time should I meet you?' Clare asked.

Bernice, she noticed, as her gaze returned from the window to the room, was fluffing up her pillow so much it looked like she was hoping to fashion a miniature white blimp out of it.

'Twelve-thirty?'

'Twelve-thirty.'

Bernice let go of the pillow and it dropped lifelessly to the floor.

'Goodbye, Clare,' Art said, feeling as if he should be a candidate for post-traumatic stress counselling.

'Goodbye, Carl.'

Seeing that he was fifteen minutes early, Carl decided to have a quick drink at the sports bar in the lobby of the Sheraton. He needed a little Dutch courage before revealing himself to Clare. How would she react? He dreaded to imagine. At least Bernice would be there, too, to soften the blow, he hoped. Bernice was the kind of girl his mother would have liked – straightforward, full of fun and pleasant to be with. Remembering his mother's reaction to Dee-Dee, Carl found that he was involuntarily hunching his shoulders.

'Doesn't she ever talk?' his mother had asked after Carl first introduced them. 'She's a good-looking woman, but there's something not quite right, isn't there?'

Carl had defended Dee-Dee at the time, but his mother's comment lurked in the back of his mind on his wedding day, six months later. He hadn't told his family he was getting married, not wishing to hear any criticisms they might have. A few hours after the civil ceremony, he telephoned his parents to break the news. 'She's a wonderful woman, Ma,' he'd said in an abrupt tone. 'She just doesn't talk very much. It's not a crime.'

'No. The crime is sneaking away to get married and not telling your family,' his mother had responded. Carl still shuddered with shame at the memory.

Bernice was definitely a talker, and Carl knew she liked him enough to help him clear up this mess with Clare.

Finishing the last drop of his Bloody Mary, Carl rose from the bar stool and tried to recall some of Dee-Dee's advice after one of her seminars – the one on the Power of Positive Thinking. She had related some story of a man who had been paralyzed from the neck down in a car accident. Carl knew there was a happy ending to it, that the man had managed to put a good spin on everything, but he couldn't for the life of him remember how.

Bernice waited for the telephone to ring three times before picking it up. It was a tiny gesture, she knew, but it was a start in her own personal campaign to be a little bit cool when it came to men.

'Right,' she said, after Carl had greeted her. 'I'll be down in a minute or two. I'll meet you in that bar there in the lobby.'

Why hadn't she said '*We'll* be down'? Carl wondered, wandering back to the bar. Had she already informed Clare of what was going on? Had Clare refused to meet him? No, he reassured himself. Bernice had made a mistake, that's all.

When she walked up to his stool, she saw him looking behind her for Clare. His face collapsed slightly, then re-arranged itself.

This wasn't a promising start.

Her heart tensed.

'Clare couldn't come. She's meeting Ca – I mean Art – for lunch.' Bernice looked at the stool beside Carl's but didn't sit down on it. Her skirt was a little too short for a stool – if she crossed her legs there would be a definite thigh problem. 'She was dead set on going. I didn't know how to stop her.'

'Oh. I see.' Carl looked at her hopelessly. He had geared himself up for his moment of truth and now it had eluded him.

'So—' Bernice stood, watching him twist his seat back and forth. She couldn't suggest that they have lunch, could she? Be a little uncool just this once?

'Does Clare know anything yet? Does she know about Art and me?' Carl asked.

'*I* haven't told her. I thought I should leave that to you. I'm sure you can sort this all out by tonight.'

'I bet Artie hasn't told her either. I should have called that bastard today. This has gotten way out of control.'

'Do you think I could have a drink?'

'Yes, of course.' Carl collected himself. 'Would you like to sit at a table? There's one over there.'

'Great.' She forced the words Coca-Cola out of her mouth when the bartender asked her what she wanted and followed Carl to yet another corner in yet another bar.

This time was going to be different, though.

This time she would stay sober and be elusive and irresistible.

'This place is totally over the top,' Clare smiled. 'Or, I suppose it's the opposite, it's under the bottom. We're fathoms down, twenty thousand leagues under the sea. I've always wondered how much a fathom or a league is. They seem such strange words to use to describe measurements.'

'I know. I have to confess that I never read Jules Verne, though. For some reason the thought of that book never appealed to me.'

'Me neither. You know, I was temporarily stunned when I found out you were a writer too, but it's not that surprising when I think about it, not really. I should have guessed.'

'Well, I always thought you had talent, too. That's why I showed your letters to—' Art hid the fact that he couldn't bring himself to finish the sentence with a short coughing spasm. 'This is shameless, what I'm doing,' he rebuked himself silently. 'Unforgiveably, desperately shameless.'

'Thank you,' Clare smiled shyly. 'But listen, Carl, speaking of confessions, I want to make mine right now and get it out of the way. It's been preying on me for so long, and I'm tired of carrying it around.' Clare was rushing her words at full speed, as if she were approaching a high hurdle. 'You remember writing to me, that letter where you told me about finding your best friend in bed with your lover?'

Art nodded slowly, racking his brain, trying to remember that bit of the correspondence. Why hadn't he read it all more carefully?

'And I wrote back saying that if I found my husband in bed with my best friend, I'd probably offer them a cup of tea?'

Yes, it was coming back to him now. He'd thought she was a typical fucking repressed, inhibited, polite limey when he'd read that one. Now he thought that reaction was breathtakingly appealing. He really wished she'd stop wearing those cute dresses of hers – this one was pale green and sleeveless with a sort of Chinese collar. Art didn't need this sensory overkill – his hand was itching to undo buttons.

'And you wrote back to tell me that, unlike me, you'd never been married.'

Oh, God, *that* had been a shock, he remembered. Carl had lied about Dee-Dee, had deleted his marriage from the letters. He'd kept meaning to ask Carl why, but had never gotten around to it.

'Well, I've never been married either. Jeremy and I are living together, but we're not married. I let you think we were because—'

Her words faded as he struggled to untangle the threads of confusion in his mind. Carl had lied about *not* being married, that much he knew. And now she was telling him what? That she had lied about *being* married? This was too bizarre to believe.

'Carl? Are you listening?'

'Yes, yes,' he said hastily, then, looking at that trusting face across the table, he decided he couldn't possibly string her along any longer, he had to be truthful. 'No, actually, I wasn't listening. I tuned out after you said you and Jeremy aren't married. I'm sorry.'

'So am I. That's what I've been trying to say. I thought it would all be easier – the correspondence, I mean – if you thought I was married.'

'I see.'

'Have I let you down terribly?'

169

'Oh, God, Clare—' he moaned. He actually moaned. The only other time in his life he could remember moaning was when his mother had died. Then he had moaned and cried and gone crazy with grief. This wasn't as terrible, he knew. Nothing he could imagine would be as terrible as that. But it was the end of his impossible dream. He had to tell Clare – asthma or no asthma – who he was. He imagined sitting beside her in the ambulance, holding her hand on the way to the Roosevelt Hospital Emergency Room. At least he'd have a little more time with her.

'Carl? I'm so sorry. Are you all right?'

'It's Art,' he muttered.

'I know.'

'You know?'

Relief, what joyous relief. She knew who he was, and she was still here.

'Yes. Art makes you do things.'

'Excuse me?' Did she think he was possessed by the devil in the guise of Art?

'Art takes over from life, from reality. Once I had written that I was a married woman, I started to *feel* I was.'

'Oh. *That* art.'

'What other art is there?'

'There's me. *I'm* Art.' He waved away the waiter who had come to take their order. Clare was looking at him as if he'd announced he was Vincent van Gogh. 'I'm Art Rolfe. I'm not Carl Lioce. OK? Carl and I went to the television studio together. When Carl realized what was going on, he switched nametags with me and I went up on stage. I'd read the correspondence, so I knew what to say.'

'I don't believe this.'

The signal for the submarine to dive sounded through the restaurant, making further speech impossible. Clare's face looked as if it had witnessed a violent death. When the noise died down, Art found that he couldn't look at her, so addressed himself to the tablecloth.

170

'Carl pretended to be me and I pretended to be him. We were going to set everything straight at dinner last night, but then—'

'But then?' Her tone had turned steely, accusing; his idea of what God would sound like when ticking off all the sins Art had committed in his lifetime.

'I don't know.' He was aware that he was fumbling for words, for excuses. 'You were a little tanked, and I guess Carl was a little upset that you'd shown the letters to your agent. I don't know . . . he kept on with the whole switch deal, so I did, too. I don't mean to blame him,' Art added hastily. 'I'm sure he's probably come to his senses by now.'

'What about you? Why didn't you tell me last night?'

Art shrugged. It was all he could do. Telling her the truth at this point seemed, for reasons he couldn't explain to himself, shoddy. The fact that he'd fallen for her would sound like another excuse.

'Of course. Why didn't I see it before? You *look* like Art – the way he described Art, but I wouldn't admit that to myself. You dress like a businessman, he dresses like a writer. And you forgot Angela's last name. He remembered. Of course. How could I have been so stupid?'

She was talking to herself, Art knew. His presence was unnecessary, probably irritating.

'So was sleeping with me part of the plan? Was that what was supposed to happen? Was that the *programme*? You take me home and seduce me – the wolf Art in the sheep Carl's clothing?'

'No. No way. No one was out to get you. The whole thing kind of evolved, so to speak. Nothing was planned.' Oh God, he thought, torn by the desire to run out of the restaurant and hide in a trash can for the rest of his life and the equally compelling need to stay as long as he could in Clare's vicinity.

'Art!'

No, it was impossible. He couldn't believe it. There was Dee-Dee, standing beside him, panting slightly, wearing a black

171

tank top, black bicycle shorts and black rollerblades, holding out sheafs of paper. This had to be a nightmare.

'Sorry to interrupt—' Dee-Dee gave Clare a cursory glance. 'But this is important. I'm so glad I managed to track you down. I remembered your secretary's name and I found her number and I called her and asked her if she could take a wild guess where you might have gone to lunch. At first she was really pretty annoyed and didn't want to say anything but I've taken a seminar in the Power of Persuasion. Anyway—'

'Dee-Dee? Please tell me the truth. Are you working for the CIA?'

'Of course not, Artie. Anyway, after our meeting this morning, I went home and I realized the beginning isn't quite right. It doesn't really set the tone for the whole story. So I flew at my keyboard and I wrote a whole new beginning – it's fantastic, you'll love it. I start in an autobiographical vein – before I get into the deeper stuff – I describe my marriage to Carl. I thought that would work well at the beginning, portray what a modern marriage is all about for a female such as myself.'

Art closed his eyes and kept them shut. He wished he could block his ears.

'Is something wrong, Art? You've been acting very untogether today.'

Opening his eyes, but unable to open his mouth, Art found himself praying for another 'dive bell' to sound.

'Excuse me? You're married to a man named Carl?' Clare asked.

'Time out,' Art signalled with his hands, but neither female paid the slightest attention.

'I *was* married to Carl. We're divorced.' Dee-Dee now turned deftly on her blades towards Clare and gave her non-smile. 'I'm sorry not to introduce myself. I'm Dee-Dee Lioce and Art is my agent.'

'Lioce.'

'Yes. Of course, I will be using my maiden name – Anderson – for the book.'

'Of course.' Clare stood up. 'Art, I think it's best if I leave you two alone to discuss business. I have to go.'

'Clare—' He was half-way out of his seat, but he couldn't maneuvre quickly enough, Dee-Dee was blocking his way.

'What's the matter, Art? She said she had to leave. This is a good opportunity for us to talk.'

'As if,' Art moaned, sinking back down into his chair.

Clare was gone.

Chapter 12

After rushing out of the Submarine, Clare hailed the first taxi she saw, collapsed in the back and asked to be taken to the Metropolitan Museum of Art.

'I don't believe this. I don't believe this,' she kept muttering, until the taxi driver turned around at a stop light and said, 'I don't believe it either, lady. So what's new?'

From that point on she kept her thoughts to herself.

She watched the windscreen wipers slapping back and forth, the crowds of people hurrying in and out of the rain, the traffic crawling along the streets. She watched and she wondered. She wondered why she had been chosen to be made such a fool of. She wondered why both Anna and Carl would treat her so shamefully – Anna in a professional sense, Carl in a personal one. What did they see her as? A natural-born object of fun and games? A sitting duck for their target practice? An incredibly stupid woman?

Well, she certainly was the latter. Of course Carl wasn't the man she spent last night with – how could he be? Art wasn't even a particularly good imitation of Carl, now that she thought about it. Carl would never say 'What's the programme?' He wouldn't wear a suit and tie. And, if he watched *EastEnders*, he would have told her so in a letter.

How gullible she'd been.

Clare was wiping tears as well as rain from her face as she

paid the taxi in the front of the museum and walked up the imposing stairs.

Instead of enjoying the paintings, she wandered aimlessly through the galleries, unable to concentrate or think of anything but Carl and his treachery. He'd behaved despicably, she knew, but a growing feeling of despair at her own actions assailed her.

Had she been so unattractive in her drunkenness? Was that his justification for playing such a cruel trick? She hadn't been what he expected, so he'd turned his back on her. All those times she'd wondered if he would let her down were they ever to meet, and now she found that she'd let him down. By doing what exactly?

By doing what her mother and father had both hated as well – by acting foolishly, acting like a child. She remembered an incident which had happened when she was around seven, before her parents divorced. Unable to control her terror one night, she'd gone into their bedroom, crying. 'Could I sleep in here, on the sofa, just for one night, just this once?' she'd asked. Her mother, reaching to turn on the bedside light and sitting up in the same movement, said, 'No, Clare. One night means two nights means too many nights. I can't make any exceptions, I'm afraid. The rule is that you sleep in your own room. It always has been. It's not like you to ask.' On the way out of their room, Clare heard her father begin a sentence with the words, 'You know, the brat—' She couldn't hear the end of it and was glad not to. Why was it, Clare asked herself twenty years later, that her father calling her a 'brat' had been more hurtful than her mother not letting her sleep in their room?

And why was this rejection of Carl's so similarly wounding now? Because she'd let her guard down momentarily and he hadn't liked what he'd seen. Hiding in a corner of her heart had been the hope that she'd been wrong to be on the defensive so much of her life. Carl, allowing Art to take his place, had effectively driven her from the room and called her a brat at the same time. She'd been right to always be so careful – this one trip to New

York had taught her that, even if the knowledge came at a very high price.

Writing those letters, revealing herself to a stranger had been a stupid, crazy act.

No, she corrected herself as she tried but failed to focus on a Degas. Writing the letters hadn't been stupid. When she'd had the correspondence, she'd felt special – she'd felt as if Carl was connected to her. When she told him about her childhood fears, when she told him her thoughts on friendship or wrote long passages on books and plays she admired, whenever she opened her heart to him on any subject, even simple ones like movies – she felt strangely relieved and happy knowing he'd respond.

He had loved her from afar. She knew in her heart he had.

But when he saw her close up, he ran away.

'I've disappointed him,' Clare thought. 'I didn't live up to his image of me.'

Finally summoning up some energy, she gave up her pretence of studying art and left the museum. For a few minutes she stood outside in the rain, gazing up and down Fifth Avenue.

What was she supposed to do now?

She wanted Angela Rae to appear out of thin air, to come and save her. She needed her more now than she'd needed her when that plane had crashed.

Clare found herself sinking onto the stone steps. She'd never had asthma in Spain – was that because, as she'd told herself a long time ago, her monsters chose other ways to get to her in Spain, or was the real reason an obvious one – the asthma, at an early age, had turned from a physical problem to a psychosomatic one.

The disease had had nothing to do with her bronchial airways and everything to do with her head. She was not only a disappointment, she was also a fake.

Standing up wearily in her damp dress, she made her way down to the street and hailed another cab. This time neither she nor the driver spoke after she'd given him the name of the hotel. She needed to get back. She wanted to see Bernice, a familiar face. A friend.

And she wanted to go home.

Five Coca-Colas into her time with Carl at the Hudson Sports Bar in the lobby of the Sheraton, Bernice felt a caffeine – sugar buzz kick in. She was listening to Carl tell her about his ex-wife, listening as if her life depended on it.

'But Carl . . . Desiree? That can't be her real name.'

'I know,' Carl laughed. He was on his third gin and tonic. Two half-eaten hamburgers rested in front of them. 'Dee-Dee is a pretty unbelievable name too. The point is, I never understood what she wanted, Bernice. When I first met her, she was quiet and sultry and – I don't know – I guess I'd say mysterious. But even though she was mysterious I thought I knew what she wanted – I thought she wanted me.'

'And then?'

'And then she started up with these seminars. All these seminars about personal fulfillment. I couldn't keep them straight. The Power of Positive Thinking, the Power of Persuasion, the Power of Self-realization, the Power of Power, I think one of them was called. Pretty soon, I couldn't understand what she was talking about. Isn't that strange? I mean, as soon as she begins to talk, I begin not to understand her.'

'But you never understood her in the first place, not really.'

'No,' Carl paused, picking up a ketchup-coated cold french fry from his plate, then tossing it back down again in disgust. 'No, you're right, I didn't.'

'You were dazzled by her beauty.'

'I was,' he nodded. 'You must think I'm a typical male idiot. I *was* dazzled by her beauty. How ridiculous.'

'I don't think so,' Bernice started to lean forward, but stopped herself. 'Women are dazzled by good looks too, you know. Did they have that commercial here – that one for Diet Coke where all the women in an office take a break to watch some construction worker strip his shirt off?'

'I don't know. I don't watch TV very often.'

'Well, I'm in the advertising business and now advertisers are beginning to see the value of hunky, handsome men. Women love cute rear-ends and rippling muscles. And in the nineties, we're allowed to admit it.'

'But you wouldn't make a mistake like I did. You wouldn't go for some guy primarily on the basis of sex appeal.'

'Absolutely, I would. I might not marry him if he didn't talk, but then again, I might, because I talk so much myself – so we'd balance each other out. The seminar business would bother me, though. I don't really think of myself as English, but I guess some national characteristics are hard-wired. I wouldn't go to a self-fulfilment seminar if you paid me. Well, I would if you paid me, but I'm sure I'd say something which would get me kicked out anyway.'

'Clare and me – our letters – they rescued me from this overwhelming grief I was feeling after Dee-Dee left.'

'Were you mourning Dee-Dee or your marriage?'

Carl, who had been concentrating on making dents in his hamburger bun with his forefinger, looked up sharply.

'Good question,' he said.

'Well—' Bernice shrugged. 'From what you've told me, you come from a happy family, a solid emotional base, and divorce must seem like a dirty word to you.'

'Yes, well, remember I'm Catholic.'

'So am I.'

'Really? Shit.'

'My parents tried the convent route after I got chucked out of the state school I went to after I'd been chucked out of the trendy, academic up-market one Clare went to. Needless to say, the nuns didn't see me as a budding Mother Theresa.'

'How long did you last?'

'Forty-eight days. I can tell you the exact amount of hours; in fact, I can tell you the seconds, if you'd like.'

'It's not necessary,' Carl laughed.

'Save my seat, will you? I need to go to the loo.'

In the ladies, Bernice studied herself carefully. She looked fine, but she didn't trust the image. Some mirrors were 'good' mirrors, she had noticed. You could look fantastic in them, then go into another room where there was a different mirror and see yourself in a whole new, nasty light. Was this mirror safe? Should she put on another layer of eye shadow, just to make sure? No. Carl, she figured, was not a fan of heavy make-up. At the basin, she washed her hands, re-washed them and then did it again. What is this? she asked herself, when she finally noticed what she was doing. Is it Lady Macbeth time? Am I trying to expunge the guilt of stealing a man who should by all rights be with my friend?

'Fuck Shakespeare, she said out loud. The woman at the basin beside her burst out laughing.

'I love this country,' Bernice decided. 'I love it to bits.'

As she walked back into the bar, she saw that Carl's seat at their table was empty.

'Oh shit,' she thought, looking around the room in a wild state of panic. 'He has gone, walked out for good. He has gone to find Clare or anyone – anyone but me.'

'Hey.'

She felt a hand on her shoulder as she heard the voice behind her. He'd been to the gents while she was in the ladies. She wanted to shriek with relief. Instead, she basked in the slight warmth of his hand as he guided her back to the table.

'Listen,' he said as they were about to sit down. 'Why don't we leave this joint? All these TV screens and baseball games are getting to me. Besides, it has just occurred to me that you're in a foreign country. You should see some of the city. I know you went sightseeing with Clare the day before yesterday, but I bet you didn't walk around Little Italy.'

He swayed slightly as he spoke, Bernice noticed. The tables were turned – now *he* was the tipsy one in the equation. That was fine by her, perfect in fact. After the second drink, he'd stopped asking her when she thought Clare would be back from lunch. Now, after the third, he'd suggested a sightseeing tour *à deux*.

'I can keep this going, I know I can,' Bernice told herself. 'There's plenty to drink in Little Italy. I know because Clare and I *did* go there. But there's no need to inform Carl of such an unimportant little fact.

'Little Italy sounds wonderful,' she said. 'As long as you can guarantee a Mafia shooting.'

'No problem—' he spread his hands. 'I'm a wiseguy.'

'You're a smartass,' she countered. 'There's a big difference. I should know.'

They headed out of the bar, and into the lobby.

'Hold on – I forgot my jacket,' he said, turning back. 'I'll be with you in a second.'

Checking the lobby for mirrors, she stopped and emitted a cry of pained surprise, the sound of a small animal caught in a large trap, as she saw, instead of a flattering reflection, a blonde, bedraggled woman walking towards her.

'Bernice, God I'm glad to see you. You wouldn't believe what the hell is going on in my life. I'm so glad you're here. I was terrified that you'd be out somewhere and I wouldn't be able to talk to you. They switched identities on us. I mean Art is Carl and Carl is Art—' Clare stopped, suddenly remembering their conversation in the room that morning, when Bernice had been so strange. Why hadn't she thought of it before? Bernice knew too. Everyone knew. How much more humiliation was waiting for her? Did Anna know about all this too?

'Hello, Clare.'

Clare looked behind Bernice's left shoulder and her eyes froze.

'Carl.'

A rueful smile started to creep across Bernice's face, the same smile she knew appeared when she would see Simon the Skunk books on the racks at W. H. Smiths, exactly the same smile she always gave when the sales lady at a store informed her that they didn't have what she wanted in any size above an eight.

She didn't want to look behind her at Carl's face, but she couldn't avoid it.

'Well,' Carl said in a quiet voice. 'I'm glad we've got our names straight, finally.'

What was it with men? Bernice asked herself. How could they sober up in a second if they wanted to? It wasn't fair.

'Yes, we have our names straight. And I even know the name of your ex-wife, too.'

'Dee-Dee?' Carl gasped.

'Mmm,' Clare replied. 'We bumped into each other at lunch. I wasn't in the mood to chat, I'm afraid.'

'Isn't that an absurd name?' Bernice said to two people who weren't paying any attention to her.

The lobby was a hub of activity, full of convention-goers, tourists and hotel employees brushing past each other in a hurry to get to their individual destinations. By some unknowable law of nature, they all left a wide berth for the English women and American man standing in the centre of the room.

'Clare, we have to talk.'

'I'm not sure we do,' Clare replied evenly.

'Come on—' Carl reached out and put his hand on Clare's shoulder. 'I have a lot of apologizing to do. Give me a chance to grovel. I'm really good at grovelling.'

Finally wrenching her eyes away from Carl, Bernice turned and saw Clare's expression soften. 'Well,' she tried to console herself. 'At least it was a quick, clean kill. It could have been a lot messier. I could have done a long stretch on Death Row.'

What had Clare said? Bernice had blanked out, she had missed whatever Clare had said to Carl in return to his grovelling comment, and now they were gone, walking towards the revolving doors and out onto the street. Carl's hand was on Clare's shoulder in the same position it had been on hers only moments before. Perhaps they had said goodbye to her as they left, but she doubted it. They were too engrossed in each other to bother. Anyway, a goodbye didn't make a hell of a lot of difference at this point.

Bernice wandered over to the bank of lifts, walked into a waiting one and pushed every button she could see.

The flat was just as she had imagined – unkempt, cramped, dark and yet welcoming in its own way. It had a womblike atmosphere, the lining of the womb being Carl's vast collection of books which were resting on floor-to-ceiling bookshelves. The living room was small, with only one sofa, one desk, one standing lamp and one chair; the bedroom was smaller, from what she could see of it through a half-closed door to the right of the living room, and the kitchen, to the left and rear, was miniscule. From the living-room window it was possible to see a tiny sliver of the Hudson River – possible if you stood on tiptoes and craned your neck into a contorted swanlike position.

'Would you like to sit down?' Carl motioned to the chair and sofa.

'I'm fine here,' Clare answered, perching herself on the narrow window seat.

Seeing Carl in the hotel lobby, Clare felt her depression evaporate and her soul rebel. He had had as much to do with this warped fairy-tale, she realized, as she had, if not more. He had written to her with an empathy he didn't seem to possess. Having too much to drink was not as heinous an offence in her mind as not tolerating that drunkenness. The thought of losing control had always terrified her, which is why she'd been so careful not to. But she had never blamed or judged anyone else who didn't have those same fears. Carl had judged her for one slip. Who was he to play the moral almighty one?

Faced with his presence, sitting on the window seat as the rain splattered the panes behind her, she wanted to hurt him the way he had hurt her.

'You didn't like seeing me drunk – was that what this is all about, Carl? Did I not come up to your expectations because I was a fallible human being? I thought you approved of people who make mistakes, I thought you had some sympathy for weakness. I can't believe how you reacted – jeering at the way I repeated myself and then leaving in a bait.'

'Clare – look – I'm sorry. I'll say I'm sorry five thousand times. I panicked at the television studio, and I behaved like a total jerk at dinner. I can't believe I pushed you into Artie's arms.'

'I like Art,' Clare bristled. 'And I wasn't in his arms. He behaved very well, given the circumstances. At least he finally told me what the hell was going on.'

'I like Art too. Although I have to say, I could have killed him last night at certain points. It's strange to watch someone trying to be you, if you see what I mean.'

'It's even stranger to find out you've spent the night in the flat of an impersonator, wouldn't you say?'

'I know—' Carl, who had been standing, suddenly fell onto his sofa, his arms outstretched. 'I was an asshole. It's as simple as that.'

'No. It's not so simple. Are we supposed to be friends now? For the past forty-eight hours I've been assailed by lie upon lie upon lie from people I trusted. I don't know whether to believe anything you say. As far as I know, you could actually *be* Art and this is some kind of double bluff.'

'How did you guess?' Carl smiled.

'That's not funny,' Clare retorted, but she couldn't stop herself from giving a small smile in return.

She studied him as he sat sprawled across the sofa. He had the dark hair she'd pictured – longish and thick. His face was dark as well, dark and angled with a straight, strong nose and mouth. He *looked* like a hero, when he wasn't sulking as he had been the evening before. Obviously his looks changed dramatically with his moods – he would be a lousy poker player.

'Maybe I was frightened of you.' He said this in an unsure tone of voice she hadn't heard him use before.

183

'What does that mean?' she asked, feeling as if she should move closer to him, but remaining stiffly on the window-sill.

'Maybe you mean too much to me, Clare. I knew that if you were as perfect as you were to me in your letters, I'd be in deep trouble. You're married. You live thousands of miles away. I think I was looking for a way out of what I feel, so I grabbed at anything I could. For self-protection.'

'Oh.' She coughed.

'Are you feeling alright? Bernice said you were smoking yester-day afternoon. Are your lungs OK?'

'I'm fine. The cigarettes didn't bother me. God knows why I had them. I think I was trying to do everything I've never done in one go. Drinking, smoking. It was lucky there wasn't any heroin around. Anyway, I'm fine. Actually, I'm hungry. Art took me to some really strange fish restaurant—'

'The Submarine?'

Clare nodded.

'Do you believe how tacky that place is?'

'I . . . I quite liked it. But then Art told me who he was and then your ex-wife came in and I left without eating anything.'

'What was Dee-Dee doing there?'

'She was chasing down Art about some book she's writing.'

'Dee-Dee is writing a book?'

'Yes.' Clare understood that the conversation had taken a turn, that she could no longer treat him as an enemy. She wasn't sure why she hadn't yelled at him, or shown more of her anger about his changing places with Art, but somehow they had slipped into the easy intimacy of their correspondence without her knowing how or when the transition had occurred. 'She's beautiful. Is she some kind of model?'

'No, she was a dancer. She almost made it big, but in the end she had to settle for teaching. I think she's watched the video of *Chorus Line* at least five thousand times. I can't believe she's writing a book. And Art is her agent?'

'That's what I gathered. I didn't stay long.'

'So. The truth will out, as they say. Now you know that I've been married too.' Carl's head dropped slightly. 'I couldn't bring myself to tell you in the letters, I—'

'I'm not.'

'You're not what?'

'I'm not married. That's *my* only lie in this whole farce.'

'But—'

'But I let you think that I was. Oh, God, I'm bored with explaining this. I told Art everything before I knew he wasn't you. Jeremy and I are living together, we have been for three years. We're not married. Not yet.'

'Are you planning to marry him?'

'I guess so.'

'You *guess* so?'

'I don't think it's any of your business.'

'No,' Carl sighed. 'I suppose it isn't.'

'Carl, I have no idea what you and I mean to each other, have you?'

Carl sat silently on the sofa for a moment, staring at the books on the opposite wall.

'Fuck it,' he said abruptly, standing up and moving toward Clare at the window. He leant down and kissed her on the lips, then pulled her up into his body.

Art couldn't face going back to his office. The little energy he had left had been spent trying to shake Dee-Dee off his back, and when he finally managed by promising he'd read her new beginning chapter and synopsis that afternoon, he left her standing on the street in the rain and walked straight back to his apartment.

The absence of Clare hit him as soon as he entered his living room, and he spent the next twenty minutes rooting through his CD collection, until he finally emerged with the song he wanted to hear . . . the Beatles singing 'The Night Before'. Listening to it repeatedly, he replayed each moment of the previous evening with Clare – their conversations at the restaurant, their short time sitting in the living room together, the momentary glimpse he'd had of her sleeping in the spare room when he'd woken up at five a.m. and gone to check that she was still there. He tried to forget the look on her face when he'd told her he wasn't Carl, but that was a doomed effort.

Rousing himself from his reverie, he pulled the telephone towards him, dialled Information and got the number of the Sheraton.

'Hello,' he said, when the hotel operator put him through to Clare's room. 'Is this Bernice?'

'I guess so,' she replied. 'Is this Art?'

'Ditto. Listen, I told Clare who I was and I just wanted to know . . . I mean, has she had an asthma attack or anything? Do you know what's happened to her?'

'She's gone off with Carl, Bernice replied. 'No huge surprise, right?'

'She's gone off with Carl.'

'She's gone off with Carl.'

'Why do *you* sound so miserable?'

'Why do *I* sound so miserable? You want to know why? I'll tell you why. It's all your fucking fault for switching nametags—'

'*Carl* switched the nametags, Bernice.'

'Carl. Art. What's the difference. And who gives a shit?'

'Calm down, Bernice. *What's* all my fault? Or all Carl's fault? I don't understand.'

'You wouldn't. You're not some stupid, idiotic, pathetic emotional wreck of a woman, are you?'

'I would be if I had a sex-change operation.'

'How much do they cost? Do I have to go to Sweden? I would, Art, I'd do it. I'm tired of being a woman and falling in love and getting nowhere. It's shattering.'

'Who have you fallen in – oh,' Art cursed himself for not picking up on it sooner. 'Carl.'

'It's hopeless, isn't it?'

'I'd say so.'

'Thanks. Thank you so much for your kind words of encouragement.'

'You asked the question.'

'I only asked the question because I was hoping you'd tell me I was wrong.'

'Great logic, Bernice. Look – I'm in the same position you are. I'm in love' – Art paused, amazed that he had uttered the L word – 'with Clare. But we both know they've got that thing going between them . . . that damn correspondence. How can we compete with that? It's impossible.'

'I know.'

Art could hear the tears in Bernice's voice.

'I'm perfectly aware that it's impossible,' she continued. 'So I'm going to go down to the bar in the lobby and get pissed as a newt.'

'I always hated that expression. It's one of those naff fucking English deals I never understood. What does getting drunk have to do with a species of frog?'

'What do you want me to say – drunk as a skunk? I refuse to say that. I refuse to have anything to do with skunks. Besides, naff is an English word, isn't it? What right do you have to complain about one English expression in the same breath as using another?'

'Can we stop arguing over naff–newt semantics for a second? I need to get out of this damn apartment and I wouldn't mind getting hammered – hammered as a hamster – myself. I'll come and join you.'

'All right,' Bernice said wearily. 'If you must. We can both cry in our beer.'

'Isn't that lager to you?'

'Listen, sunshine. It's anything bloody alcoholic, OK?'

'OK,' he answered, sounding slightly abashed. 'You're on.'

Sitting cross-legged on Carl's bed, wearing one of his shirts which came down to just above her knees, Clare listened to the relentless sound of rain.

'I wonder where Angela is now,' she mused.

'Bali?'

'I hope so.' They were sharing a beer from a bottle. Carl held it out to her but Clare shook her head.

'No, thanks. Oh, my God, what was that?'

'Thunder,' Carl smiled. 'You'll get to hear a New York City thunderstorm and see if it matches up to the way I described it in my letter – listen – hear the car alarms?'

'Yes,' Clare nodded, trying to concentrate on what he was saying. It was hard to think of anything but sex at the moment. Carl had amazed her with behaviour in bed which she was still trying to come to terms with. He was so passionate, so concentrated, so focused on giving her pleasure, she couldn't look at him drinking his beer now and see him as the same man. He was a present, a gift from the gods, one which every female in the world should receive – just to know what it was like to have a man who knew what to do and how to do it.

She would never say something as disloyal as 'Carl is better in bed than Jeremy', because Carl was doing something completely different from Jeremy. He wasn't thinking of himself, or his own pleasure, only of hers. She felt as if she were a queen bee. The attention, at first, made her nervous. She kept trying to give something back, to concentrate on him as he was concentrating on her, but he wouldn't have it. She would say, 'Let me rub your neck' and he'd say, 'No, I want to rub yours. Relax, Clare. This is what I like to do. Leave everything in my expert hands.' He wouldn't let her lift a finger, so to speak. All she was supposed to do was lie back and enjoy his attentions. After a while, she did just that.

Only now could she wonder who had been making love to her in this extraordinary selfless fashion. Was this *her* Carl, the Carl in the letters, the one who sent off missives to unknown Shanes in Australia? The man in bed with her had had a passion which was so intense and so giving she couldn't believe any woman was capable of walking away from it. Clare found herself wondering about Dee-Dee. Had he made love to her like this? If so, how could she have left him? It didn't make sense, unless Dee-Dee, like Clare herself, felt a little afraid of Carl's wild intensity. That's the only way she could describe it to herself. He was so intense, he was slightly scary.

Clare looked over at Carl and relaxed. He *was* Carl – the sympathetic and clever and funny Carl she'd been so affected by over the past fifteen months. As it turned out, he didn't chew loudly or wear too much aftershave; he was, in fact, almost perfect.

For a moment, when she remembered how close she had come to throwing herself into Art's arms the night before, she distrusted her instincts. Perhaps she would have gone to bed with anyone walking down the street who made a move in her direction. She calmed down when she reflected that Art and Carl were close friends. They must share some of the same characteristics; it wasn't that crazy to have liked Art as much as she had. Especially since she thought he was Carl.

It was time, she knew, to admit to herself that she loved Carl. All these months she'd been deceiving herself, pretending that their correpondence was a special kind of friendship, outside the boundary of normal male–female relations.

You win, Billy Crystal, she thought. There is no such thing as a straightforward friendship between a man and a woman. Sex always comes into it. Thank God.

'The Bridges of Manhattan City,' she suddenly said out loud.

'What?'

'My agent – Anna – she said if we ever made it into a book, our correspondence could be like *The Bridges of Madison County*. Actually, there were about fifteen different movies she thought it resembled.'

'Artie had the same response.'

'It's weird that we both showed it to our agents, isn't it? And weird that we're both writers.'

'I guess you'd call it synchronicity.' Carl reached out, grabbed a piece of her blonde hair and began to twist it around his finger. 'An amazing *correspondence*. So much of what has happened between us seems unbelievably fated. Think of *Notorious*, Clare, think of the beginning when Devlin first meets Alicia properly. She's getting drunk, remember, he first meets her when she's getting hammered.'

'I hadn't thought of that.' Clare looked at him in wonder. 'You're right.'

'And Devlin pushes Alicia at Sebastian, the way I practically pushed you at Art.'

'Art's hardly Sebastian, Carl. He's not a Nazi. You're taking the analogy a little far, aren't you? God, that thunder *is* loud.' Clare pulled the sheets up over her.

'I love you.'

'What?'

'I said I love you.'

She sat silently for a moment, then reached out for the bottle of beer and took a long swig.

'"And then I go and spoil it all by saying something stupid like I love you,"' Carl sang, doing a passable imitation of Nancy Sinatra.

The tiny frisson of irritation Clare experienced on hearing this evaporated almost instantaneously.

'I love you too,' she heard herself say. Did she love him? Yes, definitely. She did.

'Good. That's settled. When do we get married?'

'Carl, was that a joke?'

'Kind of.' He moved his hands in the air as if he were balancing a scale. 'And kind of not.'

'Well, on the kind of not point, you know I have to tell Jeremy about us. I have to sort things out at home. I can't think about getting married now.'

'Of course, I'm sorry. It really was a semi-joke. I'm fucking up all over the place, aren't I?'

'No, no you're not.' She took his hand in hers and kissed it. 'Everything has happened so quickly, that's all.'

190

'It hasn't for me. A part of me has been waiting for this to happen forever. Ah, the storm is moving on. Listen, the rain has stopped. Will you come outside with me now? I want you to smell the city streets. Then we can come back in and order some Chinese to be delivered.'

Clare pulled on the oversize pair of jeans Carl tossed to her, watched as he dressed himself, and, pleased to be accompanying him, to share his moment of rainswept city streets, followed him out the door, into the lift and then onto the street.

This was the sort of man she should be with . . . a man who appreciated smells and thunderstorms, a man who wouldn't make studied phone calls or hide himself away from people. A writer, she knew she should be with another writer. Someone who understood.

'Can you smell it?' he asked, his arms outstretched, his face raised to the heavens. 'Isn't it magnificent?'

'Absolutely,' she replied. 'Can we go back to bed now?'

Chapter 13

'I think this was a mistake.'

'A big mistake or a small one?' Art asked. 'Will it scar us permanently or will we recover?'

'Oh, we'll recover,' Bernice responded, fastening her bra. 'We've both made mistakes before, I'd guess.'

'It would be convenient if we could fall in love with each other, you know.'

'I know. It would solve everything. And, Artie –' she leant over and patted him on the thigh. 'I enjoyed myself, I really did. But—'

'I know,' he said ruefully. 'Ditto. We're good lovers, but we're not great lovers – of course that could have something to do with our combined intake of tequila.'

'That's true.'

'Do you want to do it sober sometime? Just to see?'

'Hold on, I'll get that. Christ, I hope it's not Jeremy.' Climbing over Art's prone form, Bernice reached for the telephone.

'Hello?'

Art observed Bernice's face as she spoke – she was a nice girl, a nice *woman* he corrected himself. Fun and easygoing and a sweet substitute to ease his battered heart. Falling into bed together had happened without either suggesting it, a natural progression which both understood to be a one-off, drunken spree. She was as close as he supposed he would ever come to Clare and he was, for her, the next best thing to Carl. The physical deal they had wordlessly struck had worked ... but only momentarily. Images of Clare were now torturing Art even more painfully than they had when he was alone in his apartment.

'Now? You're here *now?*' she kept repeating. Art wondered what was getting her so worked up.

'What was that all about?' he asked when she'd put the phone down.

'That was Clare's agent. She's here. In New York. At Kennedy.'

'So?'

'She's brought Jeremy with her.'

'Oh, shit.'

'And they're on their way here. I've got to get in touch with Clare right away. This is a nightmare. I don't know what he'll do, he's an athlete, you know.'

'Mr Cricket. I know.'

'What time is it?'

'Around ten.'

'How can I get in touch with Clare?'

'Why don't you try Carl's apartment? That's the logical place, I'm afraid.'

'You're right,' she sighed. 'Will you do it? I don't think I can cope with hearing Carl's voice right now.'

'All right. Move over, will you?' Rising from the bed, Art pulled on his boxer shorts, nudged Bernice to the side, sat down, picked up the phone and dialled Carl's number.

'Carlo. It's me. Look, I don't have time to have a long conversation. Something has come up. Is Clare there?' Art nodded at Bernice with an expression conveying shared despair. 'OK. I'm at the Sheraton with Bernice. Just tell Clare that her agent seems to have flown into town and for some reason she has brought Jeremy Cricket with her. They're on their way here now. They're coming from Kennedy, so that gives Clare about forty-five minutes to get back. If she wants to get back, that is . . . Right?' Art nodded again. 'We'll be here.'

'He says they'll both come over,' Art told Bernice, putting the telephone back down. 'Sounds like there's going to be a showdown.' Picking up a red sock from the floor, Art put it on his foot, then crouched down in search of the other. 'What's this agent like, anyway?'

'She's a piece of work,' Bernice said, as she set about searching for all the various pieces of her clothing as well. 'Clare talked to her this morning and told her . . . oh, God, it's too complicated.'

'Try me.'

'She told her that she had fallen in love with you, Art. The real you. When she thought Carl was you, that is.'

'You win, I'm lost,' Art straightened up, buttoning his white shirt as he did so.

'I know, don't worry about it. It will all come out in the rinse cycle. I don't understand why Jeremy has suddenly entered the picture, though, or how and why those two teamed up.'

'My other sock has completely disappeared.'

'How are we going to face the happy couple, Art?' Bernice grabbed her top and pulled it over her head.

'I think the happy couple will have more problems facing Jeremy, don't you?'

'My heart hurts.'

'My *head's* killing me. I thought you said tequila was so pure it doesn't have any downside.'

'That's when you drink it in Mexico, I suppose. It must lose some of that purity when it crosses the border. Oh, God, Artie, I don't think I can stand seeing them. I think we should leave this hotel room. Go somewhere else. Climb the Empire State Building or something.'

'Listen, Bernice, we've lost.' Art pulled on his trousers. 'We have to face that. You and Carl will never get together. Neither will Clare and I. So I think we should be good sports about it.'

'That sounds *frightfully* English.'

'Oh, please. The Brits don't have a monopoly on good sports-manship. You just think you do because you always lose at everything so you *have* to be good sports or you'd all have nervous breakdowns about your woeful inability to succeed.'

'Bugger off, Art.' She turned her back to him and stepped into her jeans.

'Has it come to this? From intimacy to invective in ten minutes? I'm distraught, Bernice. I really am.'

'We tell him we're in love, that's all. I know it will be painful, but he has to accept it sooner or later.' Carl had his arm around Clare in the back of the taxi, and he pulled her in closer to him as he spoke.

'But you don't understand. If Jeremy is with Anna, he must think I've fallen in love with Art.'

'You mean with me.'

'No, I mean Art. The real Art. I told Anna I'd fallen in love with Art.'

'Clare, I don't—'

'Don't even try to understand.'

'Well, I wouldn't think it mattered *whom* you'd fallen in love with as far as Jeremy is concerned. Art or me. The point is you've fallen in love with somebody else.'

'What is Anna doing, bringing him over here? What is she trying to prove?' Clare turned her head away from Carl. She didn't want him to see her guilty face.

'Whatever her motive may be, I'm glad she's come with him. The sooner this is out in the open, the better as far as I'm concerned. We can start our life together with a clean slate.'

'Hang on a minute, Carl. Am I supposed to wipe out a three-year relationship in one second in a hotel room in a foreign country?'

'You have to tell the truth.'

'Really?' Clare pulled away from his grip. 'You and I didn't tell the whole truth to each other for almost two years. There might be times it's not such a good idea to tell the truth.'

'Are you backing out of us, Clare? Are you going to fly back home with Jeremy? I don't believe it.'

'I don't know *what* I'm doing,' Clare thought. 'I feel as if I've signed up for a job I won't be able to handle. As if I'd said in a secretarial interview that I could type three hundred words per minute and now that I've been hired, I don't know how to tell the boss that thirty words per minute is my top speed. It's Carl's overwhelming nature, his *force field* which is both completely compelling and totally daunting at the same time. He looks at me as if I were the only person who exists in this world, with everyone else just a cardboard cut-out. I may not be able to keep up with him, to take his emotional pace. Can I leave Jeremy, leave London and come here to live with Carl just like that? After only one afternoon together? Am I strong enough to take such a huge risk?

'Why won't you answer me, Clare?'

'Because I fucking well want you to leave me in peace for a minute,' Clare snapped, then immediately regretted the outburst. 'I'm sorry, Carl. The past forty-eight hours have been—'

'Hell?'

'No. Total chaos. First you're Art and Art is you and then we get together and then Jeremy and Anna show up out of the blue. I need some time to think, that's all.'

'That's fair. I know. I'm sorry if I pushed you. I don't want to lose you as soon as I've found you, you understand that, don't you?'

'Yes. Of course,' Clare replied, stifling a sigh of exasperation. 'I'm glad Bernice and Art are going to be there. I . . . oh, my God—' Clare stopped.

'What?'

'I've just remembered. I've remembered what Bernice said to me this morning. Oh, my God.'

'What?'

'Never mind. Forget it.'

'*What*, Clare?'

'I'm going crazy,' Clare thought. 'Bernice said she had fallen in love with Art. Which means she's fallen in love with Carl. Oh, *shit*. This can't possibly get any worse, can it?'

'Clare? Talk to me.'

'It's a female thing,' Clare finally replied, taking refuge in the unspeakable mysteries of the opposite sex.

'Isn't it going to be a little cramped in here?' Art asked, eyeing Clare and Carl as they perched together on the end of Clare's bed. 'Don't you think we should do this down in the bar?'

'It's too noisy down there,' Carl replied.

'He's right,' Bernice nodded. 'I don't think the six of us are too interested in the baseball games, either.'

'Jeremy might be,' Art commented. 'You know, I could take him aside and explain how cricket differs from baseball and what a far superior game baseball is. He might really enjoy that.'

'Very funny, Art,' Carl said.

'Well, *I* thought it was,' Art responded, shrugging.

'Is it possible to open a window in here?' Clare asked.

'Nope,' Art answered. 'It's not possible to jump out of one, either. Desirable but not possible.'

'Are they going to call from the lobby or come straight to the room? Do you know, Bernice?'

Sitting on the end of her bed, Bernice answered Clare while looking at Art in the chair opposite. 'She didn't say. I would *think* they'd call first. But you never know with Anna.'

'Anna?' Art straightened from his slumped position.

'Oh, fuck,' Bernice muttered. 'That's them.'

The knock on the door temporarily paralyzed the two couples. No one seemed to want to get up and answer it. When the knock was repeated, Carl stood up.

'I'll go.'

'No—' Clare pushed him back down. '*I* will.'

'Jeremy,' she said quietly, after opening the door. 'Anna. Come in.'

'What the hell—' Anna entered the room before Jeremy,

surveyed the scene in an instant and turned to Clare. 'So you've got your lover here to protect you.' She turned back again and transferred the same look of loathing on Art.

'Hi, Annie,' Art gave a little wave to Anna. 'Long time no see.'

'You *know* her?' Bernice exclaimed.

Carl stared at Art. Bernice and Clare stared at Art, then Anna, then each other. Carl stared at Clare. Jeremy stared at Carl.

'You bastard!' Anna's enraged voice filled the room.

'Is there somewhere we can sit down?' Jeremy asked, standing a foot inside the doorway. 'It's been a bloody flight. And the cab ride was, if possible, worse.'

'I've got an idea. There's a deli down the street. We can go there and have some coffee and converse in peace,' Art suggested, looking brightly at the others in the room.

'That sounds reasonable.' Carl, as he rose from his position at the foot of the bed, stooped down momentarily to pick something up which had been underneath his foot. 'Is this anyone's?' He held up one red sock.

'Who the hell is he?' Anna barked.

'He's Carl,' Bernice replied. 'At least some of the time, he's Carl.'

'That's mine—' Art walked over and took the sock from Carl's hand.

'What? Were you screwing Clare here? In the hotel room *I've* paid for?' Anna sounded as if she were either about to punch someone or faint.

'Bernice?' Clare took an involuntarily step back. 'You and Art?'

'Bernice too!' Anna exclaimed. '*Both* of them? Jesus, Art. You're . . . you're . . .' Anna spluttered to an abrupt end.

'Hungry,' Art finished for her.

'What do you care who he screws?' Bernice faced Anna, trembling.

'He's my husband.'

'Wrong tense, Annie. I *was* your husband. Past, not present.'

'Excuse me,' Jeremy walked into the middle of the room and

addressed them as if they were his team-mates. 'I really am feeling shattered and I would like to go to some place where at least there might be a breath of air and enough seats to accommodate all of us, if we have to remain in a group in order to sort all this out. A delicatessen sounds fine to me. Art? Could you lead the way, please?'

'I'd be delighted,' Art replied.

At the table in the deli, Bernice, Clare and Carl sat on one side, facing Art, Jeremy and Anna. An ancient waitress dressed in a short pink nylon dress, made three trips to plonk six cups of coffee in front of them. The silence which had descended on the group as soon as they left the hotel room continued as they took turns with the milk and sugar.

Sitting next to Carl rather than Jeremy made Clare feel as if she had made a choice between the two men, when the fact was that she hadn't made her mind up about anything. She wanted to reach out and touch Jeremy's hand, but she knew he wouldn't appreciate the gesture. He would want to sort out whatever difficulties there were to sort out and then get on with it, 'it' being his life.

She was a part of that life, she knew. However, if someone were to rush into the deli and tell Jeremy his team needed him immediately, Jeremy would most probably make his excuses and leave, abandoning Clare to her fate. Was that a bad or a good thing, emotionally speaking? she wondered. What would it feel like to have a man who put your interests and feelings first every day of the week, every second of the day? Clare sneaked a sidelong glance at Carl's profile. He looked a little like a taller Al Pacino, she decided. Suddenly, she became aware of his foreignness. American men *were* different. They were, she thought, more giving and therefore also more demanding.

Clare had bought a second-hand car when she was twenty years old and despite its clapped out exterior and dodgy engine, she had stuck with it faithfully for seven years. If she won the lottery, she doubted whether she'd buy a new car. Gazing across at Jeremy, she took in his familiar face, the way he sat so composedly, all his movements and expressions she knew so intimately. How could she think she could simply trade in Jeremy for Carl? It wasn't right. And it wasn't in her nature.

'So—' Art was the one to speak first. 'Let me try to get this straight. You thought I was having an affair with Clare, Annie? Am I right?'

'An*na*,' she responded. 'I never liked the way you called me that.'

'And Jeremy, Annie must have rung you to tell you this dreadful news and to insist you come over and rescue the damsel in distress?'

'Something along those lines,' Jeremy responded, pouring more milk into his cup.

'Which, presumably, she wouldn't have done if she thought Clare was having an affair with *Carl*. True, Annie? You were the one who set the whole television meeting up, yes?'

'Yes,' she mumbled, looking a little sheepish.

'Hoping that something might happen between Carl and Clare, yes?'

'No, no, I never meant that,' Anna looked nervously at Jeremy, sitting beside her. 'I thought they should meet – that's all. The correspondence was so all-consuming for Clare, I thought if they met, she could get a little perspective on it.'

'You always smile when you lie, you know, Annie. Remember? I've told you that before. It's a dead giveaway,' Art said, in a surprisingly kind voice.

Clare forgot about her own situation momentarily and found herself trying to imagine Art and Anna married. Had the marriage foundered because Art wouldn't let Anna get away with anything? It seemed that way, at the moment, although Clare thought she could detect a little affection still in Art's eyes when he looked at his ex. Not love, but a recognition of a love that had been. And that clashed with Carl's description of Art's enduring hatred of the Swamp Creature. Perhaps Carl had not delved as deeply into Art's soul as he thought he had.

What Clare saw in Anna's eyes, despite her aggressive pose, was a sad longing.

'What correspondence are you talking about? Clare? What is Anna talking about?' Jeremy asked.

'Didn't she tell you on the plane?' Art turned to Jeremy.

'No. I listened to an eight-hour monologue about *you*, Art. I feel as if I had personally videotaped your entire marriage. I know more about you than I know about Mike Atherton.'

'Who's Mike Atherton?'

'He's—'

'Jeremy—' Clare cut in. 'Carl and I have been writing letters back and forth for almost a year and a half; we never met but we had a long correspondence. Anna thought we should meet.'

'So you did meet,' Jeremy turned his eyes to Carl. 'And you've fallen in love with her.'

'Ooh, slick cookie,' Art thought. 'Jeremy ain't half bad. I'd like to kill him, but I have to admit I admire the hell out of his sang-froid. But then I guess I would have admired the hell out of Douglas Bader if I'd met him in Colditz. Maybe the Brits are at their best up close and impersonal.'

'Yes,' Carl said simply. 'I have fallen in love with Clare.'

Bernice's head bowed. She dropped five lumps of sugar into her cup, one by one.

'Clare?' Jeremy inquired as if he were asking a question to the next contestant on a game show. 'What about you? Have you fallen in love as well?'

'Someone please rescue me,' Clare prayed. 'I don't know what to say or do. I don't know anything.'

'Clare?' Carl's voice was wounded. 'Aren't you going to answer him?'

'I don't know.'

'Of course she doesn't know.' Art seized the second of silence following Clare's feeble response. 'Listen, Jeremy. Clare came out here thinking she was going to promote her book. She was landed on a television show, a *live* television show, and told that no, she wasn't going to promote her book, she was going to meet Carl. Well, the man she met on that show *wasn't* Carl – it was me pretending to be Carl. For reasons I can't be bothered to go into now, we switched identities, Carl and I. Until this afternoon, Clare thought *I* was Carl. You can imagine' – Art paused – 'you can imagine her relief when she met the real Carl. Then you two fly in unexpectedly. The point is, she's confused and she's upset and she doesn't need any hassle from anyone right now. She probably wants to go somewhere on her own and sit and think about everything. To collect herself and her emotions. She's been through the fucking ringer, OK?' Art's voice was rising; his tempo of speech picked up speed. 'And the least, the very least all of you can do is to let her be alone for awhile, instead of chewing over her bones like rival dogs.'

'Thank you, Artie,' Clare whispered.

'Oh, brilliant, truly brilliant. You fucked her when you were *pretending* to be Carl, didn't you? How low can you go, Art? Really.'

'No, I didn't fuck her at any point, Annie. In any identity. Not that it's any of your business. The ex at the beginning of ex-wife is there for a purpose, you know.'

'But you fucked Bernice?'

'Bernice and I fucked each other, thank you very much.'

Carl put his head in his hands and rubbed his forehead. He didn't want it to be like this. None of it. He wanted Clare back in his apartment, listening to the storm, sharing a beer, keeping him company in the lonely hours after midnight. At some stage during the day he'd lost his sense of humour and his interest in other human beings. All these people squabbling around him were unimportant – everything was unimportant except Clare, their correspondence, their relationship.

'Carl?' Bernice's voice was whispering at his side. 'It will be all right. Really. You'll get Clare in the end. You just have to be patient.'

Was she right? Carl wondered. Jeremy was like a visitor from another planet, so self-contained and authoritative with his lean athletic looks. So fucking British. Perhaps Artie had some reason all these years in his negative obsession with the British character. They *were* different – more cultured, more reserved, more . . . *British*.

'I suspect Art may be right,' Jeremy commented, putting both palms on the table top. 'Clare probably wants some time to herself. It sounds as if—'

'Absolutely,' Carl cut in. 'Clare, should we leave you alone? Is that what you want?'

'I want to go home,' Clare announced in a voice drained of emotion. 'I want to go back.'

'To England?' Carl asked.

'No, to Albania, Carlo.'

'Art, would you keep out of this? You've caused enough trouble already.'

'There's a flight tomorrow morning,' Jeremy stated. 'The British Airways day flight. I'll phone for tickets tonight.'

He can't conceal the victor's smile, Art thought.

'Why have I just shot myself in the foot?' Bernice asked herself. 'Why did I reassure Carl that Clare would be his in time? Because I know I'm going to lose and I have to be a good sport? I *hate* sports.'

'Um, do you want me to move out of the hotel room then, Clare?'

'No, please stay, Bernice. I'd like to keep it the way it was, you and I together. Jeremy, you can get a room, can't you?'

'If that's what you'd prefer.' He nodded.

'Anna? Can you get one too?'

'I suppose so. What's one more hotel room on my bill?'

This time Anna had a Esther Rantzen haircut, Bernice noted. She was wearing a tartan skirt and boxy jacket. The combined effect made her look like a female lacrosse coach.

'I'd offer my spare room, Annie,' Art said. 'But I don't think it would suit you.'

Unaccountably, Clare found herself thinking of Eddy Elephant.
Had Anna slept with Eddy Elephant during her marriage to Art?
The thought bothered her. As soon as she realized how irritated
she was, she started to laugh. There she was, sitting in a deli with
her two lovers, wildly jealous because her agent might have shared
a bed with a stuffed animal.

'What's so funny, Clare?' Carl was looking at her with a crazed,
desperate expression.

'Nothing,' she replied, chastened. Nothing was funny. She'd
effectively said goodbye to Carl when she'd announced that she
wanted to go back to London. This whole trip, she knew, would
fade with time. Her one effort to break out of the personality
pattern she'd woven over the years had failed. When the crunch
came, she had opted for the comfortable choice. She didn't have
the courage to risk a new life. 'Nothing's funny, Carl,' she repeated.
'I'm sorry.'

'You don't have to go,' he said, his eyes burning into hers.

'Yes, I do,' she replied. It all sounded like a soap opera. Now
she realized that she'd rather watch than participate.

'I'll pick up the tab for this, folks,' Art announced, rising from
his chair. 'And, Annie, why don't you and I go have a drink
somewhere and do a post-mortem on the corpse of our marriage?
In private.'

'All right,' Anna said glumly.

'What are you going to do, Carl?' Bernice asked.

'I'm going home. That's what Clare wants, is that right?'

Clare nodded.

'I'm sorry, Carl. It's my turn to apologize and grovel. I know
I said before that I . . . I just want to go, that's all. As soon as
possible. Can you understand that?'

'No,' he answered. 'And it's not over yet.'

'They think it's all over,' Jeremy paused. 'It is now.'

'What?' Carl looked at him. Art couldn't believe the hatred in
his friend's face.

'It's a sporting expression, Carl. I understand that we're rivals at the moment, but there's no need to hit me, I assure you. And now I think we can depart, can't we?'

'Do you believe the way this guy talks?' Carl murmured to Art as they rose from the table.

'Yeah,' Art replied. 'I've heard it all before.'

Filing out of the deli onto the pavement, the group stood for a moment in an ensemble, strangely reluctant to go their separate ways.

'Well, it's been real,' Art commented, taking Anna's arm.

'Let me know what's happening, Clare, don't try to pretend I don't exist,' Carl said, stepping out into the street and hailing a taxi. Before getting into the cab that had come gear-crunchingly to a stop in front of him, he turned back. 'No, Artie. You're wrong. It's been *unreal.*'

'Why? Why the Swamp Creature? That's so cruel, Art. Why do you have to be so cruel?'

Anna was, as it happened, sitting on Art's sofa, in the same position Clare had been the night before. She had said she would prefer his apartment to a bar, and he had gone along with her, more out of a sense of exhaustion than politeness.

'The Swamp Creature was just an expression,' he answered, trying to concentrate on his ex-wife. It was going to be difficult, he knew. His mind was back in that room in the Sheraton, with Clare. Would she really return to England or would she stay here . . . stay with Carl? In many ways, he hoped she would leave. The prospect of seeing her continually on Carl's arm was too much to bear. Yet the thought of her thousands of miles away was no picnic either.

'A horrid expression.'

'I know,' he replied.

'I loved you, Art.'

'You loved London more.'

'No. No, that's not true. I didn't want to leave, that's right. But you could have stayed. You could have stuck with me.'

'I was miserable there, Annie. We both know that. You took to the place, you adored it. If we'd had children, if we'd had a son, you would have put him down for Eton. I couldn't go along with that, don't you see? We were heading in such entirely different directions.'

'And now you're screwing an Englishwoman. A *girl*. A girl I *know*. If that's not throwing everything in my face, I don't know what is.'

'I didn't know you knew her,' Art was struggling to be patient. 'And Bernice is not a girl. She's ten years younger than you and I. That's no big deal. She happens to be English – you've got me there. Maybe I hate the nation *en masse* but not the English people individually.'

'Please.'

'OK, maybe I've changed. I don't know.'

That seemed to be the key phrase of the night, Art thought. The old 'I don't know' sidestep.

'Do you love her?'

'Do I love Bernice? No. I like her a lot, though.'

'I made her father rich and famous.'

'Really? That's terrific, Annie. I mean it. You're obviously doing well over there, you're—'

'And that's another thing. You becoming a literary agent. When I heard about it a couple of years ago, I almost flew over and murdered you. How dare you go into the same business as me?'

'Does it really matter?' Art asked wearily. 'We're on opposite sides of the pond, remember? We're not exactly in competition.'

'I loved you.' Anna's voice dropped. 'I've missed you. It's hard, Art. It's tough being over there. On my own. There were so many times I wanted to talk to you.'

'You should have talked to me. You should have called. Annie, I'm sorry things didn't work out, I really am. I know we couldn't be friends right after the breakup, but we could be *now*. I can imagine it's tough for you. I'd like to help.'

'Really?'

'Yes, really. We shouldn't have been incommunicado for so long. We met when we were so young, it's not really that surprising our marriage didn't work – we both had a lot of growing up to do. In different directions. My guess is that your pride was hurt because I was the one who left. But you were the one who stayed, so my pride was hurt, too.'

'It was?'

'Of course it was. I couldn't convince you to move back here with me – how do you think that made me feel?'

'You suffered?'

'Yes, Annie. I suffered. A lot.'

'Oh.' Anna uncrossed her legs and lay back on the sofa.

'Does that make you feel better?'

'Yes. Yes, it does. It's amazing how *much* better it makes me feel. I really believed our divorce didn't touch you, had absolutely no effect. I thought you walked away cheerfully – as if I'd had no impact on your life. I went crazy when Clare told me on the phone that she'd fallen in love with you. I couldn't come to terms with it. That's why I rang Jeremy and got him to come over with me. I was unbelievably jealous, Artie.'

'And what do you feel now?'

'Tired.' Anna yawned. 'And relieved. It's nice to talk to you like this. It feels comfortable, as if we *could* be friends. I would never have anticipated that.'

'Me neither, but it seems to be the case.'

Rising from the sofa, Art went into his bedroom and found a pair of pyjama tops. He came back into his living room and handed them to Anna.

'Why don't you sleep in the spare room?'

'I thought you said it wouldn't suit me.'

'Well, it will save on your hotel bill.'

'Art?' Anna looked up at him, then averted her eyes. 'What do you think? I mean, we could try—'

'I don't think so,' Art put his hand on her shoulder. 'It would

207

ruin this comfortable feeling we've got now, Anna. It would be an act of nostalgia.'

'I like nostalgia,' she said softly.

'So do I. But sex, when it's nostalgic, is too sad for me.'

'You mean you wouldn't be able to laugh?'

'I wouldn't be able to laugh,' Art agreed.

'Well, knowing you, I guess that settles it.' Anna took Art's outstretched hand and rose from the sofa.

'Here—' Art guided her to the spare room and turned on the light. 'The bathroom's on the right there, and there are some fresh toothbrushes and some toothpaste. Get some sleep. We can talk business, relationships, whatever you want to tomorrow morning.'

'Art—' Anna paused at the threshold. 'I'm glad you're not in love with Bernice. And I'm *especially* glad you're not in love with Clare.'

'Why's that?' Art tried to sound nonchalant.

'Because—' she hesitated. 'I can see you two together. There's honesty for you. Imagining you in bed with Bernice is bad enough, but Clare. I can imagine you falling in love with her and that's just—'

'Annie—'

'If I'd known about the switched identities, if I'd known you weren't involved with Clare, of course I wouldn't have called Jeremy. Anyway—' Anna smoothed her hands over her skirt.

'Yes?'

'I'm glad I did come. You know, it's strange being back in New York. Do you think I should move back here? I could—' she interrupted herself with a huge yawn.

'You're exhausted. Goodnight, Annie,' Art said, putting his hand on the small of her back and giving her a little nudge into the spare room.

Anna, after brushing her teeth, washing her face and combing out her hair, went to turn down the bed.

'Oh, no, not this fucking elephant again,' she mumbled, throwing Eddy onto the floor.

*   *   *

208

His parents hadn't gone through anything like this, Carl reflected, as he lay on his bed, his feet crossed at the ankles, his hands crossed on his chest. They had met, fallen in love and married. After which they had had six children. Sometimes they argued, sometimes they would even go a few days without speaking to each other, but his mother had never run away – which is what Dee-Dee had done and Clare was on the verge of doing.

Why did the women he loved flee from him?

Artie had said that Clare needed to be alone. Fat chance of her being alone when Jeremy was in the same country, the same *house*.

Artie had become really exercised on that point. He'd talked like some knight on a white charger, come to rescue her from the clutches of two disreputable suitors. Well, bully for Art. He could afford to be dispassionate because he didn't love her. It was easy, a cinch for him to come across as some gallant fucking saviour who had Clare's best interests at heart.

'Thank you, Artie,' he remembered Clare saying.

'Yeah, thank you, Artie. Thanks a lot. You made me and Jeremy look like selfish, egotistical assholes.'

But Art didn't count, not in this story. Art was a secondary character, not the hero.

And Jeremy might be a sporting hero, but he wasn't a romantic one. He didn't have the necessary emotional fire in him, that was clear.

Carl uncrossed his ankles and arms and sat up in bed, his thoughts beginning, finally, to get him somewhere interesting.

Paris kidnapped Helen of Troy. He took her out from under her husband's nose and spirited her away. That's what he had to do if Clare did go back to London. He had to work his ass off at any job which would give him enough cash to get there.

And meanwhile?

Meanwhile he'd write to her. He'd put it all down on paper, every single thought and feeling, every word in the world.

*   *   *

'Bernice—' Clare could hear her fumbling in the dark, trying to open the minibar door without making too much noise.

'Sorry, did I wake you up? I thought a glass of wine or something might help put me to sleep.'

'No, I couldn't sleep either. Bernice—' The sound of a beer can being opened interrupted Clare's question. 'Should I turn on the light?'

'No, no, I'm fine.' Bernice stumbled back to her bed.

'Are you? I think we should talk.'

'About what?'

'About Carl.'

'Oh.'

'Are you in love with him?'

'No.'

'But you told me you were this morning – I mean, you told me you were in love with Art, but we all know now what that means.'

'Yes, well, I admit, I had a crush on Carl. That's different from being in love. You know me, I could have a crush on practically any male I meet. I'd probably fall deeply in love with Jeremy Beadle if I happened to run across him.'

'Are you sure?'

'Well, maybe not Jeremy Beadle—'

'Bernice.'

'Yes, Clare. I'm sure. Look, I'm a slut, OK? I screwed Art this afternoon. How in love could I be if I jump into bed with the next man who shows the slightest interest in me?'

'Well, I jumped in bed with Carl this afternoon. I suppose that means I'm not in love with Jeremy.'

'Are you really going back with Jeremy tomorrow?'

'I'm going back, definitely. I need to get some distance from Carl, from this entire scene, right now. I *think* I love Carl, but then I *think* I still love Jeremy. The problem is, I don't *know* anything.'

'It's amazing that Art was married to Anna, isn't it?'

'It's unbelievable. Carl told me that Art calls her the Swamp Creature.'

Bernice laughed.

'But I feel sorry for Anna,' Clare said quickly. 'She thought I was in love with her ex-husband – that must have been such a shock. No wonder she dragged Jeremy along to split us up.'

'That was a fairly drastic response.'

'Maybe she still loves Art.'

'Anna? You think so?' Bernice took a swig from the can.

'I could see it in her eyes tonight. And Art, he's someone it's possible to be in love with for a long time, I think.'

'Really? Why?'

'His mind works in an interesting way. He's unpredictable.'

'He's certainly unpredictable in bed,' Bernice laughed. 'He's funny, too.'

'Funny?'

'He made me laugh – but then I was drunk, so it wasn't too difficult.'

'How did he make you laugh?'

'Clare, do you want all the intimate details?'

'No,' Clare said instantly. 'No, of course not.'

'I'll tell you if you like.'

'No, Bernice. Really.'

'I suppose Carl was perfect.'

'Bernice.'

'God, what's the point in sharing a room with another woman if we don't talk about sex?'

'Sleep. Sleep's the point.'

'Sleep's boring.'

'Good night, Bernice.'

Clare turned on her side, and tried not to think that she would be voluntarily flying out of Carl's perfect arms at ten o'clock the next morning.

211

Chapter 14

Christmas was only twenty shopping days away, but Clare hadn't bought one present. She hadn't done much of anything, really, since she'd come back from New York. Eight months of idleness was an awfully long time, she knew, but she couldn't bring herself to start a new novel or even to think of what she might write next.

In a fit of financial desperation, she'd done what she swore she never would. She'd used the money her father had left her in his will, which had been gathering mould, but more importantly, interest, in a special account at the Nat West. This wasn't money she deserved, she knew. She'd never been close to her father, she hadn't even gone to his funeral. Taking what he had willed to her seemed like crass behaviour and she wasn't proud of herself. She should have tended bar or waited on tables to avoid betraying her own ethics, but she couldn't summon up any energy whatsoever. All she could do was watch television: GMTV in the morning, followed by Richard and Judy followed by mindless drivel until *Neighbours* and repeats of *Columbo*.

During the summer months she'd roused herself enough to go to Jeremy's Test matches at Lord's and the Oval, but she didn't venture further afield. She wouldn't go as far as Old Trafford or Headingly. No, she stayed in London, in Angela's house, waiting.

For what? she asked herself, as she watched Fiona Phillips interview Liam Neeson. Was she waiting for Carl?

Every five days or so, she'd get another letter from him. He was saving up to come to London, but he hadn't managed to make enough yet. All he could earn just managed to keep his rent paid and himself fed. No magazines accepted his freelance articles, no publishers had any interest in the various ideas for books he came up with. *He* was the one tending bar. His letters were full of nicely observed tales of bar life – the characters who came in regularly, the couples who would erupt into arguments and end up tossing glasses of wine at each other – all sorts of stories which amused and diverted her.

They were also infused with yearning. He couldn't stop himself, it seemed. He'd pour out all his love and affection, as if he were serving from a limitless barrel.

'You can't know how much I have to offer you. If you did, you wouldn't have left. You can't honestly believe that you don't belong with me. It's a psychological impossibility, Clare. You can't play at being the person you were before you met me. You can't.

'I am a superstitious man. I'm even superstitious about my super-stitions. Until now I have never told anyone how I try to trick fate.

I never say the word goodbye, at least not to someone I want to see again. I'll say see you or adios or ciao or au revoir; sometimes I'll use catch you later. Since childhood I have had a terrible fear in my heart. If I say goodbye, that's it. I'll never see the person again. My whole family teases me about this all the time. But I've never given in to their teasing . . . I've held my ground.

'I haven't said "goodbye" to you, Clare. I will see you again. And again. And forever. I will never say goodbye.'

She didn't know how to respond to emotion like this. What she should have done, she did know, was to call the whole thing off as soon as she arrived back in London. She should have written

213

to Carl and explained that their romance, their friendship, their correspondence, were all over now. She should have settled back into life with Jeremy as it had been BC – Before Carl.

Yet she'd answered the letter which arrived five days after her return from New York, and she had continued to answer all his subsequent letters. Her replies to him, however, swung wildly in terms of their tone.

Sometimes she'd have moments of clarity when she realized she did love him madly, and she'd write back, if not an equally passionate reply, at least one which tried to express her strong feelings for him. But at others she couldn't summon up any emotion, and she'd end up penning a quick, neutral letter, a letter she knew would disappoint him.

He must have been desperately confused. If so, his mind reflected hers. She had come back, after all, back to London, back to Angela's and back to life with Jeremy. She had, supposedly, made up her mind.

Yet Carl was right. She couldn't play at being the person she'd been before she'd met him. Jeremy acted as if nothing had happened in New York. He never asked her the direct question, 'Did you sleep with Carl?', but those unspoken words seeped through the air of Angela's house like a slow gas leak. Clare felt, occasionally, that she should broach the subject and confess all to Jeremy, but she wasn't sure that knowledge was what Jeremy actually desired. If he'd *wanted* to talk about it, to thrash things out, he would have done so.

Clare would watch him batting and think, 'Yes, that's what he does in his personal life as well. He guards his wicket carefully.' Jeremy was normally caught out or out LBW. Sometimes run out. Very occasionally stumped. But Clare knew that he prided himself on the fact that he was so rarely bowled out. He didn't let the bowlers get past him. He didn't let anything through.

Everything was the same between them, superficially. He was polite, considerate, loving. She was polite, considerate and loving back. When he wasn't away playing a match, they stayed at home. He cooked. She watched TV.

Only now they made love a lot less often.

'Do you think maybe we should talk about our sex life some-time?' she'd offered timidly one morning after another evening without any physical contact.

'I think maybe you've been watching those talk shows too much,' he responded. And then he smiled. 'We don't need to talk. It will sort itself out.'

'I guess so,' she smiled back.

But the truth was, she felt relieved when he left at the end of November for the tour of the West Indies. She didn't know how to live intimately with a man who was becoming more and more of a stranger.

Many times she considered picking up the telephone and calling Art. He, she felt, might have some answers for her, or at least he might soothe her troubled psyche. 'So what's the program?' she imagined him asking, and the thought made her laugh. 'The programme's screwed up, Artie,' she would have answered. 'Let's go to some ridiculous restaurant and I'll tell you about it.' 'OK, I'll be right over,' she could hear him say. Artie, emerging from Customs at Heathrow, wearing one of his polka-dot ties, would have been a welcome sight. Clare thought of all the different, fun restaurants she would have liked to take him to for lunch before she stopped herself, remembering that the person she should be picturing herself with was not Art Rolfe but Carl Lioce.

'I'm not dying of grief, Clare,' Carl had written in the letter she'd received the day before. 'I'm not suicidal. But I'm desolate. There is an ineffable sadness in my heart. Sometimes I try to shake it off, but I don't want to, not really. Because I'll be damned if I'm going to let go of any part of you, any memory of you – however said it makes me in my present state.'

How was she going to reply to that? Of course, she should have stopped the correspondence as soon as she'd arrived back from New York. Whereas at first the letters had been reasonably harmless, now they were a deep, dark and very threatening secret. When Jeremy was at home, she had to make sure she got to the post before he did. If a letter from Carl awaited, she'd take it into the study and hide it away. This deception on her part made her feel inordinately guilty. Although she'd slept with Carl only once, she felt as if she'd been having an affair with him for years.

Perhaps she should go away somewhere – away from Jeremy *and* Carl. But where would she run to and what good would it do? Her life, she decided, glancing at the weather map on the television screen in front of her, was one huge fog bank of indecision.

When the phone rang, she started, unable to think who might be calling at eight-thirty in the morning. Not Jeremy, she knew. Even knowing she was an early riser, he was scrupulously careful to avoid any possibility of waking her up. Angela, perhaps? Could it be Angela? Was she on her way back?

'Clare?' She didn't recognize the male voice.

'Yes?'

'This is Art.'

'Art!'

'Yes. The one and only. Not Carl. Art. Let's get that straight.'

'What time is it? It must be three-thirty in the morning there.'

'It is. And it's cold as shit because the heating has gone off which is ridiculous given the amount of money I pay for this place. Anyway, I wanted to ask you something.'

'What?' Clare reached for the remote control on the kitchen table and switched off the TV.

'Well, just for something to do while I freeze to death here, I re-read some of your correspondence with Carl.'

'Yes?'

'And it strikes me as strange – the way you felt when you were a kid – I mean, I understand the asthma problem, I get that. But I don't understand why that made you so frightened of *everything*.

216

The ambulances carrying dead bodies of someone you knew, all that stuff. The general fear, not the specific fear of your own disease or possible death. Do you see what I mean—'

'Yes,' Clare nodded, as if he were in the room with her. 'I've never understood that myself. I mean, lots of children have asthma and I'm sure they didn't have the same worries of the world exploding or all the electricity going off for ever.'

'You're not just worried about yourself, that's what intrigues me. And the fear – it's so damn intense.'

'It *was*. It's gone now. I had a small taste of it before that television show, a small attack of asthma which brought the general fear, as you put it, back. I saw this endless graveyard with children's bodies – it was horrible – anyway, it didn't last long. And it hasn't come back. I'm beginning to think that the asthma isn't real – I mean, that after I was six or seven or so I grew out of it physically, but not mentally.'

'Well, *I* think something happened to you.'

'Excuse me?'

'Something you don't remember – something not connected with the asthma exactly. Something really, really scary.'

'Artie, have you been drinking?'

'Of course I have, but not a lot.'

'You sound like you suspect something evil in my past. I *know* I wasn't abused by my father or any other man when I was a child. I know I would remember that.'

'I'm not saying you were abused, necessarily, OK? I'm not saying that. It's just all so strange – you don't feel any panic when your plane is crashing, but you stay up all night listening to the radio to make sure there hasn't been some Holocaust when you're safe and snug in your room in Kensington. It's weird, Clare. Really. I think something happened to upset you, to make you feel the way you did. It could be anything—'

'Such as?'

'I don't know. Why don't you ask your mother?'

'Oh, come on. She'd laugh at me. Not that my mother

217

laughs very often, but she's English, Art, and we don't go in for psychobabble.'

'I'm aware of that. Alright, forget it. It was just an idea I had. I—'

'How's Carl?'

'He's working his ass off trying to get to you. Don't you know that?'

'Yes . . . yes, I know that.'

'And how's Jeremy?'

'He's in the West Indies.'

'I asked how he is, Clare, not *where* he is.'

'He's fine,' Clare said. 'He acts as if nothing happened in New York.'

'Well, did it? Did anything happen in New York?'

'What do you mean, Art?'

'You know what I mean.'

'No, no I don't.'

'Of course you do. You're trying to sidestep it, that's all.'

'Artie, please. I don't understand what you mean. You're making me feel as if I'm in a session with a really perverse shrink.'

'OK,' he laughed. 'Fair enough. It's nice to hear your voice, anyway.'

'How's Eddy?'

'He's lost his other eye, otherwise he's in great shape.'

'How did you get this telephone number?'

'I looked it up in Carl's London telephone book under Angela's name – just in case I had to call and congratulate you on winning the Booker Prize.'

'I'm not writing at the moment.'

'What are you doing?'

'I'm wasting time. Artie . . . what are you wearing?'

'Jesus, Clare,' he paused. 'Do you *really* want to do this?'

'I didn't mean . . . oh God,' she started to laugh. 'I meant . . . are you wearing your polka-dot tie?'

'No. But I was. I took it off at about two-thirty in the morning, actually. I didn't think anyone would object. I'll put it back on if it's a problem for you.'

'It is. Put it on right now, Art. Right this second.'

'Clare?'

'Artie, I'm joking. Really. Listen, have you been to that Sub-marine restaurant lately?'

'I go there all the time. You're asking some strange questions. Did I wake you up?'

'No, no. I've been up for a while, actually. Watching TV. It's a really exciting life I lead.'

'I think you're drunk again. And you're still cute when you're drunk, even at eight-thirty in the morning. I should be advising you to call A. A. Instead, I'll tell you once more – talk to your mother. Find out if anything happened when you were a kid that could have provoked your old panicked responses. As a special favor to me. It's a long shot, but I think you should take it. It can't hurt.'

'No, I suppose it can't.'

'Good – and take care of yourself.'

Art hung up then, before saying goodbye, and Clare looked questioningly at the receiver for a moment before reaching for the remote control again.

Carl was a lousy bartender, he knew. If he wasn't sure how to make a drink, he would improvise and put whatever he'd concocted in front of the customer, saying 'No charge.' He also handed out many free drinks on a whim – if he thought the man or woman ordering had a broken heart, for example. Or if a derelict wino happened in off the street asking for a cherry brandy as if it were the elixir of life.

Peter Fitzgerald, the owner of O'Malley's bar, was a friend of Carl's older brother and Carl knew Peter was rolling in dough. Still, it wasn't fair to rip him off like that and Carl knew sooner or later he'd get fired. Probably sooner rather than later.

219

The atmosphere of the place was helpful, though, and Carl knew he would miss it. Suffering as he was from a profound sense of discouragement regarding his inability to make a living by writing, and the impossibility of seeing Clare again, Carl was happy to be in a place where most people seemed to be discouraged as well. O'Malley's wasn't Cheers, that was for sure. There weren't a lot of laughs and he wasn't a patch on Sam Malone. However, at this precise juncture in his life, he needed to be with people who were as unfulfilled as he was.

When he looked up from wiping down the bar to see Dee-Dee standing in front of him, he felt his heart lurch in the same way he did whenever he saw one of Clare's airmail envelopes sitting in his mail slot.

'Happy Christmas,' she said.

'It's only the beginning of December,' he replied.

She didn't speak, but sat down on a stool and flicked a thick strand of dark hair back off her forehead.

'Can I get you something?' he asked.

She gave a small shrug.

'Dee-Dee?'

'A glass of white wine, I guess.'

After pouring it and placing it in front of her, Carl hesitated. What did she want? What could she possibly want from him? Had she come here to gloat? Was that book of hers going to be a success? He hadn't dared to ask Art about it, not that he saw Art that often these days, anyway. A feeling of discomfort in Art's presence had made him avoid Art lately. He didn't know why Art should have this effect on him, but put it down to a hangover from those hours Art had pretended to be him. That had been an unsettling experience and Carl, though he wasn't sure why, had come to mistrust Art slightly.

'Can I help you with anything else?' he asked, leaning on the counter.

'I'm not sure.' Dee-Dee had an unnerving way of looking at you with a high-beam stare until she'd effectively shamed you

220

into bashful blinking. 'I want to know if I can trust Art. I want to know your take on him.'

'You tracked me down for that?'

'More or less. He hasn't sold my book. I don't think he's even *trying* to sell my book. I'm thinking of switching agents, but it's kind of like a divorce, you know. It's not an easy step to take.'

'No?' Carl didn't know what to say. There was an element of self-confidence in Dee-Dee's voice which made it difficult to yell at her and say, 'He hasn't sold anything of mine, either, kiddo, and I've been writing a hell of a lot longer than you have.' Being bitchy to her wouldn't help him feel any better either, he knew. Beyond all the hurt and pain she'd caused him lay Carl's familial feeling for her. He was not the kind of man who could ever, once he had fallen completely in love, fall completely out of it.

'Art's told me he's done the best he can, he's said a lot of the right things – how he was amazed by how quickly I could write, what an ambitious book I'd attempted. But that might be the usual stuff any agent says to a client, I don't know. That's why I came here. I thought you might know if he's just stringing me along.'

'Art's called me ambitious, sure. But he's never called me "quick." Which doesn't surprise me, actually. I'm not.'

'Oh, Carl.' Dee-Dee placed her cool hand on Carl's forearm, then removed it. 'I'm so tired. I've tried *so* hard. You don't know. You don't know what I've tried to convey in this work. It's—'

'Awesome?'

'Yes,' she nodded . . . somewhat sadly, he thought. 'It is.'

Making fun of her wasn't any more satisfactory than yelling at her, Carl realized, although she had probably distilled every seminar she'd ever attended into a huge tome of collected banality, which if he read, he would throw down in disgust. But she was trying – which is more than he could say for himself lately – aside from his letters to Clare. Dee-Dee was making an effort. And the way she sat on the stool, leaning forward at a slight tilt, sipping her wine with the lipstickless lips he remembered kissing, touched him deeply.

221

'Are you happy, Dee-Dee?' he asked.

She shrugged again, suddenly prompting Carl to a recollection of Jeremy Letts shrugging at the table in that deli. Jeremy and Dee-Dee were both athletes of a sort, Carl reflected. Their bones, their movements, even their shrugs were graceful.

'Are *you* happy?' She threw the question back at him. He couldn't tell from her tone whether she cared or not.

'I'm in love with an Englishwoman who is living in London with another man, a sports star,' he said, feeling as if he were back in church, confessing.

'Oh,' she said. 'I see. Well, I'm not jealous, that's not in my nature. I hope it works out for you. But I don't think you've explored the depths of your nature, Carl. When we were together, you were so stifling.'

'Stifling?' He waved away a middle-aged woman waiting to be served.

'That's what I'd call it, yes. Stifling. You never listened to me.'

'You never talked . . . until the end, when you talked all the time and I didn't understand what you were talking about.'

'That's it, that's it exactly. You never understood. You wouldn't allow any real expression, you liked me *mute*.'

'What?'

'You heard what I said.'

'Dee-Dee . . . I . . .' Carl enraged, exasperated and at a loss, leant across the bar and kissed her with a passion he couldn't believe he was allowing himself to feel.

'There—' he shouted when he drew away. 'There – I like your mouth open or shut or in *any* position, all right?'

'As long as I don't say anything.'

'Come on—' Climbing over the bar in what he knew was an uncoordinated movement, Carl lowered himself to the floor beside his ex-wife and grabbed her hand. 'We're going to bed.'

'OK,' Dee-Dee shrugged. She didn't smile.

*   *   *

Bernice hovered over her telephone, her dialling finger twitching with desire.

What excuse did she have? Could she wish him an early Merry Christmas? No, that was terminally lame. She would have to think of a better excuse. But what? Every night she struggled with this desperate wish to call Carl, and every morning when she woke up, she would congratulate herself on not giving in to it. The strong possibility that he'd sound bored, or indifferent, or – even more likely – that he'd initiate a long conversation about Clare, kept her from succumbing to temptation. At least, she thought, she could still harbour a slice of hope. As long as she didn't have her worst fears confirmed, she could indulge in her ludicrous fantasies.

The ache to pick up the phone and dial would gradually build over the course of the day, and she'd be in exactly the same position each evening, like a drug addict yearning for a fix. 'Take it one day at a time,' she kept telling herself, but she couldn't understand why time hadn't helped her. The passage of eight months should have assuaged the pain, she knew. She should have forgotten Carl's face, his voice, his mannerisms. But she hadn't. Occasionally, she'd fall off the wagon and dial Carl's number, then hang up before the first ring had even sounded.

Obviously, she couldn't confide in Clare, and all her other friends were sick of hearing her talk about it. They'd either tell her it was a lost cause or advise her to fly to New York again and look him up. Bernice couldn't bring herself to give up, nor did she want to force the issue and confront him. Her heart was doing a contorted and painful limbo dance. The bar kept getting lower, she kept struggling to go under it and come out standing straight on the other side. How low can you go? she'd ask herself. And the answer was always 'One more inch'. Soon she'd be prostrate on the floor. But she hadn't quite arrived at that position, not yet.

Clare and she still conversed on a regular basis, but they avoided dangerous topics. Unfortunately, those blacklisted topics had become so far-ranging in their scope, conversation was strained. If Clare mentioned anything to do with America, whether it be to do with politics or an item on the news, Bernice would immediately change the subject. All the while Bernice carefully avoided asking even the simplest question about Jeremy and/or Carl.

They were becoming skilled in skirting or deflecting troubling talk, but the nature of their friendship was changing organically. They were no longer confidantes, they were acquaintances.

A man shouldn't be necessary to her life, Bernice knew. A man shouldn't interfere with a female friendship. Especially a man who had no interest in her. She had a half-way decent job and a half-way decent life. She should get on with it.

What she definitely *shouldn't* do was re-visit Marie in Harlesden. Yet she'd done exactly that this afternoon. Marie had, after all, predicted that Bernice would marry a man she met abroad. Of course at the time Bernice had assumed this was Paul, but the other day, she'd been leafing through *Time Out*, come to the section in the back with ads for psychics and remembered her meeting with Marie. Marie could have been talking about Carl, she thought. Marie might know something crucial about the future.

The stained green carpet Bernice recalled from her last visit to Marie's had deteriorated to the point of almost non-existence. The flock wallpaper was peeling in sympathy. And Marie's front tooth had disappeared. Did Fergie first meet Madame Vasso in a place like this? Bernice wondered, trying to visualize the Duchess of York in these surroundings. Actually, she decided, it was surprisingly easy to imagine.

Marie had eschewed the all-white look and was dressed in what looked to Bernice like a Donna Karan navy blue suit. The effect of this discrepancy was jarring and Bernice asked politely if she could smoke.

'Absolutely not,' Marie replied and Bernice quickly stuffed her packet of Silk Cut back into her bag.

'You've got dental problems,' Marie announced, sitting down on a folding wooden chair.

Refraining from saying, 'No, *you* do,' Bernice deposited herself on another chair at the small round table. She could hear a man yelling at someone in the next room.

'You have dental problems and man problems,' Marie continued.

'Now we're getting somewhere,' Bernice thought.

'They're similar, men and bad teeth,' Marie said. Bernice waited for further illumination. It didn't come.

'Will I solve my man problems?' she asked timorously.

'You're going to marry a man you'll meet on a trip abroad.'

'Mmm,' Bernice nodded, simultaneously slightly irritated and hugely relieved. 'You've told me that before – the last time I came. Can you tell me a little more about that?'

'No.'

'No?'

'I'm not receiving anything else.'

'Do you know . . . can you tell if he's in love with someone else?'

'He's difficult,' she replied, frowning. 'I am getting something on that. He's a painter?'

'A painter? No, he's a writer.'

'Yes,' Marie sounded exasperated. 'He paints pictures with words. As I said. He's a painter. He's married.'

'He *was* married.'

'Yes.'

'And he's going to marry me?'

'How do I know?'

'But you said—'

'I said you'd marry a man you meet abroad. That could be this man, the painter, or it could be another man.'

'I see.'

'Good. Now do you want to contact any of your dearest who have departed?'

'I don't know, it's complicated, my family. You see I'm adopted and—'

'Shh. I knew you were adopted. Obviously. The point is not

that. The point is that your great-grandfather is here. Now. Don't talk so fast.'

'I wasn't—'

'Not you. Slow down—' she looked over her shoulder and waved her hand up and down in the air. 'I *hear* you. Lower your voice. That's better. Yes.' She turned back to Bernice. 'He says you should go to the dentist soon. He also says that you should write a book.'

'A book?'

'On Celtic myths.'

'What?'

The voice of the man in the next room was getting louder. 'Fuck off, you wanker' she heard him scream, then sounds of pounding on the flimsy dividing wall started up.

'Celtic myths. Go away now—' Marie twisted in her seat, and shooed the air.

'All right. How much do I—'

'Not *you*. Him. Your noisy great-grandfather. Do you want to do the Tarot cards now?'

'I think I'll skip those.' Bernice rose from her chair. 'How much do I owe you?'

'Fifty quid.'

'Fifty quid? Last time it was twenty-five and I stayed longer.'

'Is that my problem?'

'No,' Bernice sighed. 'It isn't.'

Carl would love that story, Bernice thought, picking up the telephone and punching out his number. Too bad I can't tell him.

Before it had a chance to ring, she gently replaced the receiver in its cradle for the night.

Chapter 15

'Dee-Dee—' Art rubbed his eyes. 'It's two-thirty in the morning. I've just managed to get some sleep because the idiots just managed to get my heating back on this afternoon. I am a literary agent, not Dr Kildare. I don't take business calls after I leave the office and I sure as hell don't do house calls. Can't this wait until the morning?'

'You don't understand, Art. This is important. I've just had sex with my ex-husband and that changes everything, don't you see?'

'No. I don't.'

'The book. *Shescape.* This puts a different twist on the book. I want to write it in. I think it should be the penwhatever chapter.'

'Penultimate?'

'Yes.'

'Do you mean to say you're going to describe sex with Carl in vivid detail? I don't think I want to read that, Dee-Dee, and I doubt that your public do, either.'

'What *is* Carl doing?' Art asked himself. 'He's deranged. There is no way I could have stuck with this woman for two days much less two years and now he's taken another helping.'

'This is about sex as a conceptual entity.'

'Have you conceived? Is that what you're telling me?'

227

'Art . . . please. Listen to me . . . No one ever listens to me properly.'

Ah, it was dawning on him now. Finally. Her voice. She had a homeless person's voice, combined with the looks of a Greek goddess. She was so out to lunch, she'd appeal to Carl. He would have liked her peculiar, misguided belief in herself and her Grail-like quest for meaning. She would play on all those underdog strings in his psyche.

'I'd be very happy to listen to you. In office hours, Dee-Dee. I'm tired. I can't concentrate. Give me a break.'

'Oh,' she replied, after pausing for a moment. 'I'll call you tomorrow, then. Or should I come by?'

'Call me,' Art said firmly. 'Call me anytime tomorrow – but, Dee-Dee, try to hold off until at least seven a.m., will you?'

When he lay his head back on the pillow, Art struggled to recreate the dream he'd been having. There had been a swimming pool beside a villa in some unidentifiable Mediterranean country. A small but perfectly formed submarine lay at the bottom of the pool. And a terrorist equipped with a heat-seeking missile stood poised to shoot from a neighbouring rooftop.

What the hell was that supposed to mean?

Uncomfortable in her mother's presence, Clare squirmed in the chintz chair, before sitting up perfectly straight.

'I don't understand what you're getting at, Clare,' her mother said. 'Of course going to the hospital itself may have been frightening. But the doctors were wonderful and competent; what's more I would think you would have felt safer there than anywhere else.'

'Maybe it didn't happen in hospital.'

'*What? What* didn't happen in hospital? Honestly, I don't understand. Are you seeing some kind of analyst?'

'No,' Clare's shoulders slumped. 'I used to be really terrified all the time, that's all.'

'You never told me.'

'I know.'

'Are you blaming me for something in your past?'

'No.' Clare regarded her mother. She was perfectly coiffed, perfectly dressed, elegantly simple as always. The poise and quiet her mother exuded stopped Clare from saying anything more. This had been a wasted trip, she knew. Why had she listened to Art?

'Well, I know you always wanted me to take you to those dreadful places like Blackpool, but I can't see my failure to do so as terrifying in any way. Perhaps you're thinking of the plane crash in Spain?'

'No. It started before the crash.'

'When exactly did "it" start?'

Her mother was trying to help, Clare knew, even though her effort was clinical and dispassionate. She was using the same tone she had used long ago when arguing with Clare's father. He would be screaming and ranting, and her mother would answer in the voice of a census taker. It must have driven Dad mad, Clare decided, stunned by the surge of sympathy she suddenly felt for him.

'I'm not sure when "it" started.'

'Well, that's not particularly helpful, I'm afraid.'

The conversation was coming to an end, Clare knew. Her mother hadn't asked her about either Jeremy or her work, which was a blessing. She should quit while she was ahead.

'I think I'll be going now.' She offered to clear away the teacups, but her mother refused.

'I can do it,' she said.

Her mother, like Jeremy, would not allow Clare to help. Was that why she often felt like a child in Jeremy's presence? Were Jeremy and her mother more similar than she had ever imagined? She'd never seen her mother do anything or act in any manner which was not thoroughly admirable and mature. Like Jeremy, her mother didn't drink. Like Jeremy, she didn't smoke. Neither of them ever yelled. And they didn't, as far Clare knew, ever cry.

'You wanted me to be grown up from the day I was born,' Clare thought, looking at her. 'Why was it that having to be so grown up all the time has made me more of a child?'

'Before you go, Clare, I should tell you I've been thinking of selling this house. It's far too big for me and I don't know why I've stayed here all these years.'

'Where will you go?'

'I've seen a flat in Chelsea. Markham Street.'

'That sounds nice.'

'I've put in an offer for it, actually. And a friend of a friend seems set to buy this place. So it's only a matter of time.'

'Good.' Clare couldn't think of what to say next except goodbye, but she hung back for a minute.

'I've cleared out your room. I hope you don't mind.'

'Of course not. There was nothing in it that I need any more – only my stuffed animals. I can get a bag and take them with me now, if you'd like.'

'I've given them away.' Clare's mother frowned. 'I'm sorry. I thought you'd outgrown them ages ago. I gave them to the Brompton Hospital, in fact.'

'Oh. Well, that makes sense. I remember always wanting one with me when I went there.'

'I never understood why.'

'Company, I guess.' Comfort, she wanted to add, but didn't. Her mother was standing perfectly straight with teacups in both hands.

'I remember you were ridiculously attached to one of them – that dog. I was worried for a while. It seemed unnatural.'

'What dog? Sit down, please. We can clear the cups together in a minute.'

'No. I'll do it now.' She walked off to the back of the house with the cups, leaving Clare sitting, feeling useless, like a pathetic child.

'She can do it so easily,' Clare thought. 'She can reduce me to a little girl again within seconds.'

When she came back, her mother was holding a tray. Placing

230

the Sèvres teapot, the sugar and the cream on the tray, she started to move towards the kitchen again, but stopped.

'In answer to your question about that stuffed dog. I can't remember its name, I think one of your godparents gave it to you for your birthday. You wouldn't let go of it. It was like a dummy, and I always disapproved of dummies. Unhygienic. You wouldn't be separated from the dog. Then, thank God, you gave it away.'

'I did?'

'Yes, to a girl in the bed beside you in the ward.'

'Why? If I loved it so much?'

'I didn't say you *loved* it, Clare. I said you were attached to it. And you were very grown up for your age – even then, when you were only five or so. You thought she needed it more than you. *I* thought that was a very healthy and mature response.'

'Why did she need it more than I did?'

'I don't know—' her mother looked annoyed and sounded it. 'I must put this in the kitchen.' She disappeared again, leaving Clare wanting to scream in frustration. Had it been like this all through her childhood? she asked herself. Yes, basically, it had.

'Right,' her mother said when she came back for the second time. 'That's done. The girl you gave the dog to had something wrong with her heart, if I remember correctly. It's a Heart and Lung hospital, the Brompton, you know. There were children in there with heart problems, with cystic fibrosis, all sorts of very serious complaints.'

'What was her name?'

'Clare – really – how would I know? You were friends with her, you gave her that dog and then she died. I have to admit that I was relieved when her parents took the dog with them. I was really getting quite irritated by that dog. It looked so tatty.'

'She died? Where?'

'In the hospital.'

'In the operating theatre?'

'No. She was in the bed beside yours. She died there after the

231

operation. Unexpected complications of some kind. I came in right after it had happened. Apparently it had all been pandemonium. Doctors and nurses rushing to her bed, frantic attempts to revive her. And that was complicated even further when the electricity shut down.'

'What?'

'There was a power cut, but only for a very short time. It made no difference in her case. At least that's what a nurse told me later.'

'Why didn't you tell me about this before?'

'I didn't see why I should bring it up. It's not a natural thing to talk about, and you didn't seem affected by it.'

'I didn't?'

'No. Not as far as I can remember. You probably didn't take it in.'

'Oh yes, I did,' Clare thought. 'I took it in so far I buried it. And it was resurrected as a monster.'

'What a fuck-up,' Carl said, looking at Art with a mournful expression. 'I can't believe I did it. How could I have betrayed Clare like that?'

'Listen, Carlo—' Art shifted his weight, trying to make himself comfortable on Carl's lumpy sofa. 'The odds are that Clare hasn't been chaste herself. Remember Jeremy. I really wouldn't describe this as rank betrayal. However, *I* don't appreciate being woken up at two-thirty a.m. in order to hear a lunatic woman telling me about your sex life. Try to lay off Dee-Dee, will you? It's not good for any of us. She's nuts.'

'I couldn't bear to ask you before. Is the book awful?'

'It's worse than awful. It's dire. It's dismal. It's hysterically bad. I shouldn't have shown it to anyone – there are people out there who are sniggering behind my back these days. They can't believe I took her on. Neither can I.'

Carl's phone rang and continued to ring.

'Why don't you answer it?'

'I wait until the thirteenth ring.'

'Of course. How stupid of me. This must be some kind of superstitious gesture to the ghost of Thomas Edison.'

'No, I don't want to be disturbed, that's all. If someone is patient enough to hold out for thirteen rings, then they deserve to disturb me.'

Picking up the receiver finally, Carl answered by quoting his telephone number. After a second, his previously gloomy face lit up.

'Clare, how fantastic! This is amazing. I've been thinking about you.'

Art stood up, sat down, then stood up again and disappeared into Carl's kitchen.

'I know we've never spoken on the telephone before,' Clare said, 'but I couldn't wait to write you a letter about what's happened, what I found out this morning.'

'What did you find out?'

'Why I was so frightened when I was a child. A friend suggested that I go to see my mother, that she might tell me something about my childhood which could help explain my fear. And when I did go, my mother let something slip almost accidentally. A girl beside me in the ward at the hospital died. A girl I'd made friends with. She died in the bed beside me and the electricity went off for a while, so, you see, it all makes sense now. I must have been watching, I *know* I watched everything and it was terrible.'

'Which friend?'

'I don't know her name. She had some kind of heart trouble, apparently.'

'No, I mean which friend suggested you go see your mother?'

'What a ridiculous question to ask,' Carl thought, his heart pumping. 'How stupid. But I'm jealous. Someone else helped her. Not me. That's not right. It should have been me. Why didn't I think of it?'

'A friend you don't know,' was Clare's response.

233

'What an irrelevant, stupid question for him to ask,' she said to herself. 'And now I'm lying to him again. How did this happen?'

'And you honestly think that's what's at the bottom of all your fears? Are you sure? I mean, you might not have been in your bed at the time the girl died.'

'I was on a drip, Carl. I was in no shape to wander around the wards, spreading goodwill. I was six years old.'

'You're fucking up you're fucking up,' Carl's brain kept telling him.

'Well,' he tried to appease her. 'That's amazing.'

'I thought so.'

The rebuke in her tone hit him so hard that he bent over.

'So do I. Really. I mean, it *does* all make sense.'

'You can recoup,' he told himself. 'You have to recoup. And quick.'

'It all fits into place, Clare. Every time you saw an ambulance and thought it was carrying the dead body of someone you knew. You must have been thinking of her. And your fear that all the electricity would go off forever. You probably thought the doctors who were at her bedside looked like scary monsters – especially when the lights went out. All these figures looming in the dark. Death. Destruction. I can just imagine it.'

'I keep trying to remember her name.'

Carl couldn't tell whether she'd softened towards him or not.

'Maybe you should go out and buy one of those name books pregnant women get when they can't decide what to call their child. There are lists of every name imaginable. That might jog you into remembering.'

This was a reasonable suggestion, Clare thought. So why did it annoy her so much?

'That's an idea,' she forced herself to say with some enthusiasm. 'Anyway, enough about me. How are you?'

'I'm missing you like crazy. Otherwise, I'm surviving. It's snowing

234

here at the moment. You'd love it. There is that magical time before the snow turns to slush and Manhattan looks like a winter wonderland.'

'It must be beautiful. Like the city after a thunderstorm.'

'We're back to safe ground,' Carl thought, smiling. 'Back to our correspondence, back to our real selves.'

'Exactly. I'll write to you about it this afternoon.'

'Maybe you could ring me sometime. If you felt like it. I know it's expensive, but we could keep it short,' she said, surprised at how timidly the words came out. She needed to talk to him sometimes, to get his response to her feelings straight away. Hearing his voice might help her sort out her confusion. Was she responding to him now as a lover? A friend? At this precise moment, he'd put her on edge, perhaps because they weren't used to talking to each other. Ninety-nine per cent of their relationship, she realized, was based on letters and sex. They had spent probably a maximum of two hours actually talking to each other.

'That's a good idea,' Carl replied, wondering why she needed this phone contact when what they had together in print was so perfect. How could he get across what he wanted to in transatlantic calls, when every sentence spoken was an immediate response capable of being misinterpreted? What had happened to her sense of purity? Her sense of time? Why did she suddenly want to speed-read?

If she'd written to him about seeing her mother and remembering the death of her friend, he could have responded properly. The goddamn telephone had screwed things up. They should either see each other in person and read each other's face the way they read each others' words, or not communicate audibly at all. Telephones sucked.

'So . . .' Clare paused. 'I have to go now.'

'I *will* get some money together soon, Clare, I know I will. And I'll be over there before you know it.'

'That would be wonderful,' she said. 'I'll call you again sometime soon. I know you don't say goodbye, so I won't either.'

235

'Alright. But I want the last words. I love you, Clare.'

As he was on the verge of hanging up, Carl heard a tune playing in the background, and voices singing 'Neighbours, everybody needs good neighbours . . .'

'Clare – wait a second – what's that? Who is singing?'

'Nobody.'

'Nobody? I can hear music and singing.'

'It must be a crossed wire,' she said. 'I've really got to go.'

Art emerged from the kitchen when he could no longer hear Carl speaking. He'd struggled with himself, wanting to listen in, but he'd reasoned that he didn't actually want to know what they were discussing. Whatever it was, it sure as hell wasn't Clare admitting to a new-found love for a bespectacled American literary agent.

'So. How is she?' Not asking, he knew, would have seemed unnatural.

'She was excited because she'd discovered what had made her so frightened as a child. Some friend of hers suggested she go ask her mother, which she did, and it turns out that she had been in a hospital bed beside some girl who died.'

'Really?'

'Yeah, and the lights went out or something.'

'You sound dismissive, Carl. That must have been a revelation for Clare.'

'A revelation brought upon by some so-called friend. She said I didn't know the friend, but I bet it's Jeremy.'

'I wouldn't think so.'

'Why not?'

'I don't think that's Jeremy's style – prodding someone to delve into childhood traumas.'

'How the hell would you know what Jeremy's style is?'

'I don't.' Art put up his hands in a gesture of self-defense. 'Relax. I suppose that was an observation on Englishmen in general.'

'I am sick of your English phobia, Artie. I really am sick of it.'

'OK,' Art reached for his tie to straighten it. 'I should be leaving.

I was supposed to meet my client for lunch at that restaurant around the corner from here ten minutes ago. I shouldn't keep him waiting. But Carl—'

'Yes?'

'Have you ever considered that you may not be in love with Clare after all, that you may have to *think* you're in love with her because of the weight of all that correspondence – which, after all, seems to me to constitute a kind of fantasy world? I mean, it's not reality, is it? It's not as if you had lived with her for fifteen months. You just *wrote* to her.'

'You seem to be forgetting the fact that I met her, Art. I slept with her. I saw her sitting on my bed in there—' Carl pointed to his bedroom, 'wearing my shirt. It was no fantasy. The sex was—'

'No,' Art covered his ears with his hands. 'I've heard enough about your sex life, thank you.'

'Well, don't try to second-guess my feelings, to analyze them away, then. You're against her, you've always been against her just because she's English. You're fucking zenophobic.'

'I'm fucking bored with this drama, that's what I am.' Art had risen and walked to the front door. He had one hand on the doorknob and the other clenched in his coat pocket. 'This is never-ending. And I'll tell you something else, I don't think you really want it to end. I don't believe you really want to go to England and close the deal. You like this lovesick, suffering artist persona. You get to be the underdog. What's a flight to London cost? It can't be *that* much off season. I can't believe that you haven't saved enough in seven months, Carl. I think you like it this way. You thrive on the distance. But you should know it's getting tedious for the rest of us who have to hear about it non-stop. *I'll* give you the money to go to England and get this all settled.'

'I can't take your money if you offer it in that kind of spirit. It's tainted.'

'Come off it, Carl—'

'No, Artie. You have no sensibilities. You don't understand

people. All you care about is money and "deals" and twenty-something girls. I used to think you had a generous heart. Now I think your heart was transplanted from Scrooge before he met up with the Ghosts.'

'Thanks,' Art said, pulling the door open. 'Thanks a lot.'

'You're very welcome,' Carl answered, turning his back.

Chapter 16

'I'm a lot like Cliff Richard,' Simon McKay stated, leaning back in his chair. Bernice recognized the pattern on the chintz material covering it. Clare's mother had the same in her house. 'I'm a star here. I'm a star in Europe. But the States? No one has ever heard of Simon in the States.'

'Simon the Skunk or Simon McKay?'

'We're inseparable.'

'Ecstasy. I need a tab of Ecstasy,' Bernice thought. 'Then I'd hug my father and have good feelings. I wouldn't notice the way he patronizes me, I might not mind the Paco Rabanne stench – or the pathetic teenage clothes he wears. But then I'd probably end up on the front page of the *Daily Mail*. "Twenty-eight-year-old Woman takes Ecstasy for First Time and Falls Down Dead at Famous Skunk Creator's Feet".

'You're inseparable? You're telling me that you're inseparable from a *skunk*?'

'Bernice, why do you always have to be so antagonistic towards Simon?'

'I don't like his politics.'

'Don't be facetious.'

'I'm not. He runs the Forest of Dean as if it were his own private fiefdom. Who died and made him King of the Animals?'

'Let up,' Bernice told herself, 'Don't give him yet another excuse

239

to be disappointed in you. It's not his fault that he couldn't have children. It's not really his fault that I'm adopted. It's my natural parents' fault. They're the ones who gave me up. So why do I keep making trouble for the people who took me in?'

Tuning out on her father's staunch defence of Simon the Skunk's political position in regard to the other animals in the forest, Bernice forced herself back in time, to nine years previously, when she had gone to South Africa to find her 'real' mother.

Simon had told her she was adopted at such an early age that she couldn't remember any shock or disappointment. As time went by, however, and her behaviour met with close to constant parental disapproval, she bought into the classic fairy-tale vision of a perfect real mother and father: two people who would understand her slightly wayward nature and welcome it with unconditional affection and love. When she reached eighteen, she set about finding those parents, only to discover her natural father, a Navy man, had died, and her natural mother had married and was living in Cape Town.

The McKays, to their credit, had paid for her trip to South Africa. Bernice sometimes wondered whether they hoped she'd never come back – which was what she had hoped at the time, too. Upon arrival, ringing her real mother took strangely little courage: she was so sure of such a wonderful welcome, she dialled the number without any hesitation.

Vivien Parke, when she answered and Bernice revealed her identity, sounded put out.

'Of course I'd love to see you,' she said. 'But this is my day for charity work. I have a group of underprivileged children coming over.'

'Underprivileged children? What do you think I've been?'

Bernice blurted out. The conversation deteriorated rapidly from that moment, as Vivien's voice turned icy cold and Bernice hotly continued to press for a meeting. She finally wrangled an appointment with Vivien the next day.

As it transpired, Vivien was living in Cape Town luxury. She had the swimming pool, the black servants, the whole nine yards of bourgeois comfort provided by her rich banker husband.

Vivien explained patiently to Bernice as they sat at a glass table by the pool that she'd simply been too young to keep her when she'd had the chance encounter with Bernice's natural father on a weekend in Brighton – a chance encounter which resulted in a chance pregnancy. Vivien, a practising Catholic, had never considered aborting Bernice. Bernice's father, a practising rogue, had disappeared without even a fond farewell. The pregnancy had been remarkably easy, so Vivien commented, as she sipped her iced tea. Vivien had held her new-born daughter for a few minutes before handing her over to the nurses.

'I named you Bernice.' Vivien said, finishing off the tea and placing the glass carefully on a coaster. 'I'm glad your parents kept it. I hope you like it too.' Bernice looked at her mother's face, but couldn't see any sign of emotion.

'And then?' Bernice asked, feeling like an investigative reporter trying to unearth world-shattering secrets from a stonewalling Cabinet member.

'And then, three months later, I met Roger. He's from here, so we moved here.'

Yes, Vivien admitted under further questioning, Roger knew about Bernice's existence. And yes, she'd often thought of Bernice and wondered how she was. Now, of course, she was very glad to see how well Bernice had turned out.

Vivien hoped Bernice would be discreet enough not to say who she was if one of her and Roger's four children joined them poolside. The children really didn't need to know this little secret, did they? Vivien was sure Bernice would take their feelings into consideration. And she very much hoped Bernice would have a nice life in the future.

'Well, that's sweet of you,' Bernice had said. Vivien simply nodded, as if acknowledging a deserved compliment.

One of Vivien's four children *did* appear for a dip in the pool.

She was an eight-year-old, dark-haired, freckled-faced slim little thing in a canary-yellow bathing suit. 'This is a friend of a friend of mine, Miss McKay. Shake hands properly,' Vivien said to the girl. Bernice received a strong handshake from her half-sister. 'She's called Bernice, too. Just like you.'

'You named her Bernice?' Bernice struggled to say as the little girl went for a running dive into the pool.

'Yes.'

Had Vivien been hankering for her all along? Was she trying to recreate her abandoned child in the guise of the little girl now splashing in the pool? Bernice felt all her hope for this meeting return in full force.

'Did you name her Bernice because of me?' she asked, feeling her heart tremble.

'No,' Vivien stared at her with incomprehension. 'I like the name. I didn't want to waste it. I mean, it seemed a shame not to use it again.'

Bernice left. She never went back and she never contacted Vivien again.

'You see, Simon is a natural-born leader,' her father was saying as Bernice's thoughts left Cape Town and returned to Kensington. Remembering that afternoon always made Bernice try hard to be semi-civil to her adoptive parents. They were, after all, the lesser of two evils. 'Anyway, I don't understand why he's never sold in America. Do you think Anna's been pushing hard enough?'

'How would *I* know?'

'You see her occasionally, don't you?'

'Don't *you?*'

'The point is . . . Bernice . . . I think, for reasons I am beginning to understand, Anna may be holding me back. She may be nursing a grudge against me.'

'I doubt that. Aren't you being paranoid?'

'Just because you're paranoid doesn't mean you're not being persecuted,' he replied, obviously pleased with this sentence.

'I think Anna may well be jealous of Simon the Skunk. His fame.'

'Oh, absolutely.' Bernice looked at her father with wonder. This was such a crazy idea, it almost made him interesting.

The voice of Bernice's mother floated in from the hallway. 'I'm off to Tesco,' she cried gaily. 'Bernice, when I come back. I need to speak to you about Christmas arrangements. We're having a party—'

'Fine, Mum, I'll talk to you then,' Bernice yelled back, knowing she'd be out of the house before her mother returned.

'Do you think you could get some time off work?' Bernice's father continued.

'For Christmas? I should hope so.'

'No, I mean before that. Next week.'

'Why?'

'I want you to do something for me. I'll pay you.'

'You'll pay me?'

'Yes. I need someone to go to New York, to check out possible American agents for me. Anna has a semi-partner there she usually refers her clients to, but I don't trust that woman, either. I'd like a man, preferably. Someone like that Jackal character Amis switched to.'

'I don't know if I can get the time off at such short notice,' Bernice said, her heart sprinting. New York. If she *could* go, if she were *paid* to go . . . God, she wouldn't even have to do any work when she arrived there. All she had to do was return and tell her father that Art Rolfe was his man. With a cast-iron excuse to be in his city, she could call Carl. She could invite him out for a friendly drink. They could go to that bar they'd gone to on the first night.

'One more chance. I've been given one more chance.'

'Well, see if you can get the time off and get in touch with me,' Simon said, placing his hands on his designer-ripped blue jeans.

'Why me, Dad? I mean, I wouldn't have thought you would trust me with something as important to you as this.'

243

'I can't go myself – Anna might find out and try to sabotage me. And I thought I should give you a chance to prove yourself, to show me how you can buckle down to a task. You've lasted a fairly long time in that job of yours. You must have proved yourself to your employers. Now you can prove yourself to your father and make up for all those childish, irresponsible escapades.'

'Well, thank you very much, Dad,' she smiled. 'Thank you for the opportunity to redeem myself. I hate to think of you as Cliff Richard, really I do. You might end up with those hair extensions, or leading impromptu sing-alongs on rainy days at Wimbledon. Or, worse, having some kind of strange relationship with Sue Barker. I promise I'll do my best for Simon. My very best.'

In an urgent effort to drag herself away from the television in the late afternoons, Clare signed on for membership at the Hogarth Health Club, around the corner from Angela's house. Each afternoon, she would go there for a swim, a quick jacuzzi and a long stint in the steam room. If she couldn't keep her brain healthy, the least she could do was work on her body.

At seven p.m. on 3 December, she emerged from the club and walked the ten minutes home. When she opened the door, she saw a large suitcase sitting in the hallway. When she walked further on and turned into the kitchen, she found Angela Rae sitting there, staring at the blank screen on the counter.

Who else would come back from a round-the-world solo sailing trip which had lasted nearly two years and be dressed in what looked like an Armani suit, set off by a pearl necklace and pearl bracelet? Clare asked herself. Angela was impossible. And wonderful.

'A television, Clare. Why?' Angela would never kiss or hug Clare, even after a two-year absence. And Angela always came straight to the point – in this case the introduction of television to her house.

'I wanted to watch Jeremy when he goes on foreign tours. I had cable installed so I could get Sky Sports. I'm sorry, Angela.

I knew you'd hate it. I can get it removed, probably, if you really object.'

'No. What's the point of being a cultural snob at my age? I'm sure I'll find it riveting if I ever decide to watch it. Put on a skirt, will you? It's time to go to the casino.'

'Angela—' Clare sat down. 'I want to know about your trip. I want to *talk* to you. I don't want to go gambling right now.'

'No?' Angela sounded disappointed. 'I've heard they have poker tournaments at the Victoria off the Edgeware Road, not so very far from here. We could go, then come back and talk.'

'Please, Angela, I need to talk now. I'm in trouble.'

'Then don't marry him.' Angela took an elaborate array of pins from her head and shook loose her jet black hair down to her waist. Clare wondered, as always, whether this was her natural colour or had been dyed for years.

'Don't marry who?' she asked, blinking.

'Don't marry whoever you think you *should* marry.' Angela took a brush from the bag in front of her and began working on her hair, keeping her eyes fixed on Clare as she did so.

'There are two people I think I should marry.'

'Well, that's even easier. Don't marry either of them.'

'How did you know *that* was my trouble?' Clare asked.

'What other kind of trouble is there for someone like you?'

'I could have trouble with my work. I *do* have trouble with my work.'

'Who doesn't? Are there any good new restaurants around here, if you insist on not going to the casino?'

'There's one called The Chiswick I've read about.'

'Fine. Let's go there, then. You can tell me about these men while we're eating. I assume one of them is Jeremy. Whatever the case, I'll just go put my luggage away and my hair back into place. I'll take the spare room – there's no point in you moving out of the main bedroom – I'm not staying long.'

'Why doesn't that surprise me?' Clare looked at Angela with awe. 'By the way, you're the one who got me into this trouble, you know. Inadvertently. But still, you're at the root of all my problems with these two men.'

'Really?' Angela's eyes brightened. 'How devious of me.'

Life was not making sense, Art decided, pausing outside the window of Tiffany and Co. on Fifth Avenue. He was seeing Clare everywhere these days . . . on the street, in shops, through the windows of passing buses. Her face was omnipresent. He was being haunted by a ghost; yet this ghost was a living woman, one who happened to be living thousands of miles away and one who also happened to be living with another man. Clare, if she ever left Jeremy, would most probably end up with Carl. So what was he, Art, doing wasting his time thinking about her?

For all he knew, Clare could be one of those Englishwomen who shopped, ate and had her hair done at Harvey Nichols. She might buy silly hats and drink Pimm's at Royal Ascot. Clearly, she came from an upper-class or upper-middle-class background; she'd gone to a private, all-girls' school, her mother had a house in Kensington. She had probably spent many Augusts standing behind twits with guns on the grouse moors of Scotland. How could he, Artie Rolfe, sacrifice his democratic principles and be enamoured of a woman like that?

Anna had rung him up at the beginning of December to tell him she was seriously considering moving back to New York. 'I'm tired, Art,' she said. 'I was at a dinner party the other night, and they were all going on about how badly educated Americans are, and how misguided any person could be to think an Ivy League university in the States could be on a par with Oxford or Cambridge. One of the men said, "A PhD from Harvard is the equivalent of a GCSE grade here." Of course he then turned to me and said, "I hope you won't take that personally, Anna." And I shook my head and smiled and said, "Of course not." What I wanted to do was kick him. It never used to bother me, you know. But it does now. I think it may be time for me to come home.'

Anna's story triggered an old memory from Art's days in

London. They had gone to the Barbican with a British friend of hers, a reviewer for the *Observer*. 'Have you heard of Chekhov, Art?' the critic asked him as the curtain was about to rise on *Uncle Vanya*.

'Chekhov?' he'd replied. He and Anna had been in London for six months and he was just getting used to this kind of condescension. 'Gosh. Golly. No. Who's he?'

'A Russian playwright. You might find this a little hard-going. It's very subtle.'

'What's subtle mean?' Art had asked. 'And is that spelt with two ts or one?'

They were all like that – in his experience. The toads. They assumed Americans were uneducated idiots who, if they weren't close personal friends of Hugh Heffner/Madonna/Jim Carrey, dreamt about becoming one.

'I know it must be hard there, but New York is tough too,' he'd advised Anna. 'You should be very sure before you make up your mind. And to start all over with a new list of clients – that could be murder.'

'Well, I'm thinking about it, anyway. I keep humming the Star Spangled Banner to myself – I think that must be meaningful. It's a delayed case of homesickness, I guess. It's been incubating for fifteen years. Now it's hit.'

'And I'm lovesick,' Art thought. 'I never believed Annie would want to come back to New York. That's surprising enough; but the idea that I'd fall in love with some Englishwoman – that's the ultimate irony.'

Staring vacantly at the acres of silver in Tiffany's, Art made up his mind. He didn't love Clare. He couldn't.

Even if she called him up out of the blue and professed undying love, he couldn't. He couldn't move back to London. He'd die there. Those soul-eating cannibals would devour him, inch by bloody inch. They would tie him to a stake and force him to listen to conversations about Glyndebourne. Then, as he twisted in agony, they'd segue into a riff on BBC documentaries. For the *coup de grâce*, they'd encircle him chanting Eton, Winchester, Westminster and he'd collapse, a bloody, chewed-up corpse.

Art, catching sight of a Clare James lookalike leaning against one of the jewelry counters, flinched. Then he gathered himself together and walked down Fifth Avenue humming Tina Turner's What's Love Got to Do with It?

Carl was duly fired from his bartending job at O'Malley's the day after he'd jumped over the bar and disappeared with Dee-Dee. There were plenty of other bars in the city, he knew, and he spent the next few afternoons tramping through the slush searching for one which might employ him. So far he'd had no luck and the whole process was depressing him. This was not what a 35-year-old graduate of New York University, much less a published author, should be doing with his life.

Cutting short the quest, he headed home from midtown on the subway. When he arrived, splattered by grey, filthy melted snow, he trudged up the stairs to his tiny apartment feeling very pitiful and unappreciated. No letter from Clare had awaited him in his mail slot. There had been no mail at all, not even a bill.

The sight of Dee-Dee standing outside his door, dressed in a multi-coloured overcoat and wearing what appeared to be a Russian fur hat, startled him so much he almost turned around and headed back for the street in panic.

'Dee-Dee, what a surprise! How long have you been waiting here?'

'Only ten minutes or so.'

'I'm sorry. You should have called.'

'I was in the neighborhood, as they say. I have something to give to you.'

'You do?' Carl felt his eyebrows rise. What was she going to give him? Her body? God, no – not again. He couldn't get back into bed with her again, however much he might want to.

He opened the door and watched her as she removed her coat and hat. She was wearing a long red wool skirt and black velvet turtleneck, but no jewelry. Dee-Dee never wore jewelry, and he'd always admired her refusal to bedeck herself, just as he *used to* admire Art for never wearing sunglasses. These days he'd prefer not to think about Art at all.

Opening her simple black purse, Dee-Dee removed an envelope.

'This is for you, Carl,' she said, handing it to him.

He took it feeling some fear. Was it a bill from a lawyer? No, they were well and truly divorced. All the legal work was finished.

When he saw the wad of one-hundred dollar bills inside, he sat down heavily on his sofa and whistled.

'Have you robbed a bank or something?'

'No. I sold the engagement ring you gave me.'

'Why Dee-Dee? That was unnecessary. Really.'

'I don't think so. You remember when you bought it for me? When your first novel did quite well?'

'Yes, I remember.'

'I think you should have the money now, when you most need it. You can afford to go to London and see this love of yours. I think that's important. You've never traveled, you've never explored. The new experiences will be good for you.'

'Dee-Dee—' Carl rubbed his hand over his face in disbelief. 'This is incredibly generous of you. But I remember you saying something the other night when we were in . . . I mean, didn't you mention something about wanting to go to Tibet? Shouldn't you be the one taking this money?'

'Carl, I can travel within myself. I can go to wonderful places without moving an inch. If you think I'm generous, you're right. Women are givers, Carl. Men are takers. That's the inherent nature of your sex.'

She put her hat and coat back on. Standing in front of him with her straight back and clear face, tinged by the cold, she looked like an extra from the set of Doctor Zhivago.

'But after what happened between us the other night . . . you still want me to go see another woman?'

249

'Of course.' Dee-Dee's voice was impatient, as if she were talking to a silly child. 'Please don't paint me as a jealous woman. You know I don't possess that emotion. Having sex with you again was interesting, it sparked off a lot of thought. You weren't assuming we'd be a couple again, were you? Because of one night of sex?'

'No.' Carl felt irrationally deflated.

'So take the money and fly. I never understood why you gave me that ring. You knew I don't wear jewelry.'

'Yes, but I thought it was the right thing to do anyway – whether you wore it or not. I thought you should *have* it.'

'You thought I should have a symbol of the fact that you possessed me?'

'No, Dee-Dee.' Oh, God. They were heading full speed ahead into the kind of argument they'd had so many of in the last months of their marriage. These always started out on a course Carl thought he understood, her feminist response to his supposedly unenlightened male attitudes. Half-way through, though, Dee-Dee would switch track and begin to berate her own sex for not comprehending the inherent nature of the male species. What that inherent nature was, exactly, Carl could never figure out. Sometimes men were strong, macho cave dwellers, sometimes they were pathetic, spineless wimps, and sometimes they were wholly irrelevant. Today they were takers.

And that was fine with him.

The afternoon had been a nightmare, Bernice thought, lying on her bed in a state of dishevelled, cold bitterness. Thomas, her boss, had told her she couldn't go to New York.

'You're a cunt,' she had screamed at him in their trendy office in Berwick Steet in Soho. It was so trendy, people were *expected* to scream abuse at each other.

'Well, I may be one, but you *have* one,' he had screamed back and they'd reached a standstill of separate but equal fury.

'I'll tell you what I *will* do,' Thomas said, lowering his voice and rubbing his shaved head. 'I'll let you off early today because frankly I can't stand the sight of your ungrateful face.'

Bernice, careful to flounce as conspicuously as possible when she left the office, emerged onto the street, cursing every passer-by in sight. It wasn't fair, not when she had a chance to go on an expenses-paid trip to New York. It wasn't fair at all.

The anger and frustration she felt left her so depleted that she fell asleep at five p.m., escaping into equally horrible nightmares, where rats scampered across her bed, licking her face with their grotesque rodent tongues. When she awoke to the sound of her telephone ringing, she was grateful to escape the unconscious hell she had dreamed up.

'Yes,' she answered, struggling to banish the image of mammoth, disgustingly obese rats.

'Bernice?'

'Yes.'

'This is Carl. Carl Lioce. I'm calling from New York.'

She must still be dreaming, she realized. If only this could happen in real life.

'Listen, I'm sorry to bother you, but I'm calling because I need to know something. Is Jeremy staying at Clare's house?'

'Is who staying where?' Bernice began to hit her head in frustration, trying to make herself wake up.

'Jeremy. Is he at Clare's? Or is he away playing cricket somewhere?'

'He's in the West Indies.' She might as well give in to the dream, follow it wherever it might lead her. At least Carl was making a guest appearance in her sleeping synapses.

'Ah. Well, that makes things easier. I'm coming over, you see, and I wanted to surprise her, but I needed to know if Jeremy was around. Does that sound underhanded of me?'

'Ah—' Bernice checked the alarm clock beside the telephone. Eight-ten p.m. She might have kipped for a couple of hours and been woken by the phone. In which case this conversation could actually be happening. 'Did you say something about underwear?

251

Carl? Sorry – what did you say? Did you say you're coming over? When?'

'Day after tomorrow.'

'What?'

'Day after tomorrow.'

'Where are you staying?'

'I *hope* I'll be staying with Clare.'

'Oh.'

'But I want my arrival to be a surprise, so don't tell her, all right?'

'Whatever you say.'

It was just as well Thomas hadn't given her the time off, Bernice concluded. She would have flown to New York only to discover that Carl had flown to London. Within forty-eight hours, Carl would be in Chiswick, ten minutes down the road from her flat at the back of Olympia, right under her nose. No, Bernice corrected herself, right under the duvet with Clare.

'I'd love to have a drink with you if I have any time,' Carl continued.

As all hope drained out of Bernice's a body, anger replaced it. *If* he had any time. *If* he didn't have anything better to do, she could be his back-up. Who did he think he was? Eric Clapton?

'That's very nice of you.'

'Bernice – are you OK?'

'I'm fine, but I'm in a rush, Carl. I'm going out tonight. I have to get ready.'

'Sorry to keep you. I appreciate the information on Jeremy. I'm a little wired, you know. I've never been abroad in my life. And seeing Clare—'

'Don't trip over the Post Office Tower,' Bernice interrupted him. 'And make sure you visit Legoland.'

'Bernice? You sound—'

'Goodbye, Carl.' She hung up and turned over onto her stomach, willing herself back to sleep, welcoming oblivion with closed eyes.

Chapter 17

Clare was woken by the shrill sound of the front doorbell. When she threw on a dressing-gown and went downstairs to answer it, she saw a man holding a Federal Express package, breathing out frost. The weather had turned icy overnight and Clare quickly signed for the package before heading back into the sitting room where illegal wood sat on top of newspapers in the fireplace, waiting to be lit.

'What has Carl sent me now?' she wondered before noticing that the writing on the outside was not familiar. She grabbed a box of long matches from the mantelpiece, lit the fire and opened the package. Inside was a videotape with an accompanying note held in place by an elastic band.

'Thought you might enjoy this for old time's sake. I've had it doctored so it will work on an English video. The part you'll really enjoy, the part we missed, is the Sam and Deidre segment. You and I pale in comparison.

Carl told me about what happened in the hospital all those years ago. You must have a lot to think about. Maybe now you can grieve properly.

I bet she was a great little kid.'

Art

*   *   *

While she was re-reading the note, Clare heard Angela enter the room.

'Look—' she said, as Angela, in a black and white kimono, her long hair pinned up haphazardly, sat down on the floor beside her. 'Artie sent me a video of the *Magic Moments* show.' Clare had related the entire story of her New York trip to Angela at the restaurant the previous night.

'I'd like to see that.'

'We don't have a video.'

'I'll buy one this morning.'

'Angela? I didn't think you even knew what a video was.'

'Well, that's ridiculous of you, Clare. I was once in a video, myself, actually. A rock video. One of David Bowie's.'

'Mmm.' Clare was used to Angela's wild lies by now. The problem was that Angela also told unlikely stories which had, in fact, occurred, as it subsequently transpired. Separating the truth from the fiction had become an interesting exercise for Clare over the years. If she had to bet, she'd say Angela had never even heard a David Bowie song, much less appeared in one of his videos, but she wouldn't have put a huge amount of money on it.

'I'll make us some tea, Angela, and then I want you to tell me about your trip. I spent all last night ranting on about myself. By the time you finish describing all your adventures to me, the stores will have opened.'

'I spent a long time in the Bermuda Triangle waiting to disappear,' she announced. 'But I'm still here.'

A few hours later, as they settled down in the kitchen to watch the *Magic Moments* tape, Clare was surprised by her growing reluctance to see herself on screen.

'I'm not so sure now that I want to watch this.'

'Don't be silly,' Angela scolded her. 'We've got the video, we should use it. Who *is* that dreadful man?'

'Mick Nelson – the host.'

254

'He looks as if he should be preaching a Mormon sermon in Salt Lake City.'

'Look at his smile – it's terrifying.'

Art had somehow contrived to edit out the commercials, so Clare abruptly appeared on stage, sitting beside Mick.

'I look awful,' she wailed, hiding her head in her hands.

'No – you look bewildered. Who is that, then?'

The camera had panned to the audience and zeroed in on Art, catching Carl in its frame as well. 'That's Art on the left and Carl is beside him – you can just see a glimpse of Carl's face. He's the one with the longish dark hair. Look, here comes Art.'

'He bounded to the stage quite gracefully,' Angela commented. 'Now be quiet, I want to listen.'

After Clare and Art had left the stage and Mick was in the midst of introducing Sam and Deidre, Angela pushed the stop button on the video remote control.

'I want to see that again.'

'It's so embarrassing, Angela. Once is enough, really.'

'No,' she pushed the rewind button. 'If you don't want to, you don't have to.'

'I want to see Deidre and Sam,' Clare smiled.

'Then come back in a few minutes.'

Bemused, Clare wandered out of the kitchen and stood next to the fire in the sitting room for a short time. When she returned, Angela was executing deft and complicated manoeuvres with the video control. She kept re-winding then starting the tape up at the point when the camera showed Carl and Art sitting in the audience. Then she'd freeze the frame.

'What are you doing?'

'I'm examining,' Angela answered. 'I'm examining faces.'

'And what's the outcome of this examination?' Clare asked, as Angela switched the television off altogether.

'Clare. You've never asked me superfluous questions, for which I am very grateful. You've never inquired too deeply into the causes of my return into your life after the plane crash, for example. You

255

understand that explanations are not my forte. However, now is the time for me to do some explaining.'

'You don't have to,' Clare quickly put in. Angela's serious tone disconcerted her. Telling Anna and Carl that Angela often scared her had been a half-truth. Sometimes when Angela spoke, she reminded Clare of various frightening and strict female teachers she'd had in the past, but the feeling always passed quickly, usually dissipated by Angela's girlish laugh. Now, however, it didn't sound as if Angela had any intention of laughing in the near future.

'I know that I don't have to explain. I *want* to, so I will.' Angela immobilized Clare's rising protests with a commanding glare.

'After our little adventure on the plane, I was struck by your fortitude. You didn't scream, you didn't fuss, you were perfectly well behaved – even when I told you later that your father had died. I know you weren't close to your father, but I recognized in you a character trait which reminded me of myself. And that worried me.'

'Oh.' Clare frowned, overtaken by the familiar feeling of failure. Angela was supposed to believe in her, not worry about her.

'You were joyless, Clare. Obviously you had no reason to be joyful during that time I first encountered you, but I could see the opposite side of your inability to express any negative emotion – your inability to express any positive emotion. I was fifty-seven years old when we met. I had lived the kind of cloistered spinster existence Anita Brookner describes so well in her novels. I know I've made up wonderful, exciting stories for you about my past, but those are my own little attempts at fiction.

'People now assume that I've always lived an adventurous life. Let them. In fact, I was anything *but* adventurous. I was a personal assistant, Clare. A glorifed secretary to a very rich Norwegian shipping broker.

'Every morning I would go to his office on Hill Street in Mayfair and every evening I would return to my flat in Bayswater. I ran the office very efficiently indeed – it was my life. My idea of adventure was my yearly trip to Spain. I took one week each summer by myself

– always to the same town – always to the same hotel. I had no romantic life, no children, no passion. Well—' she paused: 'I am lying again. I had a thwarted passion for my employer; but that was of no consequence as he hadn't the slightest interest in anything but my organizational abilities. Still, I loved him. I knew he didn't love me, but I loved him. You have to make a choice when you're in a situation like that. If I'd said anything about my feelings to him, I'd have had to leave my job. Or, I could leave my job without saying anything to him and so avoid the torture of seeing him. I decided to keep working, to keep my mouth closed and keep working. Seeing him, even in those circumstances, seemed at the time better than not seeing him at all.'

Angela stared out of the kitchen window for what seemed like a very long time to Clare. She didn't want to interrupt the silence, though. She sensed it was important for Angela to continue at her own pace.

'The crash changed me. Not because I almost died and so discovered the value of life, or because I instinctively reached out and grabbed the hand of the little girl sitting beside me. No. It changed because of what I saw later, what I saw in *you*. I know I wasn't of much use to you after the crash. I did the best I could, which wasn't much. But your face began to haunt me. I said goodbye to you in Heathrow, yet you refused to leave me. I saw you every time I looked in the mirror. And, Clare, that face looked so sad, I can't tell you.

'Every time I looked at myself, I saw you and I wanted to weep. I saw this composed, resigned, joyless face. And I began to realize, through you, how absurdly empty my own life was. We were both little old women, Clare, even though you were only twelve. I realized I couldn't change the fact that I was an old woman, but I didn't have to be "little". You understand what I mean by that, I know you do.

'So I left my job. My employer – my love, my hero – was shocked. Yet somehow he managed to replace me within a few hours. Strange, isn't it?' Angela smiled. 'Anyway, I took all the money I had saved up over the years. It was a considerable amount, of course, because I never used to spend it on anything except essentials. I sold my flat and bought this house as a comfortable base. I travelled. I had affairs with all sorts of strange men, most of whom were idiotic. They'd have to be to take up with a woman who had been a virgin at the age of fifty-seven. And then I came back – to find you.'

'Why?' Clare finally spoke.

'To see if you had changed as well, to see if you were still sad, I suppose. If you were still so similar to me, to me as I had been before I took off. The little old woman.'

'And had I changed?'

'No. I could see why you hadn't when I saw your mother's face. I saw in her face what I had seen in you and in myself. We all shared that blank expression which covers a horrible fear. We all had those dull eyes. Joylessness – that's the only way I can describe it. So I determined to reach out to you again. Not by grabbing your hand but by grabbing your heart.'

'Which is why you took me to the Ritz?'

'I took you *gambling*, Clare. I took you to a place which embraces risk. I wanted you to have stories to tell, not to have to fabricate them like I do. *I* started taking risks at fifty-seven, I wanted *you* to start young.'

'Why didn't you tell me any of this before?'

'I didn't think it was necessary. Once you had gone off to Bristol and out of your mother's influence – and don't misunderstand me, I think she's done the best she was capable of doing for you – I thought you would begin to come into your own.'

'But I didn't? Is that what you're saying? Are you saying I still haven't?'

'*You* tell *me* the answer to that.'

'This isn't fair, Angela. I'm not someone who would ever swim the English Channel or go island-hopping in the South Seas. That's just not part of my nature. And I *have* taken risks. I've written two novels – writing is a risk.'

'Doesn't that depend on what you write about?'

'I thought you liked my books.' Clare began to tremble. She turned her face away from Angela.

'I like your writing. I admire it. But the books are both joyless as well, Clare. You must see that.'

'What do you expect of me? Do you want me to climb Mount Everest barefoot?'

'I don't *expect* anything of you. And I am not talking about physical risks. That may be my choice, the way I like to gamble, but there are other ways. You can take risks with your emotions.'

'I have.' Clare felt tears form and immediately brushed them away. 'I fell in love with Jeremy. Falling in love is a risk.'

'Doesn't that depend on who you fall in love with?'

'You're saying that every single thing I've done in my life, all my feelings are of no consequence at all? I think—' Clare rose from her seat. 'I can't bear—'

'Sit down, Clare.' Angela reached out, took Clare's hand and gently pulled her back into the chair. 'Every single thing you do or feel is of consequence. I'm not trying to tear you apart, I'm trying to help. You told me last night that since you've been back from New York, all you've done is swim and watch television. Do you think that's healthy?'

'No,' Clare mumbled.

'Neither do I.'

'What am I supposed to do? You've just told me my writing is worthless, my relationship with Jeremy is a joke. What am I supposed to do?' Her voice, she knew, had become hysterical.

'Listen to me—' Angela pressed Clare's hand. 'I have gone off on a lot of adventures on my own. I've enjoyed taking physical risks. I know, though, that the real adventures in life are other people – relationships with other people. Honestly, I think it's easier to climb a mountain or swim the Channel than keep a marriage happy or raise well-balanced children. Living with someone every day ... that's the risk, Clare. One which I've never had the courage to take. And one which you've avoided with Jeremy because he's away so much.

'I know that you feel hurt by what I've said. And, frankly, I'm glad of it. You've *responded*. I'm leaving this afternoon, I'm off to Texas.'

'Texas?' Clare momentarily forgot her misery in disbelief.

'I want to see some oilfields. Then I'll be travelling around the southern bit of the States. I'd like to be in New Orleans for Mardi Gras. Anyway, that's not important. I'm going to leave you an envelope and I don't want you to open it until 10 January. When you do read what I've written inside, I want you to consider what I've said very seriously. I think I know something important about your life.'

'You sound like the Oracle at Delphi, Angela.' Clare tried to pull her hand away but Angela wouldn't let go. 'What are you talking about? I don't understand. This is silly. If you know something important, why won't you tell me now? You've made me feel miserable. If there's something that can help me, why can't you tell me now?'

'I want you to promise me you won't open the envelope until 10 January.'

'All right.' Why was she agreeing to this absurd deal? Clare asked herself. And how could Angela say all the terrible things she'd said, then walk out the door again almost immediately?

'I want you to believe in me, Clare. I want you to trust me – this crazy old woman who has muscled in on your life. You trust me and I'll trust you.' Finally, Angela released Clare's hand and sat back. 'Don't open the envelope until the tenth – if nothing else it's a good story to tell, isn't it? So promise me.'

'Angela—' Clare sighed in frustration, before saying, 'All right' again.

'Clare, look at me.'

Instinctively, Clare obeyed this command.

'What?' Angela asked, staring fiercely at Clare with her dark, almost black eyes. 'What is the name of the girl who died in the hospital?'

'Sophie.' The name came out as if bidden by a force from the underworld.

'Sophie.' Angela nodded. 'Now you can watch the rest of that tape, if you want to. I'm going upstairs to take a bath and get ready for my next adventure.'

'She's a witch, she really is a witch,' Clare thought as she sat staring at the kitchen table after Angela had left the room. 'She has supernatural powers. Sophie. Sophie had red hair and freckles and her two front teeth were missing. She told me a joke. "Why is six afraid of seven? Because seven eight nine." I gave her my dog the night before she went into surgery. We held hands for a long time. She had the smile of an angel.'

Chapter 18

After Angela left, Clare tried hard to cut down on television time. She'd watch it when she woke up in the morning, but not after Eamonn Holmes had signed off – nine a.m. was the latest she would allow herself. She had substituted the more worthy activity of reading the newspapers and then doing *The Times* Crossword puzzle for her post-nine a.m. activity.

The clue she was working on, Tax two thirds of landed gentry fiddled, had her stumped. The answer could be an eight-letter synonym for tax made up from two-thirds of the letters in the twelve-letter combination of landed gentry, fiddled being a hint to form an anagram. Or it could be a synonym for fiddled, in which case she had no idea what landed gentry had to do with it.

When the doorbell rang, she expected to find the milkman, asking for his weekly bill to be paid. He always came early on Friday mornings.

The sight of Carl standing outside made her think she'd temporarily taken leave of what few senses she believed she still possessed.

'Hey,' he said, smiling sheepishly.

'Carl—' she said, then ran out of words.

'Can I come in?'

'Of course. God. How amazing.' She stepped back and he

stepped over the threshold, dropping his suitcase and enveloping her in a bear hug.

While he crushed her to him, Clare thought of Angela. Angela would have loved the risk on Carl's part – showing up like this without warning. She would have loved Carl, with his quirkiness, his passions. Angela hadn't made many comments when Clare had told her about Carl over dinner, she'd listened attentively, but kept her thoughts to herself. Yet she'd kept re-winding the videotape that following morning, looking at the bit where he appeared. 'I'm examining faces,' she had said. And after that she'd talked about emotional risks. Carl must have been the risk Angela meant her to take.

'I'm so glad you've come,' she smiled up at him. Finally something was happening in her life. Finally things were moving. Angela had gone to Texas, leaving Clare feeling that she was disappointed in her. Whatever was contained in the mysterious envelope would not make up for the fact that Angela, after all was said and done, had no more belief in Clare than Clare had in herself. 'Joyless' was such a harsh adjective, and such a hard one to shed. Could Clare suddenly run out into the streets and find joy? She didn't think so. And how was she supposed to write about joy if she hadn't experienced it? Angela may have turned her own life around at the drop of an aeroplane, but Clare couldn't do the same.

Faced with some terrible truths about her personality, Clare didn't make herself go out and experience life, she took the easy, tried and trusted, option, she stayed hidden at home. Now, suddenly, Carl was on her doorstep, forcing her out of her bleak mood and bleaker preoccupations.

'I'm glad I've come, too,' he replied. 'So where's the tea, where are the crumpets? Why isn't the Queen here to welcome me?'

Bernice had smoked a packet of cigarettes in less than an hour. She couldn't remember how much she'd had to drink. It was the office Christmas lunch party, so she felt entitled. Condor and Co. had taken over Sale Pepe, an Italian restaurant tucked away behind Sloane Street, famous for its chaotic atmosphere. As waiters bustled through the room shouting expletives in Italian and throwing baskets of bread rolls and bottles of wine back and forth for no apparent reason, Bernice wished she could enter into the spirit. She was sitting beside her boss, Thomas, who was no longer her sworn enemy but rather her new best friend.

'Why do I fall for men who don't love me? It's self-abasement, that's what it is.'

'No,' Thomas countered. 'It's natural. I do it all the time.'

'He's here now. He's in this country at this moment.'

'You've told me that ten times already, Bernice.'

'Have I?' Bernice sat back heavily in her chair and looked at the zabaglione sitting on the plate in front of her.

'I suggest that you approach your romantic life in the same way that I do,' Thomas said in the voice of a seasoned listener to other people's problems. 'As if it were work. You're perfectly competent, most of the time, at your job, Bernice. So transfer your skills. Think of this man as your client. Joe Bloggs may come into our office asking us to sell Audi cars to the public. Our job is to think of a way to do this which is also a way Joe Bloggs will understand and be excited by. What you have to do is fashion a campaign to sell yourself as the ideal mate. What is this man looking for? Does he want someone solid and dependable, does he want someone exciting and sexy? Work it out – meet the customer's specifications and then exceed them.'

'This customer has gone to another agency, Thomas.' Bernice frowned. She took the paper crown off her head and began tearing it into tiny pieces.

'Then you're fucked, sweetheart.' Thomas leaned over and kissed Bernice on the cheek. 'Merry fucking Christmas and since you don't seem too interested in your zabaglione, can you pass it to me?'

*   *   *

Returning with a pad and pen, Clare leapt back into bed and started to make a list.

One: The Tower of London
Two: Parliament/Westminster Abbey
Three: St Paul's Cathedral

She stopped and glanced over at Carl who was watching her write. 'You got that wrong in your second letter, you know. It's St Paul's Cathedral, not Church.'

'Ah.' He ran a finger down the side of her neck. 'Forgive the ugly, uninformed American.'

'If I'm going to be your tour guide, I have to be precise,' she said, smiling. 'And if you're going to stay here, I have to get some food.' She put down the list. 'You are going to stay for a while, aren't you?'

'As long as you want me.'

Carl had rescued her; he'd come and saved her, lifted her out of her paralysis. Clare looked at him gratefully. All these months, all these years she had had the feeling that she'd been waiting, but she hadn't known for what. Now she did. Feeling a surge of energy, Clare jumped out of bed again and began to get dressed.

'Hey, not so fast,' Carl said. 'We can spend some more time here, you know.'

'I know,' she smiled. She had willed herself, over the past seven months, not to think about sex with Carl, partly because she was afraid of sex taking on too much significance, overriding her normal emotional response system, and partly because she thought the first time may have been a fluke of some kind, that his performance in bed couldn't possibly be as good as she'd remembered. He couldn't sustain that kind of intensity, she thought, that whole-hearted devotion to every inch of her body.

Now she knew it hadn't been an aberration. And she couldn't stop it from being significant. The sex was amazing, utterly fantastic, so why shouldn't that count? Why should she run away from it? She didn't have to, not anymore. He was beside her now and she intended to keep him there.

'We can spend all the time we want to in bed. But, honestly,' her smile widened. 'We are going to need to eat at some point. If I go out now, I can get some wine, maybe some champagne even. We can celebrate.'

'Why don't I come with you?'

'Why don't you stay here and rest? You're going to need all your energy for later.'

'Good point.'

Carl propped himself up on his elbow to watch her dress. She pulled on some jeans, a white shirt and a navy-blue sweater.

'I'm off,' she announced. 'I'll be back soon, I promise. Help yourself to whatever is available in the kitchen. There's some coffee, if you'd like.'

'That's probably a good idea,' he answered, yawning. 'Now I finally understand about jet-lag. I need a second wind.'

When she'd disappeared, Carl wandered into the bathroom next door and saw what was obviously a man's bathrobe hanging on the hook of the door. 'Jeremy,' he thought. 'Shit.' After a moment's pause, he put it on. 'I'll just go get some coffee in this thing and I'll have it off by the time she comes back.'

Downstairs in the kitchen the instant coffee was on the counter beside the electric kettle. Within a few minutes, he was sitting at the kitchen table, mug in hand.

'Thank you, Dee-Dee,' he said to the empty room. 'You've saved my life.'

Picking up the remote control lying on the table in front of him, he fooled about with it. 'Neighbours, everybody needs good neighbours,' he heard as he watched pictures of various people, obviously some characters in a soap, dart across the screen. He'd heard this song before, he remembered. The time Clare had called him, right before she'd hung up. Dismissing this irrelevant memory, Carl switched channels and continued channel-hopping until he was faced with what looked like a sporting competition of some kind. Black men in white trousers were standing around a field. He turned the sound up, and moved his chair closer to the set.

'So, Geoffrey,' a commentator said. 'What do you think of his batting at this stage of the match?'

'It's brilliant,' another commentator replied in an accent Carl had never heard before. 'Letters is defending well – he's not letting Ambrose's bouncers disturb him. He's cool as a cucumber – as usual.'

The camera now focused on a man holding an oddly shaped bat.

'Oh, shit,' Carl said. 'Oh, shit.'

'Look at that, will you, David? Look at that stroke. It's racing to the boundary. It can't get there fast enough. That's his half-century.'

Half-century? What the hell was a half-century? Did they play this game for fifty years?

'I haven't seen anyone like him. David. Not in all my time in cricket.'

'Not even yourself, Geoffrey?'

'Very funny. No, seriously, Letts is a positive pleasure to watch. I can't say enough good about him.'

Carl turned off the set, took his mug of coffee and retired to bed again, after carefully replacing Jeremy's bathrobe on its hook.

'Here – this should keep us going for awhile.' Clare came into the bedroom, carrying a bottle of champagne and two glasses. 'Have you had a little sleep while I was out?'

'No.' Carl frowned. 'Before you open that I think we need to talk.'

'OK.' She placed the bottle and her glass on the bedside table. 'What do we need to talk about?'

'Jeremy.'

'Oh.'

'I need to know what my status is. I mean, I need to know if it's

267

going to be the same as New York; if as soon as he comes back, you'll go back to him.'

'No.' Clare shook her head. 'I won't. I've been thinking about him too, actually. While I was out buying the food. I've decided that the best thing to do is to tell him, when he next rings, exactly what's going on – straight away. It's not fair to him to lie or put it off.'

'What exactly are you going to tell him?'

'That you've come over and that I'm in love with you.'

'Whoa.' Carl's hand tightened around the glass. 'Those are the words *I* want to hear, but I don't think *he*'ll be too pleased.'

'I have to tell him, Carl.'

'Of course you do. I guess I feel sorry for him, though. I know what it's like to lose someone.'

Clare was silent.

'Where will he go? I mean, he lives here with you . . . where will he go?'

'He has a flat in Fulham. He sublet it when Angela asked me to move in here two years ago. He can stay with friends or his family until the lease is up.'

'Will you see him when he gets back? I mean, if he asks to see you?'

'Of course. But if you're worried, don't be. I don't love him, Carl. I'm not sure that I ever did, not really.'

Carl had a thousand questions to ask: if she didn't love him, why had she stayed with him for so long? Why had she gone back to England with him after New York? Why had she written so many emotionless letters in the past eight months? Why had she sometimes been so passionate? What would have happened to their relationship if he hadn't turned up on her doorstep?

These queries travelled at high speed through his brain, yet he held back from voicing them.

Instead he asked, 'Why is Jeremy called "Letters"?'

'How did you know that?'

'I was fiddling around with the television when I made myself a cup of coffee. I saw him playing in a game.'

'A match,' Clare corrected him. 'A Test match in the West Indies. They do that with the last name of cricket players – it's an English thing. Ian Botham was referred to as "Bothers". Mike Gatting was "Gatters". So they call Letts "Letters". They're nicknames.'

'Oh. Right. What would they call me? "Liocers"? It doesn't really work, does it?'

'I don't think I'll ask about half-centuries,' Carl thought. 'It's eerie that he should be Letters, though. I don't like it. Still, one Letters does not a Correspondence make.'

'You don't have to compare yourself with Jeremy. I know I'm not a dancer like Dee-Dee. We have to relax about the past and past relationships or we'll make ourselves crazy. Are you ready for the champagne now?'

'Let yourself go, relax and let yourself go.' Carl started singing, mimicking what Clare recognized from her childhood as Fred Astaire's voice.

'God,' she thought. 'It's sweet the way he sings. Why did it bother me that time in New York? I must have been crazy.'

'I remember one year at school,' she said, when he'd finished his song. 'There was a rage to let yourself go, to fall from a standing position and trust your friends to catch you before you hit the pavement and broke your neck. I was the only one who wouldn't do it. It wasn't that I didn't trust them to catch me when I fell. But I could never explain that to them. I couldn't explain that I wouldn't do it because I didn't trust *myself*.'

'Why? What did you think you'd do?' Carl asked.

'I have no idea,' Clare opened the bottle expertly and poured the champagne into two glasses. She handed one to Carl. 'But I think I'd do it now. Actually, I think I *have* done it now.'

'And have I caught you?'

'I think so, Carl,' she smiled at him and took a sip from her glass. 'I bloody well hope so.'

'So will you marry me?'

This was the second time he had proposed to her when lying in bed. He obviously didn't believe in kneeling.

'Yes,' she answered. 'I will.' She expected fireworks to go off, or at least some momentous occurrence to happen to mark the occasion. Instead, she hiccuped.

The only love letters which are of any use are those of goodbye

Étienne Rey

Chapter 19

'Please,' Clare heard herself pleading. 'Please let *me* do something. Let me—'

'No, sweetheart,' Carl put his hand over her mouth. 'Leave it to me.'

'But that's all I ever do,' she thought, closing her eyes as she felt his hands run over her body. 'It's been over a month since you arrived in London and that's all you'll let me do – leave it to you.'

How could she possibly explain this feeling she had now to anyone?

'He's *too* unselfish in bed,' she could hear herself saying to shrieks of female catcalls and male jeers.

Yet it was true. Any time she made a move to give him pleasure, he would check it, as if her involvement weren't in the least necessary or desired. He was there, in bed, as a pleasure-giving machine; pleasure-taking was not of the least interest. At first Clare had been stunned by this approach. She had, she admitted, enjoyed it incredibly, but as the weeks had gone by, she began to feel that this selflessness on his part had flipped over and become selfishness. His refusal to take from her in bed made her feel like an inflatable doll.

At times she would get so frustrated, she'd physically grapple with him in order to get some parity in what was going on, to take control for a while, but he'd win the quasi-wrestling match with ease and go on to do what he always did – concentrate entirely on her.

'I should have such problems,' she could hear Bernice say.

'Carl—' she'd said one night, breaking off in the middle of making love and sitting up straight in bed. 'I need to get involved, too, you know. I want to give you something. This has to be a two-way street.'

'I get pleasure giving you pleasure,' was his response. It made sense, but then it didn't make sense, not really.

'You should let me get pleasure by giving *you* pleasure, then,' she reasoned.

'Are you saying you're not getting any pleasure here?' he'd asked.

'No, of course not, but—'

'Listen, it's impossible to talk about pleasure anyway. You just have to experience it.'

'Right,' she thought. 'Lie back and think of England. If this is what makes Carl happy, it should make me happy too. What am I complaining about?'

So Clare did, indeed, leave it to Carl yet again. She made no attempt to take any initiative. When they'd finished, or rather, when he had finished servicing her, as she had come to think of it, she rolled over and turned her face to the wall. She had thought they'd be able to giggle together, but Carl and Jeremy were alike in one way – they both took sex very seriously. And now, instead of giggling, she was hiding her tears.

'I wish we didn't have to go out – I wish we could stay here like this all night,' he was rubbing her back as he spoke. 'What time is dinner anyway?'

'It's early, seven-thirty,' she replied.

He had no idea she was upset. It occurred to her that once upon a time she could have explained this bizarre situation to him in a letter. 'Taking turns being selfish is part of a relationship,' she would have written. 'If one person is always the selfish one, and the other always the unselfish one, the roles become fixed and neither of you can really express yourself.' He would have written back a thoughtful reply and they could have discussed the whole concept of selfishness. By post. Two people not involved in a physical relationship could discuss sex rationally. As long as she hadn't met him, she could confide in him.

Now, in person, wearing the engagement ring he'd bought on hire purchase, she kept her back to him.

'It will be strange to see Anna and Bernice again. I should thank Anna for setting up that *Magic Moments* show. I wonder whether we would have ever met without her.'

'I don't know,' Clare said quietly. 'I suppose our curiousity about each other would have meant we'd set up a meeting ourselves at some time.'

'Yes, but it might have been too late. You might have been married for real. Anyway, I'm looking forward to seeing Bernice again too. I suppose she wishes Art was here.'

'Why?'

'Because of that time in New York – you know. Their afternoon of passion.'

'I don't think Art and Bernice were ever serious about each other.'

'You don't? I think they'd make a great couple.'

'Well, set them up, then, why don't you?' she said crossly. 'And then maybe you could put Dee-Dee and Jeremy together and Anna and Mick Nelson. Then we'd have a wonderful group of tidy couples.'

'Clare . . . are you all right?'

'I'm fine,' she answered, hugging the pillow.

Something was wrong. But what?

For once, Bernice thought, I'm not the cause of tension. I *should* be, given that I'm not too thrilled about celebrating Clare and Carl's engagement. But I've behaved perfectly so far; I haven't had too much to drink, I've joined in the conversation amiably enough, I have resisted all temptation to stare into Carl's eyes with desperate longing.

No. It's not me. Yet there's definitely tension here, I can feel it. I think we'd all be grateful if there were a bomb threat in West London and we had to call a halt to dinner.

This was the first time Bernice had seen Carl since his arrival in London. Clare had called her a couple of times, asking if she wanted to get together, but Bernice hid behind the answering machine, figuring she could use the Christmas social rush as an excuse, if she had to. On 1 January, when her phone had rung, Bernice forgot about the answering machine and answered with the words; 'Happy Hangover.' Clare, laughing, proceeded to inform her that she and Carl were engaged.

'I hope you'll come to the wedding, Bernice. We've scheduled it for Friday fortnight, and late next week I thought we could all have dinner – you and Anna and Carl and me – to celebrate. How about that restaurant Snows on the Green? Do you think that would be nice?'

Bernice said all the right things in, she hoped, the right tone of voice. She waited until she had hung up before bursting into tears. Later that evening, Thomas came over for a drink. When she told him how reluctant she was to go to this dinner, he insisted that she had no choice. 'If you don't go,' he explained, 'Clare will think you're still in love with Carl. More importantly, *you'll* think you're still in love with him. You know, some people don't travel well. Carl might have been Mr Wonderful in New York, but he could easily be Mr Gauche in London. You might recover from this unrequited demonic crush.'

As it happened, Thomas had been right. After half an hour at Snows on the Green, Bernice began to see that Carl *was* different. He was . . . Bernice struggled to find the right phrase to descibe him and emerged with 'toned down'. His exuberance had gone, his face was less alert. He looked as if he had wilted.

If only the change made a difference to my emotions, she found herself wishing. If only I could brush aside my old feelings for him and look at him as if he were someone I'd just met whom I didn't particularly fancy.

At least she didn't have long to go before the evening was over – that was a relief. The first and second courses had come and gone, and now they were finishing dessert. Only coffee and the bill; then freedom from further torture beckoned.

'Anna? Are you really serious about moving to America?' Clare asked.

'Yes,' Anna replied. 'It looks that way . . .'

Clare seemed nervous, Anna thought. Nervous and dowdy at the same time. Falling in love with Carl hadn't helped her in the fashion stakes; if anything, in fact, Clare's dress sense had become worse. Whereas she used to be overly conservative, now she was slightly slovenly. Surprisingly, Bernice, for once in her life, was looking quite smart in her black velvet stretch trousers and white polo-neck top.

'Well, if you *do* go to America, you should know my father is on a rampage about breaking into the market there. He thinks Simon should be Britain's biggest export.' Bernice considered telling Anna that her father was on the point of getting another agent in New York, but decided against it.

'How is the old skunk doing these days?' Carl asked.

'Oh, he's terrific. My father told me that in the next book, Simon is going to meet a wizard in the forest. That way he can get mystical for a while. I told him that if he wants Simon to get really mystical, he should have him eat some magic mushrooms. The illustrations for that could be wonderful.'

'Simon could become a guru,' Carl laughed. 'He could establish an ashram in the forest,' Bernice laughed with him. 'And do yogic flying.'

'He could be the next Nostradamus – he could predict the future, too.' Carl was warming up, Bernice thought, his eyes were beginning to smile.

'Actually, it's not a bad idea to make Simon a little more mysterious,' Anna joined in. 'I think the readers might be getting bored with the Robin Hood theme. Even kids can get tired of the same story told over and over again. Mystery is good.'

'Like Angela's mysterious envelope,' Carl said. 'That has *me* intrigued, anyway.'

'What mysterious envelope?' Anna's eyes brightened.

'Which female star had Anna chosen to copy for her hair-style tonight?' Bernice asked herself. Anna Ford – that was it, definitely an improvement on Esther Rantzen. She no longer looked like a lacrosse coach; now she resembled a competent, trustworthy and attractive female executive.

'Angela left Clare an envelope when she went off,' Carl explained. 'She told her not to open it until 10 January – tomorrow. Apparently she's written something very important in it.' Carl reached out to put his arm around Clare's shoulders as he said this and Bernice was surprised to see Clare immediately shrug it off.

'She *has* written something important,' Clare stated. 'I'm sure of it.'

'Clare refuses to cheat and open it before the tenth.' Carl, refusing to take Clare's rejection, put his arm back around her. This time she allowed it to remain.

Why was she in such a peevish frame of mind? he wondered. She hadn't even dressed up for dinner. After their love-making had finished, she'd put on the same jeans and sweater she'd had on all day. The front of the sweater still had a spot of ketchup from lunch. Normally, Carl didn't mind causal dress – in fact, he welcomed it. Yet he had a thin but strong old-fashioned strand in him when it came to something like an engagement dinner – he thought Clare might have made an effort.

'Clare's not like me,' he continued, trying to say it amiably. 'I couldn't possibly keep that kind of promise if I were really curious about something. I'd steam open the envelope.'

Bernice almost blurted out, 'So would I. God, I love you,' but miraculously stopped herself.

Instead, she gathered up enough courage to look him straight in the eye and say, 'I'm curious, Carl. Have you kissed any ugly men lately?'

'Not lately,' Carl replied, giving her the grin she remembered seeing that first night in New York at the precise moment in the bar when Bruce Sprinsteen's voice had boomed from the juke-box, singing, 'If you're looking for love, honey, I'm tougher than the rest'.

'What are you talking about?' Clare asked, shifting her gaze back and forth between Carl and Bernice.

'I kissed a sad, ugly banker at a party once.' Carl hadn't touched the coffee which had been placed in front of him while they were talking about Simon the Skunk. He had, however, drunk a fair amount of red wine.

'You kissed him? On the lips?' Clare drew back in her chair, away from him.

'Yes. Briefly. Not from any homo-erotic impulse, just to—' Carl faltered. He couldn't understand why Clare, of all people, would physically recoil at the thought of a harmless kiss. Was she *that* uptight? 'Just to—'

'To cheer him up,' Bernice finished. Clare had obviously had the same reaction she'd had upon first hearing this story. 'I know it sounds strange, Clare. But the idea grows on you. I almost did it the other day myself. There was a pathetic, desperate old woman who came into the office for an interview. I mean, she had no hope of getting the job, and I felt so sorry for her I almost kissed her on the way out.'

'Speaking of homo-erotic impulses,' Anna cut in, 'Artie sent me your ex-wife's book to read, Carl. *Shescape*. You know, she has some really remarkable passages about sex in it. I was stunned, to tell you the truth. The rest of it is basically incomprehensible.'

'I'm very fond of Dee-Dee.' Carl said, his face tightening. 'If she has been open about her sexual experiences, I think that's brave. I think *she's* brave to try to write a book, even if it is incomprehensible. Dee-Dee has been through a lot in life and she still has a generous heart. She gave me the money to come here, actually.'

278

Whoa, Anna thought. He's awfully touchy about his ex. And does he always take money from women? Poor Clare.

'You never told me that.' Clare looked Carl straight in the eye for the first time that evening. 'You never said that Dee-Dee gave you the money.'

Staring straight back, Carl frowned.

'I didn't *not* tell you. It never came up, that's all.'

'Oh,' Clare remarked. 'I see.'

'If you want to get into this, how about the fact that *you* didn't tell *me* anything about your lunch with Jeremy. I know you had it, yes. But I have no idea what you talked about.'

'I didn't take notes, Carl. He was perfectly friendly, and perfectly fine about our breakup.'

'*Too* fine, maybe,' Carl frowned again. 'It sounds unnatural to me – his nonchalant attitude about the whole thing.'

'No,' Clare shook her head again. 'It's not unnatural. That's Jeremy. That's the way he is. Maybe that's why I didn't repeat every word of our conversation at lunch to you – I knew you wouldn't understand. I'm not saying Jeremy wasn't a little upset, but he would never show it. And I don't think he feels it too deeply either.'

'Well, that's pathetic, isn't it?'

'Pathetic?' Clare snapped.

'Yes. If you love someone you should feel deeply, for Christ's sake. That's the whole point.'

'I meant that he didn't feel the hurt too deeply, not that he is incapable of feeling, Carl. Maybe he didn't feel grand passion, maybe he loves me like a brother . . . I don't know. But I *do* know he's not *pathetic*.'

'The tension is gathering momentum,' Bernice thought. 'The happy couple have been together only a couple of weeks – they should be starry-eyed, holding hands – not snappy and on edge. I should be burning with jealousy as I watch uncontrollable displays of public affection. Instead of which, I'm seeing two very testy people. And I'm not sure why, but I'm getting no satisfaction

279

out of that. I'm feeling the way I felt after reading *Breathing in the Dusk*. I'm feeling sorry for Clare, for both of them.'

The waiter, who seemed to have a sixth sense of timing, came up at precisely that anxious moment to ask if anyone wanted more coffee. The break allowed a short silence to descend after they had all refused.

'Dare I ask whether you're writing anything, or planning to write anything, Clare?' Anna finally broke the conversation deadlock.

'No, I haven't planned anything. I feel guilty about being so unproductive for so long, but I think I'll be able to start up again when we go back to New York. I need different stimuli. I think a new country, a new city will—'

'Go back to New York?' Carl looked bewildered. 'What do you mean?'

'When we go back to New York,' Clare replied as if she were speaking to a three-year-old, 'after our wedding.'

'You never said anything about going back to New York.'

'I assumed—'

'*I* assumed that we were staying here. I love it here. I love the parks, I love the way of life – it's a big city, but a livable city. There's so much—'

'I thought you loved New York. The sidewalks after the thunderstorms, the newly fallen snow, all that—'

'I've lived in New York for thirty-five years, Clare. I told you that. I told you at the very beginning of our correspondence that if I spent a few more years in New York, I'd achieve total depravity. That's not something I want. It's not something I desire. Don't you remember that line?'

'Unlike you, I don't remember every single line from the fucking correspondence.'

'The *fucking* correspondence?'

'Sorry, that wonderful, amazing, soul-enhancing correspondence. Excuse me for attacking the bible.'

'Shit,' Bernice thought, watching Carl's face crumple. 'I hope Clare hasn't splashed out on a wedding dress yet.'

'Where did you think we were going to live in London?' Clare pressed.

'In your house,' Carl mumbled.

'In *Angela's* house, do you mean? Angela *loaned* me that house, on condition that she'd have it back if she ever decided to live here permanently again. She could come back and take it over any time – she could come back after the Mardi Gras.'

'I'm amazed that you two haven't talked about all this before.' Anna stated matter-of-factly.

'Your amazement doesn't interest us,' Carl said hotly.

'Right,' Clare nodded. 'This is our problem. We'll sort it all out later. We'll be fine.'

'I'm sure you will,' Anna said in a placating tone. 'All young married couples have disagreements.'

'Boy are you two doomed,' she thought. 'I give you six months max.'

'I think we should go now, Anna,' Bernice prodded.

'I think you're right,' Anna agreed, much to Bernice's relief, since the dinner had started early and it was now only nine-forty-five. 'But the bill—'

'I'm paying,' Clare announced.

'Oh, right then. Bernice and I will leave you two to it. I suppose the next time we see you will be at the Chelsea Register Office. I'll bring some rice.'

'Don't forget the confetti,' Carl smiled wanly.

'I'll be in charge of that,' Bernice replied, then hustled Anna toward the cloakroom. When they emerged onto Shepherd's Bush Road, Anna said 'Neither of them even kissed us good-bye.'

'I'm sure they've got a lot on their minds.'

'Evidently so. God. How could it be?' She pulled her fake leopardskin coat closer to her. 'They seemed so attuned to each other in those letters. And now – tonight – they seemed to clash at every opportunity.'

'Pre-wedding jitters, probably.'

'I don't know,' Anna shook her head. 'I don't think they should ever have met.'

'And whose fault was it that they did?'

'Oh, they would have met eventually, one way or the other,' Anna said breezily. 'Let's say, I just hastened the inevitable.'

'Then do me a favour, will you? Don't hasten anything to do with my life, whether it's inevitable or not.'

'Bernice. I was trying to promote a romance. I spent my own money trying to turn a dream into reality. I really am sorry if it didn't work for them.' She gave the smile Bernice remembered, the one that transformed her into a girl. 'It worked for me.'

'What do you mean?'

'I mean I'm pregnant. And the reason I'm pregnant, if you can believe it, is the Correspondence. I met a man when I was on the flight back from New York. A Frenchman. We've been seeing each other. And I'm going to have his baby.'

'Anna, hold on a second. I thought you said you were going back to America.'

'I am. He lives in Denver, Colorado. He owns three restaurants there. Isn't that fabulous?'

'Why didn't you tell Clare and Carl?'

'The atmosphere was so strained tonight. There was never a right time. And it was supposed to be a celebration for them, not me.'

'Well, congratulations.' Bennice gave her a quick hug. She didn't have the energy to ask Anna endless questions about when the baby was due and what it would be called. And if Anna getting pregnant at such an advanced age hadn't given her hope for her own future, she would have been jealous. 'What about your career?'

'I don't know. For a while, when I got back here, I thought about moving back to New York, continuing my work there. I didn't know how serious this relationship would be. Then I got pregnant. So it became very serious. For both of us. It's strange, Bernice. Here I am, unbelievably happy because of the

letters those two wrote to each other, and there they are, arguing.'

'I think it has had a strange effect on all of us,' Bernice muttered.
She said goodnight to Anna and watched her hail a taxi. 'The
fucking correspondence,' she whispered to herself.

They'd made it up by the time they reached Angela's house. Carl
had announced that going back to New York was fine by him, and
Clare had apologized for snapping at him, especially in regard to
their correspondence. They had kissed during the entire taxi ride
back to Chiswick, and Clare opened the front door with a light
though not entirely carefree heart. She hadn't explained how hurt
she'd been that he'd told Bernice about kissing the man, but had
never told her. She hadn't admitted that the hurt had increased
when he'd mentioned Dee-Dee's paying for his trip. She'd kept
those little aches to herself and was glad, now, that she had. What
did they matter? Nothing so insignificant could shake her love for
him. Not now, not after she'd decided to marry him.

The dinner, which had been her idea, was probably ill-judged
anyway, now that she thought about it. Why had she invited Anna
and Bernice? They made an unlikely foursome, and some strain was
inevitable, given that she had hardly spoken to Anna in the past
nine months and her friendship with Bernice had taken a much
less intimate turn. She was searching to re-establish a connection,
but a restaurant was not the place to do it. Seeing Anna and
Bernice separately would have been a much better idea.

As it was, the entire evening had seem forced and out of kilter.
Before dinner, as they were getting dressed, she had felt a perverse
desire not to play the blushing, lovestruck fiancée, a desire which
had translated into her putting on the same grotty clothes she'd
worn all day.

After they'd all arrived at the restaurant, at the beginning of the
meal, Anna began discussing a rumour that Liz Hurley was going
to write an autobiography. Clare had excused herself, and gone
to the loo. On the way back to the table, Carl had caught her

eye. He proceeded to give her a 'we're in this together' look and then actually winked. That wink, Clare knew, was a response to her letter about people recognizing a soulmate in the midst of any crowd or party – the one about being an only child and missing the idea of someone being in your 'team'.

The wink struck Clare as so blatant, so obvious an appeal to their 'closeness', their 'team' spirit, that she almost turned around and walked out of the restaurant. From that moment, every gesture and word of Carl's had annoyed her; and this senseless irritation, in turn, had made her more irritated still.

She was relaxing now, though. She'd probably over-reacted because it had been the first time they'd gone out together in public. She was used to being alone with Carl.

People did not have to do what was expected of them, she remembered Carl writing to her. On New Year's Eve, they didn't *have* to get drunk and kiss everybody.

Well, she didn't have to gaze into his eyes adoringly or find everything he said riveting just because it was an engagement dinner, did she? That's what she could say to Carl if he complained about her behaviour at dinner. She could quote the correspondence back at him, chapter and verse.

The chances were, though, that he wouldn't complain, not after their amorous taxi ride.

Clare turned on the front hall light, then, while Carl walked down the passage and into the kitchen, she went into the study and checked her answering machine for messages. There was only one and when she pushed the play button she heard Artie's voice.

'Clare. Carl. Looks like you're out. If you get in before ten-thirty, please call me at my office. I need to talk to you, Clare. I've just received a letter from that Angela Rae character. Is this lady for real? You won't believe what she has written. Call me pronto. If what she says is true, I need to get over there a.s.a.p. Call me. Oh, this is Art, by the way.'

'Art? What does he want?' Carl had appeared in the doorway.

284

'Angela sent him a letter, apparently.'

'Angela? Why would Angela write to Art?'

'I don't know, we have to call to find out. He says it's urgent. Do you have his office number?'

'I have it right here—' he pointed to his head. '212–865–7256. I'll dial it for you.'

Clare waited as Carl dialled.

'Art? It's Carl. What's going on?' Carl paused. 'Yes, she's here. But you can tell me – all right.' Carl grudgingly handed the telephone to Clare.

'Clare?' Art sounded rushed.

'Yes, Artie?'

'This is so strange, I don't know what to do. I received a letter from Angela today, like I said in the message. It's complicated, but the gist of it is that she claims she had a wild, passionate affair with J D Salinger ten years ago. Which is a completely mind-blowing piece of news – if it's true. Anyway, she says she wants you to write a book about it, based on what she tells you, and she wants me to be your agent. What's the program here, Clare? Is she nuts?'

'I don't know.' Clare was stunned. Angela and the famed recluse Salinger? Could it possibly be true? 'Angela makes up things a lot, Art. This could be pure fabrication. But Angela has done some amazing things in her life, so I suppose it *is* possible.'

'She says she's left something for you, some proof that it's true.'

'What?'

'She's not specific, but she says she left something for you before she went to Texas.'

'She left an envelope. I don't know what's in it. She made me promise not to open it until tomorrow.'

'What does it look like?'

'It's . . . hang on a second,' Clare moved Carl, who had been hovering over her in her chair, to the side and took the envelope out of the top drawer of the desk.

'What's this all about?' Carl asked.

285

'Angela told Art she had an affair with J D Salinger,' Clare explained quickly.

'What?' Carl exclaimed. 'That can't be—'

'It's thick, Art,' Clare ignored Carl and was on the phone again. 'There could be ten pages inside it.'

'Can you open it now?'

'I—' she hesitated. 'No. I made a solemn promise. I can't. Not until tomorrow. I don't want any bad karma coming from Angela. There's something about her . . . I can't explain.'

'You don't have to. Look, I can catch a nine p.m. flight tonight and be over there tomorrow morning. Will you wait to open it until I get there? I mean, Salinger is the mystery man of the literary world. If he was having an affair with a woman who then swam the English Channel and takes round-the-world solo sailing trips, it could be an explosive love story, you know?'

'Absolutely,' Clare replied. 'I think you should come – but don't be too disappointed if it turns out to be a wild-goose chase. I don't know why Angela would want to trick you like that, but I can't guarantee anything. To tell you the truth, I thought whatever was inside the envelope had to do with *my* life, not hers.'

'You sound disappointed.'

'A little, I guess. Is that egotistical of me?'

'No. Look, I better get the program in action here. I've got to pack, get to Kennedy. I've got to get going.'

'Then we'll see you sometime tomorrow morning?'

'Art's coming here?' Carl asked.

Clare nodded, as Art said, 'Probably around nine a.m., if the flight's on time.'

'Great,' Clare smiled into the reciever.

'Great,' Art echoed before hanging up.

'Why didn't you open the letter?' Carl asked, after they'd moved to the kitchen and Clare had recounted Art's side of the conversation.

'You heard what I told Art about Angela. It's true. I don't want to cross her.'

'I think this woman has an unhealthy influence on your life.'

'She's the one who brought us together, remember? That wasn't unhealthy. And, don't forget, you once asked her to marry you.'

'Well, I'm glad now she didn't accept. Why has she written to *Art*, though? It doesn't make sense. She's never met him.'

'She's *seen* him.' Clare took an apple from the bowl of fruit on the table in front of them. She tossed it in the air, caught it, then threw it up again.

'She has?' Carl grabbed the apple in mid-flight. 'We're talking together, Clare. I can't concentrate when you do that. When did Angela see Art? He didn't come *here* did, he?'

'Don't be silly. He sent a tape of the *Magic Moments* show and Angela and I watched it together.'

'You didn't tell me that.'

'You didn't tell me about the man you kissed.' Clare grabbed a pear from the same bowl and began to toss that. 'You didn't tell me about Dee-Dee and the money.'

'Clare, let's not start that up again. And please—' he caught the pear. 'Please stop this fruit-throwing routine. It's getting on my nerves.'

'All right. Listen, Carl. It seems that both of us have neglected to tell each other every tiny thing that happens in our lives. I suppose couples need privacy – if they tell each other everything, there's nothing left to tell.'

'There's *always* something left, Clare. I don't like the idea of our hiding things from each other – I wasn't hiding the story of the guy I kissed, I wasn't hiding Dee-Dee's money, I just forgot to tell you. That's all.'

'And I forgot to tell you about the *Magic Moments* tape. That's all.'

'OK. Sorted. But I'm not sure I'll be any good at giving you your privacy – you should know that.'

'Privacy? Why did you pronounce that with an English accent?

And sorted . . . why did you use that word? That's an *EastEnders* word.'

'I don't know. I picked it up from you. It's some form of osmosis, I guess. You know I've been *trying* to like *EastEnders*. For your sake.'

'It sounds wrong when an American puts on an English accent and uses English expressions. It sounds phoney. And don't try to like a programme for my sake – that's ridiculous.'

'I want Grant Mitchell,' Clare suddenly found herself thinking. 'I want to live above the Queen Vic and serve behind the bar with Grant Mitchell at my side.'

'Alright. OK. I'm sorry. God, Clare, what's happening to us tonight? I think we should talk all this through, these little misunderstandings.'

'I think we should go to bed. I'm knackered.' Clare stood up.

'No, sit down. Really. I think it's important we discuss these things, not keep them inside, so they start to fester.'

'Carl, leave it alone, will you please? You're forcing a conversation I don't want to have—'

'But—'

'I'm sorry. I'm too tired.'

Clare left Carl sitting in the kitchen and went upstairs, wondering how she could be so cruel, why she was picking on him like that? He annoyed the hell out of her with his intensity . . . *that's* what it was. He smothered her.

During the weeks they'd spent together, he'd keep saying how unbelievably amazing everything was: the Tube, the historic buildings, the culture on offer, but especially their perfect, incredible relationship. No one had ever shopped together in a supermarket the way they had. No one had ever walked down a street at dusk the way they had, no love affair in the world, not even Romeo and Juliet's, could compare to theirs.

Until this afternoon, Clare had been overwhelmed by his enthusiasm, his *joy*. That's what she saw on his face when she had said 'yes' to his proposal – joy. The emotion Angela had said she lacked. He could give it to her, she was sure, he could teach her how to feel joy. Together, she knew, they would fill in each other's gaps, lick each other's wounds and make a happy life for themselves. So why had she been crying in bed? Was it because she had come to understand that joy is not like some communicable disease? You can't catch it from someone else no matter how close you stand?

Clare undressed and ran a bath. She had been so certain, so sure that he was the man who could bring out the feelings lying dormant in her. That's what the letter from Angela was going to say – she had been positive. 'Choose Carl, love Carl, let yourself go with Carl and begin to live.' Angela's conviction was Clare's conviction. Now the letter could be something else entirely – proof of a love affair between Angela and a famous writer.

'No.' Clare shook her head fiercely, as she climbed into the bath. It couldn't be. The letter *had* to be about Carl, not J D Salinger. Angela was playing a trick on Art, for some reason Clare couldn't fathom. When she opened the envelope the next day, life would be fine again. Her reservations about Carl's intensity would disappear. These feelings of irritation would stop. There was no doubt about it.

Carl sat down at the kitchen table with pen and paper. He knew how to solve any problems they might be having, even though she refused to talk to him about them. He knew exactly what to do to put things back in place.

He'd write her a letter.

Chapter 20

'We had a mega tailwind, so we landed a half hour early,' Art said, standing in front of the fire with a cup of coffee in his hand. 'And Terminal Four was practically empty. The whole trip was a breeze.'

'Don't you think it was unnecessary?' Carl asked. 'I mean, why not wait for us to call you when we opened the envelope? Why come charging over here? It seems like a waste of time.'

'Hey, Carlo—' Art took a sip of coffee, then put his arm around Carl, who was standing beside him. 'I missed you. What can I say?'

'Of course it was unnecessary,' Art said to himself. 'Do you think I really believe Angela Rae had an affair with J D Salinger? That's about as likely as Demi Moore having had a major fling with Ronnie Corbett. I came because I wanted to see Clare, OK? I would have taken *any* excuse to see her. How can you be so clueless, Carl? How can you be so deaf? How can you not hear my goddamn pounding heart?'

'I guess it's time, now,' Clare announced. She was sitting in a chair in the corner of the room, dressed in jeans and a grey sweatshirt. Angela's envelope was in her hand.

'Go for it,' Art urged.

Carefully opening the white envelope, Clare paused before taking out the contents. She wanted to know, and yet she didn't want to. Angela, at the end of the day, at the end of all these years, still scared her. Was this a Pandora's box, which would let loose all the sins of the world when opened? Hardly, she answered herself. It's a letter – that's all. A letter.

'Go on,' Carl said.

She removed a sheaf of papers, holding them close to her, then leafed through them, speedily, one by one, until she came to the last. Looking up, with a dazed expression on her face, she went back and started at the first page again.

'Clare?' Carl asked, moving toward her chair.

'No – stay away,' she commanded, unable to believe what she was reading. 'Stay away. I don't want anyone to—' she stopped, staring at the last page again. 'Forget Salinger, Art,' she said softly. 'Just forget it. I . . . I have to get out of here.' Standing up, still clutching the pages, she ran into the hall.

'Clare?' Carl ran after her, with Art close behind.

'I have to get out,' she repeated and grabbed a jacket from a peg by the door.

'Clare? Where are you going?'

'Leave me alone. I'm going out.'

'Clare—' Carl started towards the door, but Art held him back. Clare rushed out, slamming it behind her.

'She doesn't want anyone right now, Carl. Listen to what she said.'

'She needs me,' Carl said wildly.

'No. She needs to be on her own. Remember that lecture you gave me about listening to people instead of indulging your ego? Take your own advice.'

'Where is she going? What did that letter say? I don't understand.'

'Come back into the living room and sit down. Calm down. Give her some space.'

Going back in with Art, Carl sat down dejectedly.

'I should have followed her. We had some arguments last night, just little arguments, but we didn't work things out. I wrote her a letter. I wanted her to read it this morning, but she said she had to wait until after she'd read Angela's.'

'You wrote her a letter?' Art raised his eyebrows.

'What's wrong with that?'

'Nothing,' Art said quickly. 'Nothing. It just seems strange when you're actually living together to keep up with this letter business.'

'It's a good way to communicate, to straighten things out. Not that we have any serious problems. We're getting married on Friday, you know.'

'No, I didn't know, actually. Congratulations.' End of story, Art thought. End of song.

'We've been so happy – you wouldn't believe it. It's been incredible – and now – Christ, I could kill Angela Rae. What the fuck is she doing to Clare?'

'I have no idea. Carl. But I'm sure it will all work out.'

'Where do you think she's gone?'

'How would I know?'

'What did the letter say?'

'I don't know, Carl,' Art said with evident exasperation. 'What has happened to your brain? What has happened to *you*? You're like some puppy dog panting at her feet. You're obsessed.'

'No, Art. I'm in love.' Carl stared at Art's round face, which he'd once found so genial. Now it seemed to reflect a hard-hearted emptiness. 'You were always so pissed off at the Brits for not showing their emotions. Now you're giving me a hard time because I *do*.'

'I'm not giving you a hard time, Carl. You've got emotions – that's great. And I'm glad you can show them. But showing them all the time at such a fever pitch . . . it's exhausting. It's as hard to handle as not showing any.'

'Art, you just don't get it.'

'Clearly not,' Art finished his coffee. 'There's probably not a shower in this house, that much I *do* get, having spent way too much time in this country, but I'd like a bath if it's possible.

292

I have to meet someone soon, and I need to clean up after the flight.'

'Who are you meeting?'

'An old friend.'

'I thought you hated all the English.'

'This is an American who is living here temporarily. I called him yesterday. Could you show me where the bath is?'

'Yes, of course,' Carl roused himself. 'And Clare's fixed up the guestroom for you.'

'I could go to a hotel, you know.'

'I know, Artie. And I know we haven't been on good terms lately, but that was before I came here, before Clare and I got together. You can see now that I *did* want all this to happen, I wanted to "close the deal" as you put it. I think we can be friends again, can't we?'

'Sure,' Art nodded.

'So please, stay here with us. Stay for the wedding, if you can.'

'I don't think that's possible. I have to get back to work on Monday. But a night would be great. Now Bathward ho.'

After Art left to meet his friend, Carl sat in the living room contemplating the fire, trying to make sense of recent developments. Clare had run off like a wild, frightened animal, Art had called him 'obsessed', and he was sitting alone in a stranger's house, in a foreign country, a week away from getting married for the second time.

This time his marriage would last. It had to. He wanted a family, children, a home. If that meant he had to find a more stable job, then fine, he would. He could write at night or in the early morning. Anything was possible if he had a soul mate at his side. And Clare, despite her behaviour over the past twenty-four hours, was that soul mate. She was trapped by her environment sometimes, that was all. Growing up in England, she had accumulated many of the characteristics of the national psyche – an unwillingness to delve into personal problems, a reserve, a strait-jacket of White Anglo-Saxon Protestant demeanour which only he could release her from.

He could give her lessons in ethnicity, he thought, smiling to himself. Teach her to wave her hands around and hug people and cry in public. That's all she needed; as she had said in one of those first letters, she had lived in noiseless black and white. He would be the one to provide sound and colour.

She might have problems adjusting to his boisterous, loud family at first, but after a while, she'd fit in. He hadn't told them about her yet, but this time his failure to announce his wedding was different from the last time with Dee-Dee. He didn't expect his parents to disapprove of Clare – no, he thought they'd take a while to get used to her, that's all. She was, after all, foreign.

Anyway, a second marriage was not the same as a first. His mother wouldn't mind so much that his wedding was a *fait accompli* this time. She wouldn't be expecting a church ceremony, a white dress, a long walk down the aisle. This time, she'd forgive him for not informing them. He hoped.

Why he had wanted to stay in London was suddenly a mystery to him. At first he had found it welcoming and refreshingly free of brooding violence. The city was beautiful, imposing and impressive. Right now, it would have been an interesting experiment for him to have lived here, but he should have known all along that it would be a disaster for Clare to stay. She needed a different atmosphere to bring her out of herself. The pace and the craziness of Manhattan would act like a hothouse; it would force her to bloom.

Art was wrong. Art didn't understand Clare. He didn't know that Clare *needed* to be crowded, be forced to deal with her emotions and verbalize her feelings. That's what she had begun to do in the letters and now that's what she could continue to do in real life.

What would she have done if he hadn't forced the issue by

turning up on her doorstep? She would have sunk into a listless life, allowing all her truest emotions to wither and die.

Clare needed leading, that's all. Help. Instruction. What she didn't need was to be left alone.

Deciding to go out into the streets and parks to find her, Carl took one last look at the fire. It was a pity, he thought for an instant. A real shame that they couldn't have stayed in this house for a few months longer, at least. He'd miss this fire back in his tiny, freezing Upper West Side pad. He'd miss the space. And the adventure of a foreign land. Missing all that, however, was infinitely easier than missing Clare.

Art left South Kensington tube station, crossed over two streets and turned left. He walked for another few minutes before reaching Fulham Road and turning right. Passing Butler and Wilson, then the Royal Marsden, he continued heading west, until he came to the Brompton Hospital.

'OK,' he thought. 'Here goes. Let's see if I've made a complete fool of myself.'

She was sitting at a table in the cafeteria, the letter in front of her, a cup by her side. He stood observing her for a moment before plucking up the courage to approach.

'So,' he said, sitting down in the chair across from hers. 'How's it going?'

'Art – God – how did you—' she jumped, startled. The colour rose in her cheeks and he was afraid her beauty at that moment was going to give him a heart attack. At least it was a hospital, he said to himself. Help was close at hand.

'A hunch. I figured you might want to come back here. I know the Brompton is the hospital closest to Kensington which deals with asthma. I'd like to think I'm Sherlock Holmes, but it wasn't that difficult to guess, really.'

'I made a scene, didn't I? I'm sorry.'

'Don't apologize.'

'Is Carl all right?'

'Carl's fine. Don't worry about Carl. You went back to the ward, didn't you?' Art removed his glasses and laid them on the table by her cup of tea.

'Yes,' she said. 'Yes, I did. I walked in there and my heart practically froze. I still can't believe you worked out that I was here. It's amazing.'

'Did some memories come back when you were in the ward? Was it the same as you remembered?'

'Smaller, it seemed smaller of course, as everything from your childhood does when you grow up. Some memories came back – yes. Some were nice, actually. Reasonably pleasant. You know, caring doctors, lovely nurses.'

'And the others? The other memories?'

'Not so lovely. The smells – I was overwhelmed by those hospital smells. I wish I could separate them out, figure out which smell is iodine, which is disinfectant – I don't know, whatever they use in wards. But I can't. It all smells horrible, that's all I know. I wouldn't ever be able to describe it properly,' Clare smiled ruefully. 'It's too close to me. All my books, all the characters in them, they were at a safe remove. Oh, God, Artie, I'm not making much sense.'

'Yes you are.'

'Am I?' Clare picked up Art's glasses and started to fiddle with them. 'Did you know that a huge number of car accidents happen in hospital parking lots?'

'That sounds right. Think of what people must be going through as they drive in and out of places like this. Clare . . . did you remember anything about the girl?'

'Sophie.' Clare didn't look up.

Art stayed silent, studying Clare's hands on the table. She wasn't wearing an engagement ring. Had Carl given her one? As if, Art thought in a wave of anger at his own continuing stupidity, as if it mattered one tiny bit whether Carl had given her one. They were going to be married in six days, engagement ring or not.

Clare's pale blue eyes caught Art's dark eyes for a split second when he looked up, then they turned to the window at the far end of the cafeteria.

'I remembered a little of the last bit, I mean, I remembered that Sophie was in the bed beside mine, holding onto the dog I'd given her. Her mother was with her. And she said – I heard her say, "I'm so frightened, Mummy. The world is going away."'

'God.' Art said softly.

'I think she said that just before everything started to go wrong and people came rushing in from all over the place, and they closed the curtains around her. Her mother was screaming. The lights went out. That's all I remember – the lights going out and then more screams – like the screams on the plane when it was going down – those same screams except I don't know who was screaming. I mean, it couldn't have been the nurses, and it couldn't have been only her mother because it sounded as if the whole ward was screaming. Only I don't know if *I* was screaming. But there were all these figures in the dark and I tried to hide under the sheets. And just as suddenly the lights went back on and as if some magic spell had been put on the ward, the screaming stopped and there was total quiet . . . which was worse. Christ, I sound like Jodie Foster in *The Silence of the Lambs*, don't I?' Clare put her head in her hands. 'It sounds so melodramatic.'

'Maybe it was just plain dramatic,' Art suggested.

'Maybe.' Clare raised her head. This time their eyes caught each others' for a good long moment before both shifted away self-consciously.

'It's weird, Artie, because people *did* die, I mean I'd get to know a child and then, the next time I came back, I'd ask about whoever it was and the nurse would look at me with this . . . this expression which I understood even then. But they died when I was away, so it didn't seemy so real. I couldn't really comprehend it, when Sophie died, though—' Clare stopped.

'It was different. It was real,' Art finished her sentence. 'You know, I think those are the heroes. Kids like Sophie. And their families.'

'I agree.' Clare finally stopped playing with his glasses. 'Have you ever seen anyone die?'

Looking around the cafeteria before answering the question, Art thought of all the doctors he'd seen, all the nurses, all the meals he'd eaten in hospital cafeterias like this one. They all looked the same in the end, the thought. Patients, relatives, doctors – anyone who spends any time at a hospital cafeteria table looks similarly death-weary and desperate for life.

'Yes. My mother. Cancer, of course. I hate that fucking disease.'

'That must have been incredibly painful.'

'It was.' Art paused for a moment before saying, 'I think that's part of the reason I couldn't go along with the "suffer in silence" program a lot of British people seem to believe in. Nothing was silent about my mother's suffering. It couldn't be. She *couldn't* be brave and stoic, it was too goddamn painful. And neither could I, watching her go through it.'

'I'm sorry,' Clare said, reaching out for Art's hand, but switching at the last second and picking up her cold cup of tea instead.

'So am I. But Clare?'

'Yes?'

'The world does go away. There's not a hell of a lot either of us can do about it.'

They sat for a while without speaking. Clare looked down at the table, at Angela's letter.

'You don't have to tell me about that, if you don't want to,' Art said.

'I owe you an explanation, Art.' She pulled the sleeves of her sweatshirt over her hands in a nervous gesture, 'I mean, coming all this way for nothing.'

'I don't mind.'

'You *should* mind. Angela has treated you horribly. I don't understand. And me, too. She's played a joke on me and I don't understand why. It's so upsetting.'

'Well, talk it over with Carl. I'm sure he can help.'

'I can't tell Carl—' Clare shook her head emphatically. 'That's part of the problem, why I was such a mess this morning. I can't tell Carl.'

'Oh,' Art sat back.

'Angela set us up,' Clare mumbled, but Art could hear what she'd said.

'She set you and Carl up?'

'No. You and me. She set *us* up – here – I might as well show this to you. You'll be as confused by this as I was, I'm sure.' Clare pushed the pages in Art's direction.

Picking them up, Art turned over page after blank page – eight of them. When he reached the ninth, the last, he saw two words written in the middle – Art Rolfe.

'What?'

'I know. I've been trying to work it out. She's planned this carefully – sending you that letter just before I was going to open hers – I'm sure she wanted to get you over here. She must have known how exciting her lie was – exciting enough to make you fly to London. She's trying to get us together – in almost the same way Anna tried to get Carl and me together. It's unbelievable – she's behaving as badly as Anna did. I would never have thought Angela was capable of it.'

'Angela doesn't know me – she's never even seen me.'

'Yes, she has. She watched that video you sent. She kept stopping it to concentrate on the faces. I *thought* she was concentrating on Carl's but she must have been concentrating on yours. She must think – she must believe – that you and I – that—'

'Oh.'

'Which is – which is—?'

'Ridiculous,' Art finished. 'You don't have those kinds of feelings for me.'

'Exactly. And you don't have them for me.'

'I think I need some coffee,' Art said, picking up his glasses and putting them on. 'Do you want anything else?'

'No. No thank you.'

'Oh, terrific,' he thought as he queued for a minute, waiting for his coffee. 'Now I have to play the "What could Angela have possibly been thinking of, we're just good friends" game. Now *I* have to be the true Brit and suffer in silence. Where's Douglas Bader when we really need him? What if I *didn't* stay silent? What if I shouted out exactly what I'm feeling right now? I'd make a total asshole of myself, that's what.'

'Well,' Art said when he returned with his cup. 'No harm done, really. Angela hasn't hurt anyone. I had some moments of excitement and a few free drinks on the plane. I wouldn't be too upset by this if I were you.'

'But don't you see the complications, Art? How can I tell Carl? He'd hate Angela. He'd hate her for ever. And despite all this I still love her. I still want her in my life. What am I supposed to tell him about the letter?'

'Hold on—' Art held up his hand. 'Let me ponder for a minute.' Squinting his eyes, he stroked his chin and stared up at the ceiling. 'I hesitate to suggest lying to your future husband, but that may be the answer to this problem.'

'But what would I say? What lie would work? Nothing would make sense. How could I explain her letter to you?'

'That would be a tough one. Let me think some more—' This time Art stared at the floor. 'OK – how about this? What if Angela sent you blank pages – all blank pages. The idea being that you don't need any advice or wisdom from her – you should get it from yourself, from within yourself.'

'Then why wouldn't I have told you and Carl that it was blank? Why would I have rushed off like that?'

'You were upset that you'd been so dependent on Angela for advice. You realized that you should have known all along that no letter from a third party should make any difference to your life, that it should be up to you to control your own destiny. You know – back to the Wizard of Oz theme you and Carl like so much. Dorothy didn't need to go on that seriously traumatic trip to the Emerald City to see the Wizard, all she had to do was click her heels and say "There's no place like home". Or how about . . .

"The answer lies not in our stars, Brutus, but in ourselves." That's always been a good line. Throw that in at some point. Carl loves Shakespeare.'

'I don't know.' Clare shook her head. 'That still doesn't explain why Angela would have sent you that letter about Salinger.'

'For kicks. She's a weird and wacky woman – everyone knows that, right? Maybe she had too much to drink in some Texan bar and wrote a crazed letter to a relative stranger. Listen, Clare, of all the people alive and walking the streets of this world, Carl Lioce is the one I could guarantee would believe that story.'

Clare laughed. She laughed so hard she reached out to steady herself and spilled her cup of coffee. The liquid ran over Angela's letter.

'Let's get rid of the evidence,' Art said in a conspiratorial tone. He gathered up the pages, rose and went to dump them in the bin near the door.

Unusually for London, the sky was a cloudless blue. As he walked down Kensington High Street towards Olympia, Art wondered why he had no memory whatsoever of sunny days – all he could recall from his English sojourn was cloud and rain.

Why had he taken such an intense dislike to this place all those years ago? He had over-reacted, he knew. But why? Did he secretly wish *he'd* gone to Eton? Was he an envious, bitter closet Anglophile? No. Perhaps he had blamed England and the English for his deteriorating relationship with Anna. When a marriage is breaking up it can poison the atmosphere. London reminded him of failure and fights.

Also, cities and countries were strange, like women. Sometimes you fell in love with them instantaneously – as he could remember doing when he stepped off the plane and found himself for the first time in Italy. Sometimes you disliked them on sight.

If pressed, he'd have to say he had hated California as intensely as he hated Britain and found LA even more unpalatable than London. Whereas he had a bizarre sneaking affection for Iceland, which he'd visited once in his life. The reaction he had to places was visceral, just as his response to people was.

Could he trust those reactions, though? He'd fallen in love with Anna – granted at a young age, but still old enough not to be able to use callow youth as an excuse. And now he'd fallen in love for the second time in his life – with Clare. On the basis of what? Visceral response. Carl had spent over a year writing to Clare, while he, Art, had spent all of one short evening, one aborted lunch and one coffee break with her. Had Carl been right about people taking too many short cuts with each other? Was he, unlike Carl, too impatient to take the time to get to know someone before tumbling into a state of demented romantic yearning?

Or did all those words Carl and Clare had exchanged add up to far less than a shared look and shared laughter across a hospital cafeteria table?

Art, when he had finally located Bernice's flat and been ushered in, was jolted out of his musings by the sight of a surprisingly tidy, nicely decorated two-bedroom apartment.

'Don't look so stunned,' Bernice said, smiling. 'Underneath my sluttish exterior lurks a natural-born domestic paragon. I don't let many people in here, though. They'd be shocked and disappointed in me.'

Informing Bernice of the goings-on of the last forty-eight hours while she fixed him yet another cup of coffee, Art settled into a rocking chair at the head of her kitchen table.

'You're being very blasé about all this, Artie,' she commented when she save him his coffee and joined him. 'If someone had told Carl I was *the* woman for him, I'd be jumping up and down with excitement.'

'Oh, come on, Bernice. I don't have a chance in hell – Angela Rae or no Angela Rae – bless her. They're getting married on Friday. Today is Saturday. This isn't Four Weddings and a Funeral and Clare's not Hugh Grant, thank God. She's not going to bolt at the altar or at the front of the registry office. No, this is One Wedding and My Funeral.'

'One Wedding and *Our* Funerals. I wish they'd go away, I wish they'd get out of this country.' Bernice rose from the table, took her coffee, threw it down the sink and got a bottle of wine out of her fridge. 'Carl wanted to stay here,' she continued, uncorking it. 'Did you know that? And Clare wanted to go to New York.'

'Clare wanted to move to New York?'

'Absolutely. She was really unsettled when Carl said he preferred living in London.' Bernice poured out two glasses. 'Here. Join me. It's far too late in the day for coffee. Anyway, I'm sure Carl's given up on the idea of staying here. He wouldn't do anything which might upset poor Clare.'

'*Poor* Clare? Vicious tone alert, Bernice. I thought she was your friend.'

'And I thought Carl was yours. I haven't heard you say anything nice about him for . . . for . . . how long? I'd guess since the day I met you.'

'That's not fair. I like Carl. From the first moment he walked into my office with his book wrapped up like a Christmas present, I liked the guy. He has a warmth, a spirit I really admire. In fact, I *love* Carl. But this whole thing is bringing out the worst in him. He has lost all perspective – he's so focused on a fairy-tale ending to the correspondence, he can't see how ill-suited they are. This marriage is going to be a disaster. And—' Art shrugged. 'Although I love Carl, I love Clare more than I love Carl. Love for a woman has a stronger pull for me, you know? There are all those extra benefits.'

'Well, I love Clare too. I'm just jealous of her. Truly, madly, deeply jealous. People aren't supposed to be jealous of friends. Well, I am. But I still love Clare. I don't see why I can't love her and be jealous of her at the same time.'

'You have a point.'

'Right. Anyway, when I occasionally get moments of lucid thinking on this subject, I can forget my jealousy and try to see them as a couple. And I agree that they're totally ill-suited.

303

But honestly, Art, we're not the ones to inform them of this little fact, are we? I mean, we have ulterior motives.'

'You have a point there, too. Bernice, you have lots of points, but do you have anything to eat?'

'Marks and Spencer's all right by you?'

'What, are we having shirts and underwear for lunch?'

'They do food, too, Artie.'

'Oh. Fine.'

Art watched as she pulled two packages out of the fridge, opened them, pierced the film on the top and shoved them into a microwave on the kitchen counter.

'I keep thinking that Carl will be like my other doomed romances,' she said as she set the temperature and timer, 'that, eventually, he'll fade from my mind. And when I saw him the other night, he'd changed. But my feelings for him hadn't. I wish I'd never gone on that trip to New York. It sucks, Artie. The whole thing sucks.'

'Well, Annie had a good result from it all,' he commented. 'Has she told you her news?'

'Yes, it's amazing, isn't it?'

'It's wonderful. Did you tell her the way you feel about Carl?'

'No.'

'Did you tell anyone else, besides me?'

'Approximately a thousand people. I don't know why I didn't tell Anna, actually. I tell anyone who will listen. I even told—' she stopped.

'Yes? Bernice? Who?'

'Jeremy,' she said, blushing. 'He came to talk to me, to ask me questions, all about Clare and Carl and I don't know how it happened. Well, I do know. Once I started, I couldn't stop myself. God.' Bernice reached for her wine glass. 'It's so embarrassing. I told him everything. He promised he wouldn't repeat what I'd said to Clare. I trusted him – he's one of those people who wouldn't cheat if his life depended on it. At least I think he is. I couldn't bear it if Clare found out about my feelings for Carl. It would be so humiliating. Shit, I'm such an idiot. Hold on, I've just got to get a packet of fags from the bedroom.'

When she returned, Bernice lit a cigarette from the flame on the hob. The microwave buzzed and Bernice went to it, wiping her eyes as she did so.

'Don't beat yourself up, Bernice. Believe it or not, I was idiotic enough to tell Jeremy about my feelings for Clare too. A week or so ago he telephoned me at my apartment. I'd had a few glasses of wine. He was very cordial; I admired his style. Now I feel as if he lulled me into a false sense of security. Before I knew it, I'd told him the whole sad story. I felt like we had bonded, you know – both losing Clare – not that I ever had her in the first place. But he was incredibly sympathetic. The next day, when I woke up, I worked out that he must have called me at three a.m. his time. I mean, what's that all about?'

'I don't know.' Bernice grabbed an oven glove, took the packages out of the microwave and dumped their contents into two bowls.

'Maybe he has some sort of long-range game plan?'

'Maybe he'll do what we can't. Maybe he'll break them up before Friday and marry her himself.' She plonked down one of the bowls and a fork in front of him.

'I wouldn't say this to anyone else in the world, but I'd prefer Jeremy to Carl when it comes to being Clare's husband.'

'Obviously,' Bernice said, picking up the bottle of Chablis and pouring more into Art's glass, 'I would too.'

A couple of hours and a couple of bottles later, Art found himself back in Angela Rae's sitting room, attempting to look surprised at Carl's news that Angela's letter had been one long blank.

'This is ridiculous,' he said, trying to sound outraged. 'Why would Angela be so perverse? And why is she jerking *my* chain with this Salinger stuff?'

'She may have been drunk when she wrote you, Art,' Clare turned her head away from Carl, trying to hide the guilt she felt.

Art and she were in league against Carl, fooling him with lies. She wished Art would bring the conversation to an end quickly.

'This is all too much.' Art rose from the sofa. 'I need to take a little nap. I'm jet-lagged. And disappointed. But I'll be fine after a short sleep.'

'Should I wake you for dinner?' Clare asked. 'I've got some pasta. I know you like pasta. It's five now – what if we eat at eight?'

'Umm, thanks, Clare, but I'm going out tonight.'

'Really?'

'Yes. Bernice and I are hitting the town. I thought I'd take her gambling.'

'Gambling?'

'Sure. I used to be a member of the Vic. I think those are lifelong memberships – I'm going to find out, anyway. So if you would please wake me up around seven, I'd be grateful.'

'I'll wake you up, Artie.'

'Thanks, Carl. Goodnight for awhile everybody.'

'Why did you buy pasta for Art?' Carl asked as soon as Art had disappeared from the room. 'And why am I being such a jerk?' he asked himself simultaneously.

'I know he likes it,' was all she replied.

'Are you willing to talk with me now? Will you tell me what you think about *my* letter?'

'Right now?' Clare sighed.

'Yes. Right now.'

He was on self-destruct, he knew, but he couldn't stop. She was being so elusive, so distant. He wanted to pin her down and make her understand him. After she'd finally returned to the house around noon and explained about Angela's non-letter, he'd forced her to read his own letter.

'It's very sweet and thoughtful' was all she said when she'd finished it.

And then she'd insisted on going out again, this time to shop for food. By herself. When she came back, she avoided talking to him all afternoon, claiming she had to prepare some kind of fancy pasta meal for Art. He'd been silently seething as he sat in the kitchen watching her chop onions and create a ridiculously complicated sauce. But he refused to leave her presence – he wouldn't budge.

When Art arrived, Carl had been on the verge of physically grabbing Clare and shaking her until she consented to speak to him. Now, with Art upstairs taking a nap and all the cooking done, she was still trying to side-step a decent conversation.

'As I said before, the letter was sweet and thoughtful. And well-written.'

'Well-written? I'm not in some creative writing course you're teaching, Clare.'

'Well, it was. I can't help it if I notice that.'

'What about the *emotions*?'

'Carl—' Clare swept back her hair from her face. 'Angela was right about me. I don't have many emotions, or not as many as you want me to have. If we get irritated by each other occasionally, I don't think it's the end of the world. You need everthing to be so perfect.'

'But it *is* perfect. I want you to recognize that, that's all.'

'I know. You said it in the letter – that we are perfect together. But don't you remember saying in one of your early letters that you distrusted perfection? That you liked human failings?'

'Maybe I distrust perfection, but I can't deny it when it exists, and neither should you.'

'I'm not sure how to explain this to you,' Clare grabbed a cushion from the sofa and hugged it to her, 'but I'll try. People don't have to talk all the time. Sometimes they can let subjects drop. You know, it's like in films – the really erotic ones, as far as I'm concerned, aren't explicit, they're slightly veiled. I displayed my emotions in my letters. You've seen them, you've seen me. And yes, I needed to show myself more, to come out of myself. But I don't want you standing over me waiting for me to emote every second. I want to be able to cook a meal without you staring at me. I want to walk down streets with you without discussing what it's like to walk down a street together. Don't you understand?'

307

'Yes,' Carl replied, only because he knew if he didn't agree she might explode or walk out or even *flee* from him. What was wrong about talking? he wanted to ask. Why not comment on how it felt like to be together? In the early days with Dee-Dee, he'd been intrigued by her silence, but now he knew it had masked a huge desire to speak, to share – a desire he hadn't recognized at the time. Dee-Dee had had to go elsewhere to share, to all those group meetings. He needed to make it clear to Clare not only that she could speak, but also that she *should* speak and share with him.

A mania had gripped him, a mania to understand Clare's essence. He thought he'd succeeded when he arrived in London and she'd greeted him so happily. He thought he'd ensured permanent success when she agreed to many him. But now? Now she was drawing away and fighting all his efforts to bring her back in.

'I just want to be normal, Carl,' she threw down the cushion, moved across the sofa and put her arms around him.

'But you *aren't* normal,' he wanted to say. 'Neither of us is. We're extraordinary. Together, we're extraordinary.'

The telephone rang just as he had begun to kiss her. She leapt from his arms to answer it, going to the extension in her study rather than the one in the kitchen.

Was that because she could close the door in her study? he asked himself. Was she shutting him out yet again?

He stood up and sneaked into the Hallway, flattening himself against the wall closest to the study door. All he could hear, though, was her muffled voice. Creeping back on tiptoe, he was stoking the fire when she came in.

'So?' he looked up. 'Who was that?'

'That was Jeremy.'

'Jeremy? What did he want?'

'He wants to have lunch with me tomorrow. I said that was fine.'

'I think I should come, too.'

'Carl.'

'If he's trying to get you back, he should come out into the open and face me instead of sneaking around.'

'He doesn't want me back. He knows it's over.' Clare paused. 'He wants us to be friends. He's civilized. And a civilized man can have lunch with his ex-girlfriend without kidnapping her. I wouldn't mind if you had lunch with Dee-Dee.' Suddenly, she began to pace around the room. And just as suddenly she stopped, came up to him, grabbed him fiercely by the shoulders. 'Carl, listen, I'm feeling claustrophobic. Do you think we could ask Art if we can join him and Bernice tonight? I'd love to go out gambling.'

'What about the special dinner you prepared? Since Art's going out, I thought we'd be having it together. And then we could watch *Notorious*.'

'*Notorious*? For the fiftieth time since you arrived? I don't think so, Carl.' Her voice was shrill, Carl thought. Feverishly shrill. Almost screaming with frustration. 'Come on,' she said after a few seconds. He could sense that she was taking great pains to regain control of herself. 'It would be fun to go out.'

'Sure. Of course. I'll ask Artie when I wake him up.'

'Fantastic,' Clare said, breaking into a relieved smile. 'That will be terrific.'

'Artie.' Carl shook Artie's shoulder. 'It's seven. Wake up.'

'What?' Art struggled to a sitting position. 'Where am I? What's happening?'

'You're in London. You're about to go out with Bernice. And Art, listen. Clare wants us to go along with you two. I don't think that's such a good idea.'

'Why not?' Art yawned.

'We need as much time alone together as we can get at the moment. You understand, don't you?'

'I guess so.' He yawned again.

'OK. Enough. So you'll tell Clare this is a hot date. You know, just you and Bernice. Extra company not appreciated.'

'If it's that important to you, sure. But Carl, don't you think you may be smothering her a little? If she wants to go out, don't you think—'

'No. She's having lunch with Jeremy tomorrow. I want some time alone with her tonight.'

'Are you jealous of Jeremy?'

'No, no Art, I'm not jealous. What's wrong with everybody? Doesn't anyone believe in romance anymore? I want a romantic evening, OK?'

'OK, OK. No problem.' Art stretched his arms, then made circular motions with his head. 'I believe in romance. I believe in the Beatles. Shit, I believe in Santa Claus – only he didn't show up this year – why do you think that is? Maybe he's sick of the red suit?'

Chapter 21

This was not the way to behave, Clare knew.

She stood in front of the kitchen window looking out onto the small back garden noticing how clear the wintry dawn light was; a sharp, clean light which made the grass come alive again.

Needling Carl, avoiding Carl, being an outright bitch to Carl, were all activities Clare would never before have thought herself capable of. What had snapped? Could you fall out of love with someone as abruptly as you fell in love? Was there a thin elastic band holding all emotion in place, a band which could stretch and break at any second without your knowing it had even been under pressure?

Was it that one wink that had done it? Had one wink destroyed a love affair?

If that were the case, though, why should she be so angry with Carl? It wasn't his fault. He hadn't done anything dreadful or cruel to disillusion her. All he had done was to try to convey a sense of shared intimacy. It had been an obvious way to convey it. She couldn't fall out of love with him just because of that, could she?

Or had she fallen out of love with him because she'd come to know him better?

He was a sweet, wonderful, spontaneous man who was full of fun, who took an astounding interest in all things British – an interest which was almost, she thought when she came upon him one morning poring over a list of Cockney rhyming slang, obsessive – and who loved her madly. There was no real reason not to love him, any more then there had been a real reason not to love Jeremy.

She just didn't, that was all. And she was angry with him because she was angry at herself. She had promised, in all good faith, to marry him. The ceremony was due to take place in five days.

So what, exactly, was she going to do about it?

Cradling the cup of coffee against her chest, Clare kept her eyes fixed on a pigeon which had landed in the garden. It was dejectedly, half-heartedly surveying its surroundings. Evidently finding nothing of interest, it flew off again.

Did she have a right to break his heart?

Did she have a right to assume that she was so crucial to his life, that she *would* break his heart if she left him?

He was a grown man – an intelligent, attractive, funny, grown man. He wouldn't want to be married out of pity. She wasn't irreplaceable, she knew very well. There were other women he could love, even if he didn't meet them in the fateful way he had met her.

That's what confused the issue so much, Clare thought. The fact that they had corresponded so long, the fact of their bizarre getting together. The mixed identities, the uncertain waiting period before he'd come over, everything had played out like some romantic tale. Carl loved stories, he *believed* in them. He had chosen her to be the princess in this particular story and this particular story happened to be the story of his life.

No man would ever treat her better, of that she was sure. He would make her his priority. She would be able to discuss with him every little problem she had ever had in detail. In painstaking detail. For days. He would be a shrink, a friend, a lover, everything wrapped into one. How could she not take what he offered? What more did she want?

She wanted less. She wanted someone who would challenge her, someone who would shout back at her, even if, at the time, she hated being shouted at. And she wanted someone who would leave her alone sometimes.

But what she most wanted was a man who would look after her, yet, at the same time, allow her to be strong. It might be an impossible combination by definition, she knew, but that was what she was looking for. Not a white knight on a charger but a man who would help her figure out how to be a woman who didn't need rescuing.

Carl had responded to her weaknesses, she knew now. He kept referring to her letters about her childhood fears. He was drawn to them, as a doctor would be drawn to a patient's illness. That was Carl's nature, to tend to people in trouble. She adored him for that, but adoration was different from marital love. He had said that he loved a woman as he would love a child. Well, she wasn't his child. She didn't want to be his child.

She could call the wedding off. She *should* call the wedding off. She should go upstairs right now, wake him up and tell him it was impossible, that their marriage could never work.

How would he react? How awful was this going to be?

Clare opened the window and took a huge, deep breath of winter air. When she exhaled, she started to cough. Turning on the tap to get herself a glass of water, she was surprised when she coughed again. Before she could fill the glass, she'd dropped it in the sink. The coughing took hold of her, in spasms stronger than she could believe. This wasn't like the attack she'd had at the television studio. No, it was worse, much worse. She grabbed the edge of the sink to keep herself upright, but found that she couldn't hold on. Sinking down on the floor, she gasped in terror, knowing she couldn't move. There was no way to get to the study, no way to reach her handbag with the inhaler. Why? she thought, manically. Why do I have to die on a kitchen floor?

The world's going away and I'm going with it.

When the arms grabbed her, when the inhaler magically

appeared in front of her, she had no idea how long she'd been struggling to breathe. Had it been seconds, minutes, hours? The panic of being robbed of breath, strangling on an invisible rope, didn't subside until she'd managed to breathe semi-normally for ten minutes.

'Should I call an ambulance?' Carl asked quietly.

'No,' she barely managed to shake her head. 'I'll be all right.'

'OK.'

He continued to hold her from behind, clasping her in his arms, giving her the strength she needed.

'How did you know?' She finally twisted her head around to look up at his face.

'I heard you coughing. It woke me up, I guess. I came in here and saw you – you couldn't have noticed me – you were in real trouble. I remembered you telling me about that attack before the *Magic Moments* show, how you had your inhaler thing in your purse. So I found your purse in the study and I found the inhaler and that's pretty much that.'

'Carl—' she whispered.

'Don't worry,' he interrupted. 'It's all part of the service. And it's my dream come true – rescuing the woman I love.'

Jeremy had suggested they meet for lunch at Cibo's, a small Italian restaurant behind Olympia, not far from Bernice's flat. He was waiting for her when she arrived, reading the sports pages of the *Mail on Sunday*.

'Excellent,' he said, standing up to give her a kiss on both cheeks. 'I'm glad you could come.' He sounded so congenial, Clare thought, as if she were one of his friends who needed to be reassured of his continuing interest.

'I'm a little nervous, actually,' Clare admitted, thinking that she should get all the potentially painful subjects of conversation over with as early on as possible. 'I didn't tell you at the lunch we had before – I don't know why – I should have, Carl and I are getting married. This Friday actually.'

'Ah!'

He didn't flinch, didn't betray any surprise or emotion, but then she hadn't expected him to.

'I honestly hope you'll be happy, Clare.'

'Thank you, that's very generous of you.'

'Well,' he tilted his head to the side and smiled. 'The better man won. What can I say?'

'I don't see it as a sporting contest,' Clare replied.

'Of course not,' he said soothingly. 'But you know I see everything in sporting terms. That's the way my mind functions, I'm afraid.'

Clare ordered a mineral water, as did Jeremy.

'I'm interested—' Jeremy put his elbows on the table and rested his chin on his right hand. 'The *Magic Moments* programme. How did you feel when you were about to go on?'

'I—' Clare paused. She wasn't used to Jeremy asking how she 'felt' about any subject. 'I was terrified before it began. Really terrified.'

'And when you got to the stage and the show began?'

'Well, then Carl, I mean, Art came on. I calmed down at that point. Why do you ask?'

'I'm interested,' he repeated. 'After the show, you went out with Bernice, am I right?'

'Yes, Jeremy. Why are you asking me all these questions about that time in New York?'

'Indulge me, Clare,' Jeremy said, a half-smile on his handsome face. 'Nothing is going on. There is nothing sinister about my interest. I don't, for example, have any plot to break you and Carl up. Yes, I had believed we were going to get married, but I understand now that it may not have been such a good idea, after all. We had three excellent years. We can both move on.'

'That sounds clinical.'

'It's not meant to be. I suppose I should tell you that *I've* met someone else, too.'

'Really?' Clare felt a bullet pass through her heart, but then

315

she felt it make a clean exit on the other side. 'Is she someone I know?'

'No. She's someone I knew ages ago, when I was a child actually. She lived down the street. We hated each other back then, but when we ran into each other at my parents' New Year's party, well, we'd both grown up a lot. We've only been together a week, but a week can change everything.' He passed his hand through his brown hair, and he smiled self-consciously. 'Anyway, the point is, you can relax about my intentions. I'm asking you about New York because I want to know what happened, I suppose. When I'm bowled out in a match I watch the video, I study it to see exactly what mistake I made. What went on in New York had me confused. I couldn't get a grip on how you felt. Everyone involved in that episode seemed like alien creatures to me – even you.

'I was pleased when you flew home with me, but then you went into a slump which I couldn't really understand either. At that point I didn't know now to confront you or how to talk about it. So I concentrated on my cricket and pretended nothing had really occurred. Of course Carl showing up while I was away changed the picture entirely. My feeling, when you told me on the telephone, was that he had broken the rules, he had cheated – gone behind my back as it were.'

'Unsportsmanlike behaviour,' Clare commented, amazed by how much Jeremy was talking. This new woman must have unleashed a part of his psyche.

'Something like that,' Jeremy nodded. 'Although, as we know, all's fair in love and war. Anyway, I retired from the field as gracefully as I could and let you get on with it. I can't pretend I wasn't hurt and offended as well, but I've recovered now.'

A waiter came to take their orders as Clare pondered Jeremy's words.

'You know I don't like to talk about myself, that I'm a very private person,' he continued after the waiter had gone. 'I realize this may sound strange, but I would be far happier if I could play cricket without anyone watching. I don't want fans, I don't

316

particularly like applause. I love the sport, that's all. Not the trappings of it. Because of those trappings, I've built walls around myself. They're very effective, but they keep people I care about out as well. I feel as if I kept you out, Clare. And I want to make sure I haven't hurt you by doing that. I care about you, you know, I really do. I want to think that you'll be happy.'

'I am happy, Jeremy,' she said, looking down at the tablecloth.

'That's good,' he nodded. 'Tell me something. After we came back to London, I assume you were in touch with Carl?'

'He wrote me letters, yes,' Clare blushed. 'I'm sorry. I didn't tell you that. I was conf—'

'It's over. Don't worry. There's no need to apologize now. What about Art? Did he contact you?'

'Yes,' Clare replied, wondering why Jeremy had asked that question. 'He called me once and said he thought that I should talk to my mother about my childhood. I never told you, but I used to be terrified constantly when I was a child. Art suggested I try to find out if anything had sparked off that terror, any incident.'

'You never told me. You see, I *did* keep you out.' Jeremy cocked his head and studied Clare in such a way that she felt uncomfortable. 'And was there any childhood incident?'

'Yes, Art was right. A girl had died in the bed beside mine at the hospital. Sophie. She was a friend of mine. Jeremy, I—'

'Did you let Art know he'd been right?'

'No. I told Carl. And Carl told Art. Art sent me a video of the *Magic Moments* show, along with a note saying he hoped I could grieve for Sophie now.'

'Well,' Jeremy said as their lunch arrived. 'That's all I really wanted to know, actually.'

'But—' Clare felt dazed. 'You haven't asked about Carl. I mean, you keep making me talk about Art.'

'Really?' Jeremy sat back as the huge plate of pasta was placed in front of him. 'That wasn't my intention.'

Befuddled, Clare stared at her chicken breast.

'Do you hate Carl so much?' she asked in a frightened voice.

'You said he had cheated, that he hadn't behaved honourably. Is that what you think of him?'

'No. I told you, all's fair. He was playing by his own rules. So be it.'

'You may not believe this, but Carl saved my life this morning – literally. I know that sounds over the top, but it's true. I was having an incredibly bad asthma attack and he found me, he saved me. He's different, Jeremy, I know. He's not like me. Or you. Carl took a risk when he showed up here. He's a gambling man. I admire people who gamble. I need to learn how to gamble myself.' She knew there was a desperate note in her voice.

'That's excellent, Clare, really. I'm not here to disparage Carl. And obviously I'm grateful to him and I admire him for saving your life. That's heroic. Although, I have to say, I'm surprised you had an asthma attack in the first place. Were you under some kind of stress? What set it off, do you know?'

'I—' Clare rubbed her eyes hard with her hands. She let out a little puff of air. And she didn't finish the sentence.

'Anyway, tell me, how's Bernice these days? What's she up to?'

'She's fine,' Clare replied, relieved to be on to a different subject. 'She went out last night – with Art, actually. He's in town. They went to a—' Clare stopped.

'To a . . . ?'

'To a casino.'

'Oh.' Jeremy twirled strands of spaghetti expertly on his fork. 'That must have been fun. Art and Bernice make a good couple, don't you think?'

'Why does everyone keep putting them together?'

'Excuse me?'

'I mean, I don't think they're really a couple. They're just messing around. Honestly, they don't suit each other.'

'Really? Why do you say that?'

'Art's not Bernice's type. She goes for better-looking men, you know, *superficially* better-looking men. Art is handsome in

318

a very subtle way. He has incredible eyes, and he has a sense of playfulness that's really attractive without being too boyish. Benice wouldn't understand the nuances, what's underneath his sharp businessman-like approach. He's complicated, but he's also empathetic. He's capable of lying, when it's necessary, but he has scruples. It's hard to explain, but he's—'

'He's . . . ?'

'Nothing. Never mind. I just don't think he and Bernice would make a good pair.'

'Oh,' Jeremy shrugged. 'I thought they would, from what I've seen of them, which, granted, isn't much. Anyway, that's for them to sort out, isn't it?'

'Yes,' Clare said. 'It's none of our business, really. And he's not here for long. In fact, he's going back to New York late this afternoon.'

'Right,' Jeremy nodded, devouring another forkful of pasta.

She couldn't eat. She kept staring at her plate as thoughts crashed through her brain, knocking against each other like dodge'em cars. Why did she feel as if Jeremy had put her through the wringer? He hadn't asked anything particularly intrusive. He had steered well clear of her sex life with Carl. He hadn't pressed her for any intimate details. Yet she felt as if she'd been a corpse in an autopsy, dissected bit by bit, all her organs removed and stuffed into bottles.

'Jeremy?'

'Yes.'

'Would you mind terribly if I left now? I'm not hungry. I feel a little ill. I think I should go home and lie down.'

'Of course, I'm sorry you're not feeling well. Pre-wedding nerves, perhaps.' He smiled sympathetically, but his face suddenly struck Clare as inappropriately amused.

'What's so entertaining?' Clare wondered as she rose from the table and received his goodbye kisses. 'What don't I know now?'

When Clare returned home, she found Carl and Art sitting in the living room, surrounded by Sunday papers. Art's face was pale, his eyes weary.

'You're back early,' Carl said, jumping up. 'Anything wrong? Are you feeling OK? I know you shouldn't have gone out after this morning.'

'I'm fine,' she said hastily, taking off her jacket. 'It was fine. Jeremy had to get back early. Net practice at Lord's.'

'But it went alright?'

'Yes. I told him we're getting married, he told me he's found another woman, so everything is absolutely fine.' She looked at Art, still sitting cross-legged on the floor in front of the fire.

'You look dreadful,' she addressed him, her voice sharp.

'Thanks. I feel it.'

'You slept in. You must have had a hell of a time.'

'It was fun.'

'I bet.'

The blatant sarcasm in her voice made Art look up from the *Observer* with a questioning gaze.

'We got tanked. And we won a lot of money. I figured that allows me to feel simultaneously hungover and happy.'

'Don't you think you might have a problem?'

'Clare?' Carl looked at Clare in disbelief.

'What kind of problem?' Art asked. 'I have to catch a plane soon. That's the only problem I can think of. Terrorist bombs might be awaiting me midair.'

'A drinking problem. A gambling problem.'

'Oh, I see. Well, drinking *and* gambling – that makes two. So that means I have *problems* plural.'

'What does Bernice think of your problems?'

'Clare, what's wrong with you? Why are you weighing into Artie like this? He hasn't done anything wrong.' Carl was staring at her as she stood in the middle of the living room, her hands on her hips, looking like a pissed-off housewife who had been unhappily married for thirty years.

'He's going out with my best friend and he's taking her gambling

320

and he probably got her drunk as well. And now he's leaving, flying off.' Clare repeatedly shook her head in anger as she said these words. 'I don't think that's right. I think that's dishonourable. It's not the way a man should behave.'

'Whoa—' Art but both hands up in the air in a gesture of surrender. 'Sorry to offend your sensibilities, Clare. I didn't know—'

'You don't know anything,' Clare yelled, then burst into tears and fled the room.

'Sweetheart, what's wrong?' Carl was by her side on the bed, stroking her hair. 'What was that all about?'

'I don't know,' Clare replied, burying her head in the wet pillow.

'You're concerned about Bernice, is that it?'

She nodded.

'Well, I can understand that, but I'm sure she's OK. You're probably still recovering from this morning, too. I really wish you hadn't gone out. I'm sure you didn't mean to, but I think you hurt Artie's feelings just now. I mean, he's a decent bloke, really. I don't like to see him hurt.'

'Bloke?' Her head lifted.

'Sorry, he's a decent *guy*. He and I have had our problems recently, but I'll always love him.'

Clare remained silent.

'Are you sure it wasn't something Jeremy said at lunch? Did he upset you?'

'No. I'm sure.'

'Well, Artie's leaving in a little while, so we'll get back to normal.'

'Normal,' she mumbled.

'Do you think you can say goodbye to him? Or do you really dislike him that much?'

'I think I should drive him to the airport,' Clare said, sitting up. 'I was so nasty to him. I didn't mean to be, I don't know what got into me.' She balmed away tears from her cheeks. 'I just lost it.'

'Pre-wedding nerves,' Carl said, kissing the top of her head.

'Yes,' Clare replied, biting her thumbnail. 'That's it. Pre-wedding nerves.'

'I'm sorry,' Clare said, staring straight ahead as they approached the Chiswick roundabout. Neither she nor Art had spoken after they'd climbed into her car.

Until it was time to leave, Carl and she and Art had conversed pleasantly enough – making jokes about Angela's mythical affair with Salinger, about some of Art's more outrageous authors, about anything but Clare's recent outburst. Carl had pulled Clare aside and whispered, 'I think you should go without me and make it up' when Art announced that he should really get going.

'No problem,' Art replied to Clare's apology, staring ahead as well. They merged onto the M4 and sped towards Heathrow, in silence. When they arrived at the airport, Clare pulled into the Terminal Four car park.

'You don't have to come in,' Art said.

'I want to,' she replied.

His flight, they learned from one of the many overhanging information screens, was delayed by an hour.

'Do you want a cup of coffee or a drink?' Clare asked.

'A drink would probably help, yes,' he answered.

At a table in the bar, they sat in silence again. Five minutes passed before Art said, 'Maybe I should go now – check in, go through Immigration and into the pleasure palace of Duty-Free land.'

'Art—' Clare put her hand on his wrist. 'Don't go. Not yet.'

Another couple of minutes passed without either speaking until Art looked at his watch.

'Art—' Clare inhaled, then exhaled heavily. 'Are you *really* fond of Bernice? I mean, I've known her for a long time. I don't want her to be hurt. After what happened between you in New York, I mean, obviously you two have some kind of relationship.'

'And?' Art looked at her. 'I don't think I understand what you're trying to say, Clare.'

'I don't want her to be hurt, that's all.'

'So you're . . . asking me what my intentions are?'

'Oh, God. I don't know.' Clare knocked her forehead with her fist. 'It's none of my business, is it?'

'Well, I don't plan on marrying her, if that's what you want to know. But then she's not planning on marrying me, either, I think you'll find, Clare, that the man who hurts Bernice is not the one sitting with you now.'

'I'm sorry.'

'You've said that.'

'I know. I know. God. I don't know what to say. I have all these things to say and I don't know how to say them. If you and Bernice—'

'Can we skip me and Bernice? We've covered that subject.' Artie straightened his navy blue and green polka-dot tie. 'If you want to talk about Bernice and me and you don't know what to say, why don't you write it? After you and Carlo get married, write me a letter, Clare. Tell me what to do with my love life. Give me friendly advice.' Art's annoyed voice rose in pitch. 'I tell you what. Let's have a correspondence, why don't we? I know it won't be anything like as good as the one you have with Carl, but you're not going to continue that when you're married, are you? Or are you?'

He slapped his forehead.

'Oh, how silly of me. Of course you are. Carl and Clare can't exist without a correspondence. Nothing counts unless it's on paper, does it? Right.' He grabbed the napkin beside his drink, took a pen out of his jacket pocket and wrote 'To Clare: Goodbye. I love you, From Art.' Stuffing it into her hand, he strode off towards the check-in counter. Clare, after seeing what he'd written, burst into tears, crumpled the napkin in her hand, threw it on the table and walked, head bowed, in the opposite direction.

*   *   *

323

'I feel disloyal telling you this,' Carl said into the telephone, 'but I'm confused. She's been acting so strangely lately. I can't talk to her. She's unreachable. I don't understand her.'

'You didn't understand me, either,' Dee-Dee replied, but there was kindness, not reproach in her voice. 'I don't blame you, Carl. I was crazy in those days, I really was. I feel now as if I've woken up from a bad dream.'

'What do you mean?'

'I mean, the way I kept struggling to find something, anything, to believe in. And then the book—'

'I thought you were proud of the book. Just because it hasn't sold yet, Dee-Dee, doesn't mean—'

'I know, I know. That's not it, though. *Shescape* was so confused. No wonder it hasn't sold.'

'What's made you change your mind about all this?'

'I met someone who made me see things clearly, finally.'

'A man?'

'Yes.' Carl could hear the smile in Dee-Dee's voice. 'But not that kind of man. Not a boyfriend. A teacher, Carl. Someone who can guide me through life.'

Carl stifled a groan.

'He's different, his seminars are very different to the ones I went to before. I told him about trying to find myself, you know, and he said, "Why do you need to find yourself when you have your legs?"'

'What?'

'I know that sounds bizarre. What he meant was that I really went wild trying to find myself at exactly the same time I gave up on being a professional dancer. When I knew I wasn't going to be a star. Remember?'

'Yes, that's when you started teaching. And you began the seminars at the same time.'

'Exactly. So he said, "Look, Dee-Dee, you may not be the best dancer in the world, but you can be the best dance teacher. Do what you're best at." And I realized – I mean, I was never a great communicator, I barely spoke when you and I were first together and then, after that, all I could talk about was all this junk about men and women. That's because I thought I'd failed as a dancer. I tried to communicate by writing. That failed too. But I know I *am* a good dancer. I communicate by dancing and I can do that when I teach.'

'Wait a minute.' Carl was genuinely stunned by Dee-Dee's surprisingly sane and rational tone. 'Does this man have a name for his theories?'

'Yes. He's running a series of seminars called Doing What you're Best At.'

'Oh,' he said. 'I see.'

'Are you really in love with Clare, Carl? Or are you doing what I did? Trying to make up for what you see as a failure in your life? The fact that your books haven't done so well. Is Clare your version of my past attempts to find myself?'

'God, that's a strange question.'

'Think about it. You seem so hyper, so *desperate*. It doesn't sound like you – you don't sound like yourself when you talk about her. You were never desperate. I hate to say this, but there's a snivelling tone in your voice when you talk about not being able to understand her.'

'Really?'

'Yes, really. Even when I left you you didn't sound like that. You were upset, yes, but not snivelling. You sound as if you'd lost yourself somewhere along the way. Maybe that's because she's not actually the person you want to find.'

'Dee-Dee, what's happened to you? You never used to talk like this. You never used to make any sense, no offense.'

'I don't know. I'm thinking more about other people now that I don't have to think so much about myself.'

'God,' Carl thought. 'It's come to this. I'm paying attention to words of wisdom from some guy who runs seminars called "Doing What You're Best At." This really is desperate.'

'I've got to go now, Dee-Dee,' Carl said hastily, hearing the front door open. 'Thanks.'

'Think about what you're doing, Carl. Think about what you're best at.'

'I will,' he said. 'Sure thing.'

He was just hanging up when Clare came into the kitchen.

'Who was that?' she asked.

'Wrong number.'

'Oh.'

'How was Art? Did you patch things up?'

'Art's fine,' Clare replied.

'Good.'

'Would you mind if I took a nap now?' She threw her bag on the kitchen table. 'For some reason, I'm shattered.'

'That's fine, I think I'd like to take a walk.'

'By yourself?'

'Yes,' Carl nodded. 'By myself.'

'Where are you?'

'I'm in a phone booth outside some place called the Shepherd Bush Empire, beside another place called the Bottom Line.'

'All right. Look, there's a pub on the corner called the Bush. I'll be there in about ten minutes. Order me a gin and tonic, will you?'

'Sure – I'm not upsetting your plans, am I?'

'No, it's Sunday evening. There's not much going on. In fact, I'm recovering from my rave with Artie last night. A drink might make me feel better.'

'Thanks,' Carl said. 'Thanks, Bernice.'

She found him in the corner of the pub, nursing a lager. The glass of gin and bottle of tonic were waiting in front of an empty chair.

'So, what are you doing out wandering the streets in a foreign country in the dead of winter?' she asked, taking a seat, pouring the tonic into the glass and removing her leather jacket. She'd deliberately dressed in absurd clothes for the weather, wearing, for the sake of superstition, the same outfit she'd had on when they'd had their first evening at the bar in Manhattan. It had been a New York spring then and now it was a London winter. Sleeveless wasn't such a good idea. Shivering, she took a big gulp of gin.

'I'm trying to figure things out,' Carl answered. He wasn't wearing the same clothes as he had in April. No, he was dressed sensibly in heavy brown corduroy trousers and a bulky tan jersey.

'What things?'

'Bernice – tell me – do you think Clare and I should get married?'

'Excuse me?'

'I want to know your opinion.'

'Carl,' she sighed. 'I'm the last person you should ask.'

'Why? You know Clare really well. And you know me a little, so why shouldn't I ask you?'

'Because . . .' Bernice but down her glass and looked Carl straight in the eye. 'Because I have feelings for you myself, and I know I'm not supposed to say that, but I'm tired of not saying it. I'm not drunk, I'm hungover. In headache veritas. I always hated fucking Latin.'

'Bernice? Are you joking?'

'No. I wish I was. I've had these ridiculous feelings since that first night at the bar, OK? And then I had to stand by and watch you fall in love with Clare. Which hurt like hell. Maybe I'm telling you this now so you'll understand that I can't come to the fucking wedding, I just can't. I'll make up some excuse. I'll lie. I don't care. I'm not coming.'

'I thought you and Artie—'

'No.' Bernice finished off her drink in another huge gulp. 'So marry her and be deliriously happy. Just leave me out of it.'

'I didn't know. I don't know what to say.'

'There's nothing to say,' Bernice announced, standing up. 'You came to me to ask me something I can't answer. So be a nice fellow and leave me alone, all right?' Tears had now appeared and Bernice furiously brushed them away with the back of her hand. 'Just leave me alone.' She ran out of the pub. Carl stared helplessly at the leather jacket she'd left behind.

Clare was sitting at the kitchen table, her head in her hands.

'That was a very long walk,' she commented dully.

'Yes, it was, I needed to think things over.'

'Oh.'

'Don't you want to know what things I needed to think over?'

'Not now, Carl, if you don't mind. I told you – I feel shattered. Lying down for a while didn't help.'

'You don't really care, Clare, do you?'

'Of course I care. I'm tired. That's all.'

'And you're annoyed with me again.'

'No,' Clare said through clenched teeth.

'Yes you are. We *have* to talk, Clare. This isn't optional anymore, it's compulsory.'

When he heard the footsteps approaching the kitchen from the hallway, Carl went into immediate New York City response mode. He grabbed a knife from the rack on the wall behind him.

'Carl,' Clare shouted.

'Carl—' Jeremy said very quietly as he appeared in the open doorway. 'There's no need for that. Unless you have a cannibalistic bent I would appeal to.'

'I can't *believe* the way you talk,' Carl turned his back on Jeremy and put the knife away. When he turned and faced him again, he said, 'I'm sure it's supposed to be amusing and witty, but it isn't, Jeremy, I promise you it isn't. How the hell did you get in here anyway?'

'I still have a key. Here—' Jeremy handed a silver key to Clare. 'Now I don't. Listen, you said at lunch that Art was going back to New York today, Clare. Was he on the BA flight?'

'Yes.'

'Well, I just heard on the radio that it had to make an emergency landing. Apparently one of the engines caught fire twenty minutes or so after take-off, so it had to turn back to Heathrow.'

'Is it all right? Did they land safely?'

'As far as I know.'

'But you're not sure?'

'I think they would have said something if someone had been hurt. You know the drill with those emergencies – they have fire engines lining the runway. I've been in one myself. In India.'

The telephone rang, interrupting Jeremy. Clare, her hands beginning all of a sudden to tremble, answered it.

'Yes? Bernice? What are you talking about? What jacket? Yes, of course. Come over, if you'd like. Jeremy has just told me that Art's plane had an emergency landing at Heathrow. An engine caught fire. I hope to God nothing has happened to him. Do you think he'll be all right?'

'How would Bernice know?' Carl said, turning to Jeremy, then back to Clare as she hung up. She was leaning against the wall, her hand covering her mouth.

'Don't you think you're over-reacting a little, sweetheart? I'm sure Artie's fine.'

'You don't know what it's like to be in a plane in trouble. You don't know how terrifying it is.'

'But your plane crashed, Clare. Art's hasn't. It may have had a bumpy landing, that's all.'

'Why don't you sit down, Carl, and let me get you a drink,' Jeremy suggested. 'And you too, Clare.' He took her hand, led her over to a kitchen chair. 'Sit down.'

'It's not right. This is so wrong. It's just *wrong*,' she said violently.

'What's wrong?' Carl asked, looking at Clare, and then, with a reluctantly grateful face, at Jeremy who had found a bottle, uncorked it, poured a glass of wine and put it in front of him.

'What do I do?' Clare focused her gaze on Jeremy as he placed another glass in front of her. 'What do I do if he's been hurt?'

'I'm sure he's fine.' Jeremy rested his hand on Clare's shoulder.

'I don't understand.' Carl glanced back and forth between Clare and Jeremy.

'We're talking about Art,' Jeremy responded.

'Yes, I know. I can sometimes comprehend the English language, believe it or not. But Art is *my* friend. I don't mean to sound selfish or hard, but don't you think *I'm* the one who should be the most upset if Art had been hurt in some way?'

Jeremy simply shrugged. Carl thought of getting the knife again. Instead he downed his glass of wine in one go.

'Clare, I know you were rude to Artie today, and you must feel awful about that, but I honestly think you're seriously over-reacting. Art's been in an emergency landing and he's fine. You've been in a real crash and you're fine. I mean, bad luck is supposed to go in threes. So why not good luck? Is that so absurd?'

Carl gave up. He looked at the misery in Clare's face and wondered, for the first time since their relationship began in earnest, whether she might be difficult to live with. Her moods were so unpredictable, but not unpredictable in a pleasant, wacky way. No, she could be surly and actually unattractively pessimistic. This business with Artie – it was a little worrying, but Clare was turning it into a crisis. She looked as if she were about to go upstairs, put on black and prepare for his funeral. And she and Jeremy had some kind of understanding which excluded the rest of the world. They were staring at each other as if they were fellow masons attending an initiation ceremony.

'It will be on Ceefax, won't it?' Clare said, agitated. 'We can see if anyone was hurt on Ceefax.'

Looking frantically around the kitchen for the TV remote control Clare suddenly turned her head to the doorway.

'What's that noise?' she asked. 'Who is singing?' The sound of a male and female voice combining on the theme tune of *EastEnders* came rumbling down the hallway and into the kitchen, causing Jeremy, Carl and Clare to look at each other in astonishment.

'Hey—' Art Rolfe said as the Da da da da da Da da singing

stopped and he appeared in the doorway, his arm around Angela Rae. 'Look, Angela. The whole gang's here.'

'Artie – my God – what the hell is going on?'

'Carlo, sorry, I'm back. I was on my way to check in and I ran right into your original pen pal, Angela Rae. I thought that since I've been in on this correspondence from the beginning practically, I should stick around and see the two originals meet face-to-face. I could always catch a flight tomorrow. What's one more day? So, Angela Rae – meet Carl Lioce. He used to want to marry you. Now, as you know, he's been unfaithful to you. He has other ideas. He—' Art stopped when he swivelled his eyes from Carl and saw Clare. She was sitting in a chair, her head on the kitchen table, quietly sobbing.

'Clare—' he said, his voice instantly moving from cheerful tipsiness to anxious sobriety, 'Clare, what's wrong? Are you alright?'

'She was worried about you, Art.' Jeremy, who was sitting in the chair at the end of the table beside Clare, explained. He stretched his long legs out and crossed his ankles. 'She thought you might have been hurt. One of the engines of your plane caught fire and there was an emergency landing.'

'What?' Art took off his glasses and began to blink frenetically.

'Your flight – the flight you obviously didn't get on,' Carl repeated. 'Where have you been? I mean, if you didn't get on that flight, why didn't you come back sooner?'

'We decided to have a drink at the airport bar,' Angela said. She was standing by the kitchen sink, dressed in a long woollen black skirt, black silk blouse and black woollen shawl. She was watching Clare cry but made no move to go to her. In one swift movement, she hoisted herself up on the kitchen counter and made herself comfortable there. 'And then the traffic into town – on a Sunday night, it's loathsome. All the way back to the Heston service station. Still, we're here. And Art obviously has reason to be glad of that. So do I. Carl – at last we meet.' The doorbell rang just as Angela reached out to shake hands with Carl, who was a few feet away from her. Jeremy immediately leapt up to answer it.

331

No one in the kitchen spoke until Jeremy came back with Bernice at his side.

'See. I told you. He's fine. And he's with Angela.' Jeremy smiled. 'Now do you believe me?'

'Clare—' Bernice had spotted Clare's crying form. 'Clare, what's happened?'

'I'm all right.' Clare raised her tear-stained face. 'Really, I'm sorry. It's all been too much. I think I need to go up to bed. I don't think I can—'

'Yes, you can,' Angela said in her schoolteacher's voice.

Boy, she *is* scary, Carl thought, taking an involuntary step back from Angela as he fully registered her witchlike appearance.

'Now, don't back off, Carl,' Angela laughed.

Clare had been right, Carl reflected. Angela did have a girlish laugh, a giggle almost.

'Don't back off because I'm here to tell you that I accept your proposal of marriage. Two years after you made it, granted. But I accept. And since your proposal to me preceded your proposal to Clare, I believe I have priority.'

'Right.' Carl started to laugh as well. There was something about this woman, he said to himself. Something scary, yes, but wonderful at the same time.

'So you and I can tie the knot on Friday,' Angela continued. 'I'll simply substitute for Clare.'

'Right. Absolutely.' Carl's laughter grew. He was beginning to feel giddy, with all these people crammed in the small kitchen. What was Jeremy doing? Hanging around to see if he could steal Clare back at the last minute? And Bernice? After what she'd said at the pub, wasn't she slightly embarrassed to be here? And Art? Why, after she'd made a fool of him with that spurious Salinger letter, had he teamed up with Angela?

'Well, that's a relief. For a while I feared you might worry about the age gap.'

'Who me?' Carl smiled at Angela. 'Never.'

'Oh, fabulous,' Bernice thought. 'Now he's flirting wildly with the old bag. This does wonders for my ego.'

'That's perfect, then,' Angela smiled. 'Because, you see, I know you don't really want to marry Clare.'

'Sure, Angela, I—'

'You never wanted to *meet* Clare,' Angela cut Carl off. 'You went to great lengths to *avoid* meeting Clare. You should see the video, Carl. Watch it closely, as I did. You'll see Art, his eyes on the stage, lighting up when he sees Clare. Bounding up to meet her. And you? You look as if it's the last place you wanted to be.'

'It *was* the last place I wanted to be.'

'But Clare – Clare, the woman whom you'd corresponded with all that time, the woman with whom you'd shared so much – she was there. Why didn't you want to be with her? To help her on that stage?'

'It wasn't the right place to meet, Angela. It was false. Ridiculous.' He felt completely ridiculous himself having an argument with a seventy-something-year-old woman sitting on a kitchen counter. Yet he didn't know how to stop this cross-examination of hers. Everyone else was silent, as if they were the studio audience of yet another god-damned television show.

'Any place is the right place to meet, Carl. You didn't tell Clare who you were afterwards, either, did you? Not after the show, not at dinner. You went out with Bernice instead. Am I right?'

'Yes. But Clare and I have had this conversation, Angela. We've sorted – sorry – straightened everything out. I don't mean to be rude, but it's none of your business.' Carl was trapped in the corner, between the hob and the sink. He wanted to go over to Clare who had, by now, stopped crying and was clearly riveted by his conversation with Angela, but he didn't want to appear to be running away from Angela's questions. He glanced over at Art, who was leaning against the refrigerator. Art should have done something to help him, Carl thought. Art was being useless. Why *had* he come back?

'And you went out to lunch with Bernice the next day as well, didn't you Carl? You didn't scour the streets to find Clare. In fact, you ran into Clare only because she ran into you. Were you two going off somewhere, Bernice? Before Clare came into the hotel?' Angela swung to face Bernice, who was still standing in the doorway.

'We were going to Little Italy,' Bernice replied immediately, feeling that she was somehow betraying Carl by telling the truth.

'I *was* going to tell Clare who I was, Angela,' Carl was almost shouting. 'I *was* going to find her. As soon as I got the chance.'

'You didn't want to tell her who you were for good reasons, Carl.' Angela lowered herself onto the floor and approached him, until she was only a few inches away. Then she reached out, took his hand, looked up into his face and said, 'You didn't want to tell her because you weren't in love with her. You knew, deep down, that the whole correspondence was one long lead-up to the perfect romance. You also knew what a disaster it would be if you met and *didn't* have that perfect romance. Failure to fall in love would make a mockery of the correspondence. All that time, all that effort would be wasted.

'You wanted to get to know another human being, but more than that, you wanted to fall in love with the perfect human being, the soul which corresponded completely with yours. But love's messy, Carl. It doesn't come in paragraphs or have full stops at the end of sentences. People never match exactly. And you sensed that from the beginning, which is why you never wanted to meet Clare. When you finally *had* to meet her, you actually *forced* yourself to fall in love with her. And she eventually forced herself to fall in love with you. To be true to your vision, not your heart.'

'That's not fair, Angela.' Carl felt tears starting up at the corners of his eyes. 'That's totally unfair.'

Bernice lit a cigarette. Jeremy uncrossed his ankles and sat up straight. Art didn't take his eyes off Clare's stunned face.

'I love Clare,' Carl said. 'I love her.'

'All right, then.' Angela took a pin out of her hair, then replaced

334

it in almost the same spot. 'That's probably better for everyone concerned. You won't have to cancel your family's trip over here for the wedding. When are they arriving, Carl?'

'What is this, a trial?' Carl jerked his hand away from Angela's and went over to Clare. He grabbed her hand. 'You keep shooting questions at me. Trying to prove something. What? My guilt? I'm not guilty of anything but loving Clare. Just because I haven't invited any of my family to the wedding doesn't mean I don't love her. It's a private wedding, all right? Just friends.'

'But you've *told* your parents?' Angela pulled herself back onto the counter and crossed her legs and arms.

Carl knew that he could walk out of the room at that point and be totally justified in doing so. Yet he also knew that he was still being watched, his answers were being judged in what had now become a show trial. His jury consisted of Clare, of course; Jeremy, equally naturally, given his status of rival; Bernice, forgivably. And also, unforgivably and incomprehensibly, Artie.

'No, Angela,' he finally answered, all eyes upon him. 'I haven't told my parents.'

'You don't think your parents would approve?'

'I think—' Carl narrowed his eyes. 'I'm sure they would approve. It would take them a little while to get to know Clare, that's all. My mother would . . . I think at first she'd think Clare was a little unemotional.' Carl caught sight of Jeremy as a half-smile appeared on his face. 'Like him.' He pointed at Jeremy. 'Like that pompous asshole who has never met an emotion in his life. Oh, God.' Carl tightened his grip on Clare's hand. 'Clare, I didn't mean you're a pompous asshole. You know what I mean. You're just very self-contained. You've said so yourself, in the letters.'

'But she wasn't self-contained a little while ago,' Angela remarked coolly. 'She was sitting at the table crying her heart out.'

'That's because she thought Artie might be hurt.' Carl was making a huge effort to control his temper. He was on his own, his back against the proverbial wall, facing the enemy. He had to remain calm under fire. 'Clare, don't you want to say something? You've been sitting here listening to all this. Don't you want to say whatever's going through your mind?'

She shook her head.

'I'm going now,' Bernice suddenly announced from the doorway. 'Do you want to come with me, Carl? Because you know if you stay any longer I think you're going to get seriously hurt.'

'No, thanks, Bernice. I'm staying.'

'Are you sure?' Bernice asked, thinking, 'This is it. The last chance.'

'I'm sure,' he nodded.

'I'm going now, too,' Jeremy announced. 'Clare – take care of yourself.' He leant over and kissed her on the cheek then rose from his chair. 'Art – why do I think you actually have been involved in an emergency landing?' Jeremy paused. 'And managed to land safely? Anyway, it was nice to see you again. Goodnight, Angela, goodnight, Carl,' he added, before moving to the doorway and taking Bernice's arm.

'Carl—' Bernice didn't move. She studied his resolute face, 'Do you have my jacket here, by any chance?'

'It's on the chair in the living room,' he replied, avoiding her eyes.

'Why do you have her jacket?' Clare asked.

'I had a drink with her when I went out before.'

'Don't worry, Clare,' Bernice raised her chin as she spoke. 'I'm not trying to steal him from you. Not that it would make any difference now, when Artie's stolen *you* from *him*. Well done—' she turned to Art. 'Some day you'll have to tell me how you did it. Come on, Jeremy, let's get out of here.'

'Bernice—' Clare called out, but it was too late.

'What's she talking about?' Carl stared at Art, still propped up against the fridge door. 'What does she mean about you stealing her from me?'

'I don't know if I can answer that right now, Carlo. I don't know how Clare feels about me.'

336

'What?' Carl gave up all hope of controlling himself. 'What the fuck are you talking about, Art?'

Art didn't reply.

'Clare?' Carl took her by the shoulders and turned her to face him fully. 'What is Bernice talking about? What is Art talking about?'

'I fell in love with Art,' Clare answered. 'I don't know when or how, I don't know why, even.'

'Great,' Art mumbled, and was thankful no one heard him.

'I don't believe this.' Carl let Clare go and rounded on Angela. 'This is all your fault,' he snapped at her. 'You've tricked her into thinking she's in love with him. She can't be in love with him. They have *nothing* in common. They don't even know each other. He's a fucking *business* man. He wears suits. He *hates* English people. He thinks they're all xenophobic zombies – and that's an exact quote. This is a joke, isn't it? Please tell me this is a joke.'

'It's not a joke, Carl,' Angela said quietly.

'I'm sorry, Carlo, I—

'Oh, shut up, Art.' Carl gripped Clare's shoulders once again. '*You* tell me. Tell me this is a joke.'

'I'm sorry—' Clare hung her head. 'I'm really sorry, Carl. I didn't know, not really, not until just now – when he walked in. I had thought before that maybe . . . but I didn't know. I know it seems crazy, I mean, I told you I was in love with you. I thought for years I was in love with Jeremy. I know it must seem as if I'm some flighty, heartless bimbo, but I've never felt the way I felt when I thought Art was in trouble. And then when I saw him, God, I've never wanted to be with anyone so badly in my life.'

'Oh, Christ.' Carl stood up abruptly. 'What the hell am I supposed to say? Am I supposed to wish you two good luck? Is that what a true Brit would do? Tell me, Artie. Is that what I'm supposed to do?'

'No, Carl,' Art replied. 'You're probably supposed to hit me.'

'I have a better suggestion,' Angela quickly put in, hopping off the counter. 'I think you should come with me, Carl. I'm going to Morocco. Tomorrow. I don't expect you to fall in love with me, of course. But I *do* feel responsible for all this in some odd way. Come on an adventure with me. I can afford to pay for you – easily, in fact, given that I did a lot of gambling on my trip to Texas. Come with me, and if you enjoy it, we can continue for a while. We can go to New Orleans, for the Mardi Gras. Or Rio. The Indian Ocean. Wherever you want, Carl.'

'I despise you, Angela. I don't think I can travel with you when I hate you.'

'Don't be so silly,' Angela laughed. 'It's when you travel with people you think you love that the trouble starts. You don't know how easy it is to go off people you *thought* you liked when you travel with them. Whereas, with you and me, our relationship can only improve. And I promise I'll let you sulk about Clare for at least a week, despite the fact that I know you don't love her as you think you do.'

'Oh, please,' Carl muttered.

'You see – you're relenting already. I can tell – your voice softened a little just then. Sleep on it and tell me tomorrow,' Angela strode over to the table and kissed the top of both Clare and Carl's heads. 'Goodnight, you two,' she said. 'And goodnight, Artie,' she added, giving him a quick smile. 'I'm glad we bumped into each other.'

'So am I, Angela. It was an amazing coincidence.'

'Wasn't it just?' Angela responded as she exited the kitchen.

'Do you two lovers want to be alone?' Carl asked. 'Is that the program, Art? Or should I stay and we can pretend to be a happy threesome talking over old times?'

'I don't expect you to be my friend, Carl.'

'You know something, Art? I would have preferred to lose to Jeremy, if I had to lose to someone.'

'I feel the same way,' Art replied evenly. 'I would have rather lost to Jeremy than to you.'

'And what fucking sport am I?' Clare glared at the two men.

'Basketball? No, you're too short.' Art looked at Clare's grudging smile and wondered when he was going to be able to feel her hand in his. 'Bernice is in love with you, Carl,' he commented. 'Does that make any difference?'

'No. Clare, I'm finding this impossible to believe. What happened? What went wrong? I mean, forget about him – what happened between us?'

'I don't know how to explain.' Clare hung her head. 'I don't know, Carl. Maybe I tried too hard. Maybe you tried too hard. I'm not sure.'

'I tried too hard,' Carl murmured, closing his eyes. 'Me and Danny the Dope Dealer. Shit.' When he opened them again, he said, 'I think I'd better go now. Before I *do* hit you, Art.'

'Where are you going?' Clare asked, sounding frightened.

'I'm going out to a pub. And then I'll crash at Bernice's, if she lets me. As a friend,' he added, putting a great deal of emphasis on the last word. 'Don't think you can get away with not feeling guilty because you've palmed me off on Bernice.'

'You can stay here, Carl. Really—'

'No chance.' Carl cocked his head to the side and suddenly, astonishingly, smiled. 'It's all my fault, I suppose. Reading *People Magazine*. I mean, it serves me right, doesn't it?'

'Why,' Clare asked herself, 'why hadn't he smiled like that more often? Why hadn't he showed that sense of humour more often? Then maybe . . . no,' she stooped herself, glancing over at Art's deep, dark eyes. 'This was the way it was meant to be.'

'I'll come back tomorrow and pick up all my things and also tell Angela whether I accept her offer or not.' Carl was halfway out of the kitchen when he added, 'And Art, maybe someday I'll forgive you. But I doubt it. I really do. The only reason I'm walking out now is that I do not ever in my life want to snivel. Goodbye, Art. Goodbye, Clare.'

'Goodbye? Did he say goodbye?' she asked as she heard the front door close.

'Yes.'

'Well, that's it, then. Neither of us is going to see him again. He has a superstition about the word goodbye.'

'Snivel?' Art asked. 'What was all that about snivelling?'

'Oh, God.' Clare raised her eyes to the ceiling. 'He saves my life this morning and I betray him this evening. I can't believe it.'

'How did he save your life?'

'I had another asthma attack. A bad one. Just after I'd decided I had to tell him the wedding was off. He found my inhaler and he found me.'

'At which point you decided to marry him after all?'

'I couldn't break it off, Artie, not then. I didn't know what to do. He's so special.'

'I know.'

'Do you think he'll be all right?'

'He'll be fine, Clare. I know Carl. And I think Angela has the right plan, if he'll only accept her offer. He'd love to travel, you know, why do you think he had all those telephone books in his apartment? He's yearning to go on an adventure. That's why he wrote to Angela in the first place – because of her sense of adventure. You see, people's first responses are usually the right ones. Carl *should* have a relationship with the person he wrote to. The *first* person he wrote to. I think Angela will end up being his Muse. And a damn good one.'

'You adore her, don't you?'

'Angela's incredible,' Art grinned. 'I wouldn't put anything past her. I mean, bumping into me at the airport. I can't believe that was coincidental. The only thing about Angela that would surprise me now is if she *didn't* have an affair with Salinger.'

Clare giggled. The two linked eyes then quickly looked away from each other.

'I'm nervous,' Art said. 'This is worse than that first night in my apartment when I was pretending to be Carl.'

'I know,' Clare said. 'It's all happened so quickly. Again, just like in New York, things are happening too fast.'

'Listen, I think you should go get yourself checked out by an asthma specialist. Tomorrow. It's time you found out exactly what is going on. You need information, Clare, if you're going to deal with it properly.'

'You're right.'

'And I've wanted to tell you for a long time that I've read your novels. I like them. I see what you're doing and I respect it – at the same time I also understand why they haven't sold. What I'd like to do is find you another agent in New York. There's a woman I know who would be perfect for you. I think she'd be right on your wavelength. Would you come to New York? For a while, anyway? To see how it goes?'

'Yes,' Clare nodded. 'I would. Do you want to know something really odd? Carl and I, we've never read each other's work. We both kept saying we were going to, we gave each other our books, but we never did read them. Both of us had all sorts of good excuses. Maybe we felt competitive on some instinctive level and neither of us wanted the other to be better. Is that possible?'

'I'd guess so.' Art reached for his glasses, then stopped before taking them off. 'You should read them now, though. You'd like Carl's work. You two do have a lot in common, you know. There *is* a correspondence, just not a romantic one.' He stopped and stared at the floor, before looking up with a shy expression. 'Anyway, here we are like teenagers at our first party. Do you want to turn on the TV? That might give us a chance to calm down a little. And I'd like to find out what happened to the plane I was supposed to be on.'

'Of course.' Clare picked up the remote control from the bowl on the table and pressed the on button.

Turning to the relevant page of Ceefax, Clare and Art learnt that the BA flight had had a completely successful emergency landing at Heathrow. No one had been hurt.

'So I would have escaped from a wounded plane unharmed, too,' Art commented. 'Now *we* have something in common.'

'Yes,' Clare smiled. But within an instant the smile turned into a frown. 'I still feel dreadful about Carl.'

'So do I,' Art agreed. 'Up to a point.'

'Do you think I should do something?'

'Like what? Write him a letter? I wouldn't advise it, no. To tell you the truth, I think Carl may have been a little worried about the marriage, too. I mean, not telling his parents is strange. The whole family is really tight. It says something that he *didn't* say something. I think deep down he knew you two weren't right as a couple but he had already made you his mission, his cause, the object of his quest. Leave him to Angela, really. As I said, she's the one person who can help him best, I think.'

'And do you think this is going to work, Artie? Us, I mean?'

'I don't know. But if it doesn't, if we break up, I figure I'll get invited by Angela on a fully paid exotic trip to cheer *me* up. That's something.'

'That's not a very romantic answer.'

'Romance? You want romance?' Art finally moved away from the refrigerator door.

Sir, more than kisses, letters mingle souls

John Donne

Chapter 22

He sat on the balcony, feeding bits of his roll to a tiny, multi-coloured bird. The palm trees obscured part of his view to the ocean, but he could see a boat in the distance, with a mono-skier behind, 'That has to be Angela,' he thought, smiling.

The day before, they'd gone out together in a speedboat to visit uninhabited islands dotted with idyllic, deserted beaches. The waves had been so large and threatening even the experienced hotel boat captain had suggested they turn back.

'No,' Angela had said. 'Let's keep on.' She'd turned to Carl then, and he hadn't dared demur. 'Think of it as a roller-coaster,' she'd advised.

'I hate roller coasters,' he'd replied, but his words were lost in the wind.

The hellish trip to get to the island turned out to have been worth it when they finally landed on one of the beaches.

'I didn't know places like this existed,' he'd commented. 'Paradise Unlimited. You're amazing, Angela, you know that?'

She'd nodded and stretched herself out on the beach, her eyes closed. He lay down a few feet away.

'Carl,' she'd said, after a few minutes. 'You're a good travelling companion.'

'Thank you.' She had taken off her shorts and shirt to reveal what she always wore on the beach – an old-fashioned one-piece black bathing suit with a little skirt. A few weeks before, in New Delhi, she had cut her waist-length hair into a short bob. Now she looked less like a witch and more like a well-preserved old woman.

'You were right, you know. I've been meaning to tell you.'

'Right about what?'

'Why I swam the Channel. Or you were close to right. A psycho girl bully didn't throw me in a pool, but a teenage boy did push me down and hold me underwater for what seemed like for ever when I was thirteen. I thought I was going to die. I was terrified.'

'Christ, that was a joke when I wrote it.' He turned from his back onto his side and faced her. Was she telling the truth? Did it matter? 'Isn't swimming the Channel going a little too far in getting your own back?'

'No. I'm like you. I take things as far as I can.'

'But you're not like me, Angela. I fail.'

'You're wrong, Carl. You don't know when you've won, that's all. There's a big difference. If you think about it, I'm sure you'll see that the entire episode with Clare has given you what you want.'

'Well,' Carl began to trace letters in the sand, 'I've begun to write again. For the past couple of weeks, I've been writing late at night. I think I have a good start for a book. That's something.'

'Mmm,' Angela said. 'That *is* something. I'm going for a swim now.'

Carl, remembering this conversation, wondered what the 'Mmm' might mean. He had come to understand, over the past month, that every word from Angela's mouth meant more than it seemed at the time.

And he had come to respect her as a remarkable human being. She was never thrown by the fact that people they encountered on their travels assumed he was either her son or her toy boy — she was, in fact, so blasé about it that her attitude communicated itself to him. By all rights, he should be feeling guilty that Angela was paying all his bills at wonderful hotels in wonderful foreign places, but she wouldn't allow him to be.

She is the goddess, Carl thought. Descended from the heavens in human form to take him on the trip of his life. His only worry was what he would do when it was finished.

The sky clouded over in a matter of minutes, making Carl wonder how clouds could travel so fast. He saw the boat with the mono-skier behind turn and head back to shore. People on the beach were also packing up their suncream and books and going towards shelter. Carl didn't move from the balcony. The rain, when it came, drenched the food on his tray, drenched his bathing suit hanging on the rail and thoroughly drenched him. He couldn't believe how quickly it ended, how intense it had been, yet how short-lived. Shaking his head like a dog coming out of the water, he laughed. The smell was like no smell he had ever encountered. The freshness, the beauty of it struck him as a wonder of creation.

'Heaven,' he began to sing. 'I'm in heaven.'

Ambling back into his room, he grabbed a towel and dried himself off. He pulled on a dry pair of jeans and a T-shirt and sat down at the desk. Taking up a pen, he began to write:

Royal Palm Hotel
Mauritius
Indian Ocean
Bottom left-hand
side of Africa
I think

February 14

Dear Bernice,